All Debts, Public And Private

Chad Sanborn

For Monk and Bean

Saturday

One

"That hurt?"

Pearce not responding to the question, instead keeping his eyes on the house up the street. The details of the house going blurry through the drizzle layering the windshield.

"Hey, I said does that hurt?" Chubba giving Pearce a hard, no bullshit stare. This freakshow sitting in the driver's seat next to Chubba, fucking with him.

Chubba, real name Horace Self III, in his early twenties. A fat baby who grew into a chunky kid, everyone calling him Chubba long as he could remember, even after he'd shed the weight for muscle.

Still a big boy, just solid. Though lately, he'd started turning soft around the edges again. Not hitting the weights, eating too much junk. Chubba figuring it was related to the stress of everything going on.

Chubba looking at Pearce behind the steering wheel. Pearce, dressed all in black, metal sticking out of his face here and there. Ink peeking out from under his collar and sleeves. A one-man walking freakshow, Chubba liked to say. Chubba not caring if Pearce was around when he said it. Damn sure no friendship blooming between them in the couple of months since this deal had brought them together. Just about the money. After, both would be glad to move on.

It was Pearce's fucked-up earlobes that really weirded out Chubba. Both of the lobes sporting a hole slightly bigger than a quarter. Each hole inset with a black metal ring, as if someone with meaty fingers took off their wedding ring and jammed it in there for support. Chubba unable to stop himself from looking at them and every time he looked at the holes Chubba thinking *goddamn.*

Chubba saying, "That's got to hurt, right?"

Pearce still ignoring Chubba. Reaching up, flicking on the windshield wiper, for a moment resetting the outlines of the stone house they'd been watching for an hour or so. Didn't look like a rich woman's house. Comfortable maybe, but not big time lottery winner rich.

Pearce in his mid-twenties but still waiting on the ability to grow a full mustache. Stroking his wispy goatee. The drizzle again began warping the jagged edges of the bungalow's front porch. The afternoon gray and damp with a chill that sank into the knuckles.

Pearce bored, finally giving in, asking Chubba does what hurt?

Chubba in disbelief that he has to be specific, saying those goddamn holes in Pearce's ears, that's what.

Chubba in his custom-made red and gold Nikes and his

bottom lip jutting out thanks to a soggy lump of tobacco. Every now and then spitting brown tobacco juice into an empty beer can between his legs. Chubba was a natural born mouth-breather and with a dip in looking even more like a gorilla than usual.

Pearce lightly fingering the large hole in his right lobe. The barbed border of a black-and-red tattoo snaking out from under the cuff of his black, long-sleeve t-shirt. Chubba watching, fascinated, a little sickened. Not paying attention where he was spitting tobacco juice, missing his spit can, a trace of brown saliva hitting the cloth seat.

Pearce glaring at Chubba, a look warning him to be careful.

Chubba grinning back at him, bits of tobacco lodged in the cracks of his stained teeth. Chubba rubbing between his legs at the spit, driving it deeper into the cloth of the passenger seat.

"All better," Chubba said. Chubba spit again into his can. "Like I give a rat's ass about some stolen piece of shit Volvo." Chubba said. "Where'd you pick up this piece of junk anyway?"

"OP," Pearce said.

Overland Park, that checked out. Chubba remembering the Johnson County plate on the back of the Volvo. Pearce had claimed to be from Kansas City but it turned out he wasn't from KC proper. Actually, he was from OP, just outside of Kansas City on the Kansas side. Not a big deal but Chubba catching it when Pearce let it slip a few weeks back, and Chubba thinking it meant something at the time.

"This thing got enough trunk space?" Chubba said. "We get down to it, I don't want to all the sudden find out she don't fit back there. She's a big girl, you know."

"So you told me."

"Not tall-big but thick-big. Stumpy, like a fire plug. She's short but not short-short. Less than average height, you might say. But thick, know what I mean?"

Pearce watching the house but giving a fake smile along, a big condescending nod. "Yes, I know what you mean. Chubba."

"The fuck's that supposed to mean?"

"What's what supposed to mean?"

"Calling me Chubba like that."

Pearce turned in his seat to look at Chubba. "That your name, right? Chubba?"

"My name is Horace, like my Daddy. Like my granddaddy. Folks just call me Chubba. Just a nickname. But right then when you said it, I think you meant something by it."

"What did I mean, Chubba?"

"Like maybe you meant who am I to be calling someone else thick?"

"You said that," Pearce said, laughing. "I didn't say that."

"Don't act like you didn't when you did."

Neither of them saying anything for a while, Pearce smirking, Chubba fuming. Drizzle quietly covering the Volvo until finally, Chubba suggested they go over it again.

"Follow her around tonight," Pearce said, "Wait until she's drunk, then toss her ass in the trunk. Not real complicated."

"Old hat to a pro like you, right?" Chubb said. Chubba plunged his tongue down into his bottom gum and extracted the spent lump of tobacco. Raising the spit-filled beer can, he stuck out his tongue and expertly dropped the wet chunk into the mouth of the can.

Pearce saying oh shit, looking in the review mirror.

Chubba about to tell him not to get all pissy, he didn't spill any on the precious seat of his stolen car. Then noticing Pearce slumping low in his seat. "No not that," Pearce said. "Fucking cops!"

An SUV rolling past them, a gold star and the word SHERIFF emblazoned in gold on the side, two cherry lights on top. The SUV pulling into the wide driveway of the stone house they were watching.

Chubba laughed. "Hell, that ain't no cop. That's Billy Keene."

They watched as a young man stepped from the Escalade. Pearce hit the wipers, still not getting a good look at him. Could tell he was tall, though, even taller with the Stetson sheriff's cowboy hat wrapped in plastic to protect it from the rain.

Chubba spit into the can even though he didn't have a dip in his lip. "He ain't jackshit."

"He's good sized."

"Don't make him tough."

"Don't make him *not* tough either."

"Billy?" Chubba said. "He was couple years ahead of me in high school. Big shot athlete. Only reason he won the election is because it ain't nothing but a popularity contest. Like high school itself."

Chubba going on, claiming his daddy backing Billy's campaign, that's the only reason he's Caste County sheriff. "Hell, ain't like the sheriff does anything around here anyway," Chubba said. "Other than running county road speed traps and tracking down a lost cow every now and again."

The two of them watching the sheriff ducking his head against the rain, trotting around to a gate along the side of the house. Met there by a young woman. Long, curly hair pulled back and tucked under a ball cap. She was lugging a large black bag and coming the other way through the gate. The sheriff stepping aside, holding the wooden gate for her. The woman smiling as she passed through.

Chubba and Pearce watched the sheriff watching the young woman as she ran to her car parked on the street. Then he disappeared around the back of the house.

"That her?" Pearce said, nodding toward the woman driving away in a Buick.

"Now does that girl look thick-big to you?" Chubba said. "She's curvy, I'll give you that. But nothing wrong with that."

"If it's not her, who is it then?"

"Am I supposed to know everybody in town?" Chubba said. "Caulfield might be small, but this ain't fucking Mayberry."

"Yeah, well that big son of a bitch isn't Barney Fife either. Pearce said. "Our girl on the inside, she okay in there?"

At the mention of "our girl" Chubba's cheeks flushing red. "Sharla's fine," Chubba said. "And she ain't *our* girl, freakshow. You best remember who's running this deal."

"Oh, I remember," Pearce said. Grinning, not all that surprised he'd gotten in Chubba's kitchen so easily. "Daddy."

That getting Chubba's attention. Chubba turning his big ham head to glare at Pearce. And Pearce hooking his middle finger through the hole in his dangling lobe, giving his ear a tug.

"Goddamn, don't!" Chubba bending over in his seat, queasy with phantom pain.

Two

Sheriff Billy Keene, mid-twenties, stepping into the small foyer of Arlita Hardy's beauty shop, removing his raincoat. His nostrils flooded with the acrid smell of hair chemicals.

Placing his plastic-covered gray Stetson upside down on a small pine bench. Billy glad to have his hat off. Seven months on the job and Billy still self-conscious about wearing it. Growing up he'd never worn a cowboy hat like a lot of farm kids around Caulfield. The hat made him feel top heavy. But the people of Caste County considered the hat as much a part of the sheriff's uniform as the badge and the gun. So Billy wore the hat.

Billy hanging his raincoat on a hook screwed into the wall before wiping his boots on the foyer rug.

"Wipe your shoes!" Arlita yelled from the shop.

"I am," Billy yelled back.

"Do it again," Arlita said. Billy hearing that deep laugh of hers.

Billy checking nobody in the shop could see him, then yelling, "There, I did it."

"No you didn't," Arlita said.

"Damn it," Billy said.

The sound of two cackling women coming from the shop.

Arlita busy as usual. Billy wiped his boots again. Most people did what Arlita told them to do. Life was just easier that way.

Billy heading through the open entryway toward the laughter. The beauty shop was attached to the back of Arlita's house. Arlita keeping her work and her life closely aligned the way she liked it. Billy appreciating that Arlita had upgraded the things in her life while managing to keep a sense of the way things were before she won fifty-four million dollars, after tax, in a multi-state lottery.

Arlita telling Billy to have a seat; she'd be with him shortly. He sat down in one of the hair dryer chairs to wait, legs crossed. He watched as she worked at a customer in the swivel chair, Mrs. Woodcock. Came in once a week so Arlita could "fix her hair." Other women came in to "get their hair done."

No one called Arlita's business a parlor or a salon either. It was a beauty shop.

Arlita was not a stylist. She was a beauty operator. Insisting she was, is and always would be.

The beauty shop, like the house it was connected to, was pretty much the same as it had been before Arlita came into money. Same warm, welcoming country style, but remodeled and expanded. Maybe a touch gaudy here and there. Everything with a little too much design in it.

But no doubt there was quality work in the details. Hollow doors replaced with solid ones, linoleum replaced with tile, New Jersey Formica replaced by South American granite. Everything in Arlita's world was better, at least the parts money could fix.

Money fixes a lot, of course, but not everything. Billy

learning a few money lessons too, after signing with the Yankees. Two million dollar bonus straight out of high school and set up to make a lot more until his shoulder gave out.

Now Billy with plenty money left so that he could do what he pleased whenever he finally figured out what that was. He had a lot less in the bank than Arlita had, but they'd both learned some of the same lessons along the way.

Once you come into any amount of money, you truly appreciate its power, something you always expected. You also come to understand its limitations, something that's surprising at first but makes sense later.

And of course, there's finding out the hard way who your friends are.

"Billy, how's the sheriffing business?" Arlita said.

Arlita in a short-sleeve blouse and the flabby underside of her arms flapping and jiggling as she went at Mrs. Woodcock's dyed hairdo with a hair pick, putting some height into it.

"Business is not too bad," Billy said, watching Mrs. Woodcock's hair grow with each stab of the pick. Mrs. Woodcock one of those ladies Billy had trouble imagining at any age younger than her current one. As if all her life she must have seemed to be in her fifties. And an old fifties, at that.

"This morning I had to help Don Tucker track down a heifer that got loose," Billy telling how the heifer got herself caught in barbed wire down by the creek over on Frank Foley's property. The animal wild-eyed and scared but it turned out all right for everybody involved.

"You could say justice prevailed," he said.

Arlita letting out a deep, whooping laugh. Spinning

around Mrs. Woodcock in the chair and Arlita behind her holding up a hand mirror, letting Mrs. Woodcock inspect the back of her piled hair. Mrs. Woodcock judging it perfect, just like last week.

"Sharla!" Arlita said, "Connie's ready for her nails!"

With her plastic salon cape flowing behind her, Mrs. Woodcock moved over to the recliner set up for manicures. Arlita swept up the bits of hair on the floor around the chair before patting the seat for Billy to sit down.

"Remember when you used to have to hop up into the chair?" Arlita said, fastening the cape around Billy's muscular neck. It was on the last snap and still snug. He swallowed and breathed, fighting a brief sensation of claustrophobia before it passed.

Arlita wetting Billy's hair with a spray bottle, she caught the reflection of the as-yet-unattended-to Mrs. Woodcock flipping through a magazine in the mani-pedi recliner.

"Where has that girl gone off to? She in the bathroom again? I swear," Arlita said. "I'm sorry Connie."

"Oh, it's no problem, Arlita," Mrs. Woodcock said without looking up from her magazine. From the way she said it, overly sweet and slow with a lilt in her voice at the end, Billy could tell it was a problem.

Arlita yelling for Sharla again, just as the young woman came into the beauty shop through the doorway connecting the shop to Arlita's home.

"I'm right here, dang," Sharla said, making her way over to the chair next to Mrs. Woodcock. Wherever she went, Sharla lead with her chest out. She, along with most people considered it one of her best features. Sharla always had been attractive so she casually expected she always would be. Taking a seat in a chair next to Mrs. Woodcock in the recliner. “Don’t have to yell at me.”

Arlita shook her head. Everybody in the room but Sharla knowing she was on thin ice with her job. Sharla eventually finding her way to thin ice with any of the jobs she’d had. Bank teller, retail clerk, administrative assistant. Arlita ran a black comb through Billy’s hair. Four weeks since his last cut.

Billy watching in the mirror as Sharla set up the tray, various oils and towels and files and clippers. Seeing Sharla’s face go white when she noticed him in the mirror and wondering what the hell that was all about.

He glanced away quickly, like he’d been caught looking at her even though Sharla wasn’t shy about flirting with him or most any guy for that matter.

“Oh, hey Billy,” Sharla said. Her voice cracking. Hoping the look on her face at seeing Billy in the chair hadn’t said *holy shit*. Like the voice in her head had. Remembering now that she forgot to check the appointment book that morning. Sharla telling herself to get on top of her game because their little project is happening, *today*.

Sharla clearing her throat before asking Billy what he was up to today. Billy shaking his head, saying getting a haircut.

“Hold still,” Arlita said. “Head down.”

Billy looking toward his lap, holding still. Feeling the cold steel of the scissors pressing against the hairline along the back of his neck.

When he was a kid he’d always been proud of himself for

his ability to hold still for a haircut. Other kids crying and squirming but Billy disciplined about it. Sat still and not needing to be told to put his head down or raise it back up. Just a slight nudge from Arlita was all. He and Arlita were in sync. It was teamwork.

Until he'd gone away to the minor leagues, Arlita was the only person who'd ever taken scissors or shears to Billy's hair. It was Arlita who had given him his first haircut, something he couldn't remember but she could.

Billy's mom, Sara Jane, and Arlita didn't run around together as much as they used to, but the story of Billy's first haircut came up in conversation now and again, whenever Billy's mom came in to get her hair fixed.

"Hey, who was that outside?" Billy said. Then jerking his head around at the sound of nail clippers smacking the tile floor.

Sharla, pale faced now, thinking Billy might have spotted Chubba and Pearce set up out there watching. Apologizing as she picked up the clippers.

"You've had the butterfingers all day. What's up your butt?" Arlita said, but not waiting for an answer from Sharla, just steamrolling right back in Billy's direction. "Who was who outside?"

"That girl toting a big bag," Billy said. "On the way out as I was on my way in."

"You don't recognize her?" Arlita said.

"Should I?"

"Sounds like you might want to," Mrs. Woodcock said, and everyone laughed.

"I might," he said. "Who is she?"

"You telling me you don't remember Paige Figures?" Arlita said.

Billy saying no way, that was little Paige? Arlita laughing saying little Paige is all grown up, ain't she? Billy letting that lay, instead saying last he'd heard Paige was back east somewhere.

Boston, Arlita confirmed, but back for a while to help her mother recover from her heart attack. "I did hear about that," Billy said. "Funny, but it seems like you don't hear about women having heart attacks as much as men. And she's not that old, is she?"

"She's my age," Arlita said, "so no, she is not."

"That big ole black bag, what was that all about?"

"Cameras and stuff," said Arlita. "She's some kind of photographer, artsy-fartsy stuff I guess. Her momma says Paige has some pictures hanging in some little galleries back east."

"She taking your picture?" Billy said.

"Not mine, Connie's," Arlita said, tossing her high-haired head in Mrs. Woodcock's direction. "Some arty project she's got going. Comes in here regular, takes pictures of customers getting their hair done. I don't know a thing about it other than Paige's sweet and the customers don't mind. Hell, half the time they don't even know she's snapping away."

Billy hearing footsteps scuffling toward them from the house. Arlita's granddaughter, Patty, entering the beauty shop through the same doorway Sharla had come through. Sharla making a point of not looking up as Patty came in.

"Gramma, can I get some gel for my hair," Patty said. She was twenty-one but wore too much make up for any age. Heavy-set like her grandmother but with a flashy streak – for instance, the showy diamond rocks set in gold decorating her ears – that Arlita would let show on special occasions only.

Patty sidling up alongside her grandmother, noticing Billy in the chair. "Hey there, Mr. Sheriff Man. Shoot anybody today?"

"Not yet," he said. "Just Saturday afternoon though. Give it until evening time."

Arlita handing her granddaughter a tube of hair gel."Put some real shoes on, Patty," Arlita said. "Them flippity-flops won't keep your feet dry. Hell, it's only March. Not that warm out yet."

"Gramma, don't you know wearing warm weather clothes actually brings on the warm weather faster?" Patty said, teasing.

"That sounds scientific," Arlita said, then taking a look in the mirror at her granddaughter. "Them jeans painted on?"

"They fit," Patty said, scrunching the gel into the uniform curls of her permed and bleached shoulder-length hair.

"When you were in junior high, maybe.

"Gramma, they're brand new."

"Why don't you go put on some different jeans?"Arlita said. "And while you're at it, pick out a shirt that covers you."

Patty looked down at her white t-shirt wrapped snuggly around her cleavage. She tugged at its bottom, pulling it down over her soft muffin tops spilling over her jeans. A blue-black tramp stamp vine tattoo twisting across the small of her back. In less than a second, the shirt crept back up, exposing her tanning-bed brown belly.

"Not ashamed of my body, Gramma. What you see is what a real woman looks like. A big ole girl in a big ole world."

"Not saying anything about your size, honey," Arlita said. "Nothing wrong with meat on the bones. Hell, one the reasons your granddad loved me because I was a big girl. You know I think you're beautiful. Just saying cover it up a little. So you don't look like a back-alley Sally."

"Gramma!" Pretending to be shocked by her grandmother. Patty finishing with the tube of gel and putting it back on the shelf in front of Billy. "You going to be out working tonight, Billy? I don't want to get any DUIs."

"Don't drink and drive then," Billy said. Trying not to sound preachy, but coming across that way.

Both Patty and Sharla were just a few years younger than him, had been freshman in high school when he was a senior. Though not close, they'd all known each other pretty much their whole lives. Billy not wanting to come off as an authority figure, knowing they wouldn't accept it if he did.

Then again, he was county sheriff and had obligations.

"Do what the man says," Arlita said. "Don't you drink and drive. You hear me? You get drunk tonight, you call me. I don't care how drunk or where you are, you call me. You got a cell phone and Lord knows you know how to use it. On the dang thing all the time like you are. So, you call me if you need to."

Sharla clearing her throat so her voice wouldn't crack again when she spoke. "Where y'all going tonight, Patty?"

"Probably just up to The End Zone, maybe. Or Jack Lynch's. Heard there's a party out at Koy Reed's house, so might swing by there at some point. You heading out tonight?"

"I don't know," Sharla said. "Kind of tired."

"You? Sharla Ricketts staying home on a Saturday

night?" Patty said. "You sick or something?"

"You been in the bathroom enough today," said Arlita.

Sharla rolling her eyes before realizing Mrs. Woodcock had seen her do it. Shrugging an apology and smiling. Mrs. Woodcock not smiling back.

Patty asking her grandmother for some money, saying that way she wouldn't have to stop by the bank machine. A hundred, pretty please.

"My fat fanny, a hundred dollars," Arlita said. "You buying for everybody?"

"Well, we don't want people thinking we're cheap, Gramma," Patty said. "I mean, you've got it."

"Yeah I've got it," Arlita said. "And you're flaunting it. Tell you what, I'll give you a hundred to change your clothes."

"That's not fair," Patty said, pouting. The shrillness in Patty's voice leading to another uncomfortable silence in the shop. Arlita pursing her lips, working the gleaming scissors over Billy's wet hair.

Not saying anything. Everyone noticing the redness in Patty's cheeks, so vivid it smoldered through the layers of makeup covering her cheeks. Billy unable to tell if she was mad or embarrassed. Billy couldn't stand it, needing to break the silence.

"Be nice to each other now," he said. "Else I'll have to haul you both in for a DD."

"What the hell's a DD?" Arlita said.

"Domestic disturbance. We get those sometimes."

"Some drunk farmer smacking around his wife?" Arlita said.

"Most the time," Billy said. "More than a couple times though, it's been the wife smacking around the drunk farmer."

"Amen to that," Patty said, chipper again now that the tension was gone from the room. Patty and her Gramma never staying mad at each other for long. Patty about to ask for the money again, politely this time, when she heard Mrs. Woodcock yell.

"Ouch! Watch it, Sharla!"

Everybody turned to look. Sharla scrambling to press a damp cloth over the blood running from where she'd nipped Mrs. Woodcock's ring finger with a pair of nail scissors.

"Damn it, Sharla, what is with you today?" Arlita said.

Arlita moving over to help Mrs. Woodcock. Telling Sharla to take a break. Arlita saying she'd finish the nails once she was done giving Billy a haircut. Sharla nodding before leaving the beauty shop. They heard a bathroom door close and lock somewhere inside the house.

Before returning to Billy's hair, Arlita pulled five twenties from her leather purse. Handing the money to Patty, kissing her and urging her to be careful.

"Don't be out too late," Arlita said. "Remember we're supposed to go up to Kansas City to go shopping tomorrow. I don't want to be dragging your hung over ass all around the Plaza."

"Love you too, Gramma!" Patty said. Tucking the money into the snug front pocket of her jeans. Patty disappearing into the house. A few moments later, they all heard the front door close.

Mrs. Woodcock, still compressing the cloth around her

finger, got up from the recliner. Arlita looked her up and down, asked her where the hell she thought she was going.

"I'm getting a glass of wine," Mrs. Woodcock said loudly, already on her way to the kitchen.

Arlita yelling after her,"Good idea. Bring me one!"

Just the two of them in the shop now, Arlita's voice dropping into a confiding tone as she worked the scissor blades delicately around Billy's ears.

"I tell you, I got one pissed off dead husband," she said. "Pat, bless his soul, worked his ass off, a railroader for thirty years3. Then he up and got cancer and died. Six weeks later I win the fucking lottery, pardon my French."

Billy laughing, asking would she trade it all to have Pat back?

"Hell no," Arlita said. "I'd trade three-quarters of it to have him back, then me and him, we'd go blow the rest together. Now hold still."

Without being told, Billy put his head down, exposing the back of his neck to Arlita. Arlita running hot lather over his neck before scraping it clean with the sharp edge of a straight razor.

Three

The whole damn afternoon spent watching a house. And now, Pearce thinking, a whole damn Saturday night watching a car and some other damn house.

The car was Patty's Mercedes roadster. Parked down the block from the one-story shit-box of a house they were watching. The shit-box house belonging to Dale Longnecker, Patty's lover.

Dale's wife not there at the moment, so Patty was.

Coming up on ten o'clock though. Pearce knowing Dale's wife would get home soon from her usual Saturday night shift behind the register at the Phillips 66 out by the interstate. Pearce getting anxious. Patty would need to get moving soon. Or get caught by one very tired, pissed off but probably not all that surprised wife.

Either way, things were going to start happening soon.

Until things started happening, a day's worth of boredom and anticipation continued grating on both Chubba and Pearce. Who else to take it out on but each other?

Chubba asking, "You did steal this car, right?"

Pearce not taking his eyes off Dale's house. "Think I'd use my own ride for a thing like this?"

"You tell me," said Chubba. "You're the expert. I forget, when was it you kidnapped someone?"

"A while back," Pearce said, "Year or so."

"That's right. In Kansas City."

"No. Down in Tulsa."

"Oh, Tulsa," Chubba said. "Must be why I don't remember hearing anything about it."

"You didn't hear anything about it because it worked," Pearce said. "Do it right and no one knows other than the people involved on both sides. And none of them want anyone to know."

"Like I said," Chubba said, "you're the expert." Chubba opened the glove compartment, watching Pearce for a reaction.

Nothing.

Chubba's meaty hands sifting through the compartment, pulling out pens and scraps of paper, tissues, a tire gauge and some change before finally removing a thick brown envelope about the size of a hardback book.

Tossing all the junk back in the compartment before looking down into the envelope. Still no reaction from Pearce.

Chubba removing the Volvo's owner's manual, flipping through it. Digging in the envelope, looking for the title or proof of insurance, anything with the owner's name on it.

"I got rid of it," Pearce said, still watching Dale' place.

"And why is that?" Chubba said. "Afraid someone might go looking for it?"

"Actually, yes. Something goes wrong—something better not go wrong, but you never know – but something goes wrong, I want to make it as difficult as possible for them to trace this car back to where it came from. Make it that much harder to pin it on me. See, Chubba, that's how pros work."

Chubba considered this before finally asking, "The plate?"

"Switched from another car."

"And the VIN?"

Pearce shook him off. "If they're gonna get you, they're gonna get you. So try not to fuck up, okay?"

Chubba wasn't convinced but decided to let it slide for the time being. Switching gears, saying "You know that thing you said earlier, about hiding in the back of Patty's car?"

Pearce finally looking at Chubba. "Yeah?"

"That is the stupidest fucking idea I ever heard," Chubba

said. “Who are you, Jason from Friday the Thirteenth?”

“No. It’s not,” Pearce said. “I watched. She didn’t lock her car when she went in to screw Jethro. So why not just crawl into the back seat, pop up and grab her? It’s easy.”

Chubba saying no wait, not Jason. Pinhead from Hellraiser.

“With all that metal sticking out of your face.” Chubba laughing so hard he started coughing. Had to take care he didn’t swallow his dip. “Get it?”

“Ha ha, very funny. Care to focus on our job here?” Pearce said. “Try to be a pro. You keep this up, I’m walking. I’ll drive your ass back to your daddy’s house and I’m gone, project aborted.”

Chubba stopped laughing. Taking satisfaction from getting under freakshow’s skin. But Chubba not about to take lip off this motherfucker either. Chubba giving a long, stringy spit into his spit can before speaking.

“You are one pissy little bitch, know that?”

“You’ll end up the bitch, something goes south and we find our asses in lock up all because you’re jacking around.”

“Me jacking around?” Chubba said. “Just worry about your own self.”

Chubba going on with how stupid Pearce’s hide-and-grab brainstorm was. Saying first of all, those roadsters, they don’t have much of a back seat to speak of.

But say Pearce did manage to fit back there. Chubba saying suppose Patty takes off driving before he got her? Suppose she stomps on the gas when he grabs her, wrecks the car, killing them both?

"Can't just go popping up like Pinhead," Chubb said. "Ain't no movie."

"Cut the Pinhead shit."

"Look, you got to admit," Chubba said, trying to get all the words out before the giggles came, "It's pretty damn funny, you having all those rings and rocks poking out of your face and all *and* you being named Pearce. That shit is, what do you call it? Irony, right? It's funny, all I'm saying."

"Chubba, kiss my ass," Pearce said. He opened the car door. He'd made sure to grab the keys from the ignition first.

"Do not do this!" Chubba hissed, careful not to yell. "Get your ass back in the car."

Pearce slamming the car door shut. The corner street light was out and with no moon they at least had the darkness on their side.

Chubba looking around to see if any neighbors were stirring at the sound of Pearce slamming his car door. No lights coming on. No one peeking out through their blinds to see what all the ruckus was about.

No movement anywhere except the curious sight of freakshow wandering down the middle of the darkened side street. Not even sense enough to move along in the shadows of the sidewalk.

Chubba thinking expert my ass, drooling some tobacco juice in his spit cup.

Since he'd met Pearce, Chubba had thought all Pearce's self-gloss about his criminal bona fides was nothing but a load of horseshit. Had said as much when they were arguing about bringing Pearce onto The Project. That's what they'd all come to call it, The Project.

The first time Chubba and his daddy met this Pearce guy, he'd immediately rubbed Chubba the wrong way. This was about a month earlier, in the parking lot of a fast food joint along the interstate just west of Kansas City.

Awkward handshakes all around as the winter prairie wind whipped across their faces. Sharla acting all excited to see Pearce, saying more than once it was great to meet him in person after all their chatting on the Internet.

Sharla's blatant flirting adding to the general unease running through the group because everyone understood, if not the specifics of what they were meeting about, then at least its general criminal outline.

At the first meeting Pearce asking about the money target, was she loaded? Chubba saying shit yes, how stupid you think we are, like we'd pick someone without money. Pearce saying you never know. Then asking how well they knew the target, well enough to know she'll play along rather than call the law?

Horace finally piping up, telling Pearce not to worry about it. Chubba smirking at that, his daddy putting this freakshow in his place. Horace saying he and Arlita went back a long ways.

Pearce at the time catching something more personal than business in the way the short man said it. But figuring that kind of thing was none of a hired gun's business and that was the part he was playing here.

Then the second time they met – at Horace's ranch outside of Caulfield to go over The Project in detail – Pearce had let it slip that actually he lived in Lenexa, not Kansas City. Not a big deal, but still. Lenexa and OP both sprawling suburbs of Kansas City on the Kansas side in Johnson County.

Figures, Chubba said later to Sharla. A fucking Johnson County snob.

Each KC suburb had its share of petty crime and heat of the moment killings, but neither was hardly a breeding ground for major league criminals.

But Sharla, she seemed willing to buy the way Pearce had played it off, the way most Kansas City suburbanites do when pressed for particulars on where they live in Kansas City. Pearce backtracking with that old, "Well, not in Kansas City proper. Just outside it. Nobody lives *in* Kansas City."

Chubba thinking yeah, nobody except about half a million people.

Truth of it, there was more to Chubba's dislike for Pearce than simply because it was Sharla who brought him in. Didn't like that one bit.

Didn't feel his instincts were wrong on that neither, no matter how much Sharla kept denying anything was going on between her and Pearce.

Who in the hell in his right mind would like it? All the sudden your girlfriend shows up for a felony crime with some out of town guy? Some guy you've never even heard her mention before and now, out of the blue, she's vouching for this guy?

Chubba had argued hard against bringing in Pearce from the beginning. Making the case that a kidnapping calls for what he call, "a full-growed load of trust among conspirators."

Asking Sharla so just how come all the sudden she's got

all this confidence in some guy he's never heard of? She never answered that one. Just called Chubba a jackass and stomped off. Like that was the end of it.

And it pretty much was the end of it, once Chubba's daddy said so. Horace agreeing maybe Pearce's was full of horseshit. But it made sense, bringing in an outsider to pull off something like this in a town where everybody knows everybody.

"Once we snatch her up, somebody's going to have to keep an eye on Patty full time," Horace had said. "One of us goes AWOL for a few days, like maybe you or Sharla don't show your face in town, you can damn sure bet some busybody will notice. Start asking questions. *Haven't seen Chubba lately. He feeling okay?* When they're really asking what the fuck is he up to?"

That was that. Pearce was in.

And the third time they'd met with Pearce was yesterday, preparing for today. Go time. But the love, it certainly wasn't growing between them.

Chubba laughed as Pearce slipped on the wet street bricks, landing on his back. Whenever it rained the red bricks of the street grew slippery with a thin, mossy film.

Anybody watching, their instincts would have been alarmed at the sight of this skinny freakshow picking himself up off the road. All dressed in black, weird-ass holes in his ear lobes. Tats up and down his reedy arm and jewelry sticking out of his long, narrow face.

"Expert my ass," Chubba said, leaning over to spit tobacco juice in the driver's seat, rubbing it in.

Four

Patty loved the look of her legs splayed in the air.

Dale humping away, and Patty looking up at her jiggling limbs in the yellow lamp light. Admiring the curved lines of her tan calves, her thick ankles, her toenails with the French pedicure Sharla had given her that morning. Feeling sexy.

Their entwined bodies throwing writhing shadows on the peeling, flowered wallpaper of Dale and Lucinda Longnecker's bedroom. Dale smelling of cigarettes and sweat. His mustache tickling Patty's neck. Dale getting a bit winded, she could tell, trying to make up for a lack of pace and endurance with force.

It was Dale's rough edges that first attracted Patty. Strong, nicked up mechanic's hands. The powerful way he entered her, then banged away at her. The kiss-my-ass-if-you-don't-like-it way he spoke his mind. But eventually, Patty coming to realize Dale spoke with the conviction of someone who doesn't feel the need to give anything much thought.

Lately, fast or slow, hard or gentle, it didn't matter. Again tonight, Patty wasn't feeling much pleasure with Dale. Unsure if that was an effect of the booze she slammed at the bar or just a sign that it was about time to move on from Dale.

Patty thinking it was just a sex thing and if the sex wasn't doing it for her then what exactly was the point?

Still, it was nice to be wanted. Even if it was Dale Longnecker. Patty looking at the burning red numbers of the digital clock on the nightstand.

"Better hurry," she said.

"You close, baby?" Dale said.

Patty about say no but his wife probably was. Instead, she went along with it. "Oh yes, baby. Bring it home. Now!"

Dale went to work. Patty began moaning, playing at first but the act of acting bringing her a very real sensation of pleasure. Not euphoria, exactly. But something better than what she'd been getting from Dale recently.

The heat between them increasing as they started climbing the hill together. Patty hoping for once Dale wouldn't reach the top before her. Both of them hearing a car door slam on the street.

Patty and Dale stopping, holding on to each other. Quiet. Listening.

"What was that?" Dale said.

"Car door. She home?"

"Shhh."

They listened for footsteps, the door. Nothing, just a dog barking somewhere in the distance. Once they decided the coast was clear, Dale started up again.

But it was all gone for Patty, and she could tell it wasn't coming back. Deciding to just hang on, ride it out for the minute or two left on this flat roller coaster.

When the dull journey was over, they lay on the bed naked, smoking Dale's Marlboro Lights. Patty could tell that Dale was itching to turn on SportsCenter.

Patty considering telling him it was over between them, right now. She thought of herself that way; a person who, once a thing is decided, it's done. Telling herself she got that from her

Gramma. That and her thighs.

Patty sitting up slow, the room spinning. At the first a hint of nausea, Patty stubbed out the cigarette. Needing water but, short of that, better to keep her buzz going. Taking a swig from a long-neck bottle of Bud Light on the nightstand. Dale only drank out of long-neck bottles on account of his last name.

She wiped at a trickle of beer in the corner of her mouth, about to launch into a breakup speech when Dale said, "Shit!"

They both heard the car pulling into the driveway. Patty didn't know the sound of Lucinda's car but was pretty sure from the terrified look on Dale's face that he did. Without a word, Patty scooped up her clothes, heading for the door.

"No!" Dale said. "The window."

"You got to be shitting me, Dale. I ain't crawling out no window like some whore. You did the deed, now own up to it."

"Please, Patty. Damn it, she'll kill me."

Patty rolled her eyes, shook her head. "Fine," she said, starting to put one leg into her jeans.

"No time, baby," Dale said, herding her toward the window on the side of the house.

"Let me put my pants on—"

The front door closing and Lucinda calling out, "Dale. I'm home."

Dale had the storm window up but the screen wouldn't budge. It had stopped raining but cold, damp night air blew into the bedroom. With his index finger, he poked a hole in the corner of the screen and then ripped it upwards.

"Go."

"Nice fucking you too, Dale. Hope you enjoyed it because

it was the last time you're getting any of this."

"Whatever, Patty. Go!"

Patty going feet first through the window, scraping her back on the bottom of the window as she dropped. The window closing quickly behind her.

Patty's bare feet hitting the wet ground and Patty thinking it was lucky for her Dale was too lazy to get a job where he could afford to buy a two-story house. The day's rain had turned the dirt yard to mud, and Patty felt a cold ooze rise up between her toes.

Naked in the chilly air, her body was overrun with goose bumps. She folded her arms over her naked breasts, her flesh like chicken skin. Still, the crisp air felt good to her head.

Patty looking around in the darkness. No moon out and didn't appear to be anyone around. Slipping on her thong underwear, jeans, bra and t-shirt before realizing she'd left her flip-flops in the bedroom. For a moment considering tapping on the window. Or better yet, marching around to the front door, knocking. Ask Lucinda if she'd found a pair of unfamiliar flip-flops. Instead, Patty deciding to cut her losses.

Making her way to her car down the street and around the corner. Patty kept looking back at Dale's to see if anyone was following or watching her. Wouldn't have surprised her to turn around and find Lucinda flying out of the house, coming at her with a knife. Patty thinking if Lucinda came after her, she damn well better bring a knife.

"Kick her ass, that bitch tries to mess with me," Patty said to herself, as she pushed the remote to unlock her car.

Just then realizing she forgot to lock her car. Christ, had

she really been that eager to crawl into bed with Dale? Or just that drunk?

Speaking of, she could use a beer. All the excitement and adrenaline had cleared her head. Things were probably starting to bounce out at Koy's party.

Patty taking one last look around before stepping into her Mercedes. Patty had wanted a Dodge Viper but her Gramma insisting on the Mercedes because it was safer.

It was the CLK-class roadster, a step above the C-class, Patty often pointing that out when people seemed interested. They seemed interested a lot. People were always asking her about her fancy German car. Usually, Patty could hear their real question in their voice: *Who do you think you are and what are you doing with this car?*

Sitting in her safe, starter Mercedes, her heart pounding. Looking around and half-expecting to find a livid, cleaver-waving Lucinda coming at her. Patty feeling safe now in this car. No one could get at her now. Couldn't catch her neither. *All y'all go fuck yourselves.*

Starting up the roadster, revving it. The low growl of the engine roaring before Patty tore away with a loud squeal on the wet brick street.

That ought to bring Lucinda to the window.

Five

When the headlights were half a block away, Pearce had jumped for cover in a row of evergreen bushes.

Chubba, still slumped down as far into his seat as possible, watched as the lights turned into Dale's drive way. Saying holy shit here we go when he spotted Lucinda walking up her front stoop and into her house.

Pearce nowhere to be seen. Chubba wasn't sure if maybe he was still in the bushes or if somehow he'd managed get to Patty's Mercedes, maybe wedge himself into the back of it.

Chubba not seeing Pearce but then catching sight of Patty's thick, naked body shooting out a window on the side of Dale's house. At the sight of her, Chubba feeling both panicked and aroused. Watching Patty quickly dressing herself. Chubba helpless to do anything as she made her way down the block and around the corner to her car. Then the sound of squealing tires and their target was gone.

The sound of Patty's car fading into the night. Chubba seeing someone pull back the living room curtain in Dale's house to see what the noise was all about before letting it go slack again.

Chubba waiting. He didn't have the keys. Didn't know where Pearce was. Didn't know where Patty had gone. Chubba realizing his mouth was bone dry, despite his dip.

This was Chubba's first truly criminal act and he was suddenly feeling ill. Speeding, drunk driving, doing donuts in a snowy church parking lot, that was about it for his criminal past. Even those had been taken care of by his old man, keeping his record spotless.

Chubba searching the darkness outside the passenger window when the interior of the car exploded in light, scaring Chubba so badly that he let out a shriek. A wet and muddy Pearce climbed into the driver's seat.

"Where the fuck did you go?" Chubba asked.

"Circled around the block," Pearce said, breathing hard. "Where'd she go?"

Chubba took out his dip, shoving it into the mouth of his spit can. "Well, um, let's see. I was here. She took off in her fast car. I was still here. You were somewhere with the keys to this car. So, honestly, your guess is as good as mine, ain't it dumbass?"

Unsure where they were going, they just drove off down the street, the bricks rattling the interior of the Volvo.

"Just drive around, maybe we'll run into her," Chubba said.

"I have a better idea. Where's Koy Reed's house?"

"You know Koy?" Chubba said. "How in the hell do you know Koy?"

"I don't," Pearce said, turning a corner and heading toward Main Street. "Sharla said Patty mentioned a party at his place. She might head out there. Which way is it?"

Chubba stared hard at Pearce for a long, uncomfortable moment. Street lights wheeling by overhead, casting inky shadows over their faces. Chubba finally telling Pearce to take a right when he got Main Street.

"Koy's place is east of town, out on the old highway." Chubba staring at Pearce even as he said that most likely Patty would take the old highway. It had a lot of curves, was fun to drive.

Chubba saying if they took the main highway then cut over, they might be able to catch up to her before she got there. If not, they could wait until she left the party, snatch her then.

Pearce feeling Chubba's eyes on him. Ignoring him as long as he could until finally saying, "Dude, can I help you?"

"Tell me something, dude," Chubba said. "When did you talk to Sharla?"

"What?"

"About Koy's party and Patty going there. When did you talk with Sharla about all that?"

"Earlier. She called."

"She did, huh?" Other than a text message here and there, Chubba hadn't heard from Sharla since that morning, when he'd tried to kiss her goodbye and she put him off, saying she was too nervous about The Project Later trying to call her and she hadn't answered, instead texting him that she was too busy working to talk.

"We been together most all day," Chubba said. "I don't remember you talking to her."

"What? No, I didn't talk to her. She left a message on my cell."

They passed the city limit sign leading out of Caulfield and sped north on the new highway, heading in the direction of Koy's house outside of town. Chubba remembered Pearce checking his messages a few times during the course of the day.

"Funny," Chubba said, "You never said nothing about a message from Sharla."

“I didn’t? Well, she called. Left a message. There you go.”

Chubba directed Pearce to take the right coming up on them fast. Pearce hit the brakes hard.

“How about a little warning next time,” Pearce said, turning off the new highway onto a dirt road.

“Got to stay alert,” Chubba said. “Never know when it’s coming.”

The Volvo fishtailed its way down the gravel road. Its wayward high beams struggling to bore holes into the moonless night. The farmland on either side of them was invisible. In the distance on their right, Chubba could see car lights speeding along a path perpendicular to theirs.

“There she is. Hit it.”

“I don’t want to wreck,” Pearce said, both hands gripping the wheel

“Put your goddamn foot into it!”

Pearce goosed the engine up a bit. Chubba cursed Pearce, ordered him to stomp on it. Instead, as it became apparent they would reach the intersection at the same time as the other car, Pearce laid into the brake again.

The Volvo sliding a long ways on the gravel road before its tires finally gripped the asphalt at the intersection with the old highway. They jerked to a halt just as Patty’s Mercedes went racing by the nose of the Volvo.

Chubba saying go, go! Pearce turning the Volvo onto the old highway, flooring it. Watching the Mercedes’ red taillights growing smaller.

“Good idea, stealing a Volvo,” Chubba said.

“You could have mentioned she’d be driving a goddamn

race car!"

"Just keep the pedal down," Chubba said. "There's a corner up here she'll have to slow down for. When you get close, start flashing your lights and honking. Maybe we can get her to pull over."

Neither one saying it but both thinking it...*What if Patty does pull over?...What then?*

Six

Patty swigging on a Coors Light and cursing the stupid cocksucker who'd almost T-boned her at back at the intersection. She'd picked up two cases of beer after leaving Dale's. Didn't want to show up at a party empty handed.

Easing her dirty bare foot off the accelerator as she slowed for a curve. Taking another long swallow. As she tilted her head back, seeing the flashing headlights and hazards in her rear-view mirror.

That bitch, Lucinda.

Patty ready to put her foot up Lucinda's ass sideways. This wasn't about Dale. Lucinda could have the worthless son of a bitch. Right now Patty wasn't in the mood to put up with attitude from anybody, especially not some mouthy hag like Lucinda Fucking Longnecker.

Patty trying to decide: *Pull over now and kick Lucinda's ass? Or better to lead her into Koy's party, kick her ass in front of everyone there?*

Patty getting through the curve on the road but the flashing lights closing on her quickly. That pissed off Patty even more, Lucinda on her ass like that. Patty close to the point where she was ready to bring it.

Pulling over hard to the side of the highway and a few seconds later the car with the flashing lights coming to a hard stop in front of her, cutting off her Mercedes. Patty seeing it wasn't Lucinda's car after all. A sedan she didn't recognize. Able to see there were two people in the car but unable to make out their faces.

The driver got out of the car, a guy, and started toward her. He was staying toward the edge of the light cast by her headlights but Patty could see odd little glints of light dancing across the man's face as he walked.

Patty pressing down on the clutch and putting the roadster in gear, just in case.

Pearce taking his time getting to Patty's car and hoping that somewhere between the Volvo and the Mercedes, he'd figure out what to do next.

This was it. Grab her? Where, the hair? Punch her? Would she fight back? He really hoped she wouldn't.

He'd fooled them this long. Still not too late to go back. But Pearce telling himself he could do this. A first time for everything. He wanted to do this.

Pearce pretty sure he could hit her hard enough to knock her out. Really? Or just believing his own bullshit now?

Think about Sharla. Girls as hot as Sharla never went for him, ever. Best to keep fooling them. Might be too late to back out.

Telling himself don't be scared. Mostly scared that something was going to happen to his mom's Volvo. Hoping this rich bitch in the Mercedes was more scared than he was.

Chubba wrenched around in the passenger seat, watching Pearce taking his time getting to Patty's vehicle. Chubba unable to make out much detail in the Mercedes' headlights, just dim shapes and movements.

"Hurry up, chickenshit," Chubba said to himself. "Let's get this thing done."

Chubba saw Pearce motion for Patty to lower her window. He saw the light reflecting off the jewelry in Pearce's face as he spoke but couldn't make out the words.

Watching Pearce pointing back down the road, then at the back of her car. Chubba lowered the window in the Volvo to hear.

Seeing Patty poke her head out the window to look back down the road. Pearce with a slight step back before lunging at her with a straight right. Catching her on the side of the head, a sickening sound of knuckles bones against skull.

Chubba hearing Patty scream. At first assuming Pearce's shot had knocked her cold but then Chubba seeing Pearce's top half ducking into Patty's window. The two of them struggling. Pearce yanking her by the hair, slamming her face into the steering wheel. Patty flailing, scrabbling, hollering, cussing.

Chubba hearing the Mercedes' engine snarl just as the roadster launched itself at the Volvo. Smashing into its rear end. Slamming Chubba into the dash as the world spun around him.

He could hear metal clawing metal, drowning out the sounds of people screaming. Just as suddenly, the world stopped spinning and everything was quiet except for the idling engine of the wounded Volvo.

Chubba a little stunned as he stepped out of the Volvo. Standing there realizing the car had been spun one hundred eighty degrees and was now pointing in the opposite direction.

Pearce sitting up on the shoulder of the road, speechless, appeared to be looking out across the darkened pasture. Chubba following his line of sight, seeing it wasn't the land he was looking at, but the sight of Patty's vehicle. It was now ahead of them rather than behind them. Flipped upside down in the ditch. Its engine was quiet, though the lights were still burning. Chubba walked toward Pearce.

"You all right?"

Pearce nodded but didn't say anything. Then realizing the Volvo was now pointing at him. "She hit the car?"

"Yeah," Chubba said. "You think she's okay?"

"She's going to need body work," Pearce said.

Chubba frowned at Pearce. "To hell with the car. I'm

talking about Patty. Think she's alive?"

Pearce shrugged. Gingerly he picked himself up off the ground. Soreness began to creep into his body. He remembered extracting himself from the Mercedes and hitting the ground hard just before Patty slammed into the Volvo. He'd lost a few seconds somewhere in there before coming to.

A sound coming out of the blackness of the field next to the highway, and Pearce a little slow to place it. Noticing Chubba perk up, meaning he heard it too. The slap of footsteps running through mud.

The freezing mud swallowed each step all the way up to Patty's ankle. Struggling to extract her legs from the earth's suction and get away.

She didn't know what was happening. Knowing she was covered in mud and trying to run through a muddy field for her life.

She just didn't know why this was happening. At the moment caring less about the why and more about getting away.

Her head was throbbing. Her teeth felt too big for her mouth. The skin of her face stretched to contain her swelling cheeks, nose and forehead. It was too dark to see her hand in front of her face, so she couldn't tell is she was bleeding. Pretty certain she tasted blood in the back of her throat.

Fighting to free her feet from one muddy suck-hole after

the next and the stupidest thought flashing through head—her pedicured toenails were going to be ruined. Just as quickly her mind refocused on the matter at hand, urging her to just keep running.

Hearing voices behind her. Glancing back at the Volvo's beams on the highway. Two shadows navigating the barbed wire fence that had cut her arms and legs as she'd crawled from her overturned car and through the fence and started running across the field.

Nothing but wide open space and darkness all around her. Patty kept moving, just getting as far away as she could. The adrenaline fading, taking with it the last of her energy. Patty guessing she was smack in the middle of the field.

Quietly sliding flat onto her belly, pressing herself into the mud. Stars light years away burned pinholes in the sky, but down here on earth Patty glad for the darkness. Eyes adjusting now, watching the two figures clear the fence and start blindly toward her.

Coming closer. Hearing their voices but unable to make out what they were saying. Trying to catch her breath silently, waiting to see how near they would come.

"**See her** anywhere?"

"Nope."

"Well, she's out here somewhere," Chubba breathing

hard as he fought the gummy mud at each step. “I mean, look around. Where’s she gonna go?”

“We are so fucked,” Pearce said, trying to keep his balance in the mess.

“That’s your professional opinion, right?” Chubba said. “Next time, freakshow, try actually getting your hands on the person you’re kidnapping.”

Chubba saying Patty will try to work her way back to the road so they should head back to the car.

“We’ll drive around ‘til we find her,” Chubba said. “She ain’t going far.”

“Let’s just abort, dude,” Pearce said.

Chubba saying they’re weren’t aborting shit.

Again Pearce saying, “We are so fucked.”

Chubba nodding his head, saying that might be the first thing Pearce was right about all day.

“We don’t find her, and quick, we are fucked,” Chubba said. “Absolutely dry-fucked.”

Seven

Watching for something different.

Saturday night and Billy cruising downtown Caulfield. Kicking back in the seat with his thumb and forefinger hooked around the steering wheel, guiding his sheriff’s Escalade up and down Main Street.

Street lights reflecting on the asphalt still glistening with that day's rain. Billy passing by the bank, noticing the hands on the moon-faced clock pointing toward eleven thirty.

Not on duty, technically speaking. Not patrolling, just driving, something to do. Whiskeytown playing low on the truck's stereo. Billy's Stetson off, lying upside down in the passenger seat. Billy taking another sip of beer from his Big Gulp cup. It was his Saturday night too.

Another long, slow pass through town, then Billy turning around at the end of the drag, heading back to where he's just come from. Watching for something different in a small town that never seems to change.

Traffic thinning now but earlier in the evening the fifteen blocks that made up Caulfield's downtown had been buzzing. People anxious to get out and about after being cooped up beneath three days of drizzle, driving up and down Main Street.

Packs of teenagers from Caulfield and from nearby towns even smaller than Caulfield, most of them driving mom's sedan or dad's pickup truck.

Young adults sitting low and keeping their beers lower.

Mom and dad out on the town for a steak then maybe catch a movie or run over to the Indian casino in Pierette County for some gambling.

Everyone waiting for something exciting or interesting or just *something* to happen.

But by this time of night people were either heading home or hunkering down for some serious drinking. At a bar, out at the country club, or at a house party. That time of night when you either fuck or fight.

But Main Street so quiet now that every couple of blocks, Billy caught himself slipping into a trance as he drove.

Passing the familiar stores and shops tucked into the limestone or brick buildings that he'd been passing since before he could remember, then abruptly pulling himself back to the present. Reminding himself to watch for something different.

Seeing the small differences, that was the key to law enforcement. So sayeth Sheriff Otis Cady. He was the sheriff of Eden County, the county next door to the west and a sort of mentor to Billy.

Before being elected sheriff, Billy had never met Sheriff Otis Cady, had only heard about the man. But everybody in the state knew of Sheriff Cady after that business a few years back. A crazy, drug-dealing bisexual stripper fakes her own death by murdering and setting another woman on fire in her place. A story like that has legs and travels far and fast.

It was soon after Billy was elected sheriff of Caste County in an emergency election the previous August that he'd received a personal phone call from Sheriff Cady. The gruff voice on the line inviting him to discuss the sheriffing business over a cup of coffee.

On that first visit over to Eden, the Escalade rising and falling with the sparse, rolling hills of the grassland, Billy had steeled himself for a lecture. Or worse, ridicule. A life-long law enforcement officer was bound to be annoyed to have a wet-nosed civilian as, term used loosely, a peer.

They'd met at a storefront café, one of those places where farmers gather to bitch about droughts killing the crops or heavy rains making it too muddy to harvest the crops or perfect weather yielding a bumper crop and driving down prices.

Sliding down into the red vinyl booth and laying eyes on Sheriff Cady for the first time, Billy was surprised to find the man across from him wasn't older. He wasn't youthful really, just not as old as Billy expected. Sheriff Cady looked to be in his early fifties, hard and lean but in a healthy way.

He started off saying that, like Billy, he'd come onto the job at a young age.

For his part Billy had started off almost apologetic, stopping just short of shouldering *all* the blame for his election to an office he had no business holding. He was green, he admitted. But he intended to do his best to uphold the law, bring no disrespect to the office.

"That's nice," Sheriff Cady said, stirring sugar substitute into his coffee before taking a sip. "Election's over. Now, how about you pull your head out your ass so your ears can hear?"

It was during that first conversation when he'd passed along the advice to Billy about noticing differences.

Billy snapping out of his driving trance as he passed Waxman's Drycleaners. Lights were off inside, the dry cleaners dark, closed for the evening. But Billy certain he'd seen a flashlight moving inside.

Slowing his vehicle to a crawl in the middle of the empty Main Street, Billy studied the corner storefront in his side mirror. After a moment he saw it again, light arching around inside the cleaners.

Billy circled the block, turning off the music, putting his Big Gulp of beer in the cup holder. Still not truly believing he was about to interrupt an in-progress B and E. Noticing his heart racing.

Seven months on the job and up to this point it mostly had been all speeders, drunk drivers, wife beaters, husband beaters and small time weed and meth dealers. All people he could handle because more often than not they were people he'd known most of his life. People who knew him.

The old boys who had put Billy up to the job had underestimated the power of his local celebrity. It not only got him elected on short notice in a special election, but people's familiarity with him somehow put them at ease, even during some of the ugliest episodes of their lives.

Sure, there were the occasional drunk young men who took Billy's status and celebrity as something to be challenged. But most often when people realized who was knocking on their door or handing them a ticket or suggesting they put down the tire iron, they tended to relax, a smile creeping across their guilty faces, shoulders loosening.

As he parked the Escalade, an idea hit Billy like a shock from a cattle prod: there was a damn good chance he knew the perp rummaging around inside Waxman's cleaners.

Walking along the sidewalk toward Waxman's, passing Mason's drugstore, Dow's jewelry store, Hipple's hardware store. Billy stopping once or twice, hand on a parking meter, surveying Main Street. Other than an occasional car or truck passing by, Main Street was deserted. So quiet that Billy could hear the click of the traffic light as it changed signal colors.

A fleeting moment of panic as Billy thought he'd forgotten his gun. His right hand shot to his hip, confirming it was there.

Billy and Sheriff Cady had talked a lot that first morning they met over coffee and had met at least once every month since. Sheriff Cady talking, but not lecturing. Mostly asking questions. What did Billy think law enforcement was really about, anyway? Did he know the law? Was he prepared to stay current on it? And, of course, did Billy know how to use a gun?

Billy saying yeah, he could shoot, even before his week-long crash course in law enforcement basics at the Kansas Bureau of Investigations. In fact, Billy said, he'd been issued a Kimber Custom II .45 caliber.

When he'd reached to pull it out of his side holster, show it off in the café, Sheriff Cady had just waved him off. Said it was a good idea to know how to handle one, if only so he didn't shoot himself on accident. Adding that Billy probably wouldn't ever need it to use it. Certainly hoped not, anyway.

Billy coming up quietly now on the dark dry cleaners, unsnapping the safety strap on his holster. Hand on his gun, thinking next time they met over coffee, he'd have to let the old boy know he wasn't right about everything.

Billy stopping just short of Waxman's plate glass window. With his back to the building. Waiting for what? He wasn't sure. Another flash of light? A noise? A sign from God?

He got all three. Something crashing to the floor inside the cleaners. A flashlight's beam arching through the air. Muffled cursing.

Billy peeking around the edge of the window, trying to steal a glimpse of the ruckus inside the cleaners. Seeing the flashlight rolling on the floor. Billy thought he made out the shadow of a figure rising to its feet.

The shadow figure righting itself and picking up the flashlight. It took Billy a half-second longer than he would have liked to realize the figure was pointing the flashlight right at him.

The figure with flashlight starting toward him. Billy blinded, freezing like a white-eyed deer on a highway, watching the approach of the next important thing to happen to him.

The light cast by the flashlight, held waist-high by the figure, spread wider as it approached the front of the cleaners. At the last second, the figure reaching out with the flashlight, banging on the window, jolting Billy from his daze.

A laugh coming from inside the cleaners. Billy recognized it as the high, mocking tone belonging to Leonard Waxman himself. Waxman moving to the door, flipping the lock.

"Didja fill your britches?" Waxman said. The thin man obviously amused as he stepped out to join Billy on the sidewalk.

"Why?" Billy said, "You know a good dry cleaner that can get the stain out?"

Billy playing it off but shifting his weight from foot to foot so that Waxman wouldn't see his knees shaking.

Billy thinking, hell if that wasn't different.

Eight

Sharla sitting in Chubba's idling Mustang parked in her dark driveway. Sinking two roofies in her Diet Coke. Holding them up to the street light, watching them fizz.

Then backing out too fast, hitting the gas, tires squealing, heading north out of town. Help those fucknuts Chubba and Pearce track down Patty.

Flying down the old highway. She always drove Chubba's car, sticking him with her dinged and dusty Pontiac coupe. A fair deal as she saw it. True, his car was nicer than hers, but she slept with Chubba and her body was nicer than his.

In between puffs on the menthol cigarette clutched in the fingers of her steering wheel hand, Sharla put down the cell phone in her other hand. Using her now free hand to grab the Diet Coke from the cup holder. Holding up the plastic bottle, checking to see if the hypnotic pills had dissolved yet.

Sharla really needing something to round off the sharp edges of her nerves. She was agitated, but then that's what a full day of smoking methamphetamine and a kidnapping gone awry can do to a girl.

It was graduation day for Sharla. More dope in her today than in any other day in her life. A handshake and here's your drug addict diploma

All day disappearing again and again into the bathroom at Arlita's beauty shop, smoking a bowl at a time. Just one bowl per visit, that was her self-imposed limit. Six visits to the toilet, Sharla only breaking her one-bowl-per-visit rule three times.

At least all the smoke breaks had minimized the time Sharla had to spend in the shop trying to act like today was no different than any other day. Trying not to look at Fatty Patty too often or too long.

Afraid a tense glance or her darting eyes might give away the whole thing. Then Sharla reminding herself to look at Patty just often enough so that it didn't seem suspicious to Arlita that Sharla wasn't looking at Patty. Arlita never missed a goddamn trick. Nerve-wracking trying to find that balance.

Sharla would be the first to admit that balance wasn't a strength of hers. Not even on her best day B.C. That is, Before Crystal.

Sharla always throwing that in when talking about anything that took place in that long-ago time before she started using meth. About a year ago. It seemed long ago, anyway.

Sometime about three months before, she'd graduated from weekend nostril-burning toots to daily smoking. Easier on the nose and a better kick. But no needles, she promised herself. Never cross that sad line. Lately reminding herself of this promise almost daily. Sharla choosing to take that as a sign of strength rather than weakness.

After leaving the beauty shop, Sharla had dropped by her second-string dealer's trailer to score more meth. Her First-Team All-American dealer was currently on the bottom floor of Caulfield Memorial with third-degree burns over forty-five percent of his body, the result of an explosive episode of his own personal cooking show.

So Sharla had given her business to Layne, a mechanic who couldn't fix a flat tire but could fix up a decent batch of ice. Then it was home to her small rented house to wait with her dope and pipe for Pearce and Chubba to contact her.

The rest of the day and evening spent bouncing around the cluttered two-bedroom house. Bare feet pacing the dull hardwoods of one room, moving onto the worn carpet of another. Smoking cigarettes, flipping channels on the TV.

Waiting for Chubba's call confirming that Fatty Patty was stuffed in the trunk of the stolen car and on her way to the hideout as planned.

Chubba finally calling Sharla on one of the pay-as-you-go phones they were using for The Project. The damn thing started buzzing there among the dirty dishes on the kitchen table, and Sharla swore she could tell from the *sound* of the buzz that everything was all fucked up.

Sharla driving down the old highway now, keeping an anxious eye out for Fatty Patty wandering down the side of the road. And for any hallucinations all the dope and fear might bring.

A drag on the menthol dangling from her lips now as she fiddled with the defroster. Hot or cold air to defrost the inside, damn it? Satellite radio was broken, Chubba too lazy to get it fixed. Nothing but commercials on all the local stations.

A buzzing again coming from her cell phone, a text message from Chubba: *still nuthn.*

Chubba. Sharla thinking she should never have let him go along. Next time she talked to that soft, stupid bastard, Sharla planned to ask him - and this time get an answer - just how he had gotten in Pearce's way to screw it all up.

And then more questions whizzing around inside her head, wondering was there still time to get out of this? Sharla's head swirling, thinking that just maybe there was a way they could just go on like nothing ever happened.

Holding up the Diet Coke, watching bubbles still rising from the shrinking white Rohypnol pills.

Sharla suddenly skeptical of all those stories of frat boys

spiking some sorority girl's drink without her noticing it. Not if it took this long for a date rape drug to dissolve. Unless your date went to take a long dump.

The roofies offered Sharla a glide down from the meth rather than a crash. It would get Sharla back to normal but, face it, there was no normal anymore.

Sometimes Sharla even popped a ruffie or two before she and Chubba had sex. You weren't supposed to build up a resistance to roofies, but Sharla had noticed lately that the tranquilizer seemed to be taking longer to kick in. Mistime her intake and she'd be left with cloudy memories of Chubba's clumsy, groping foreplay before the drug finally threw a blanket over the birdcage of her consciousness.

Once Chubba protested, saying that if she needed ruffies before sex, well, maybe she didn't like him all that much.

Sharla just saying, "Different kinds of love in this world, baby." She didn't elaborate, and he didn't ask.

"Goddamn Chubba!" Sharla said, picking up her cell phone, speed-dialing Chubba's cell number.

"Yellow!" he said.

"Really?" Sharla said. "Answering the phone like you're at a party or something? You mess this whole thing up and that's how it's going to be?"

"I screwed it up?" Chubba said, coming right back at her. "Your boy Mike Tyson here, he's the one who couldn't knock her cold with a clean shot."

"And where were you when all this was going on?"

"In the car," Chubba said, not sure he liked where this was going.

"In the car," Sharla repeated. "Just sat your fat ass there in the car? Listening to the radio? Does the radio in that car work? Or did you break it too? You just sat there, didn't help one bit."

"You want her to see me? That wouldn't have been too helpful"

"What I wanted, Chubba, was for you to not fuck this up. I guess that was asking for too much. Put Pearce on the phone."

"Sharla, listen—"

"Pearce. Now."

Sharla heard Chubba's voice tinny over the phone telling Pearce he was wanted on the phone. Then some rustling as the phone passed from one man to the other. Sharla was surprised at how frail Pearce sounded when he said hello.

"Hi Pearce, everything okay, honey?" High as she was, Sharla had the presence of mind to be cautious, like checking a cut to see how bad it is. She imagined Pearce could be volatile and brutish, even violent. Sharla was as excited by him as she was wary of him.

"Yeah, I guess." There was a pause, a sigh. "I mean, there's some damage to the car but it runs. It's fixable, I guess."

She was embarrassed that a career criminal like Pearce had to work with small-town hicks like them. Sharla afraid of how disappointed he must be. He sounded cool and calm though. Not letting his frustration with these hayseed amateurs get the best of him. Pearce, he was working the problem, Sharla thought. Like a pro.

"Who's car?" Sharla said. "Patty's?"

"No, the car. The one we're in."

Sharla thinking, okay, maybe not working the main problem.

Letting it slide, instead asking how their search was going. Pearce saying not good. They were just driving up and down muddy roads, no trace of Patty yet.

"She'll turn up," Sharla said. "Think Patty got a good look at you? Or the car?"

Pearce said he wasn't sure, didn't know, maybe.

Sharla noting the whiny tone creeping into his voice. Wondering if maybe Chubba was right about Pearce—all talk and no walk. But Chubba was seldom right about much of anything, and she kept her faith in that.

Just then, startled, Sharla jerked the steering wheel to the left. The Mustang swerved, barely missing the herd of black, three-foot spiders scurrying out of the ditch.

"Gotta go," she said killing her cell phone.

Sharla slowed the fishtailing car to a halt on the side of the road and slammed it into park. Reassuring herself that, in fact, there were no giant spiders crawling onto the muddy road.

Checking the Diet Coke again, seeing that the ruffies were finally dissolved. But too late. Now that it was spider time, she needed something that would deliver hard and fast.

And why was it always spiders? Or bears? Sharla wondering if hallucinations were as symbolic as dreams.

Dumping the contents of her purse on the passenger seat. Sharla rummaging through the makeup cases, hair brushes, gum wrappers, liquid hand sanitizer, pens and other items that accrued in her purse. Finally coming up with a pill bottle.

When she shook the bottle, a lone pill inside it rattled like a snake. Only one Oxycontin, eighty milligrams. But Sharla knowing how to make it work quicker and better.

Turning awkwardly and laying the green tablet on the console between the two seats. Cupping a protective hand around the pill, she used the corner of her cell phone to grind it into rocky bits. Breaking apart and rendering useless its time-release coating. Patience being not much a virtue when you're seeing spiders the size of Labradors.

Careful not to disturb her pile of crumbly dust, Sharla re-situated herself backward in the driver's seat. On her knees, ass up against the steering wheel.

Popping the index finger of her left hand in her mouth, getting it good and wet. Pulling her finger from her mouth, pressing it down on the pile of synthetic opiate. Tamping it around the pile until most of the powder clung to her slobbery finger.

Careful not to knock any of the drug from her finger, Sharla working her hand down the back of her low-rise pants and, as gently as possible, sliding her finger as far up her butt as she could.

Reminding herself you really only get one good shot at this. Not enough hand sanitizer in the world to give it a second try. She didn't have to wait long.

With its time release coating crushed - and without the delay for it to be absorbed by her stomach lining if she had swallowed the pill - the Oxycontin went to work almost immediately.

Sharla crouched there, finger up her ass, as the drug pulled the RPM needle of her central nervous system out of the red and down into the black in a couple of minutes.

First a rush of pressure in her bowels, a slight nausea in her stomach. Both going away just as suddenly as they had appeared. Her toes tingling, legs weightless. The first warm, trouble-free wave washing over her body. Her muscles melting.

"Guess I can take my finger out of my ass now," she said, giggling.

Sharla amused by her beliefs—needles were pathetic but somehow there was no shame in poking a finger up your butt for an efficient high.

Got to draw the line somewhere, she figured. That's as good as any. Until you cross it too.

Sharla turning, plopping down on the driver's seat. Her nose itched. Catching herself before she scratched it with her unclean finger. Grabbing the travel-size bottle of hand sanitizer from the passenger seat, working some of the viscous liquid in between her fingers, around the backs of her hands.

Throwing everything back into her purse before licking her finger – a finger on her other hand, just to be safe – and using it to collect the last traces of Oxycontin dust from the console. Rubbing the bitter drug on her gums.

Putting the Mustang in gear and easing it back onto the sloppy gravel road. Checking but no sign of spiders anywhere. Turning on the radio just in time to catch the start of her new favorite song, a dance track from the latest Mariah-wannabe.

The beats pumping their way into her head and chest. Her new favorite song blending into another song she liked. Driving and feeling the music, so deep into the beats that Sharla almost ran over Patty.

Patty standing in the middle of the road, waving her arms.

Sharla slamming on the breaks, the car sliding a bit before coming to a complete halt. Sharla stunned, at the sight of her. Been driving around all night looking for her, now here she stands in the headlights, looking like hell and out of breath, shoeless. Patty's porta-fridge body covered in mud. Eyes wide with fear.

Sharla lowering the power window. "That you, Patty? You okay?"

Slow at first to recognize the Mustang, then Patty warming quickly to the voice coming from inside it. Running around to the driver's side.

"Sharla! Thank God."

"Look at you," Sharla said, still unsure how to play it. She hadn't decided on how she really wanted the night to end, the question still being: Could they still get out of it? "What's going on?"

Patty swallowed hard and shivered. "I don't know. Someone tried to...I don't know. They punched me and they chased me. I don't know."

"Well, get in the car, girl."

Patty ran around to the passenger side, the dome light almost blinding in the rural darkness. Patty slamming the door shut, craning her neck, searching the road behind them. Begging Sharla to get the hell out of there.

Sharla saying that is awful, trying her best to sound shocked and concerned.

Not easy with the full, wonderful effects of the drugs

coursing through her now. Not to mention the distraction of the twin giant grizzlies on either side of the road. Sharla trying to hide her smile at seeing the brown and shaggy bears towering on their hind legs. Roaring as flames came shooting out of their asses.

Sharla stifling a giggle and enjoying the warm embrace of a fleeting wish that there really was such a thing as fire-farting bears. To right herself, Sharla focusing on keeping the Mustang in the middle of the road.

Asking Patty who it was that attacked her?

"No idea," Sharla said. "Didn't get a good look at them."

"Them? There was more than one?"

Patty nodded. "Two voices. I heard them when they came after me."

"How'd you get away?"

"Hid in a field until they were gone. Crawled all the way out the back of a goddamn muddy pasture." Patty eyed the Diet Coke in the cup holder between them. "Can I have a drink? I'm crazy thirsty."

Sharla considering the ruffie-infused soda, still unsure which way to play it. "Oh, Patty, of course. Take it."

Sharla drove, one eye on the road, the other on Patty chugging gulps of spiked soda.

"Tastes funny," Patty said the bottle now half empty.

"Been sitting"

Driving down the road and Patty calmer now. A little safer, dryer, warmer. "Why're you out here anyway?"

Sharla not missing a beat, in the groove and everything clicking as she surfed along the top of the drug. "Was heading to that party out at Koy Reed's place."

"Damn, you get lost?"

"Lost, yeah," Sharla said. "Been awhile since I been on the old highway at night. Confusing as hell, you know? You still want to go to the party?"

"What?" Patty stunned by the question. Shaking her head as she poked around the console between the seats. "Fuck no. I'm calling the sheriff. Where's your cell phone? I left mine in my Mercedes."

Not my car but "my Mercedes."

A slow burn running up Sharla's cheeks and it wasn't just a narcotic wave. Fat, spoiled little bitch. Why not work the car's sticker price into the conversation? And there it went, the chance to get out of it shrinking fast, receding, sucking in on itself until there was no escaping.

No getting out of it. For either of them.

"You sure?" Sharla said. "You been drinking. Billy might try to pin a DUI on you."

"I don't give a rat's ass. I'm sober as shit right now after all that, trust me." Patty taking another slow drink of soda. She made another half-hearted attempt to find Sharla's cell, then stopped as if forgetting what she was looking for.

Sharla catching the sluggishness settling into Patty's plump face, her round shoulders drooping a bit. "My cell's dead," Sharla said. "What about yours? We can go to your Mercedes, get your phone."

Patty saying no way in hell was she going back there. Having trouble mustering the energy for anger but keeping at it as best she could. "Whoever these motherfuckers are, they're going to pay."

Sharla quiet, just driving. At ease with her clarity now that everything was decided. Without looking at Patty she said, "You look tired, girl. Go ahead, close your eyes."

"Get me home," Patty said, words slurring a bit. She leaned her head against the passenger door window.

"Get comfy," Sharla said. "I'll take care of you."

Sharla drove around the country roads until Patty was snoring softly. Pulling her cell phone from under her leg, she sent a text message to Chubba's burner cell.

btch n bag meet @ car

When Sharla pulled up alongside Chubba and Pearce, they were both crouching down, assessing the damage to the Volvo's back end. Sharla rolling down her window. Didn't say hello, just laying down how it was going to be.

"Nobody says nothing, got it?" Sharla said. "We got her and that's all. Horace don't need to know all dirty details."

Nine

Back in his Escalade cruising Main, Billy still a little freaked out. Goddamn Waxman, trying to fix an ancient circuit breaker in the dark on a Saturday night.

"Get a damn life, Waxman." Billy saying it out loud even though he was alone.

Billy recounting his missteps. Didn't check the alley

where Waxman always parks his beat up station wagon, did you? Didn't call for back up, like you should have, did you? Didn't use his head one damn bit, did you numbnuts?

Billy trying to push away the thought that this was a mistake, this whole goddamned notion of playing sheriff. Billy well aware no one felt confidence in him as Sheriff. Yeah, the people elected him.

But it was a fluke.

All it took an untimely death, a pair of size-10 stiletto heels, an honest farm wife and a few manipulative business leaders to make it all happen. Wasn't a plan, just one thing leading to another like most things in life. Then, bam, look where we are.

The death was Big Jim Olden.

He'd been Caste County sheriff for almost twenty-five years. The man had a quick wit and a personality even bigger than his gut drooping over his silver oval belt buckle. A man who liked to eat, drink, cuss, smoke, fish and hunt. Billy liked him. Hell, everyone liked him, right up to and beyond the day he died of throat cancer.

Big Jim's deputy of seven years, Bob Gaffney, had been considered a lock to be the next sheriff. He'd served for several months as interim sheriff while the cancer ate away at Big Jim.

Of course, Gaffney was different from Big Jim. Gaffney was smaller physically. And he lacked Big Jim's personality, his way and sway with people.

Gaffney wasn't from the Caulfield originally. Came from somewhere up in Nebraska; that didn't work against him but didn't help him either.

Mostly Gaffney had been loyal to Big Jim. He was a direct link to the big man himself. That is, Gaffney was a known commodity to his neighbors. Or so they thought.

Gaffney was running unopposed in the special election in August. Then a week before the election, he flipped his truck on a country road.

He had been speeding, but that didn't dent his candidacy.

It probably didn't even hurt his chances too much that he was drunk.

But it definitely did not help that he climbed from the wreckage wearing a sleeveless black cocktail dress, thigh-high stockings and a lone red, mama-is-a-dirty-girl pump, size 10. Its mate having flown out the window during the crash, coming to rest about fifty yards deep in Harv Lindstrom's alfalfa field.

It was Harv who ran over from a nearby pasture to help. Daintily taking the interim sheriff's hand, all blood and broken fake nails, helping him from the wreckage.

Ask him and to this day Harv always swore he intended to keep quiet about the whole scene. Partly out of kindness and partly out of the realization that a kind gesture now could set him up for life with the law.

But his wife, Dorthea, had witnessed the wreck from the window over her kitchen sink and immediately called 911. The county ambulance arrived shortly thereafter, bringing with it witnesses to the end of Sheriff Gaffney's career in law enforcement.

Forever after this became known around Caulfield as The Drag Racing Incident.

Some of Caulfield's more conservative power brokers –

chamber of commerce types with a Baptist distaste for transvestites – quickly moved to place a competing candidate on the ballot.

Or as Leonard Shook, a jowly banker who claimed roots reaching back to the frontiersman who had helped settle the surrounding land and found the town, put it: "We want an alternative for sheriff—not an alternative lifestyle for sheriff!"

Leonard considered himself a funny man, as bankers go. Nobody was sure how many names were tossed around but eventually the men settled on Billy Keene. The suggestion was made to Billy over early-morning coffee at Trace's Place, the hot spot café in Caulfield. The suggestion knocking the sleepiness right out of Billy.

At first, he thought he misunderstood the men at the table. Then he thought they were pulling a joke. When he finally realized they were serious, the first thing out of Billy's mouth was no way.

He was too young. He'd only been back in town a few months.

"Hell I'm still living with my parents," Billy said. "A sheriff can't live with his parents. Doesn't look right, right?"

The men told him to get his own place.

Billy wondered aloud, wasn't it kind of important that he lacked the training or experience that most likely people preferred in their sheriff? Surely there was somebody around more qualified. What about one of the other deputies? Say, Lon Harmon?

At that a few of the men exchanged glances. Peter

Dickenson, publisher of the local paper, let Billy know that name had already been considered. Left unsaid was on what grounds it had been rejected. Billy didn't ask.

None of it mattered, the men assured him. They told Billy that he had something that couldn't be bought. Well, maybe it could be bought but they didn't have time for that.

"Billy, you've got what it takes to win this election," Horace Self had assured him. "You got name recognition."

His baseball career was behind him, thanks to shredded rotator cuff. Now, Billy said, he was just trying to figure what comes next.

Well, the banker Shook had countered, here was something to do while he figured out what comes next.

Finally, Billy got it—nobody at the table expected it to be a long-term solution. This was triage, plain and simple. Nothing more than the quickest, best way to keep a transvestite out of office.

Besides, they assured Billy, nothing ever happens around here. Next to selling stink bait, it was probably the easiest job in the county.

Driving up and down Main after his run-in with Waxman, Billy didn't find the job so easy at the moment or, frankly, at all.

He took a long pull on his Big Gulp of beer. Didn't feel like being sheriff just now.

Driving until he reached The End Zone. A quick glance in the mirrors before flipping a U-turn across Main and shooting the Escalade into an open parking spot just down the block from the tavern.

Sitting for a while, watching all the young people around his age drinking, talking and laughing behind the large windows of The End Zone.

Billy thinking he felt like being just Billy for a little while. Leaving his Stetson on the passenger seat as he headed into the tavern.

Ten

Horace Self sitting out back on his deck.

Sipping bourbon and listening to coyotes rip apart a cat somewhere in the darkness. Wild, vicious snarls before a death squeal. Then nothing but quiet night.

Horace thinking not like there's a shortage of cats in the world, anyway. Didn't care much for the way cats always look at you funny. Horace taking another sip of bourbon and turning to look for headlights on the road.

Chubba was late. The only light was from the fluorescent over the kitchen sink, its glow radiating through the sliding glass doors and out onto the deck. Giving off just enough light to reveal the outline of the bottle of bourbon on the table, waiting there for Horace to pour himself another.

Horace sat hunched at the glass patio table, absentmindedly folding a checkered dishtowel. Fold, unfold, fold again and so on. Something to do with his hands while waiting for his son to get home.

Horace considered himself a dog person. They - Horace and his second wife, Tammy - owned two dogs: Lola, a thirteen-hundred-dollar pure bred black Labrador retriever with bad hips and, J.J., some kind of rat terrier mix with too much energy and barely enough sense to stay away from the vehicles barreling down the road that ran past their ranch.

Both Lola and JJ with ears up at the sounds in the darkness but staying put there next to Horace's boots. Then there was Tom, a big-balled gray tomcat who ruled the barn. Nobody really owned Tom.

Horace thinking it's different with dogs. Lola and J.J., they understand their place in respect to who you are, what you do for them. But Tom? Could love him to death and he'd still just give you the stink eye. Horace checking the road again for lights, nothing. Another sip of whiskey. Fold and refold the dishtowel.

With everything going on tonight, Horace expected his son to be out late. But figured he'd be home by now. Unless something went wrong.

They couldn't afford for anything to go wrong.

So most likely something did.

Horace unable to keep himself from looking toward the road running from his ranch house to the east side of Caulfield. Checking again, hoping to see pin lights in the night growing into headlights as they came closer. By the time they reached his long driveway, the headlights would be wide white beams casting over the landscape of his property.

He'd know it was Chubba even before the lights reached the end of his driveway because the lights would be coming way too fast toward his house. Chubba always moving too fast.

Fancying himself a NASCAR driver. Or some kind of redneck Romeo. Or a professional gambler. That boy had a healthy fantasy life.

A fantasy is one thing. A two-hundred-thousand-dollar-plus gambling debt was one stark reality. As real a kick in the nuts. Or coyote teeth ripping your flesh.

Chubba always coming back from the casino, boasting he was a winner. At blackjack. At craps. At Texas Hold 'Em. Chubba losing a thousand to win maybe two hundred. Walking through the front door saying, "I'm a winner Daddy!"

When his boy came to him to explain away all the money he owed the casino over in Pierette County, Horace just shook his head. Said to his son, "Chubba, what are you going to do about it?"

Chubba doing what he was going to do about it—asking Daddy to pay for it.

Horace thinking there was nobody to blame but himself. Unsure if he would or wouldn't do it differently if he had it to do over again because what the hell does it matter? No damn do-overs in life.

Horace let the dishtowel alone. Turning his chair and scooting up close so he could prop up his short legs on the deck railing. Pulling up the collar of his wool-lined coat against the damp night air. Taking a long swallow of his bourbon.

Again glancing hopefully at the road and wondering, *Can a father start this late telling his kid no?*

There are many things you can't tell your kid. For instance, that there's no more money. Or that there's land, but even if you didn't already have loans against it, the land still would be off limits.

Then there are the things you do tell your kid. Stories about his -great-great-great grandfather helping to settle the land, build the town. And definitely tell your kid the land is precious. The land is the family and the family is the land. Never sell, you tell him.

It's what your daddy told you and what his daddy told him and on up the line, back to those tough bastards who fought Indians and settled the prairie. So no, can't tell your son there's no money.

You can explain to him how feed prices are eating up the profits you used to see from the small herd of cattle kept around mostly as a reminder of what used to be. That the oil under the land is long gone. You had to close the filling station because it couldn't keep up with the convenience store chains that moved in.

If your boy was paying attention, he'd work it out on his own that there's no money left to pass on to him. That's one thing. But telling him there's no money?

Horace thinking that's just not something a father does.

Could go to the bank, of course. Try to borrow even more against the land. But a loan for what? Horace's face burned just thinking about the look that would creep across Leonard Shook's fat face, sitting there behind his mahogany desk at the bank downtown on Main Street.

No way was Horace about to put himself in the situation of explaining he needed money to pay off his son's gambling debt. They would love that, all the sons-a-bitches who sneer at you behind your back. Would love to sink their teeth into a juicy piece of gossip like that.

Horace finishing the bourbon in his glass, a warm blanket coating his insides. Sons-a-bitches like Arlita Hardy. Come to think of it, she sometimes looked at people funny like a cat does. Even before she got lucky and hit the lottery.

Just where in the hell did she get off pulling shit like that *before* she won all that money anyway? Like she and Horace didn't have a history.

Horace thinking tomorrow morning she might wake up like she owns the fucking day. But by the time she goes to bed Sunday night, she'll know her goddamned place. Horace tipping back his rocks glass, then remembering it was empty.

Reaching for the bottle and catching sight of lights on the road. Recognizing the round bulbs as the headlights on Sharla's Pontiac. Soon the night with filled with the whine of the coupe's engine.

Horace very much disliked that Sharla always drove Chubba's Mustang, but it bothered him less this time. The warmth of the bourbon mixed with his relief that Chubba was home. When the engine cut off in the drive, silence again took over the night.

A minute later Chubba, bottle of beer in hand, closed the sliding glass door behind him. Coming out to join Horace on the deck.

"How'd it go?" Horace said.

Chubba with a long pull on the bottle before answering. "Pretty good."

A silence between father and son. A few noises in the night, a rustle in the brush, a soft hiss from the wind. Finally,

Horace spoke again.

"So it's done then."

"Yep."

Chubba's silhouette nodding in the affirmative, a little too vigorously. Even in the darkness Horace could sense the boy was holding back. Horace noticing the bright white of Chubba's athletic socks as his son stood drinking his beer.

"Why you in your sock feet, boy?"

"What?" Chubba said, looking down. "Oh, boots are all muddy. Took them off out front."

Again silence, Horace letting the silence and years of fatherly dominance work on his son. Horace considering the muddy boots, how they might have gotten that way. The fact that his son actually took them off outside. Tracking mud all over the house usually never a big concern of Chubba's.

Horace tossed the dishtowel he'd been folding earlier to Chubba. "Pant legs are muddy too. You track it into the house, Tammy's going to have a fit."

Chubba saying nothing, just wiping at his jeans with the dishtowel. Horace finding Chubba's silence at the mention of his step-mother interesting. The two didn't get along.

Tammy was only three years older than Chubba. Horace, proud of his youthful catch, always joked they didn't get along because Chubba and Tammy were so close in age, something akin to sibling rivalry. Often just the act of Tammy walking into the room, bottle blonde hair piled high on her queen's head, evoked a mocking face or noise from Chubba.

"Everything went as planned, right?" Horace said.

"Pretty much."

"So, Patty's taking her trip to Kansas City?"

"Yep."

"How'd our city boy do?

"Pearce?" Chubba said, still wiping at his muddy jeans. "He did all right."

"Just all right?"

"Yeah, he did great."

Silence, even the animals and wind waiting for the two to continue.

"Now I know you're bullshitting me," Horace said. "You think less of that weirdo than I do."

Chubba stopped wiping at his jeans, stood upright. Repeating Pearce had done all right. Chubba, towel in one hand, bottle in the other, taking a pull of his beer.

"How's Sharla holding up? Didn't crack up, did she?"

"No, she's cool. She sort of..." Chubba's voice trailed off, realizing too late that he didn't want to go down that path.

Horace sitting forward in his patio chair, elbows on knees, rolling the rocks glass in his hands. "She sort of...what?"

Chubba's silhouette shrugged. "I don't know."

"Sure you do. She sort of...what?"

"I don't know. Saved the day, I guess."

Again, Horace was quiet, mulling what he'd just heard. Rolling it around in his mind just as he was rolling his glass of bourbon in his hands. Finally, he spoke. "Day needed saving, huh?"

And with that it all came out of Chubba, a flash flood of words. The weak punch, the botched grab, the flipped Mercedes, the hunting party and Sharla stumbling on to Patty.

When Chubba's story finally slowed to a trickle, Horace asked about Patty. Didn't react when Chubba, eager to answer, stressed that she was fine.

Then Horace asking about Sharla. This one Chubba wasn't so enthusiastic to answer.

"She went to Kansas City with Pearce and Patty," Chubba said. Said it as if Pearce and Patty had been planning a weekend getaway and at the last minute they invited Sharla along.

"Really?" Horace said. "I thought after you grabbed Patty, you were supposed to drive her car to Arlita's, have Sharla come pick you up? Make it look like something happened between the driveway and the front door of her house, not out on the highway."

"Told you, the Mercedes is sitting upside down out on the old highway."

"I remember," Horace said. "And Sharla, she's run off to KC with the weirdo and the hostage? Do I have it about right?"

Chubba nodded.

"And let me guess," Horace said, "Sharla, she suggested you not tell me about what went wrong?"

Chubba nodded.

"She think I wouldn't find out? I mean, a fifty-thousand dollar car flipped and deserted? Somebody's going to find that, I don't care what back road you were on. And her suddenly disappearing, on the same day as Patty no less? She think I wouldn't notice that? She think the whole damn town won't notice that? What about you, Horace Jr.? What do you think?"

Chubba shrugged.

"Boy, I'm envious."

"Why's that Daddy?"

"Because you're lucky. Obviously, she's fucking you stupid."

Horace drained his bourbon. "Anyway, boy, you told me. Smart, not putting that...not putting her over me. Anything else you need to let me in on?"

"Pearce, he seemed kind of upset about his car getting dinged up."

"*His* car?" Horace said. "Thought he was stealing one?"

"Yeah, but I don't think he did. He took it kind of personal-like, the damage."

"Good for him, the piss ant."

"I thought you liked him?"

"Oh, I do," Horace said, laughing. "I like him as the sucker who wears this whole damn thing if it goes south on us."

Not saying it but Horace thinking Sharla had put herself in the horseshit with Pearce. And Horace couldn't say he was too sorry about that either.

Even in the darkness, Horace could sense that his son's feelings were hurt. "Oh, hell, don't worry about it. Nothing's gone *that* wrong. I mean, who's going to mess with us? The law? Even if Arlita does go to the law – and she won't – you really think Sheriff Pretty Boy's going to touch us?"

Rising from his chair and Horace standing full to every inch of his five-five height. Placing his hand on his son's shoulder, giving him a reassuring squeeze. "We're The Selfs, boy. All's going to work out fine, so long as we keep trusting each other. Anyway, it's done. Better get to bed."

Chubba looking around for a place to leave the muddy

dishtowel. Horace held out his hand, offering to take the tainted rag from his son. Chubba handed it off before heading back inside.

Horace pouring himself another short glass. Kicking back into his chair, boots propped up on the railing. Somewhere off in the darkness a coyote let loose with a howl, a disturbing song of feral and forlorn notes.

Horace held up the muddy dishtowel. Sipping his whiskey and wondering if the stain would come out ever.

Eleven

Billy walking into The End Zone, feeling that odd blend of familiarity and displacement.

Still young enough to get a charge every time he walked into a bar. A small thrill like he was getting away with something just by being there. The expectation that good times were right inside the door.

And there stood a walking, talking good time—Tracey Beaman at the end of the long, dark bar. Trace was a friend. An ex-friend and then a friend again, really.

The two of them best friends in elementary school, grew apart in middle school and high school. Billy running with the pot-smoking jocks, Trace with the pot-smoking arty/theater types.

But since Billy had moved back to town, he and Trace

were as tight rolling joints now as they had been building forts and playing army as kids.

Billy making his way toward Trace, weaving through the tavern crowded with tables of loud, yammering people. A few people dancing on the small dance floor. Music blaring, coming from giant speakers around the room. The DJ stationed off to the side, playing a mix of dance hits for the young women and southern rock for the young men.

Trace at the bar, sensing something, turning around just in time to catch sight of Billy halfway there.

Trace's mustache drooped around the corners of his mouth. His pale stick arms were inked, a chef's knife down one forearm, the other sporting the line drawing of cow partitioned into a butcher's guide to beef.

Trace rolling his eyes at Billy before turning away. As if to say, "Don't know you. Don't want to know you."

A pint of beer arriving at the bar at the same time as Billy. Billy looking up, surprised. Seeing the bartender, Wendy, flitting around behind the bar and already off helping two other customers. Giving him a sideways wink. Billy winking back, raising his free beer to her in thanks.

Trace yelling over the music, "Hope you're not going to drive after you drink that."

"Nope," Billy said. "Going to drink another. Then I'm getting behind the wheel."

"In that case, I recommend that wherever you're going, you drive bat-shit fast. Shortens your time on the road. Gives Johnny Law less time to catch you."

"Excellent advice, counselor," Billy said, bringing the

glass to his mouth. But Trace put his hand on Billy's arm, interrupting him before he could wet his beak in the frothy beer.

"How come a cop is never around when you need one?" Trace said. "I thought it might be different when you became one. But just like all the rest, you miss the interesting parts."

"What I miss?"

"Nothing much. Just Lynnette Scroggins threatening to kick the living shit out of Patty Hardy."

"Why's that?

"Guess she found out Patty's fucking her sister's husband."

"She is?"

Trace's face collapsed in disgust at Billy's ignorance. "Nice work, detective."

"Hell, I can't keep track of who all's sleeping around with who in this county."

Billy looking around the bar. As always, seeing a bunch of familiar faces talking, laughing, drinking, dancing. A few faces he recognized as too young to be in there at all. Those faces turning away from him, avoiding eye-contact, trying to decide between laying low or making a casual beeline for the back door.

"Anyway, Patty, she left before she got her ass kicked," Trace said. Trace going on, saying how nobody wants to mess with any of them Scoggins girls. Didn't matter how tough you were, you weren't coming out of it unscathed.

"I can't figure out," Trace said, "Why's Patty banging him anyway? He's no prize and his wife meaner than hell. Don't make no sense."

"Maybe she likes him," Billy said. "Or at least she likes

banging him."

"Ah, romance."

Billy raising his glass, a mock toast to romance. The glass on its way to his mouth when someone bumped him from behind, sending a little of the beer spilling over the sides of his glass. Billy turning around to catch who bumped him, coming face to face with Tina Stark. Her slightly crossed eyes telling Billy she was drunk.

"Shouldn't be drinking on duty," Tina said. Her face raised, nose pointed in the air with as much superiority as a shit-faced, scorned ex-girlfriend can muster.

"Well, I'm not drinking," Billy said. "No matter how hard I try."

Making another attempt at sipping his beer but interrupted again. This time Tina lurching forward up, bringing her face up to his.

"I want those balls back," she said, crooked eyes flaring.

"Excuse me?"

"Yeah, excuse me," Trace said.

"The balls," Tina said, lips snarling around the words. "Those signed baseballs I gave you."

For Billy's birthday one year in high school, Tina had given him a set of baseballs autographed by some of his favorite players. A year later Billy left the balls and Tina behind in Caulfield. He was drafted out of high school by the New York Yankees and reported for rookie ball in Tampa.

Then during his second year in the minors, Billy broke off their relationship. Turned out he made the break just before his call up to the majors, right before a once-in-a-lifetime spot start that turned into a run with the big league team through the playoffs.

From the outside looking in, the timing of it seemed selfish: Billy dumping the girl who had stood by him just before making the big time.

The truth was more complicated. They'd dated all through high school. They were both growing up, growing apart. Missing each other, and the distance between them hard on them both.

Oh, and Tina had cheated on him with some goat roper from Pierette County.

Billy finding out from his high school catcher, Doug Larsen. To this day Tina had no idea that Billy knew about that.

Much as it hurt, he saw no reason to confront Tina directly about her cheating. Never said a word, instead taking it as a sign they both should move on.

Besides Billy hadn't been sure how much longer he was going to be able to hold out against the baseball groupies now that she'd handed him a free pass.

When Billy finally told Tina it might be better if they each went their own way, she immediately shifted into the role of scorned woman. Protesting way too much but Billy not saying a word about her cheating. Her reaction only confirming to Billy he'd made a wise move. And if it made her feel better to play the part, then so be it.

It was soon after he broke it off, that Tina had demanded he return the autographed baseballs.

"Already gave them back, remember?" Billy said over the voices and music in the bar. "Remember, I had my mom boxed up the display case, give them back to you?"

"Not all of them. One's missing," Tina said, swaying against a wind only she could feel.

Then just like that, her angry mood vanishing as if it never existed. Tina speaking in a solemn voice.

"I don't blame your mom. I really don't. She's a sweet lady. But one's missing. Schmaltz, I think."

"Smoltz."

"Whatever," Tina said, angry mood snapping back front and center. "I want all my fucking balls back!"

"I don't have it," Billy said. Done with the whole conversation and desperate now for that beer. Tina lunging forward, stopping him from drinking.

"Yesyoudomotherfucker!" Tina poking a hard, long-nailed finger into Billy's chest, barely missing his badge. Poking so hard she would have jammed her finger if she had hit it.

Billy setting his unsipped glass of beer on the bar. Sighing, dialing down his tone and locking eyes with Tina as he spoke.

"Look, this is stupid. Are you serious? Because, really, I thought I gave them back. I honestly don't think I have it, but I will look again. Okay?"

Tina noting the sincerity in Billy's voice, the change in his tone. Billy seeing a softening of the hard angles of her drunken face. Just then Billy sensing movement alongside them.

No need to look. Billy knowing who it was even before he heard the high, hick voice. Billy noticing Tina didn't look away either.

"Problem here?" Cody said. Cody in silver-toed cowboy

boots and wide, black cowboy hat.

Standing there in his cocky, short-legged stance. Irked that no one felt compelled to answer him. Not even his girlfriend.

"I said, is there a problem here?"

Billy, eyes still linked with Tina's, saying, "Not at all. Think your lady friend here is feeling single and seeing double."

"Emmylou Harris!" Trace said, slapping the bar as if buzzing in to answer a trivia question.

"Emmy who?" Tina said. Her tipsy face went hard again as she launched herself at Billy, grabbing him by the collar and accidentally bumping his beer glass on the bar, half of it spilling over the side. "That who you're fucking now?"

"Get your damn hands off my girlfriend!" Cody said, fists clenched but not making a move toward Billy.

Trace laughing and saying, whoa, whoa as if trying to calm a spooked horse. Jumping up to pull Tina off Billy.

Billy looking at her with disbelief. Then at his half empty beer glass. Then back at Tina squirming in Trace's arms.

"You better get your hands off her before I kick your ass too," Cody said to Trace.

"Too?" Trace said, still laughing. Knowing Cody wouldn't come at him face to face, and Trace too smart to turn his back on the sneaky little bastard.

Plus, his friend the sheriff was standing right there.

Tina struggling to free herself from Trace's bear hug.

Trace taking a step toward Cody.

Cody taking a step back even though his voice took a step up in bravado. "Said let go of her!"

"Man, that's what I'm trying to do," Trace said, finally handing Tina over to Cody.

Cody pulling her away, leaving Billy and Trace standing at the bar. Watching as Cody directed Tina into the dancing crowd, toward their table at the back of the bar.

Making it halfway across the room, Tina turning around, shouting, "I want my balls back!" Cody trying to haul her out of the place.

"Don't we all," Billy said. Picking up his half-empty pint glass that he had yet to take a drink of.

"You really going to drink that free beer?" Trace said.

"If everybody will fucking let me, yeah, I'm planning to."

"Drinking that could be considered corruption. Your office would be tainted by graft. Your position as an impartial community leader compromised. Good lord, man, drinking in uniform—what kind of message does that send to the children?"

Billy sighed, giving up. Sliding the glass over to Trace.

"Even if I drink it," Trace said. "You still have to pay for it, you know that right?"

"Why do I have to pay for it?"

"Otherwise it's still graft," Trace said. "And because I just pulled a liquored-up, angry woman after your balls off of you."

"Point taken," Billy said, dropping a crumpled five dollar bill on the wet bar.

Outside now. Billy's face bathed in the cool, damp air. A couple of deep breaths before making his way down the wet sidewalk to where he'd parked.

Billy thinking about something Sheriff Cady had hit on more than once, about differences. Something other than noticing them.

"Goes without saying," Sheriff Cady had said, "But I'm saying it anyway. Sheriffing is a bitch of a chore. When things are not the same, when they're different—that's when you're needed. And that makes you different. A sheriff is a part of the community and, at the same time, apart from it. Not above it, you understand, but apart from it. People, they need you to be one of them right up until those times when they need you to be more than them. See what I'm saying? Neither in it nor out of it, neither here nor there. You just are."

Billy climbing into his Escalade, heading toward his bed. At the moment feeling pretty damn good to be apart from it all.

Sunday

One

It was one hell of a mess.

Arlita mopping up the spilled coffee spreading out over the surface of her glass coffee table, ruining a favorite dishtowel. Spilled her coffee at the sound of a car coming down the street, jumping up to see if it was Patty.

Arlita was a mess. Drinking coffee all Sunday morning as she kept watch out the window, looking for Patty pulling up in the driveway. The first sunny day they'd had in a week. Early-spring-crisp, jacket required, but at least the rain had passed, the clouds gone. The ground sloppy but slowly drying.

At first, Arlita had assumed her granddaughter was sleeping late again. Must have gotten in very late (or very early), because Arlita hadn't heard her granddaughter come in.

As the morning wore on, Arlita had grown irritated. Frustrated with her grandchild's thoughtlessness, her refusal to consider others. The girl shouldn't have stayed out so late, partied so hard. It was just plain rude. They had made plans. Up early, drive to Kansas City to go shopping together.

By late morning, Arlita's annoyance was festering. Went from moving quietly around the house to allowing herself to make noise. Letting doors click shut rather than muffling them. Allowing dishes to clang rather than clearing breakfast softly. Letting the pot clank against the cup when Arlita poured herself more coffee.

Finally, simmering with anger at her ungrateful granddaughter, Arlita had burst into Patty's room. Finding Patty's bed unmade as usual but empty. The first slight grip of panic squeezing Arlita's chest.

Another cup of coffee as lunchtime approached, Arlita too nervous to eat. Arlita working to calm herself, assure herself that Patty would call soon.

Why wasn't Patty answering her cell phone?

Why didn't she call home? Patty always called.

Arlita jerking back and forth between panic for Patty and exasperation with her. Tired of peering eagerly out the front window, Arlita had called around to a couple of Patty's friends. None of them had seen her since the night before.

Then she'd heard the sound of a car turning onto her street. Arlita bolting up from her couch, searching out the window as coffee bled over the edges of the coffee table behind her.

Now Arlita wringing coffee out of the stained dishtowel over the kitchen sink. Fighting the dread crushing her heart and lungs. Arlita telling herself it was probably nothing, everything was probably perfectly fine.

But it wasn't perfectly fine, goddamn it, because Arlita

had no idea of her grandchild's whereabouts.

Arlita reaching for the telephone even as she knew Patty would be upset. Accuse Arlita of overreacting by calling Sheriff Keene.

Patty would say *The Sheriff, really?*

Arlita would come back, *Oh hell, it's just Billy.*

Sending out a thought message to her granddaughter: kiss my ass child, you don't want me to call the law, then you come home. At least call home when you don't come home.

Arlita already having their argument in her head as she dialed the number to the Sheriff's office.

"**What the hell's** Dad doing?"

Billy standing in the kitchen of his parents' farm house, watching Bill Sr. through the window over the sink. Bill Sr., head bowed, face furrowed in concentration, appeared to be inspecting the yard.

Already his father had made several trips around the waterlogged yard and now he was wandering along the back fence line where the backyard gave way to a small pasture where the Keenes grew small crops of wheat and beans.

Billy had no idea what his father's investigation was turning up, but every now and then – and for no obvious reason that Billy could discern – the elder Keene would stop and tamp gently at a piece of soft ground with his boot.

"Your father's doing what your father does," Billy's mother said, moving around behind him, working at the stove. The tantalizing aroma of Sara Jane's Sunday fried chicken filling every room of their two-and-a-half-story farm house.

"He's bored, huh?" Billy said. "Since he retired?" Bill Sr., a high school history teacher and the longtime baseball coach, had retired at the end of the previous school year.

In addition to working his small farm to keep busy, Bill Sr. now filled his time by running the public golf course, which stayed open year round so long as the grounds were playable. It was a job that fit in nicely with his other job, hosting a weekly golf show on the local AM radio station.

Bill Sr. launched his radio show after noticing that people never got tired of telling golf stories, even if people did get tired of listening to them. Said he thought there might be the makings of a good show in it.

Now every Thursday afternoon he hosted *Mulligan's Island*. The show covering any national and regional golf news Bill Sr. cared to talk about. But mostly it was local people calling in to tell personal golf stories and other people calling in to say that last caller was full of shit.

Bill Sr. was proud to say the show was a modest hit and all profit.

Billy thinking all that on his plate and still his dad looked for more ways to keep busy.

"Oh, your father's always meandered around the yard like that. Not just since he retired. Ask him what he's looking for, he'll say gophers or weeds or, hell, I don't know, Martians. Gives you a different answer every time."

Sara Jane picked up a serving plate of fried chicken with both hands, then nodded at a bowl of mashed potatoes on the counter. "Put the potatoes on the table, will you Chipmunk." Billy's mother calling him by the pet name she'd given him when he was a baby. She and his two older sisters were the only one who still called him that, thank goodness.

Billy did as he was told, following his mother and the scent of her fried chicken across the newly renovated kitchen that had been opened up to the dining room. When Billy received his signing bonus right out of high school, his parents had refused his offer to buy them a new house. After finally getting his proud father to see the offer wasn't an insult but a gesture of love, Billy had convinced them to at least let him pay for some updating.

Billy setting the bowl of potatoes on the dining room table and looking out the windows at his father still mucking around out back.

"But is he bored?"

Sara Jane double-checking to make sure the salt and pepper were on the table before glancing out at her husband. Flashing her only son a wry smile.

"No more than usual. I'll get the string beans. Go call your dad for lunch. Tell him hurry it up before the chicken gets cold."

The first bite of crispy-juicy chicken thigh tasted even better than it smelled, and Billy was thoroughly enjoying what he always declared his "death row meal."

Enjoying it until his father, sitting at the head of the table, asked him about work.

"It's Sunday, Dad. Not supposed think about work on the Sabbath."

"The hell you talking about, Sabbath?" Bill Sr. said. "No one at this table's been inside a church in the last twenty years, except for marrying and burying. Things okay?"

Billy nodding, taking another bite of chicken so he wouldn't have to answer. The truth was, thinking or talking about work made his stomach queasy. He was afraid it would ruin lunch for him.

His careless work the night before at Waxman's cleaners was still eating at him. It only piled onto Billy's utter certainty that he was just plain terrible at his job. Billy wanting to tell his parents that he'd only saved face so far because Caulfield was so sleepy. It made the job easy. Wanting to confide in them that he felt like he was faking it.

But he kept quiet. Giving in to the responsibility he'd always felt to protect the perception his parents had come to have of their fearless son—star athlete, charming kid, the handsome, quick-witted young man. Their golden child whom they knew could accomplish anything he put his mind to because they had seen him do it time and time again.

Worst of all, he was haunted by the prospect that he was going to be tested. Knowing that at some point, without warning, he would be called out in front of his family, his neighbors and especially his colleagues, and challenged to prove himself up to the job they had entrusted to him.

He was not looking forward to that day.

Fear of failure had always driven him. Could never bear the thought of letting others down, especially his parents. Fear driving Billy even as it gnawed at him. Just like he was tearing meat from the chicken bone in his fingers.

Sundays were the worst. Because Sundays were followed by Mondays and Mondays kicked off with a staff meeting. Billy convinced that no one doubted him more than himself, but if anyone did, it would be his deputies.

"So tell me," Bill Sr. said. "How *is* work going?"

The ringtone on Billy's cell phone interrupting their lunch, saving Billy from having to answer his father. Billy checking the number; it was forwarded from the office.

"Going fine," Billy said, holding up his cell phone. "In fact, that's work calling now. I'll take this out back."

Billy answered the cell phone as he made his way through the kitchen and out to the patio.

"Billy?"

Billy noted the undercurrent of stress in the voice but wasn't sure who it was. "This is Sheriff Keene. May I ask who this is?"

"Billy, this is Arlita."

"Hey Arlita, sorry, didn't recognize your voice. How are you?"

"Well, I tell you, I've been better," Arlita said.

Billy heard a click on the line, cutting out part of Arlita's voice.

"Hold on," Arlita said, "I got a call on the other line."

A sparse basement apartment in a rundown apartment complex in a suburb on the Kansas side of Kansas City. Pearce checking the gray duct tape stretched over the sock in Patty's mouth.

Making sure it wasn't coming loose, what with all her squirming on the bed she was tied to, face down.

In the dim light coming through ground-level windows, Pearce could see Patty's eyes were wide with fear. Rolling around savagely in her head as she raised her head and craned her neck to look around. Each time they fell on Pearce - wearing long sleeves to hide any identifiable tattoos, his face hidden behind a Bugs Bunny Halloween mask - he saw the terror in her eyes.

Had to admit it gave him an unexpected charge.

Pearce had rented the apartment with Horace's money. Signed a six months lease, the shortest he could get, for a basement apartment across the courtyard from his own third-floor apartment. Being so close would make it easier to keep an eye on Patty while keeping up appearances of his real life.

A life he seemed to be leaving quickly behind. Shit getting crazy, no doubt about that.

They had arrived at the apartment complex in the darkest hours of the morning. Pearce and Sharla hauling the heavy, drug-dozing Patty into the apartment without any witnesses.

Dumping her face down on the bed Pearce had set up in the middle of the bedroom, away from any windows or walls she might bang for attention.

Pearce looking down at Patty now. Still spread eagle on the bed, face down. A human X stripped down to her thong panties and bra. Sharla's idea. Pearce sensing the humiliation factor appealed to Sharla.

Each hand and each foot bound by a thick, rough rope running over a corner of the bed and down to the dull, cheap bedroom carpet, where each rope was looped around the bed frame before being tied to concrete blocks. Patty straining against her restraints, grunting through her gag.

"Shhh," Pearce said, putting a finger to the Bugs Bunny teeth of his mask, "Gotta make a call."

Closing the bedroom door behind him and moving into the small, empty living room. The door muffling Patty's futile racket.

Pearce tossing the Bugs Bunny mask to the floor as he pulled a cell phone from his jeans pocket. Another of the prepaid cell phones, anonymous and untraceable, that Horace had given each of them. Reaching in his other front pocket, removing a scrap of paper with Arlita's number scrawled on it.

She answered on the second ring.

"Is this Arlita?" Pearce said, attempting to flatten his voice to a cold-blooded, unemotional tone.

"Who's this?" Arlita said.

"I said, 'Is this Arlita?'"

"And I said 'Who is this? Now that we got that clear, who the hell is this?"

Pearce pulling the phone away from his ear and looking at it. As if checking to see if it was working properly.

This wasn't going like he'd planned. But so far, what the

hell had?

"I'm a friend of Patty's. She said I should call Arlita," he said. "This Arlita?"

"Yes," Arlita said. "Which friend? Who is this? Is Patty all right?"

"Shut up and listen. We have her. We're keeping her until you give us what we want.""

An uncertain pause before Arlita spoke. "Cut the bullshit. Who is this?"

"Bullshit?" Pearce said. "Tell me, what time did Patty come stumbling in last night?"

Another pause and Pearce almost certain he could hear the breath escaping from Arlita's lungs at the precise moment she accepted what he was saying.

"We clear now?"

Arlita's voice coming soft and thin over the phone. "What do you want?"

"We'll let you know pretty soon," Pearce said, realizing he was in control now, enjoying the feeling. "Meantime, just keep this between us. We're watching. You go to the cops, Patty dies. You tell anyone, Patty dies. We clear?"

A long silence, no speaking, no breathing. Pearce wondered if the call had dropped.

"Please don't hurt her," Arlita said. "Please don't hurt my baby girl."

Pearce was moved. Damn, she really believed they might seriously hurt Patty. A good sign this just might work after all!

Pearce thinking G*ood times, good times.*

Pearce saying, "Just do what we say, everything works

itself out fine. It's not about hurting Patty, it's about the money."

Soon as he said it, Pearce cursed himself.

Horace had specifically instructed him not to let on it was about money until later. Horace saying he wanted to keep Arlita on her heels, guessing, confused.

In Pearce's mind, it was a close race as to who was more twisted, Horace or Sharla. Sharla hotter though, that was for sure.

"Oh Lord," Arlita said, "Please just don't hurt her."

"Got to go," Pearce said. "Be in touch soon."

"Please, don't hang up."

"Remember, no cops, nobody, no how, no way. Otherwise, no Patty."

"Please—"

Pearce shutting off the phone.

That wasn't too bad. Letting out a deep breath. For the first time in several hours, Pearce feeling okay about The Project. Head clear, nerves calm. Needing some sleep but first something to eat, hunger suddenly coming at him out of nowhere.

Pearce about to call Sharla on a Project cell phone but couldn't remember the number to her disposable phone. Horace had instructed them not to enter the numbers into speed dial either.

Fuck it. Pulling his personal cell phone from his other pocket. Pearce speed dialing Sharla, who was across the way in his real apartment.

Sharla spread out on Pearce's futon couch, bare feet up on the coffee table, watching a shopping channel.

Her just-used meth pipe sat cooling among the magazines and dirty dishes on Pearce's coffee table. Agitated from the crank, she jumped at the sound of her ringtone, a dance song that had been popular last month. Sharla thinking she needed to get a new ringtone as she plucked her personal phone off the coffee table.

Checking the incoming number, smiled at it.

"Hey baby,' Sharla said. "How's it going?"

"It's done," Pearce said.

"She's dead?"

"What? No, no, no. I made the call. Her grandmother knows she's been nabbed."

Sharla not saying anything, distracted by a set of diamond earring on the television. The jewelry displayed on a long-necked model that reminded Sharla of a giraffe.

"You there?" Pearce said.

"Uh-huh." Sharla cradled the phone against her shoulder as she leaned forward to retrieve her pipe.

"I'm hungry," Pearce said. "You hungry?"

Thanks to the dope, the idea of any texture on her tongue, of any matter in her teeth, of any substance in her stomach, made her queasy.

Fixing her pipe for another meth hit. Mouth dry, finding it hard to swallow. After a moment of fixating on her dope, Sharla was able to speak again.

"You know what I want?"

"Burrito?" Pearce said. "I could go for a couple of bean burritos. I know this great vegan place—"

"Fuck that shit," Sharla said. "If I'm eating Mexican, I'm eating Taco Bell."

"C'mon, just try them," Pearce said. "You'll like it, I promise."

"Know what I'd like?" Sharla drawing it out, still cradling the phone, slowly bringing the pipe closer to her lips, "I'd like you to...go make that fat pig squeal."

She waited to see what Pearce's reaction would be.

He always tried to come off like he was twisted, with the piercings and the tattoos. And they had talked about all kinds of freaky things, sexual and otherwise, first online where they met, then in long phone calls and finally, face to face.

Up to this point it had been all talk. Sharla knew she could fuck him, but Sharla knew she could fuck just about anybody if she put her mind to it. It wasn't about that or at least not just about that.

What appealed to her about Pearce was the whole air of dominance he gave off when they first connected. Sharla had been surprised at how much his I'm-in-charge attitude had turned her on. Even the way Pearce was straight-edge, didn't drink, do drugs or even eat meat. Didn't like to be out of control, ever.

When she thought about it, it made some kind of sense; it had been a long time since she wasn't the one holding power in a relationship.

But in the last twenty-four hours, since they'd hit go-time

on The Project, Pearce had been anything but firm and in control. At times even a whiny little bitch.

Now Sharla figuring this was the moment—find out if Pearce was all talk, like Chubba kept saying. Or was Pearce as twisted as she wanted him to be?

"What do you mean?" Pearce said.

Sharla thinking this isn't looking good for Team Twisted and Freaky. "C'mon, you know."

"You mean Patty?"

"You mean Patty?" Sharla said, mocking him. "Yes, I mean Patty. I want you to go kick her in that fat ass of hers."

Pearce hearing Sharla inhale deeply, holding it in for a few seconds, then exhaling. "You puffing meth? In my apartment?"

"Want me to smoke it outside on the deck? Wave at your neighbors as I'm hitting my pipe?"

The rush from the dope not as intense as she'd hoped, close but not over the hump.

Sharla saying, "Look, you doing it or not? Remember everything we talked about, all those fantasies? Well, we're in control, right? Got us a toy. Let's have some fun with it, baby. Go kick her. Her ass is so fat it won't hurt her anyway, not that much. Just enough so I can hear her squeal through her gag."

"Why would I do that?" Pearce said.

"Because I want you to, baby." Another inhale, another exhale. "Tell you what—do this for me...and I'll do something for you."

A pause. Pearce thinking it over. "Like what?"

"Well, when you get back over here, I just might not have

my top on."

"You're really bent, you know that?"

"That's what everyone likes about me, baby."

Sharla, glassy eyed, cell phone still crammed in the crook of her neck, took one more hit on the pipe. The smoke hitting her lungs. Methamphetamine seeping into her bloodstream, traveling upward, setting off a dizzying Fourth of July fireworks show in her synapses.

All the while listening over the phone to the muffled movements and grunts of helpless fear and confusion and terror. Up inside her head, Sharla finally and fully clearing the hump, her mind shifting into a high-gear ecstasy. Sharla astonished at just how damn good she felt.

When it was over, Sharla telling Pearce to get himself some burritos to go, suggesting that when he returned, he might consider eating them off her tits.

Then killing her call with Pearce before speed-dialing Chubba.

Chubba biting off a corner of his turkey-on-white. Staring at his paper plate as he chewed.

Even though the day was a tad chilly for it, Chubba, Horace and Tammy were taking advantage of the sunny Sunday, having lunch – sandwiches, chips and salsa, grapes, root beer – outside on the deck.

Chubba looking up from his plate, casting his gaze at the budding oak tree by the barn, then out over the fields of brush and wild grass stretching out behind their house.

Looking anywhere but directly at Tammy sitting across from him. Afraid he might lose his appetite if he did.

“What the hell is this?” Horace said, holding up the cross-section of turkey, cheddar cheese, lettuce and tomato wrapped in a flour tortilla.

“Turkey wrap,” Tammy said. “Something different.”

“Thought I told you I wanted a sandwich,” Horace said. “If I want something new, I'll get myself a new wife. One who knows how to make a goddamn sandwich.”

Tammy lowering her nose at Horace. “Well, honey, you're always welcome to fix your own goddamn sandwich yourself.”

Tammy smiling, taking a bite of her wrap, glancing at Chubba.

“Horace Jr., how's your sandwich? I put enough mayonnaise on there for you? It's the light stuff but it's still pretty good.”

Chubba shrugged, saying it was fine. Didn't look at her though.

“Boy, you thank your stepmother for making your lunch yet?” Horace said. “Wouldn't kill you to say thank you once in a while, would it?”

Chubba shrugging again, continuing to avoid eye contact with anyone at the table. “Didn't hear you saying thanks for your sandwich.”

“Because I didn't get a sandwich. Got a bland burrito,

that's what I got."

Suddenly Chubba jumping up from the table like maybe he'd been stung by a bee.

Horace saying, "What the hell, boy?" Chubba was allergic to bee stings, and Horace lived in constant fear that somewhere a bee was making plans to sting his son. "You all right?"

Chubba saying, "Phone's on vibe. Got a call." Digging in the front pocket of his black track pants.

When he finally managed to extract the phone from his pocket and saw it was Sharla, he shot his father a glance that communicated it was the call they'd been waiting on. Without saying a word, Chubba went into the kitchen for some privacy.

"How's it going, Shar?" Chubba said. He was surprised at how happy the sound of her voice made him, even though she sounded odd at the moment. Sharla talking at him really fast.

"Same old, same old, you know? Hanging out. Everything's good. It's all good. You know?"

Chubba letting her know it was good to hear her voice. Apologizing for the way things went down the night before. Telling her he missed her.

"Miss you too babe. Hey, you think you could wire me some money? Just for food and stuff?"

"That's probably not a good idea. Things like that create a paper trail. How long you planning to be up there anyway?" Chubba said. "Thought you said you're coming back tonight?"

"Might be better if I stay on this end for a while," Sharla said.

"What about work? Don't show up, Arlita's going to think something's funny."

"Shop's closed on Mondays. Anyway, I been thinking about what you were saying. You might be right about Pearce, about him not being up to the task."

"Now's one hell of a time to come to that conclusion," Chubba said. "He make that call yet?"

"He done done it, yeah." Sharla laughed. "Done-done. Done-duh-done-done.
DONE! Hold on a sec."

Chubba heard Sharla put down the phone, then shifting around in the background.

"Okay, that's better," Sharla said, getting back on the line. "So damn hot in here I had to take my shirt off."

"Where's here?" Chubba said.

"Pearce's apartment."

"What?"

"Don't worry, Chubba, this place is a pit."

"A pit? Sharla, I don't give a damn if he picks up after himself or not. Just put your damn shirt back on!"

"Relax, he's not here. He's out picking up burritos. I'm just teasing."

Chubba rubbing his forehead. "I'll bet you are."

"The hell's that supposed to mean?"

"Forget it. When you coming back?"

"Tuesday maybe," Sharla said. "We'll see how it goes. Like I said, might be best if I stick here, at least for awhile. We can't afford any fuck ups, baby."

Chubba thought he heard a door opening and closing in the background behind Sharla. "What's that noise?"

"Nothing babe. Gotta go."

Chubba saying, "Sharla put your damn shirt back on!"

The line going dead.

"Did you just hang up on me?" Chubba said into the phone. "Damn it, Sharla."

Stowing the phone back in his pocket and heading back out to the deck. Chubba's appetite long gone.

"What's wrong, Horace, Jr.?" Tammy said. "You don't look so good."

Horace's eyes shooting up to meet his son's worried eyes. Chubba giving a little head shake to reassure his father. "Nothing. Everything is the way I figured."

Horace gave his son a long, raised-eyebrow look, making sure.

Chubba catching the look, nodding reassuringly. Horace wiped his mouth, then laid his napkin on his plate.

"Gotta take a piss," he said, rising from the table.

"Gee, thanks for sharing," Tammy said to her husband's back as he disappeared into the house.

In the bathroom, Horace sitting on the closed lid of the toilet seat, using his home phone to dial the number to Arlita's shop.

Not expecting her to answer because she was closed Sundays. Planning to leave a message for an appointment for a haircut. Also saying he'd call her home number, just to try to catch her. First call was the groundwork. Second one was the real call.

He dialed her home number. If it came to it, it wouldn't seem so out of place now, him calling her at home number on a Sunday. The Sunday her granddaughter disappeared.

Risky to call at all, but now that he was certain Arlita knew the situation, damn if he didn't want to hear the tremble in her voice. All along he'd insisted to Chubba and Sharla it was just about the money.

And mostly it was about the money. Mostly.

The phone ringing and Horace realizing just how badly he wanted Arlita to know who it was who was stepping on her world. Reminding himself to be careful. Arlita's telephone rolling over to voice mail, and Horace muttering damn it.

Arlita sitting in stunned silence on the flower-print couch in her living room. Ignoring her ringing phone, that jackass Horace Self number popping up on caller ID.

Her cordless house phone right there on the coffee-stained table in front of her. All she had to do was lean forward, pick up the phone. She couldn't make herself move.

If she thought about it, she'd have found it odd that Horace didn't just call the shop, leave a message. Later she would discover that, in fact, Horace had left a message on the phone in her shop too. She'd think to herself, "The son of a bitch thinks the world should bow down to him whenever he wants it to."

But she wasn't thinking about any of that at the moment.

Sitting in the same spot on the sofa where she'd nearly collapsed, right after talking with the voice claiming to have kidnapped her granddaughter.

Her home phone ringing again, Horace calling back again. The ringing filling her home.

But all Arlita heard was that voice on the phone telling her "...go to the cops, Patty dies. You tell anyone, Patty dies..."

At some point Horace finally ran out of gas and stopped calling. Arlita didn't notice. She just sat, listening to the tick-tock of her grandfather clock in the foyer. Outside, birds chirping. The sun shining brighter than it had in days. Another car floating down her street.

Arlita's phone ring yet again, pulling her out of her daze. Leaping forward, grabbing the phone with both hands as if choking a neck.

"What! What do you want!"

"Whoa easy Arlita," Billy said. "Just calling you back."

Billy had been pacing around his parents' patio waiting for Arlita to finish the call on her other line and get back to him. After a few minutes waiting, the line had gone dead; Billy had let a few more minutes pass before dialing her back.

"Everything all right?"

"Who is this?" Arlita said.

"It's me, Billy Keene. You called me, remember?"

A pause, Arlita putting it all back together on her end. "Billy. Yeah. Did call you, didn't I? Sorry about that. Plum forgot about you. I'm so sorry."

"You okay, Arlita? Something wrong?"

Another pause. "No, no, everything's fine."

"Before you got that other call, you were saying that you've been better."

"Oh, that's just something us old, fat women say."

Billy unsure how to respond to that so he moved on, asking what he could do for her.

"Oh, I...um, I was just trying to remember when your mother's birthday is. It's coming up soon isn't it?"

"Yeah, you could say that." Billy scrunched up his face, looked up at the blue, March sky as if looking for some sort of clue. "Technically, October is coming up, I guess."

"October? Well, that's funny. I don't know why I thought it was in the spring. Better make a note of it in my calendar, I guess. Think I'm going to start sending birthday cards to all my clients. Good customer relations and all that."

"Sounds good to me," Billy said, nothing about this conversation making any sense to him.

Then, before he could give her the date of his mother's birthday, Arlita saying she had to go and was off the phone. Billy wondering if Arlita had been drinking.

Back at the dining room table, Billy had a second helping

of his mother's fried chicken. Eating and hoping his father wouldn't ruin his appetite by bringing up work again. Sunday's were the worst, that aching dread about work camping there in the pit of his stomach.

Then finishing off a slice of his mother's apple pie and a pleasant thought flitted into Billy's head: Maybe Sunday was the worst day for his work dread. But Sunday also happened to be the best day for an on-call sheriff to get stoned.

Deciding at that moment to head out to Trace's house later, smoke some weed, take his mind off his anxiety over staff meeting waiting for him on Monday morning.

Billy at ease now knowing he could blaze today. Because in a small town where nothing much ever happens, even less happens on Sunday.

Monday

One

Billy sipping his coffee from a flimsy Styrofoam cup, surprised at how well his Monday morning staff meeting was going.

Everyone else was drinking from a ceramic cup, *their* cup. Billy kept telling himself he needed to get himself *his* cup. Seemed a little too permanent though.

At some point in his first sit down with Sheriff Cady at the coffee shop over in Eden, Sheriff Cady had asked Billy one of those so simple it's complicated questions: What was the first thing he was going to do?

Not big picture, but the first thing on his first morning in the office?

Billy answering maybe start by reviewing files, something like that.

"First thing, pour yourself a cup of coffee," Sheriff Cady

had said, gesturing at his own cup of coffee in front of him. "In towns like ours, everything gets done over coffee. So make yourself at home. Sit down, talk with your people. Let them know your job is to make their job easier. Your predecessor, Big Jim, he was a good man. But something he needed to work on—trusting his people. Always up their ass about the littlest this and that. Way I look at it, you don't trust people to do the job you hired them to do, that's your own damn fault."

Billy had thought that over. At the time a name, Lon Harmon, popping into his head. Billy had asked what if he hadn't hired them, what if they were already there? Could he still trust them?

Sheriff Cady smiled at that. "That'll work itself out right quick, promise you that. Also promise you, if you don't start out trusting them, giving them a reason to trust you, the dance is over before the first song is sung."

Billy sitting now at the head of the long table in the corner conference room at the sheriff's office. Reviewing the files in front of him.

Already they'd managed to cover updates on crime trends from the state and federal authorities, a local trash fire, a labor accident (a Mexican migrant worker got his arm caught in an auger but luckily would keep his limb) and two reports of packs of wild dogs running out east of town and killing chickens. Also, an amber alert from the state highway patrol regarding towheaded twin boys snapped up by their daddy, last seen on the run in a blue Ford Explorer.

Second to last item was a report of suspicious activity – constant comings and goings at all hours of the day and night – at a trailer out at the Silver Spur mobile home park. Most likely meth, or prostitution. They'd keep a close eye on it, patrol it regularly until they had a reason to knock on the door.

Glancing to his left where Deputy Lon Harmon sat. Billy thinking Lon was doing a decent job of holding back his contempt this morning.

Lon with his shaved head, trying to come off tough and bull-necked. But too round and soft to pull it off. Looking like a thumb with a face. Lon taking a drink from his "Semper Fi" cup even though he never served in the military.

"Last item," Billy said, looking over the file, "the widow Hines' raccoon. Call came in Saturday evening. Dustin, you ran on this?"

"Huh?" At the sound of his name, Dustin snapping out of his faraway gaze out the window. "Um, yeah. Yeah, I did."

Deputy Dustin Rouse, all arms and legs folded into an office chair. Rocking in the chair yet somehow managing to slurp coffee without spilling a drop. His mug emblazoned with the official Professional Bull Riders logo.

Dustin's thin face looking bored, a constant expression that Billy suspected might be the result of hitting the hard ground of too many amateur rodeo arenas. Or maybe a moderate case of adult attention deficit hyperactivity disorder. Or maybe both.

Billy pausing, wanting to approach this one the right way. "Shouldn't this have been tossed over to Linda at county animal control?"

Dustin frowned, thinking hard. "Well, yeah, I thought so maybe too. But then Lon said we should just run on it."

Billy made a point of not looking at Lon. Not an easy thing considering he was sitting hunched over, plump elbows planted on the table, leaving his melon head right in the line of sight between Billy and Dustin.

Leafing through the few papers in the manila folder, Billy scanning, not seeing Lon's name anywhere. "So you and Lon both ran on this?"

"That's right," Lon said, leaning back in his chair, putting his hands behind his head, a big *whatchagonnado* smile spreading across his face. “Thought Dustin might need some back up apprehending the perp.”

“Makes sense,” Billy said. “Which is why it probably should have gone over to animal control. Linda’s got all the right gear for it and done it a hundred times. By herself.”

Movement on Billy’s right, Deputy Zane Teeter taking an uncomfortable sip from his plain, bright white ceramic cup. Boyish face and blond hair making him seem younger than Billy even though he was three years older. As usual, Zane hadn’t mumbled a word the entire meeting unless asked.

Zane was mindful to sit back in his chair, not wanting to block the view of Cookie Reins. Cookie leaning forward in her chair, not wanting to miss a second of this. Resting her abundant bosom on the table, both cold hands wrapped around a hot cup that read, “Alcohol isn’t the answer but it helps you forget the question.”

Her official title was “administrative assistant” but Cookie insisted on being called Billy’s secretary. That was the title she was hired under right out of high school some thirty odd years earlier. Though she was in her fifties now, Cookie still dressed like the eighteen-year-old party girl she was then—low-cut clothes fitting snugly over her widening, ample curves.

Lon remained kicked back in his chair. Not moving a muscle on his face but his eyes hardening, transforming his smile into a big *gofuckyourself* leer.

Lon saying "Seems to me it's a waste of taxpayers' money to have animal control run on something we can handle."

"Actually Lon," Billy said, eyebrows raised to try and soften the blow, "it seems like a waste of taxpayers' money to have an animal control unit that don't get much use."

Billy letting that hang in the air for a bit before shifting gears, saying next time pass something like this onto animal control. "Anyway, how'd it go with Mrs. Hines' masked menace?"

Lon, still reclining, pouting. Looking at Dustin, letting him know he could answer the damn question.

"Well, he tore up her seats and wiring in her Continental," Dustin said. "A mean little bastard. Once we were able to get him out of the vehicle, we shot him."

Billy looking up. "You what?"

"Shot him," Dustin said, unsure if he was in trouble.

"Who shot him?" Billy said.

"We did."

"So you and Lon, you both pulled your weapons and shot him?"

Dustin glanced at Lon. Lon rolled his eyes as he sat forward in his chair. “I shot him, all right? What’s the big deal?”

“Did you need to shoot him? Was he rabid? Because I don’t see that in the report. Just like I don’t see anything in the report about a weapon being drawn, let alone fired. How many times you shoot him? Nothing here about the number of rounds fired. And if he wasn’t rabid and he didn’t come at you, then why’d he need to be shot?

“Worried about getting sued on your watch?” Lon said. “Just a damn raccoon.”

“This is not about being sued,” Billy said, voice rising a bit. “You didn’t follow procedure. You didn’t file paperwork on a call you shouldn’t have even been on in the first place. And yeah, it does bother me that maybe you killed an animal when there was no call for it.”

Lon murmuring something Billy didn’t think he liked the sound of. Billy saying excuse me, but calm.

Lon seething but keeping quiet.

Billy saying, “I’m sorry, Deputy Harmon, did you say something?”

The unruffled sincerity in Billy’s voice speaking louder than anger could scream. Everybody in the room avoiding eye contact with everybody else. Except Billy, who kept his eyes on Lon.

Finally Lon said, “I didn’t say nothing.”

“Didn’t think so,” Billy said. Their eyes locking for a moment before Billy smiled and adjourned the meeting with, “Thanks, everybody. Have a great day.”

As the three deputies filed out, Cookie stayed behind to go over any remaining administrative business with Billy. Moving up to the chair next to him.

“Lon just call you a pussy?” she said, lowering her chin, whispering without moving her brightly painted lips.

“Who knows?” Billy said. “It’s over.”

“Piece of advice,” Cookie said, leaning in close, again her chest resting on the table. “Never miss a legitimate chance to fire someone. You don’t, it’ll always come back to bite you right in the ass.”

Billy taking another sip from his Styrofoam cup, the coffee, now tepid, washing bitterly over his tongue. Considering his assistant’s advice.

No reason to doubt that Cookie might be right. It wasn’t very often she was wrong.

Two

"**Honey, that just might** be the goddamned stupidest question anyone's ever asked me."

Arlita speaking into the telephone, face scrunched up in disbelief at her daughter's thick-headedness. Arlita breaking the news to Mona about Patty. Mona being Patty's mother, Arlita decided she had a right to know about the situation.

Two minutes into their conversation and already Arlita was second guessing her decision to inform her problem child.

"Mona, if I knew who did it, this would all pretty much be over, now wouldn't it? Is your head clear? You on dope right now?"

"Oh momma, please," Mona said over the phone, an admission by lack of denial.

"Damn it, Mona. I thought you said at Christmas that you were getting yourself cleaned up for good."

Arlita talking on the phone as she paced around her living room, a little distracted. Kept pulling back the drape, letting in dreary light, watching for the visitor she was expecting this morning.

"I am. I will," Mona said. "Let's not get into all that right now. What are we going to do about my daughter?"

Arlita thinking *We*? No one had seen Mona since she showed up two days before Christmas. Tweaking on meth, alarmingly thin, dark pupils dilated and bobbing around in her sockets. Arlita and Patty had managed to get Mona cleaned up a little by the time she took off again New Year's Eve day.

Had heard from her a few times since. Mona calling to say she was living in Tulsa, then Ft. Worth, now back in Tulsa. Just now Arlita surprised her daughter even answered her cell phone. Mona usually letting it roll to voicemail whenever Arlita's number popped up, figuring if Patty wanted to talk she'd call on her own cell.

Patty, she didn't call her mother that often. Now all of the sudden it was Mona asking what are *we* going to do?

"*We* aren't doing jackshit," Arlita said. "You're doing drugs. I'm taking care of things. That's how it seems to work most of the time."

"I'm her mother, I should be there."

"Yeah you should, but not just for kidnapping part," Arlita's said. "First baby steps, prom, graduation, wedding day—them's the usual milestones a mother wants to witness in her daughter's life. Not her first kidnapping."

Silence coming back at Arlita over the line.

Arlita picturing Mona stewing. Arlita wondering if she'd

really struck a nerve. Or if her daughter was just offended because she thought she was supposed to be. A miracle if Arlita had somehow managed to slice through all the dope, get her daughter to actually feel some kind of hurt.

The silence on the line continuing. Arlita looking out the picture window, seeing a mud-splattered red pickup truck pull up in front of her house. A wiry man in his late forties stepping from the truck.

Wearing blue jeans and muddy cowboy boots. Gibbon arms dangling from the too-short sleeves of an untucked flannel shirt. Slowly, the man clomping his way up the sidewalk, something jarring, violent even, in his heel-toe gait. His sallow face growing grimmer with each step he took toward Arlita's front porch.

Arlita, phone still cradled in her neck, opening the door. Whispering *hello*, ushering this menacing guest into her home.

Mona hearing her mother's whisper on the line, asking who's there? The man took a seat on her couch, not even pretending not to listen in on Arlita's end of her telephone conversation.

"Company," Arlita said. Then she heard a deep cough in the background on Mona's end. "Who's that? You with somebody?"

"That's just Gerald," Mona said, then yelling away from the phone. "Gerald, I'm on the goddamn phone here. Keep it down, all right?"

"Boyfriend?"

"Just a friend."

"Drug friend?"

"Fuck, mom, a friend. All right already? Can we just put all the usual bullshit aside? My baby's been kidnapped."

Arlita thinking oh for Pete's sake, here it comes. Mona's ramping up the poor, poor mother bit. Mona's talent was turning any situation into a crisis, then painting herself as the wounded party at the center of it. This one had the makings of a masterpiece.

"Mona, let's be clear about something," Arlita said, "There's a victim here, but it ain't you. You think you should be here, then come home. I want you to come home. But only if you're coming to help. I only got room for one big bag of bullshit, and the one I already got is real and overflowing. It's all I got time for. Sorry for being so direct honey, but no sense in mincing words."

Arlita looking at her guest. He was eyeing the coffee stains on her carpet beneath the coffee table. Arlita not really seeing him though; instead trying to read her daughter's breathing over the line.

Finally Arlita saying, "So? Coming home?"

Mona saying yes, and Arlita saying all right, see you tomorrow, bye baby, love you. Arlita hitting the power button on her phone, shaking her head at her guest.

"Mona's coming home?" he said.

"Of course she's coming," Arlita said. "This where all the drama is right now. Vic, can I get you a cup of coffee?"

Without waiting for his response, Arlita heading for the kitchen. While filling his cup, she asked if he was hungry, offering to fix him some eggs and toast.

"No thank you," Vic said loud enough so she could hear him in the other room. "Ain't had much appetite lately."

Arlita emerged from the kitchen with his cup of coffee. Rather than politely standing up, Vic staying seated on the couch. His long, sinuous arm reaching out to receive his cup.

"I can't eat neither," Arlita said.

She standing for an awkward moment before taking a seat in the brown leather recliner across from him. The ugly chair had been her dead husband's chair. Normally she found it comforting the way the soft leather retained the contour of Pat's husky body. Arlita figuring it was as close as she would ever get to being in his arms again, at least until they met up in heaven.

But at this moment the chair only reminded her how much she wished her dead husband were around to help her deal with all this. Never more alone than now, husband dead and gone, daughter on dope, granddaughter held prisoner God knows where.

Arlita trying to shake the thought out of her head. Out of habit, her eyes drifting to the hair of the person she was looking at, in this case, the shaggy, brown tufts peeking out from under Vic's trucker's cap.

"Could use a haircut, Vic," she said, hopping up from the recliner. "Let's head on back to the shop."

Vic stayed put on the couch. "I'm good. Don't need a haircut."

"You might not think you do, but you do. Look at it, sticking out like weeds."

"Thanks, you're looking good yourself, Arlita." Even when Vic smiled at his own joke there was something threatening in his jagged face. "I like my hair sticking out. Like people to see it. That way they know I ain't going bald."

Arlita got it just then, what Vic was saying. Of course he didn't want people thinking he was losing his hair. To the cancer.

More precisely, to the chemotherapy he chose to skip

once the Kansas City doctors had set him straight on how much of his prostate the cancer had eaten away. Given the odds, there just didn't seem much point in ruining what time he had left.

Vic had told Arlita about the cancer right after he found out, back in November when the last of the leaves were falling off the trees. Now that the trees were budding with early growth, Arlita wondered if Vic was thankful for getting to witness another spring?

Knowing Vic, all the sprouting life probably just rubbing it in, pissing him off.

"Well, I won't take you short, just clean it up a bit," Arlita said. "Bring your coffee."

Arlita starting for the beauty shop at the back of her house, not bothering to look back to see if he followed. Sometimes there was no option and no debate with Arlita. Vic stood, careful not to spill his coffee.

In the beauty shop, Vic set his coffee on a small side table before plopping down in the barber's chair. He couldn't resist taking it for a whirl, grinning like a kid.

Arlita let him make a couple of spins before stopping him on a dime, face to face with himself in the big mirror.

"All right, all right," Arlita said. "Lose the hat. I'll wash your noggin."

Vic holding his hat in his lap as Arlita twirled him around backward. Arlita draping a towel around Vic's neck before lifting the countertop under the mirror to expose a porcelain sink, unlocking the back of the barber's chair to expertly ease Vic's head back into the sink. Tested the water temperature before running it over his hair.

Arlita considering whether she should launch into what she wanted to discuss with Vic or ease into it. She decided to let him enjoy the washing before she getting to it.

Working the warm water and shampoo into his scalp with her fingertips, making little circles, then drawing long lines from front to back with the sharpest parts of her fingernails.

The aromas of mint and sage playing in the air. Vic's hard face softening, serene and passive. Arlita could almost feel Vic's scalp tingling at the ends of her fingers.

Arlita working the shampoo for an extra long time, silent, not wanting to disturb him. By the time she finished, she figured he would be nice and peaceful. As pliable as a mean son of a bitch like Vic Shears could ever be, anyway.

She wrapped his head in a fresh towel and righted him in the chair.

"So what's on your mind Arlita?" Vic said, using the towel to dab at the water running in his eyes and ears.

"Why'd you call me over here? I know it wasn't for no free haircut."

Vic's eyes narrowing. "This is free, right?"

Arlita assuring him the haircut was on the house. Arlita feeling sick all over again. For a while there she'd been almost as relaxed and lost in Vic's hair treatment as he was. Lost enough to forget the mess around her.

A wave of guilt washed over her. Forgetting it all, even if only for a moment, felt to Arlita as if she had deserted her granddaughter.

Now, hoping to drag Vic into the horrible reality of her world.

Arlita saying, "Something's happened, Vic. Something real bad."

Not knowing where to go next, just jumping in. Starting off telling Vic about the caller who said Patty had been snatched, then working backward from there.

While she told it all to Vic, Arlita worked on his wet mane. Quick scissor snips, firm strokes with the comb. Arlita moving with thoughtless ease.

Holding the comb and an uneven section of damp hair between two fingers of her left hand. Then a slick trick of the trade: Arlita holding the scissors with her thumb and ring finger rather than her thumb and index.

This grip allowing her to slip the scissors off her thumb and, with the dexterity of a gunslinger, twirl them to the back of her hand. Freeing up her scissor hand, shifting the comb into it as she ran the comb through Vic's hair. Partitioning the next section of hair to be leveled.

Then with one fluid motion expertly shifting the comb back to the hand holding up the hair, a flip of the scissors back around and re-hooking her thumb into them to making the next cut.

Doing all of this by rote, not even thinking about it.

Telling Mona about it the situation had been a painful extraction, like yanking a rotted tooth, just to get out the story. Then again, any conversation with Mona, no matter how important or trivial, usually turned into a struggle.

But now, telling Vic, it all came out in a flood. Even bringing a tiny rush of relief. Maybe because filling in Vic on the situation was akin to doing something about it... maybe.

When she was finished, neither of them spoke for a while. The snip-snip of her scissors working at Vic's hair the only sound in the beauty shop.

Finally Vic saying, "Sorry to hear it. Anything I can do?"

"I'm glad to hear you say that. Yes, there is."

Vic's face blank but a hint of curiosity creeping into it.

Now comes the tiptoeing part, Arlita thought as she went on.

"Well, don't take this the wrong way, all right? But there are, you know, rumors. Rumors about you. And about Jimmy Bowe, how he died."

Jimmy Bowe, a mean mouthy redneck. Growing up, he'd earned a reputation as a tough kid by bullying weaker boys. When he became a man, he continued to pick fights with weaker, smaller men. Wasn't above hitting women and boys, either.

Once, in front of about fifty witnesses at a keg party in a wheat field, Jimmy Bowe cold-cocked a drunken teenager for interrupting a story Jimmy was telling about killing a cat. A sickening smack of knuckle on jaw, lights going out inside the boy's head, his body falling rigid as a log to the ground. The kid was Vic's cousin's boy.

Six months later they found Jimmy Bowe's body in a ditch alongside a highway out west of town. He was beaten so badly it was a closed casket funeral.

Vic didn't say a word now, just watching Arlita's face in the mirror. She focused on Vic's hair as she went on talking.

"Now half of what comes out of people's mouths around here is lies and the other half can't be believed. I don't know if there's truth to them rumors about Jimmy Bowe, but I do know that nobody, not even his mother, misses that cocksucker, that's for sure."

Arlita let that hang in the air for a long moment. Nothing but the sound of her scissors still snipping at his hair.

"Sounds like some real bad people," Vic said. "What do you want from me?"

"Track them down," she said. "Get Patty, bring her home. That's most important."

Vic considered the request before asking Arlita what *else* she wanted. Arlita stopped with the scissors, looked Vic right in the eye in the mirror.

"Hurt them," she said. "Make them pay. Do what you do. I don't need to know nothing about it other than that when it came time, they felt it. Hear what I'm saying?"

Vic thought it over. Vic saying maybe before but not now. Not with his health the way it was. Now probably wasn't the best time for something like this. Being so close to the pearly gates and all.

At first Arlita thinking now's a hell of a time for someone like Vic to find religion. Then realizing it made sense.

"This might sound funny," Arlita said. "You're one

mean son of a bitch. But that's the way God made you. It's like violence is God's gift to you. You want to glorify Him? Then I say use the gift He gave you."

Vic laughing. "When I get there, if He don't agree, can I tell Him it was all your idea?"

"Sure," Arlita said, "but I'm pretty sure if He don't let you in, it won't be just because of this one thing."

Vic nodding in agreement but not laughing at her joke.

Arlita sensing he wasn't on board yet so playing another card. "How's your mother doing?"

Vic's mother, Lurleen, was seventy-eight years old and lived in an aging house across the alley behind Vic's sagging place. Vic spent most of his time either fixing golf carts, fixing something around his house or hers or fixing something for his mother to eat.

"Momma's pretty frail, don't hardly eat much these days," Vic said. "Last night I cooked her up some red beans and rice, walked it over to her this morning. Should last her a week."

Arlita slowly spinning Vic around in the chair. Looking down into those arctic eyes of his.

"You do this for me, I promise you Lurleen will be taken care of when...when you're gone."

Vic looking up at her, wincing with hurt and disbelief.

At first Arlita thought she'd stung him with the coming of his death. But realizing something else hurt him.

Arlita quickly saying, oh hell, she'll be taken care of whether Vic did this or not.

"You know I love that woman, Vic. Wouldn't ever see her do without. I'm sorry, I'm just...I don't give a shit if you do this or not. Just forget I even brought it up."

"You consider going to the sheriff?" Vic said. "It's his job, ain't it?"

"Oh hell no. Billy's nice enough, but he's just a kid. Besides, they said if I go to the law, they'll hurt my Patty."

Arlita choking on the words as they passed through her throat but hiding it. Without missing a beat, she whipped the cape off of Vic, using the blow dryer to clean the bits of hair from the back of his neck.

"Sorry, Vic. Was a stupid idea. Thing is, I wouldn't even know which direction to point to start you off."

Vic gazing at himself in the mirror. Arlita's trim had made him look clean, a little younger, even healthier. Made him feel good about being himself.

Vic saying, "I have a good idea where to start."

Three

"This cheese smells like a homeless person's feet."

The customer on the other side of the deli case, saying this to Pearce, was a lean, leathery woman.

From his side of the glass deli case, Pearce watched the woman, for some self-torturous reason, shoving her beak down into the plastic bag of cheese for another whiff.

Her head jerked back in revulsion. With a flourish that said *take it away*, she tossed the bag on the deli counter.

Pearce noticed how this annoyed member of the Wives Who Don't Work Club was careful not to say *bum* or even *hobo*. No qualms about using the homeless as a yardstick for stink though.

Pearce, the vegan delicatessen meat slicer, hoping the serene look on his face let her know clearly that he was not surprised by the many contradictions in this world. Like how most stinky cheeses actually taste deliciously mild.

Also hoping the blank look on his face conveyed to this woman that some people in this world really don't give a shit what she thinks.

His was one of the few jobs, like coffee barista or bartender or telemarketer, open to a person with so much metal poking out of their face, so much ink squirted under their skin. Pearce worked in the premium delicatessen stuck in a back corner of a small, high-end grocery store, the store jammed into an upscale strip mall in the middle of a debt-heavy suburb. This was how Pearce usually described his work on those rare occasions when he actually admitted where he worked.

Certainly hadn't let Sharla, Chubba and Horace in on it. Didn't fit with the image he'd sold them of himself as Pearce, the red-ass thug.

Earlier that morning on his way out the door to his job – carrying his apron, cap and, hidden in his backpack, a badge with his real name, Matt – he'd expected Sharla to still be asleep. But she was awake and jumpy, still riding the meth.

It had been a long, druggy night. He'd finally gone to bed around two in the morning after hours of trying to gauge whether Sharla was going to have drug-fueled, crazy chick sex with him.

Even now in the light of day, Pearce wasn't sure if Sharla had been playing him. Letting him watch her eat her tacos with her titties hanging out. That was as far as any sex went. The rest of the long night was The Sharla Show.

Jumping up between hits of meth whenever she thought up another new torture idea for their hostage.

Sharla constantly egging on Pearce to get up on the meth.

Rambling on in that disjointed tweaker's dialect about how great it felt, how alive, what a rush, ramble, ramble, ramble; all without any awareness that at the moment she was a walking, yammering, panting, twitching Just Say No poster.

Pearce realizing at that point he was too tired for sex and finally slinking off to bed. As he went, snapping at Sharla, reminding her again that he was straight edge. No booze, no drugs.

Pearce adding, "And I'm vegan, remember?" Like he was representing his gang affiliation. Pearce going on.

"If I refused to put meat and dairy and all kinds of other worthless food in my body, what the hell makes you think I'd put that poison in it?"

At that Sharla just doubling over with the giggles, bluish smoke from a meth hit streaming out of her nostrils.

Then in the morning Pearce finding Sharla still up as he was leaving for work. Explaining away his exit by hinting at his criminal connections, giving her some vague story about "checking in on some other projects I got going."

No doubt things had taken a weird turn after meeting Sharla online. He'd entered into their far-fetched kidnapping scheme figuring to play along for a while, at least long enough to screw Sharla.

That part still hadn't happened though it was kind of going according to plan. Topless tacos, that's something.

Of course, Sharla had turned out to be even crazier in person than online. Usually, it was the other way around, people pushing their fantasies online where it seemed safer than playing it out in the real world.

Not Sharla, she was real-world nuts. And, Pearce discovering, he found her that much hotter for it.

Then she'd introduced him to Horace and Chubba. Pearce still couldn't believe she was with that Jethro. At some point Pearce had realized, sort of, how serious they were about this whole kidnapping venture. Still, he assured himself he could back out anytime.

Even now, standing here in his apron at his real job in the deli, examining the log of cheese from which he'd cut the offending slices, somewhere in the back of his Matt/Pearce's mind he was telling Pearce/Matt it was still not too late to bail.

Some damage had been done, no doubt. His mother's car, for instance.

Pearce was supposed to steal a car for the grab on Saturday night. But when it came time, grand theft started to feel like a real crime, never mind so was kidnapping.

In some part of his pierced head – the real Matt's head – he still thought of it all as pretend. A live, really fun version of online role playing. So he'd chickened out.

Rather than boost a car – something he theoretically knew how to pull off thanks to the Internet – Pearce borrowed his mom's Volvo. Now her sedan had a dangling bumper and needed a new rear quarter panel. When he'd returned it to her Sunday morning, he told her it had been hit-and-run in a Sears parking lot.

Nope, no surveillance cameras mom. Guess your insurance will have to cover it.

As usual his mom kept up with the questions. She left him no choice but to storm out of the house, also as usual. Storming out always worked. Parents hassling you? Storm out of the room. Boss becoming a pain in the ass? Storm out of your job. Felony crime getting too hot?

Pearce wondering if it was possible to storm away from a situation like this. He'd been ready to bail Saturday night, when things went haywire with the grab.

But now he was sort of getting off on it. Surprised at how good it felt to be a thug, even a pretend one.

Pearce sniffing the log of cheese in his plastic-gloved hands. All morning at work he'd been distracted by a call he needed to make. Maybe in his lack of focus, he'd grabbed a funky log of cheese.

He sniffed again. Smelled fine, just some nice Muenster, for chrissakes. Pearch thinking it's not like it's some stinky French cheese, Époisses de Bourgogne or something like that. Mispronouncing the French name in his head as he thought it.

Pearce thinking now that's a cheese so rank it's illegal to eat it on public transportation in France. Tastes much better than it smells. It would have to, wouldn't it? Otherwise, what would be the point?

Pearce feeling the deli manager, Dana, slip up behind him. She may as well have brought a carving knife to stick in his kidney.

"Matt, there's some way more better Muenster in the back," she said, cranking up the condescension in her voice.

In Dana's mind, belittling her staff in front of shoppers passed for customer service.

Pearce turning to head for the cooler in the back, able to tell from the smug look on his customer's leathery face that she shared Dana's idea of excellence. Dana knew her stuck up customers, he'd give her that.

Pearce disappeared into the back. Normally he would have stewed over Dana's petty management style. Or gotten back at her out by recalling how her breasts had felt in his hands that one time when they made out after several after-work beers. Just the one time, before she had been promoted and promptly began treating him like the help. Instead Pearce let it all slide.

This was a good time to make that call he'd been fretting over all morning.

Pulling the heavy latch handle on the cooler door and stepping inside. Leaving the door open and checking the signal on the prepaid cell phone. His own cell phone usually worked inside the insulated walls of the cooler, but he hadn't thought to check the pieces of junk they were using for the job.

Pearce reading the digits from a scrap of paper even though Horace had insisted Pearce memorize the number rather than write it down. Punching the numbers into the cell phone.

As the ringing started, Pearce jammed the paper with Arlita's number back into his pocket. Kiss my ass, Horace.

The rich lady picked up on the third ring. Didn't sound as desperate as Pearce had been expecting.

"This Arlita?" he said, deepening his voice, half to disguise and half to intimidate.

"Hello?" said the rich lady again. Then dragging it out

in sing-song. "Heellooo?"

"Can you hear me?" Pearce said. Moving closer to the door of the cooler for a better signal. "How about now?"

"Hello?"

Pearce swore as he killed the call, then hit redial. Figuring she would still be near the phone, pick it up on the first ring. But again she picked up on the third ring like she wasn't even expecting a call.

"Arlita?"

"You called here," she said. "Who's this?" Like she was pissed off at a sales call.

"You know who this is," Pearce said. "It's your wakeup call, rich lady. Change your tone, right goddamn now. Or I hang up and this is all over and all ugly."

"I doubt it," Arlita said, not missing a beat. "You're too far down in it now to walk away with jackshit. Unless you're dumb as a fencepost. You're not fencepost stupid, are you...what do I call you?"

That one threw Pearce. He hadn't thought to come up with another fake name. Didn't think it would come up. After all, this wasn't really a social call.

Pearce the vegan looking around the cooler of meats and cheeses, spotting the log of Muenster he'd come to retrieve.

"Call me Monster. Because that's what I am, a monster from your nightmares come to life, Arlita."

"Oh hail no," Arlita said. "I'm calling you Piss."

Pearce wondering what is up this lady's ass? Piss? That's a little too close to Pearce. Lucky guess? Had to be.

Pearce saying, "Whatever. Call me what you want. Just remember, Arlita, we know who you are. We know where you are. And, lady, we know how much you have."

"We?" Arlita said.

The way she said it made Pearce think he'd slipped up somehow. His mind scrambling for what he might have given away.

Did it matter if she knew there was more than one person in on it?

It was kidnapping. You would expect there to be more than one set of hands in a kidnapping, right?

"Yeah, we," Pearce said, "And don't forget *we* have something near and dear to you, don't *we*?"

"About that," Arlita said. "I want to talk to her."

"Why?"

"So I know you have her. Who knows? You might be lying. After all, you're kidnappers. Can't be trusted."

"Lady, are you insane?"

Arlita hesitating before uttering her first hesitant words

of the call. "I want to know that she's...all right."

Pearce smiling, the rich lady unable to bring herself to say the word *alive*. Like saying it might jinx it.

Goosed with energy, infused with pleasure from knowing he was in control—of her, of the entire situation.

"Tomorrow," Pearce said.

Thinking quickly about his work schedule the next day, getting off at noon. "We'll call you sometime after lunch. Just stick by the phone. Don't have anything more important than this to do, do you? Other than start pulling the money together."

"What money?"

"What money?" Pearce said, voice rising. "What money you think, lady, the Wheel of Fortune money? The damn ransom money!"

"Hey Piss," Arlita said. "You ain't told me the amount yet. How much, Piss? How much makes it worth your while to be looking over your shoulder for the rest of your miserable life?"

Now Piece didn't miss a beat.

"Three million. In one hundred dollar bills. The next part, it's very important, Arlita, so listen up. Put the money in a Dominez box."

Pearce mangling the French pronunciation of the brand

name but not letting that slow him down. On a real roll now. Saying one of them big black boxes.

"The ones you get every month, with all the hair color stuff in them. Me, I like red heads. So why don't you put it in a Cherry 99 box."

"That figures," Arlita said. "Slutty shade of red."

Pearce didn't respond. Instead letting the details sink in, telling her that they've been watching her, knew what products she carried, when they arrived.

Pearce finally continuing. "The next part...also very important. Once the money is in the box, tape the top edges with gray duck tape."

"It's duct tape," Arlita said.

"What?"

"Not duck tape," Arlita said. "D-U-C-T. Duct tape"

Unfuckingbelieveable. "Whatever you call it, lady, just know that right now it's stretched tight over your granddaughter's mouth. So be sure to put the *duct* tape on the edges. And one strip down the middle seam on top of the box. Got it?"

"What then?"

Pearce telling her to drop the package in the garbage bin behind the Dairy Queen. Telling her to do it on Thursday, between 11 am and noon. That should give her enough time to get the money together.

"Just get your ass in gear rounding up that cash. We'll call tomorrow so you can speak to your priceless granddaughter," Pearce said. "What am I saying, I just put a price on her."

Killing the call before the rich lady could respond.

Pearce hearing Dana coming his way, asking him what the heck's taking so long?

Holding up the new log of Muenster as if to say, *found it!* Pearce heading back to the counter and slicing off another three-quarter pounds for his leathery customer.

As soon as he handed over the cheese, she took another nosedive into the plastic bag, like a gangster sampling an illegal product.

"Still smells nasty," she said, tossing the new bag onto the glass counter.

Pearce managing not to roll his eyes. Instead smiling, taking back the bag of cheese. Telling the lady he thought he'd seen another log in the back that, hopefully, would be more to her liking.

The lady answering him with a sarcastic, "Hopefully."

Retreating again to the cooler, in no hurry. Pearce dialing up Sharla on his personal cell phone. She answered brightly on the first ring.

"Hey honey, what up?"

Pearce telling her he'd made the call, their Project moving ahead accordingly. He could sense Sharla wasn't really hearing him. Probably tweaking out of her gourd. Pearce knowing she liked talking about herself though, so asking her what she was doing. Just then he hearing a muffled yelp in the background.

"Tossing quarters," Sharla said.

Even whispering, somehow her words still popped out of her mouth like firecrackers. "At Miss Piggy."

"Can she see you?" Pearce said. Hearing Sharla let out a breath followed by another muffled yelp in the background

"No worries," Sharla said. "I'm wearing Bugs Bunny. Besides, I'm all the way in the living room. Damn it! Missed completely. Thing is, you got to whip them just right to get past the corner of the hallway and through the bedroom door if you want to hit her square in her fat neck. It ain't easy. Damn it, missed again."

In his head Pearce seeing Sharla in the Bugs Bunny mask, heaving quarters through the basement apartment at the frightened young woman tied to the mattress in the dark bedroom. Sharla probably glistening with sweat. That's how he saw her anyway.

"Nailed her!" Sharla said.

Pearce hearing some kind of half-groan in the background. Then Sharla yelling shut it, bitch!

"Watch it," Pearce said into the phone, "she might recognize your voice."

"She might," Sharla said. "So what?"

Before he could respond, Pearce heard Dana coming after him. Telling Sharla he had to go, didn't wait for a goodbye sweetie.

Stepping from the cooler with yet another log of Muenster. Now the customer's face was a gristle of impatience and indignation. Pearce sat the log of cheese on the carriage, then ran the slicer back and forth several times.

Once he had eyeballed about three quarters of a pound of slices, he left it there beneath the slicer where only he could see it.

Instead, Pearce handed over to the customer the original bag of Muenster slices, the one that had set her off in the first place. Again, she dove in beak-first.

"Much better," she said, tossing the plastic bag into her cart and moving down the aisle. "Next time, you should start with the freshest cheese. Toss out all that old crap."

"That's a great suggestion, ma'am," Pearce said, eating one of the tasty slices he'd just cut. "I will do that.

Absolutely."

Four

"**Even** me?"

Trace's voice shrill with disbelief. "You'd arrest me? Really?"

Billy giving Trace a lift out to his house. Trace had done a wake and bake. Then, when he arrived in the gray hours of the morning to open up his diner, Trace's Place, he'd accidentally locked his keys in his truck.

Later, as the lunchtime rush was winding down, Trace had approached Billy while he was sitting at the counter, finishing his meatball and basil Stromboli, the lunch special of the day.

Trace's menu offered a mix of traditional and gourmet diner food. Meeting the straightforward tastes of his Kansas clientele but subtly expanding their taste buds to satisfy Trace's own creativity in the kitchen. Billy savoring the last of the Stromboli when Trace hit up Billy for a ride out to his house so he could fetch his spare keys.

Billy offering to use the slim jim to unlock Trace's truck. Trace saying no way did he want Billy messing up his truck, even if it was a piece of shit. Better to run him out to his house for the spare keys.

Now Billy driving him out that way, telling Trace hell yes he'd arrest him.

"In a heartbeat. Might not like it, but I'd lock you up."

Then Billy correcting himself, "Hell, I shouldn't say that. I probably would like it."

Getting anywhere in Caulfield took no more than five to ten minutes, no matter whether you took Main or one of the brick side streets. Trace lived out south of town, less than fifteen minutes of travel time, there and back.

Their conversation had taken this dark turn when Trace noticed how everyone watched the black and gold sheriff's Escalade prowl past them. It set the two of them off on a spirited conversation, darting from topic to topic.

The true nature of power.

The balance between safety and civil liberties.

And so on like that, until finally, Trace had struck a nerve. He questioned Billy's commitment to upholding the laws, especially laws he didn't agree with.

At that point (and as usual) their conversation had devolved into just one more way to fuck with each other, the truest sign of friendship.

"Really?" Trace said, thoughtfully stroking his Fu

Manchu mustache, baiting Billy. “A nice progression you’ve made. From high school jock asshole to pro jock asshole to washed up jock asshole. And now you’re a small-town Nazi sheriff asshole. And all before the age of thirty. I believe you’re what my grandmother would call one precocious motherfucker.”

“Look, if you’re just smoking weed, I can look past that,” Billy said. “Long as you’re not behind the wheel. But you’re dealing? I find that out, I got to run you in.”

“But you’ve scored weed from me before!”

“Not since high school.”

“That’s right,” Trace said. “You don’t buy it now. Just mooch it off me. Cheap bastard. So you’re saying you’d slap the cuffs on me? Fine. Then I’m cutting you off cold turkey. No more loose joints for the sheriff of Nottingham.”

They turned off Main, heading south out of town on Jefferson Street, past the modest, well-kept homes of Caulfield’s blue- and white-collar middle class.

Trace going on, saying that’s the problem with the law—generally it ignores reality. Doesn’t factor in the innate fallibility of people, the reality of their secrets.

Trace saying, “The thing about secrets, they’re like elbows and assholes—everybody’s got them.”

Billy jumping on that like a mad cat, countering that the

law very much acknowledges reality and people's secrets.

"You could go so far to say there are laws *because* of people's secrets," Billy said.

"I call bullshit on that." Trace getting heated up now. "Only thing the law does, it drives everything underground. Look at Vic Shear. It's the second worst kept secret in town that he killed Jimmy Bowe."

"What's the first worst kept secret?"

"That Donnie Dean Randall's kid isn't really his. But don't try to knock me off the subject at hand. Everybody knows Vic beat the hell out of Jimmy, shot him and tossed his body in a dumpster. But where's the law? Vic's walking around a free man. And Jimmy, he's still dead as dead can get. Why don't you look into that, Sheriff Asshole?"

" I don't need to open up a cold case murder file," Billy said. "Got my hands full with speeders, lost cattle and known drug traffickers such as yourself."

Just as Trace opened his mouth for what was sure to be a smart-ass comeback, Billy cut him off. "How did we get to Vic Shear anyway? That was random."

"On my way into work this morning I cut up Maple. Saw his truck parked out front of Arlita Hardy's place."

Billy giving Trace a look of disbelief. Then wondering out loud why Vic Shear would be at Arlita's on a Monday.

Everyone knew her shop was closed Sunday and Monday. He wasn't getting a haircut.

Billy feeling a pang in his stomach but couldn't put his finger on what exactly it was. No way was it hunger, not after that Stromboli.

Some people in the world had lives so hard, so difficult, it seemed that Trouble followed them like an unwanted mongrel. But with Vic, it was more that he dragged Trouble around on a leash like a stubborn dog.

Rather than head straight out of town in the direction of Trace's farmhouse, at the next corner, Billy taking a quick right.

"You lost?" Trace said sarcastically. Billy taking another right, then doubling back toward Main before taking a quick left at Maple. They continued on two blocks, slowing as they passed Arlita's house.

Other than Arlita's Lincoln Continental, no vehicles were parked out front. Driveway was empty too.

"Vic's not here now," Billy said. "Looks like nobody's around but Arlita, not even Patty."

"There's another one with a secret," Trace said. "Screwing Dale Longnecker."

"So you told me Saturday night. How do you know all this again?"

"I told you, it's a small town. Sticking our noses in other people's business is all we got for fun."

A voice came squawking over the police radio. "Hey Dustin, looks like Todd Murphy's got that Camaro of his running again."

A pause as everyone within earshot of a police radio or scanner waited for Deputy Dustin to answer Deputy Lon. Billy, annoyed but indecisive, glanced at the radio.

Trace watching his friend deciding to ignore the chatter. Finally Dustin's voice squawked back, wondering if Lon was referring to the '69 or the '74?

"He don't own no '74 Camaro," Lon said, disgusted. "The '74's an El Camino, not a Camaro. I'm talking about the green and white, '69. Used to belong to Wesley Wayne Weston."

"Wesley Wayne bought it off Chubba Self, didn't he?"

The conversation over the '69 Camaro's genealogy filling up the airwaves. Billy reaching over to turn down the volume. As casually as turning down a bad song on the radio.

"You're going to let that bullshit slide?" Trace said, honestly indignant now.

Billy shrugged, didn't say anything.

"Nice," Trace said, working himself into a lather now.

"My tax dollars at work. You'll run *me* in for weed, but these bozos can use official equipment for chit-chat? Who the hell's running the asylum, anyway?"

Billy not responding, focusing on the road. He made his way back to Jefferson, and they resumed their route out to Trace's house.

The well-kept, middle-class homes in the heart of Caulfield gave way to smaller, run-down houses fronted by broken, uneven sidewalks. Those shabby homes yielded to manufactured modular homes planted by their owners on the outskirts of town.

Just beyond that was a small trailer park that sat across the highway from an industrial section of Caulfield. The industrial park consisted of a sulfurous-smelling oil refinery, a twelve-tower grain elevator and various small, blue-collar trade shops for welders and machinists.

Once past the industrial section, the land opened up into a seemingly unending series of fields and pastures. All were sectioned off with barbed wire hammered into old wooden fence posts. Some of the fields were fuzzy with young winter wheat, others with beans or sorghum. Still others grew wild with prairie grass there for the grazing pleasure of small herds of Hereford cattle, chewing, faces brown and white and dumbfounded.

Given all the spring rain, the fields were an oozy mess. But at least the dust had been washed away, leaving a shiny gloss over the world.

Billy turning off the two-lane asphalt road into the gravel drive way that ran up to Trace's house.

Even before the Escalade came to a complete stop, Trace hopped out with a "Be right back!" Bounding up the wooden stairs he'd built himself, pausing only to unlock the door before disappearing inside the farmhouse.

Billy waiting in the truck. He turned up the volume again on the police radio. His deputies still babbling away.

"...SportsCenter last night?" Lon said. "See that shot that high school kid made on Top Ten Plays?"

"Hell yes," Dustin said. "Lucky shot.

Lon saying he'd rather be lucky than good any day of the week.

Billy grabbing the radio handset. About to chew them out but instead pausing. Taking a breath.

"Hey guys, can we keep the chatter to a minimum? Please?"

A long, pregnant silence coming back at him. Were they laughing? Cussing? Finally, Lon called back.

"Who's this?"

You know good goddamn well who this is, Billy wanted

to say.

Instead he said, "Hey Lon. This is Billy. Just want to keep the airwaves clear. Never know who might be listening."

Another extended silence before Lon's answered back, oily with sarcasm. "Yessir boss."

Irritated by his deputies and growing impatient with waiting. Billy mumbling to nobody, "Goddamn, how long does it take to grab a set of keys?"

Another thirty seconds or so before Trace finally appeared. Where before he had bounded in, Trace now moved in a slower gear as if tracking each of his own footsteps.

Hopping back into the Escalade. Immediately Billy picking up the acrid aroma of what had delayed Trace for so long.

"Damn, did you spill the bong water on your jeans?" Billy said. "Or did you just blow the smoke into your shirt? You reek."

Trace laughing and apologizing through foggy, red-rimmed eyes. Reaching for the power window button, hitting the power lock instead.

"I'll keep the window down, air it out. Can't have a sheriff's vehicle reeking of that goody-goody."

Trying again, this time finding the window switch, but confused when he pressed it and nothing happened. Taking him a second to put it all together.

Finally, with the calm of a driving instructor, Trace saying, “You need to start the vehicle.”

“Whatever you say, Cheech.” Billy firing up the Escalade.

As Billy was turning around to head back out the drive way and into town, he thought it best to make sure Trace had remembered to actually grab his spare keys.

Trace digging into one jeans pocket, coming up empty.

Billy paused the Escalade at the mouth of the driveway, waiting. With just a look demanding to see the keys before they left.

Trace digging in the other front pocket of his jeans until finally coming up with a single silver key dangling from a paperclip. Trace losing himself in its shine. Holding it up, grinning proudly at Billy.

“It’s all good, Sheriff,” he said, launching into a dry-cough chuckle.

Billy shaking his head as he pulled the Escalade onto the county road.

Heading back into town, a long silence filling the truck. Trace blinking his dry eyes. Lost and wandering in his stoned thoughts. Billy's thoughts stuck on the notion of Vic at Arlita's.

Something odd about it, but damned if he could nail it down. The silence finally broken by a mumble from Trace.

"What was that?" Billy said. "It sounded like you said 'momma.' Either that or you burped."

"Wrong," Trace said. "I said Chubba."

"Chubba Self?"

Trace nodded. Billy waiting for more, but Trace didn't elaborate. Billy losing patience with his stoned friend.

"Well, what about Chubba?"

"They, on the radio, they were talking about him earlier."

"Yes," Billy said slowly, as if speaking to a child. "They sure did talk about him on the magic talky box. Very good, Trace."

"Fuck you. Stop fucking with me. I ain't that fucked up."

"That's three fucks in three sentences. Kiss your mom with that mouth?"

As soon as the words were out, Billy regretted them. Trace's mother had passed away from breast cancer two years back, just six months before Trace's dad's heart gave out one hot July day while he was mowing an acre of grass.

Trace had been a little lost since then, more so than

usual. Billy apologizing quickly, lightly.

"Oh man, don't worry about it," Trace said. "But to answer your question, I kiss *your* mom with this filthy mouth."

Billy laughing. No harm, no foul. "So what about Chubba?"

"We were talking about secrets and all. Made me think of Chubba."

"He got a secret does he?"

"Hells yeah!"

"Well, tell it youngblood!"

"Gambling! Evidently, he's in deep over at the casino."

"Bullshit," Billy said. "His old man's got more money than God. He'd pay it off for him."

Trace shook his head. "I don't know about that. You'd think, sure. But I was talking with one of the line cooks over in that shitty restaurant they got over there. Said Chubba was in pretty deep. And evidently, his old man's not as loaded as everybody around here thinks."

"You're stoned."

"Yes, but that has no bearing on Horace Self's finances," Trace said. "You know how it is with farmers and ranchers: all their wealth is tied up in the land. Word is, Horace had to take a mortgage on some of their land to pay off

Chubba's previous debts. Fat boy's dug himself a new hole, a little deeper. Ain't the card shark he thinks he is. Telling you, you'd be surprised. Lot of people from Caulfield in deep over there. Playing games with their savings, their homes. "

Billy thinking that over. "Guess that's why they call it gambling."

As they passed into Caulfield city limits, Lon's voice came over the radio. "Dustin! You have got to get your ass over here to see this. Connie's out doing yard work again."

Dustin's voice calling back over the radio, "In her sports bra and them stretchy running pants she likes to wear?"

"Ten-four. As usual," Lon said. "Best do a drive by, check out the situation."

Billy about to get on the radio, tell them again to quiet the unofficial chatter. But before he could reach it, Trace grabbed hold of the handset.

"You boys should eat at Trace's Place!" Trace yelled into the radio.

"Who the hell was that?" Lon said.

Billy grabbing for the handset but Trace turning away, causing Billy to swerve a little.

"You all sell advertising on the airwaves?" Trace said over the radio. "It sounds like there's a lot of airtime to fill."

Finally Billy managed to snatch away the handset from Trace. "I thought I told you all to clear the airwaves," Billy said into the radio, voice firm. "Enough now, goddamn it."

Without missing a beat, Lon's voice came back at him.

"Shouldn't swear on the radio, boss."

Next came the sound of laughter. Laughter he was meant to hear, Lon on the other end was holding down the transmit button on the handset while he laughed.

Billy racked his handset. He and Trace driving in silence the rest of the way into town. No conversation in the truck, no idle talk on the radio.

By the time Billy dropped Trace off at his diner, Trace's eyes and mind had cleared enough for him to function. He was practiced at it. Trace saying thanks and hopping out of the Escalade.

Billy deciding to make another pass by Arlita's house. Considered stopping in for a visit but deciding against it. Instead, heading into the office to catch up on some paperwork.

Five

Horace standing out back on his deck, grilling KC

strip steaks for dinner. Tammy tried to limit him to beef one night a week on account of his cholesterol. So when he ate beef, he ate steak. The dogs playing in the yard, stopping occasionally to sniff the air for the aroma of meat over flame.

Chubba wandering out to join Horace. Horace immediately noticing his son was eating Doritos straight from a bag about the size of a pillow case.

Until a couple of years ago, the sight of Chubba eating directly from a bag of chips would have gone unnoticed. But that was back when Chubba was still a reflection of the nickname he'd been given as a fat baby.

Chubba had carried the nickname and the weight with him through childhood, adolescence and into his early twenties. Then one day he'd just had enough. Didn't mind the nickname so much. Just disgusted with his obese body.

It was then he started running and lifting weights with the obsessive discipline of a monk. Eventually losing the bulk but still far from the body builder's physique he craved. Every day Chubba reminding himself he was a work in progress. That was Chubba's way—once he got onto something, it was hell getting him off of it.

It was also Chubba's way to seldom fixate on something practical. He had a tendency to find a way to turn something beneficial into something destructive. Eating. NASCAR. Working out. Or, lately, gambling.

The instant Horace saw his son walk out onto the deck snarfing Doritos, he knew Chubba wouldn't stop until the big bag was empty. Horace also knowing his son ate compulsively whenever something was eating him.

Noticing his boy getting a little soft around the edges lately. Horace deciding it would be up to him to put a stop to that before his son reverts to doughy.

Rather than lecture his boy, Horace cutting straight to the bone. "What is it?"

Chubba looking up, cramming a handful of triangle chips into his mouth. Buying time before he answered.

Crunching for a bit.

Swallowing.

Finally saying with a shrug, "What?"

"Spill it," Horace said.

Now Chubba stalling by licking bright orange cheese powder from his fingertips.

Saved from answering his father by his step-mother. Tammy's blonde beehive head popping out from behind the sliding glass door, asking when will the steaks be ready?

"When I say they're ready," Horace said. "You mind?

I'm trying to have a conversation with my boy here."

Tammy rolling her eyes as she ducked back into the house.

Horace not saying a word, just turning back to Chubba. Giving his son that *I'm your dad, goddamn it* look. Eyes hard, lip pursed, jaw set. Horace had gotten into his son's head at a young age, and the look automatically making Chubba crack.

"Sharla," Chubba said, defeated. "She called. Says she's staying up in Kansas City a few more days."

Horace put down the oversized meat fork.

"That's not the plan," Horace said. "She's got to be back to work tomorrow. Everything like normal. That's the goddamn plan."

"Yeah, that's what I told her. But she said the plan needs to be, uh, fluid. React to the situation as it changes, is what she said."

"Horseshit," Horace said. "What's changed?"

Again Chubba shrugging. Once more Tammy's head popping out of the sliding glass doorway. "Horace, really, I got to know when them steaks are going to be done."

"Woman, all you got to know is that I'm fixing dinner!" Horace said.

"*You're* fixing dinner?" Tammy said. "Hell, all you're

doing is scorching meat. I'm in here baking potatoes, fixing green beans, making up a salad, slicing up bread. You, you're just making one damn course!"

Horace shaking his head, turning away, back toward the grill. Refusing to answer his only defense now that, clearly, Tammy had won the point.

When she realized he was giving her the silent treatment, Tammy scoffed loudly, again disappearing back into the house.

Horace saying to Chubba, "Thing is, you can't give the meat too much attention. Sear it on both sides, but then you move it away from the direct heat. Just let it lie there and cook. Only flip it once. Give it too much attention, it'll turn tough on you. Now give me your cell phone. Not yours but the other one."

With his Dorito-cheese hand, Chubba reaching into his sweat pants and pulling out the prepaid cell phone he was using for The Project. Passing it over to his father, who wiped it against his jeans to clean off the cheesy powder.

"Press and hold 2," Chubba said.

Horace held out the phone at arm's length, squinting at it. "Need my reading glasses. They make these things any smaller, people will start carrying them in their ass cracks."

Squinting his way to the 2 button, Horace pressed it

until a word popped up on the screen as the phone autodialed the number. Horace straining to make out the name *Sharla* on the phone's screen. His eyes not believing what they could barely read.

"You put her actual name into the phone?" Horace said. "Crimony boy, do you have a brain in that head of yours? Get it off there."

Sharla answering on the fourth ring. "Hey baby!"

Horace wincing at the false note of affection she'd intended for his son. As always, Sharla was overplaying it.

Horace was the last person to cast stones at people for pretending to be something they weren't in order to manipulate other people. But Sharla was always so damn obvious about it. It was a matter of style. Plus, it pissed him off that his own son couldn't see it.

Or maybe Chubba had simply chosen not to see it. Horace wondered which was worse.

"Not baby, honey," Horace said, "It's daddy."

Sharla saying his name in surprise, dragging it out. Quickly righting herself by saying it was good to hear from him.

Horace still not hearing the change in her voice that he demanded, a subtle mix of respect and reverence.

"Sharla, where are you right now?"

A pause. In the background Horace could hear the sound of Sharla moving things around as if looking for something. Knowing Sharla, probably scrounging in her purse for drugs.

Finally, she answered with a mix of lies, half-truths, excuses and redundant ramblings:

Still in KC, keeping an eye on Patty....

...she is fine, really, everything is okay, really...

...but Pearce wanting her to stay in KC a little longer, help him keep an eye on Patty.

The words pouring from her mouth into the phone, relayed to a cell tower, blasted up to a satellite, back down to another cell tower and finally flooding through Chubba's phone held a few inches from Horace's ear.

All the while Horace shaking his head disappointedly at his son, as if to say, *Really? This is the one you've chosen?*

"Sharla...Sharla," Horace trying to find a gap in the words. Finally barking into the phone for her to shut the hell up. That Sharla did close her mouth as commanded both astonished and pleased Horace.

"Darlin' we had a plan, remember?" he said.

Sharla starting to answer but Horace cutting her off.

"That was a rhetorical question, Sharla. Now you didn't pay much attention in high school, if I remember correctly.

Probably you have no idea what rhetorical means. Means it's a question I ask but you keep your mouth shut. Got it? That one's rhetorical too, so keep it zipped. Here's what you can do—get your sassy little ass back to Caulfield. Tonight. You will be at work in the morning, as we planned. Do you understand?"

No answer from Sharla, just more of the sound of her searching frantically.

"You can answer that one," Horace said. "That last question was not rhetorical."

Still no answer from Sharla. Now the frantic sounds had ceased too. Horace waited her out.

But Horace unaware that Sharla was only now realizing that the baggy of meth she had just polished off was, in fact, her last baggy.

Sharla doing a tweaker's quick calculation—it would be easier to make the drive back to Caulfield to buy more ice off her dealer than it would be to try to find a dealer in KC.

Already she'd pressed Pearce for a connection; he said he knew a hookup but he would have to vouch for her. And didn't it seemed untidy to create a witness that would tie them together?

At the time all Sharla could think was *untidy*? *He really use that word?*

Sharla starting to think Pearce was a real pussy, even if he was a cute one. So home to Caulfield it was.

"When you're right, you're right, Horace," Sharla said. "Be home in a couple of hours, back at work tomorrow. As planned."

Horace killing the call and tossing the phone to his son.

"See that, boy? All it takes is a firm hand. Got to let them know who's boss. Can't let them distract you. You should try it, instead of being led around by your dick all the time."

Horace turning back to the grill to check the steaks. "Goddamn it!"

Surprised by his father's outburst, Chubba jumped, accidently dropping his bag of chips. Doritos scattering across the deck.

"What is it, Daddy?"

Horace spearing one of the strip steaks with the meat fork and holding it up. It was charred and hard and aflame.

"These goddamn women in our lives caused me to burn the goddamn meat."

With a look of disgust, Horace flinging it into the yard for the dogs to fight over.

Tuesday

One

Early on a sun-glazed Tuesday morning. Vic catching site of Dale Longnecker standing at the gas pumps at the convenience store on the north side of town.

Vic hadn't gone looking for Dale. Didn't have to. It was a small town, and Vic knew he'd run into Dale eventually.

Vic had no idea if Arlita knew about Dale cheating with Patty or how she might feel about her granddaughter being the other woman in Dale's marriage. None of that mattered to Vic, other than it made Dale a damn good place to start looking for Patty.

Vic driving past the convenience store, then flipping a quick U-turn.

Dale, half-eaten breakfast hot dog in one hand, his other hand pumping gas into his Taurus, turning to look in the direction of the squealing tires. Spotting the mud-covered pickup just as it finished pulling its U-turn.

Dale realizing it was Vic. Dale looking away. People tended to look away whenever they recognized it was him. Vic having that effect on people.

Dale hearing the truck pull in, park at the pump behind him. Knowing he had a split second to make a decision...

...Say a neighborly *hey* to Vic and run the risk of an uncomfortable conversation that — at any moment and for no reason at all other than it was Vic he was talking with — could turn violent...

...Or ignore Vic, run the risk of upsetting him, have Vic kick the shit out of him?

Dale praying for a third option involving Vic just going away.

But something telling Dale that option wasn't available to him today.

"Hey, Vic," Dale said.

The digital counters on the gas pump tracked the amount of gas pumped and its cost. Dale staying focused on the counter because he only had fifteen dollars cash on him, couldn't go over. No credit cards on him. Not since Dale, never a fisherman, once dragged home a used and useless bass boat they couldn't afford. Right then and there Lucinda confiscated his credit cards. Dale was a cash-only man from then on.

Taking his eye off the gas pump counter in time to see Vic approaching him with a squeegee. The squeegee dripping a trail of windshield cleaner on the pavement.

"Dale, your windshield's filthy," Vic said in the nicest voice Dale had ever heard come out of that ugly, threatening face. "Here, let me get it for you."

Dale telling Vic thanks but no need, really.

Vic going to work as if Dale hadn't said a word.

The counter on the pump approached five dollars. Dale setting the lock on the pump handle so it would run automatically. Instinct telling him it might be best to have both hands free. Scarfing down the last half of his hot dog like a mutt unsure of his next meal. The pump counter flying past six dollars.

"Can you believe the price of gas these days?" Vic said, still working the squeegee over the windshield of Dale's beat up Taurus.

"Scary, ain't it?" Dale said.

"They say in a few years we won't even be driving gas-powered vehicles," Vic said. "We'll all be farting around in them electric cars. Or water maybe. Who knows?"

"Yeah, who knows?" Dale too nervous to be embarrassed by how stiff he sounded.

"Tell you what," Vic said, "I ain't driving no electric car until they design one that looks cool enough to get me laid. That's what cars are all about. I bet you get some strange thanks to this here Taurus, am I right? You know what I'm talking about."

Dale managing a nod, forcing a chuckle.

Rounding the front of the Taurus, Vic stood there watching Dale squirm next to the pump. The counter reading in the eights now.

Then Vic saying, "What am I talking about?" The tone of his voice taking a hard turn.

Dale confused, saying "What?"

"Said: What am I talking about?" Vic standing there, like he's waiting for an easy answer to an obvious question and getting agitated. Like Dale is fucking with *him*.

"Cars."

Vic shook his head. "Nope. Pussy. You get a lot of pussy, don't you, Dale."

"Not since I got married." Dale's lame attempt at a joke. False hope of defusing whatever the hell was going on at the moment.

There was no way he would ever do it, but there was part of Dale that wanted to cry at the unfairness of it all. Hand shaking, Dale reached up for the cigarette stashed behind his ear.

"You don't want to smoke that here," Vic said. "Blow us both up. Even you're not that dumb."

The gas counter crossing over nine dollars.

"Seen Patty in a few days?"

Dale offering his best confused look, like the name didn't ring a bell. "Patty?"

"Patty Hardy," Vic said.

"Oh, Patty!" Dale said, "Nope, I haven't seen her around. Why would I?"

Dale thought he was ready for it.

But Vic striking with such speed and power that it didn't matter that Dale was expecting it. A boot heel to the side of Dale's knee sent him crumpling halfway to the ground.

Vic coming down hard on the back of Dale's head with the squeegee. It was a ridiculous weapon, but Vic swung with such force that it may as well have been a cop's billy club.

Vic's swift, violent movements and Dale's yelps attracting the attention of the cashier and a customer inside the store. Their attention but not their help. Neither moving to intervene or call for help. A young man in a new Mustang who had pulled in to get gas just as the ruckus started pulling right on through the station. Kept going down the street until he disappeared from sight.

It was community consensus: whatever the issue, it was between these two so best to just let them work it out themselves.

The gas counter rolling over twelve dollars.

Dale writhed on the ground, simultaneously trying to hold his throbbing knee, his dizzy head and cover himself from more blows. All the while shrieking over and over, “What the fuck? What the fuck?”

Vic stopping the beating. Bending over Dale. “Like I said, even you’re not that dumb. Now, have you seen Patty?”

Evidently, Dale was that dumb. Even with Vic casting a shadow over him, ready to continue stomping him, all Dale could think to do was continue to play like he had no idea what Vic was asking him.

Vic was more prone to philosophical questions than most people would ever imagine, and at that moment — as he grabbed Dale by the hair — a question flashed through Vic’s mind: *Which is more intoxicating, cheating or covering it up?*

Vic considering asking Dale his thoughts on the subject.

Instead just banging Dale’s face into the rear quarter

panel of the Taurus a few times.

"Okay, now you're just insulting me," Vic said.

Banging Dale's head against the car had knocked the cigarette from behind Dale's ear. It rocked to and fro over the pavement, catching Vic's eye.

Vic yanking the gas pump handle from the side of the Taurus.

"You're starting to really piss me off, Dale."

Pointing the pump handle at Dale. Vic squeezing the trigger and a flood of gasoline pouring out.

Dale marinating in fuel, thrashing around as the gasoline burned deep in his cuts. Trying to turn away to keep the gas from stinging his eyes. Finally the torrent of gasoline ceased.

Dale lay still on the ground, curled up in a ball. Vic reached down and flipped him onto his back. Rummaging through the front pockets of Dale's jeans.

Vic finding Dale's Zippo and pulling it from his pocket. Vic grabbing the cigarette off the ground and shoving it between Dale's lips.

Dale eyes still squeezed tight but hearing his Zippo open with a click in front of his face.

Vic saying, "Smoke 'em if you got 'em."

It was a slippery mess. Gasoline running all over the

place and both men soaked in fuel. Dale had no doubt Vic would light him on fire.

But an even deeper level of terror washing over Dale as he realized Vic didn't seem to mind going all flambé along with him.

"Okay, okay!" Dale said. "Last time I saw her was Saturday night."

Dale telling the short version of the story, Patty sneaking out the window when Lucinda came home from work early. Saying he remembered Patty mentioning something about a party she was heading to later. Dale swearing he hadn't seen nor heard from Patty since. Begging Vic not to tell Lucinda. Telling Vic he had to believe him.

"I don't have to believe shit," Vic said, closing the Zippo. It landed with a thud on Dale's chest. "But I find out you're lying to me, I'm going light you and your whole family up like an old man's birthday cake. Understand?"

Vic not waiting for a response. Getting back in his truck and pulling out of the filling station as if nothing had happened. The clerk and the customer still watching safely from inside the store, neither making a move to help.

Dale struggled to his feet, slipping on gasoline. Unable to stand on his swollen knee. Leaning back against his car, trying to catch his breath. The gas pump counter catching his eye, reading $22.54.

Dale yelling to the people in the store, "Can anybody loan me seven dollars and fifty-four cents?"

Two

Billy wasn't surprised when he arrived on the scene to find Patty's Mercedes lying in a ditch. The car on its back like a helpless insect.

But definitely surprised, and a little pissed off, to find people stepping all over his crime scene.

"Crime scene" being the default status of a site under investigation until proven otherwise by evidence...evidence that at the moment that was being compromised by Anthony Ramirez and Marvin Welch.

Anthony and Marvin dressed in matching dark brown coveralls, their uniform for their septic tank cleaning business (Unofficial slogan: "You Shit 'Em, We'll Git 'Em").

Earlier Cookie had radioed to tell him Vonnie Gibson called in to report an overturned car in a ditch next to his west pasture. It was Patty Hardy's car. There was no sign of Patty.

Billy asked Cookie how Vonnie knew it was Patty's car, and Cookie answered that he knew it was her car because everybody knows her car, the only Mercedes coupe in town.

Now Billy sitting for a moment in the sheriff's Escalade, surveying his crime scene and the gawkers it had attracted.

Anthony standing in the ditch next to Deputy Dustin, surveying the scene; Marvin leaning his ass against the overturned Mercedes. All three men throwing a neighborly wave at Billy.

Billy placing his gray Stetson on his head as he stepped from the SUV. Walking toward the men, glancing around. Getting closer now, catching the last snippets of whatever the hell Marvin was being so adamant about.

"That's the only thing it could be!"

"Don't make no kinda sense," Anthony said. "That stuff's all bullshit."

"You guys mind stepping back up on the road," Billy said, "before you foul up my crime scene, please."

Rather than make a move, the men continued debating the theory currently on the table.

"I mean, Patty's not here, right?" Marvin said. "So obviously they took her with them."

Billy asking who took her with them? Then had to think over Marvin's answer, making sure he'd heard Marvin correctly. Asking him did he just say intelligent beings from elsewhere?

Mavin nodding vigorously. Yes, that's exactly what he said.

Before Billy could shoo them up to the road and away from his crime scene, a clicking noise drew his attention. The sound coming from the far side of the overturned car.

Billy stepping around the back end of the upside down Mercedes, toward the clicking noise.

The clicking noise coming from a camera clutched in the fingers of the young woman stepping out from behind the car.

If he hadn't seen her just a few days before at Arlita's, Billy might not have recognized her. Paige Figures, all grown up.

Paige saying "Hey Billy." Looking up from the viewfinder of her camera. "I mean, Sheriff."

Tucking a loose strand of dark curls behind her ear before going right back to snapping shots of the car and surrounding ground.

Billy saying hi and watching her for a moment. Then catching himself, turning toward Dustin.

"You selling tickets?" Billy barking at his deputy on the far side of the upside down Mercedes.

"It's okay, Sheriff," Dustin said, loping around the car on his long legs. "She's with the newspaper."

Billy looked at Paige as she squatted to take a few shots of the upside down interior of the car. Paige glancing up just long enough to give Billy a shrug and smile.

"Newspaper, huh?" Billy said. "That makes it okay?"

Dustin giving a nod, his own deputy's Stetson bobbing almost as much as his Adam's apple when he spoke.

"Yeah, it's a deal we got with the paper. They take the photos of crime scenes, then give them to us. They get to use a few in the paper."

"I never heard about it."

"Well, no offense, but you ain't never had a crime scene before neither, Sheriff."

Billy assumed Dustin was being a smartass, then saw by the earnest look on the deputy's face that Dustin was simply stating a plain fact. A bit too bluntly maybe, but no disrespect intended.

Over on the far side of the car, Anthony and Marvin's debate was heating up.

"Buuullshiiiit," Anthony said in singsong. "If aliens took her, where are their footprints?"

"How should I know? I'm from around *here*," Marvin said. "Maybe they hover or glide. Maybe they used a tractor beam or something to suck her up."

Anthony was far from convinced. Said that would mean they were in their spaceship. So where were the scorch marks in the field?

Marvin answering him back, saying just because he don't know everything about how it went down, don't mean it didn't happen.

Marvin saying, "Hey man, if I'm the smartest person in the room, we're all fucked."

"Got that right," Dustin said, heading back around the car to join them. Everyone laughing, having a good old time at the crime scene. Billy giving a polite laugh to mask his frustration with the men, most of all his deputy.

"Hey, can I get everyone to step back up on the road," Billy said. Moving back around the car, intending to usher the men up to the road. Spotting a deep shoe print in the drying mud down in the ditch. It was flat, smooth like the bottom of a utilitarian work shoe.

"Hey, any of you boys been mucking around down in the ditch?" Billy said.

The men all saying no. Bill stopping, examining the ditch.

Spotting a few more footprints like the first one he saw. Next to those, a few more sole imprints but with a waffle imprint like a court shoe.

Then seeing a third set of foot prints. Imprints of bare feet, the mud peaked where it squished up between the toes.

With his eyes, Billy tracked the barefoot prints into the field. Noticing that the shoe prints followed about half way before falling into a random pattern, like something moving around willy-nilly, no thought to their movements, maybe panicked. He would have to follow the tracks into the field to see where they ended.

"Paige, you do me a favor?" Billy said. "Can you make sure you snap a lot of shots of those shoe prints down there?" He asked it like a question but it sounded like a command.

Paige saying sure thing, starting down the side of the ditch. Billy stopping her with a light hand on her elbow.

"Any chance you can get some close-up shots from up here?"

Paige getting his meaning right away. "Yeah, I have a lense that will bring them in close," she said. "Keep me from trampling all over it."

Billy let her know that once she got the close shots from up high, then she could step down into the ditch for shots down there. But it might come in handy to have some shot of the undisturbed ground. Paige pulling a long lense from her camera bag and clicking it into place on her camera.

After Paige had taken pictures of the various tracks, Billy climbed down into the ditch.

Following the barefoot tracks into the field, turning where they abruptly turned. Following the footprints as they headed off at a right angle from where Patty's car sat upturned.

Leaning into the wind, Billy followed the barefoot prints all the way across the field, where they jumped a fence before disappearing by the side of the road.

Back at Patty's car, Billy found Anthony and Marvin still matching wits, Dustin laughing. Paige still taking pictures. Billy liked how thorough she was at her work.

"So what do you think, Sheriff?" Marvin asked.

"I already told you what I think," Billy said. "I think you need to get off my crime scene."

"Well, I think it's damn suspicious," Anthony said, not moving. Choosing not to hear the irritation in Billy's voice, the way a person might ignore a child's crankiness before nap time. Going on about what might or might not have happened here.

"No dang aliens though. Maybe she swerved to miss a deer or a possum, lost control of the car. She was thrown from the car, unconscious. When she came to, I bet she was delirious or, no, I bet she had amnesia. I bet she wandered off."

"Okay, I'm going to agree with you," Marvin said, but in an aggressive tone that most people would use when they vehemently disagreeing with someone, "and I'm going to tell you why."

Paige cutting Marvin off before he could continue. Saying how about they all join her up on the road. Said after she finished taking pictures of the crime scene, she'd shoot a couple of group shots of everyone all next to the car. Even print them all copies.

Sounding like a pretty good deal to the two men and the deputy, they all climbed back up onto the road, continuing to debate Patty Hardy's whereabouts.

Paige giving Billy a look and a smile, and Billy feeling himself blush.

"Thanks for that," he said.

Paige saying not a problem, bending down to her camera bag on the ground at her feet, coming back up with a business card. She handed it to Billy.

Said the best way to get hold of her was the cell number. Then getting back to work with her camera.

Billy inspecting Paige's card for a moment before

turning back to inspect the car. Kneeling down, peering into the interior.

Some broken glass.

Fast food bags and lipstick and spare change and other car trash strewn across the upturned roof of the car.

Walking around the car again, Billy unsure what he was looking for. Moving in close to examine the exposed underbelly of the car. Thinking damn, those Germans know how to make a vehicle. Even the bottom of this thing is gorgeous to look at.

As he backed away from the car, Billy's uniform khakis caught on a jagged edge of metal. He unhooked his pant leg where it was caught.

Kneeling down to inspect the crushed part of the Mercedes near the driver's side headlight that had caught his pant leg. Wondering if it was from before or if Patty had smashed into something that caused her to flip?

Billy standing, now inspecting the tear in his pants behind the knee.

"Damn it, these are brand new," he said.

Paige coming around to join him at the front of the car. Smirking saying, " Really, aren't all of your uniforms new?"

Billy feeling stupid now, saying yeah, guess she had a point. But liking the way she called him on it.

Billy showing her the rip in his pants.

Paige saying, "Oh, you can sew that right up."

Billy looking at her like she was crazy, looking to see if she was still messing with him. About to say he'd have his mom take a look at it, see if she could mend it when Paige cut him off.

"A grown man, an independent one anyway, ought to be able to handle the basics. Things like sew up a tear or sew on a button. Groom his hair. Pick out the right suit and tie, or at least a pair of shoes. Funny how that's all gone now, all these so-called real men only concerned with their fantasy football leagues and using the right wood chips for their thousand-dollar barbecue smokers."

Billy looking her up and down. "No really, tell me what you think."

Making her laugh now. Paige liking the way he was calling her out now. Apologizing, saying she has strong opinions and sometimes just feels the need to share them.

"Sharing? Is that what you call it?" Billy still giving her a hard time but both of them not even trying to hide their smiles. Billy turning, heading back up to the road. Leave her laughing, hopefully wanting more.

Climbing out of the ditch when he saw the other set of tire tracks drying in the mud along the edge of the road.

Billy moving back and forth between the new tracks and the Mercedes tracks, making an eyeball comparison.

The new set of tracks looked thinner than the Mercedes tracks. But one as dry as the other, as if they'd been made around the same time.

An odd thing about the thinner tracks. Billy noticing a place in the middle of the tracks where they just disappeared. About a two-foot gap before the tracks reappeared in the mud again, though a little more to the left, closer to the road. As if the car had leapt a couple of feet.

Billy had no idea what the gap in the tire tracks meant but something told him those tracks pretty much explain everything. A second car must have come along the wreck and given Patty a ride. She was probably home now, still sleeping.

Billy again considered the dryness of the tracks. Like everything had happened a few days ago. He'd have to give Patty hell for not reporting right when it happened. Probably she was driving drunk, putting off reporting until she was sober so they couldn't write her up. Nothing he could do about that now. Making a note to himself to swing by Patty and Arlita's later.

Looking over the scene from the top of the ditch now,

Billy watched Paige shooting pictures of the Mercedes. Hollered down to her and asked her to please be sure to get shots of that crushed headlight on the driver's side.

"Need it for your expense report," Paige hollered back, teasing. "Get the department to cover your tailoring costs?"

"An independent man knows how to work an expense report," Billy said. "By far the most creative part of my job."

Paige laughing at that, and Billy really liking the way she laughed. Surprised at how much he liked making her laugh.

Billy approaching his deputy, Anthony and Marvin, all gathered near his SUV. They were still yammering but had moved onto whether there was any truth in Marvin's swear-on-my-mother's-grave story about the time he'd noodled a hunnert-and-fifteen-pound catfish at the reservoir.

Anthony calling bullshit on it like he did on everything Marvin said. And Marvin saying he could understand how someone would doubt the story. Because who in his right mind would stick his hand in a channel cat's mouth, especially one that goddamned big?

But, Marvin pointing out, he wasn't in his right mind at the time. He was drunk. Plus it was dark so he didn't know it was a one hundred fifteen pound catfish he was about to noodle. Thus, his story had to be true.

Marvin saying, "Who would make up such a thing?"

"You!' Anthony said.

The deputy laughing, not even trying to hide it from Billy.

"Having fun, Deputy?" Billy said.

Deputy Dustin not getting it. "Hell, Billy, you know how it is when these boys are around. Good times all the time."

Billy giving up, telling Dustin to string some yellow tape and keep these boys off the scene. Just then Gil Bettencourt rumbled up with his tow truck.

Gil breaking to a hard stop. Leaving it running as he hopped down from the truck. Taking a quick look around before announcing to everyone, "Well, I can tell y'all what the hell happened here...."

Three

"**What brings you** back so soon, Sheriff?"

Arlita saying it brightly, hoping to ease the knot twisting in her stomach as Billy stepped into her beauty shop. "Just in here the other day."

Billy choking on the acrid smell of hair chemicals. Only half hearing what Arlita said. Wouldn't be until later, thinking back on it, that he realized Arlita had called him sheriff. Not Billy like she usually did. Like most everybody did.

Arlita standing at the swivel chair pasting goop all over Gladys Carter's small head, giving a perm to the woman's freshly-dyed chestnut hair. Sharla sitting at her manicure table, a little desk on casters so she could wheel it around.

Billy thought Sharla looked a little haggard. Dark circles, hair up in an effort to hide that it needed a wash. Noticing her unsteady hands working some kind of fancy file on the fingernails of Mrs. Carter's left hand. Mrs. Carter with her crooked feet soaking in a small tub bubbling with foaming water. Arlita and Sharla attending to the little old lady like servants.

"Looks like you signed up for the dee-luxe package," Billy said to Mrs. Carter. Mrs. Carter smiling at him. Accustomed to enjoying attention for most of her life and too far along to give it up now.

"Just came in to get my hair and nails fixed," she said. "Sharla honey, you got any of that cinnamon hot tea you had last time I was in here?"

Sharla putting down her file and glancing up at Billy,

saying hey. Then standing up and at the same time lifting her cell phone from the top of her manicure table. Taking her cell phone so she could text Pearce while making the tea. But Sharla, not paying attention, accidentally bumping the corner of her manicure desk, causing the files and clippers and gougers to jump a bit.

Billy watching as Sharla disappeared into Arlita's house to make the tea. After a long moment, Billy hearing the sound of water filling a kettle.

"So you need me to take your hair shorter?" Arlita said to Billy.

"No, just thought I'd pop in and talk to Patty," Billy said. "She around?'

Arlita shook her head, that metallic taste gurgling up in the back of her throat again. "She's out of town."

"Out of town? How long?"

For a second Arlita almost faltered. She considered asking Billy into the house, away from Mrs. Carter, to confide in him. Seemed like it might be easier to just tell him the whole thing. Let him take over. Allow Arlita to just worry rather than have to plan and worry. But the kidnapper's warning about keeping the law out of it percolated in her head.

Arlita glancing up at Billy and remembering the day he

was born. Remembering giving him his first haircut. Seeing him as she always had and unable to see him any other way other than as that sweet, funny kid. Arlita knowing a kid couldn't help her in this deal going on now. It would take some kind of grown up.

And likely a mean one, given the people attacking Arlita and her family. Arlita finally answering Billy that Patty would be back in town soon.

Ever so slightly, Arlita changing the subject. Asking Billy what did he need to speak to Patty about?

Before Billy could inform Arlita about Patty's car, Sharla came back into the beauty shop from the kitchen. Pointing at his pants Sharla said, "Looks like you ripped your britches back there, Billy."

Billy said yeah, he'd have to get that fixed. Glossing over that to get to the flipped Mercedes. An uncomfortable silence once Billy was through describing the wreck. Everybody making sure not to look anybody else in the eye.

Billy shifting his weight a little in the uneasiness of the room. Nothing but the sound of water bubbling around Mrs. Carter's feet. The silence broken when Sharla's phone buzzed. Sharla stopping her work on Mrs. Carter's nails long enough to text the person back.

Sharla letting Pearce know the sheriff was in the beauty

shop so now might be a fun time to call up Arlita and prove to her they really had her precious granddaughter.

She'd been watching Arlita all day, gauging her mood. The fat lady seeming no different really, just calm and collected as usual. Until Billy showed up. Sharla noticing how that put Arlita on edge. Now Sharla was tickled by the idea of maybe pushing her boss over that edge.

"Mind if I ask: Is Patty okay?" Billy said.

Arlita looking confused for a moment, like she'd just woken up in the middle of the conversation. "Okay?"

"From the wreck," Billy said. Billy wondering why everything felt so awkward.

Arlita saying Patty was fine. Not even a scratch.

Billy saying that was good to hear. Taking his time approaching the next part. Wanting to be careful not to lecture Arlita but still make clear the seriousness of the situation.

But before he could get to it, Arlita's house phone rang. Arlita deserting Mrs. Carter and her gradually kinking hair. Heading into the kitchen to answer her phone.

Sharla stopping her work on Mrs. Carter too. Abandoning the old lady's nails in order to text Pearce on his personal phone. Knowing he was using his prepaid phone to talk with Arlita in the other room.

Sharla texting him: *fat ldy bout shit britches whn fone rang*

Then Sharla wandering off somewhere in the house, leaving Mrs. Carter sitting half fixed in the chair.

A celebrity magazine lay open in Mrs. Carter's lap. She looked up at all the people not attending to her. Saying to Billy, "Christ almighty, what's it take for a lady to get some consideration around here?"

Arlita never thought it possible for a woman to feel so exposed while standing in her own kitchen.

Recognizing the voice on the line from the other day, just as deep and with that same waver in it. Arlita fighting back against that feeling of weakness in her chest.

"Hey there, Piss. Nice to chat with you again," she said. "Let me talk to Patty." Arlita hearing his thin, forced laugh.

"Still think you're in control, huh, grandma?" the guy said.

But Arlita heard him cover the phone. She noticed her mouth was dry. The water in the tea kettle on the stove starting a low rumble.

Pearce, wearing the Daffy Duck mask, bent down so he was level with Patty's blindfolded face.

Patty not sure how long she'd been strapped spread eagle on the bed in her panties and bra. Only let up now and then to use the toilet.

When they fed her, always fast food burgers or burritos and they didn't let her sit up. Just crammed a few bites in her mouth before jamming the sock back in and taping it in with duct tape.

As delicately as he could, Pearce removed the duct tape that stretched from cheek to cheek across Patty's face. Moving to take the sock out of her mouth but reconsidering it.

"You try anything funny, I'll smack you. Got it?"

Patty nodding. Of her two captors, the guy was the easier one. Not nice, but something about him was weaker than the gal. But weak or nice or whatever, Patty figured if the guy was criminal enough to kidnap her, he wouldn't have any trouble knocking her around.

Now the gal, she was mean. All the little tortures like hitting Patty with quarters or putting out matches on the tops of Patty's feet. Patty hadn't gotten a look at either of them. The gal, she maybe sounded kind of familiar, maybe not.

Patty hearing a vibration, like a cell phone. A half second later, she heard the guy snicker. Patty guessing he'd received a text he found funny. Finally, the guy pulled the sock, wet with saliva, from her mouth.

Patty just a little bit freer now. That little bit of freedom allowing how pissed-off she was to grow larger than her fear. Patty deciding she was about done with being scared. Wanting to tell the guy that in her life she'd already been hit harder than he could ever bring it.

But when she went to speak nothing came out. Just a dry rasp. Her throat all parched and raw, her spit absorbed by the sock. Patty trying to work up some saliva. Finally Pearce figuring it out, giving her a squirt of water from a bottle.

"Can you take off this blindfold?" Patty asked. A long pause before the guy told her no. Holding the phone against Patty's face. Hearing her grandmother's voice calling her name from far away.

Patty saying "Gramma, I'm okay."

Arlita hearing Patty's voice and having no doubt it

was her granddaughter. Arlita's eyes welling with tears.

Happy Patty was alive. Afraid for her granddaughter. Angrier than ever that someone would try to pull something like this.

And more certain than ever that the dumb sons of bitches would suffer for this.

"Sugar, you okay?" Arlita said.

Patty's voice coming back saying she was okay, just tired. Arlita hearing movement, then the guy's voice coming back on the line.

"All right, there's your proof," he said. "Now do I need to go over the instructions for the money or do you remember them?"

The guy sounding more helpful than menacing, Arlita thought. Like he was some sort of kidnapping customer service rep.

"Bullshit," Arlita said. "I couldn't hear her very well. That could be someone just kind of sounds like her. Put her back on the phone."

Pearce thrown off by that one. Not even sure how to respond.

Finally saying, "Now let me get this straight. You think we got someone who *sounds* like your granddaughter?"

Arlita ignoring that, demanding he put her

granddaughter back on the phone. Hearing him curse, then more movement. Then Patty's thin voice back on the line.

"Wh-what Gramma?"

"Listen, closely, sugar," Arlita said. "Stay strong. You have any idea who these people are, where they're keeping you?"

Patty starting to say something when Pearce jerked the phone away. "Don't even!" he yelled into the phone. "You want her to get smacked? Try that shit again."

Arlita telling him to keep his skirt on. Just want to be sure it's really her. Maybe could he ask her something, something only Patty would know. Really prove it's her. Pearce asking like what?

Arlita thinking about it. Convinced it was Patty but wanting to keep them on the line anyway. Jacking with the guy because she could. Finally, she had him ask Patty what's her favorite restaurant. Knowing full well it was Red Lobster but anything to stall.

Patty, in the darkness of her blindfold, hearing the guy ask what's her favorite place to eat? Patty about to say Red Lobster but catching herself. Recalling the guy and the gal talking from before. Unsure when it was, guessing it must have been nighttime. Because the gal had kept suggesting they "go out, have some fun tonight."

But the guy stood his ground, saying they'd better stick to the plan. The girl kept on insisting they hit Westport.

Patty had partied more than once in Westport, a cluster of bars in Kansas City. Patty figuring they must be somewhere in KC. Or at least close enough that a person could get her drink on in Westport and still keep an eye on her hostage.

Arlita hearing the guy back on the line. "She says it's Stroud's."

Arlita thinking what the hell?

The guy covering the phone but hearing Patty saying something to the guy. Then he's back on the line. "She says you know how she loves their mix up of gizzards and livers."

Pearce's vegan instincts taking over at just the thought of it. Saying to no one in particular, "Man, I'm about to puke."

Arlita thinking about it too.

Stroud's? That pan-fried chicken place in Kansas City? Then remember she and Patty had eaten there a couple of times when they were up that way shopping. Patty had loved their chicken-fried steak.

Damned if her granddaughter would eat any gizzards and livers though. Patty had been just as sickened by the sound of gizzards and livers as that dumbass there on the phone. Not Arlita. She had a taste for organ meat.

Arlita wondering why all this business about Stroud's and gizzards and livers?

It came to Arlita quickly: the bastards were holding Patty somewhere up around KC.

The first honest smile in days crept across Arlita's face. Goddamn, she had one smart granddaughter.

Pearce's personal cell phone buzzed with another text from Sharla but he ignored it.

Later he'd read that text, *red lbstr*, and wonder why Sharla was asking if he wanted to eat seafood. Sharla was hot and all, but she really needed to look up the definition of vegan.

Arlita's voice coming full volume over the phone, drilling into Pearce's ear. "All right, Piss, all right. It's her. You'll get your money. But don't you put a hand on her. In any sort of way, you hear me?"

Pearce looking down at the fat girl in her underwear strapped to the bed and realizing he hadn't even had a sexual thought toward her. That is, until the grandmother brought it up just now. Damn, he *could* do anything he pleased.

Not that he found Patty attractive. Had to admit

though, he was attracted to the idea of doing whatever he pleased to her. Finally starting to see what Sharla had been getting at with the quarters and the random kicks and punches and such.

Sharla *knew* Patty. For her, messing with the fat girl was personal.

For Pearce, it would be distant and cold, objective. Like an experiment. The coldness of it appealing to him.

"I'll do whatever the hell I feel like," Pearce said, not needing to fake a chill in his voice for once. This time it occurred naturally, like a frozen creek in winter.

Arlita hearing it too. "Piss, I mean it. I think maybe you're in deeper than you've ever been. Try being smart for once in your chicken shit life."

Pearce ignored her. Like she could do anything to stop him.

"You just worry about the money," Pearce said. "I need to walk you through the drop again? Between 11 in the morning and noon. Drop it in the garbage bin behind the Dairy Queen."

Arlita saying she had it all straight. Then the line going dead.

Arlita pushing the off button on the phone. She would find a quiet moment as soon as possible to call Vic, fill him in on the Kansas City tip.

Despite the tip and the joy of knowing her granddaughter was alive, Arlita sensed that she'd lost a small measure of what little control she'd had. This situation needed to be resolved quick. Most ricky-tick, as her husband Pat, a marine, had always said whenever he wanted something pronto. He'd picked it up Vietnam, one of the few things from the war he ever talked about.

Arlita spending a few seconds bathing in useless longing, wishing that her Pat were there now to take charge and to hold her. Arlita thinking that if she could, she would gladly trade all the lottery money to have her husband back.

A futile thought, but it brought her around to a realistic one: If it came down to it, she would pay whatever money they asked to get her granddaughter back safely.

But she would spend the remainder of her time on earth making sure they eventually paid her back with their hide. Telling herself she had the means and the mean to make it happen.

The tea kettle starting to howl and Arlita turning to snatch it off the burner. Startled to find Sharla standing at the stove, just watching it go off.

Back in the beauty shop, as Arlita and Sharla each took up their respective work on Mrs. Carter, Billy finally got to it about the serious nature of Patty's offenses.

He tried to sound flat and direct. Not scolding, but authoritative. Saying Patty should have called in the accident as soon as possible. Pointing out that she could be written up for leaving the scene of an accident, among other things.

Billy not mentioning that he suspected Patty was under the influence at the time and had put off reporting it so they couldn't breath and blood test her. He couldn't prove it, though, so didn't see a point in bringing it up.

Arlita nodding as she touched up the goop on Mrs. Carter's hair. Sharla pretending to only half-listen as she worked a buffing board on Mrs. Carter's nails.

Billy concluding by saying he was inclined to let it slide this time. But did Arlita understand what he was saying?

"Yes, Billy, I hear you," Arlita said. The condescension in her voice as thick as the stench of hair chemicals hanging in the air.

Billy ignoring it. Had one final point he wanted to cover. "Now, I'm going to need to talk to her when she gets back in town. Where'd you say she ran off to?"

"Oh, she's in up in Kansas City," Arlita said.

Just then Sharla fumbling the buffing board. Sharla apologizing, bending over to pick up the board. A little freaked at how certain Arlita sounded concerning the whereabouts of her granddaughter.

Billy looking puzzled, thinking about Patty's flipped car "How'd she get up to KC?"

Not missing a beat, Arlita saying friends came down to pick her up.

"Mind if I ask what she's doing up in Kansas City?" Billy said.

Arlita looking over at little Billy playing police.

Arlita laughing, saying, "Shopping for a new car, I imagine."

Four

Billy patrolling Caulfield after leaving Arlita's. Just driving and thinking.

Mulling the uneasiness he'd sensed back at the beauty shop. Some kind of weirdness going on there, but damned if Billy could put a finger on it.

He drove up and down Main, turning off on this and that side street, following one until instinct told him to turn down another.

Crossing over train tracks in one intersection and eventually back over the same tracks in another part of town. The awkwardness at Arlita's too vague to hold Billy's attention for long. As usual when he patrolled, his mind went rambling back to childhood memories.

Just about every house, street or building Billy passed reminded him of something or someone. Like the big public park on Main.

When he was a little kid, he used to catapult himself out of a swing, sailing as high as he could. Hanging in the air for a split second, tickled by weightlessness, before free-falling to the ground.

Driving by a smaller park down an east side street, near his boyhood home. He used to go almost every day to throw a baseball with his dad, for fun first, then with an additional purpose once it became clear Billy's right arm was special.

Billy finding himself now cruising slowly past the house where his grandmother, his mom's mom, had lived. Grandma June's place looking a little shabby now. The people living there now too lazy to give it a coat of paint.

They needed to get back to how he remembered it.

Billy making a mental note to have a deputy swing by, cite them for a housing code violation.

Before he started kindergarten, his Grandma June watched him every day while his mom and dad taught at the high school. Billy could still remember the long, boring weekdays, no cousins around like on weekends. Only a few other preschool kids in the neighborhood to play with and a couple of them mean to the bone.

Especially that dirty-faced boy, Monty something. Always torturing bugs and on the lookout for cat victims for his cruelty. Billy's grandma always shooing Monty out of her yard and warning Billy to stay away from "that worthless, ignorant little brat."

His Grandma June, she was a fun and funny lady. Saying what she thought, always laughing. Turning household chores like ironing and washing dishes into games to ease their monotony. Teaching him to bake brownies. Scratching his back whenever he asked.

The only rule she ever made of Billy follow was that he leave her alone while her stories were on television. That's what she called her favorite soap operas.

Grandma June always telling Billy stories too, fairy tales and family legends. Billy's favorites were the ones she told of her hard, happy childhood on a dirt farm less than twenty miles east of Caulfield.

Billy's mind flashing now on a faded black-and-white picture of his grandmother, a little girl in a dingy white sack dress seated atop a mule.

Involuntarily Billy's mind calling up the image of his Grandma June lying wax-like in her coffin just two years previous.

Billy thinking now that it was funny how a mind makes those jumps so effortlessly: young to old, child to elderly, born to dead. Billy wiping away her coffin image, replacing it with the thought of his grandma's fried chicken.

As Billy passed the rental storage lockers out north of town, he remembered riding out to them once with his dad and his dad's brother. A young boy wedged between the men in the cab of his uncle's pick up.

They were hauling a bunch of items from his Great-Grandma Ida's sewing room. A sewing machine, dress mannequins and such, all going into storage. That was right after they had moved Ida into the rest home.

The old woman surprising everyone and lasting there several years before passing on. Billy thankful now for his memories of visiting her. Thankful his mother made him and his sisters visit the old woman at least once a week.

A curious trick of spending most of his life in one place: many of the places of Billy's childhood eventually turned into places from his adolescence, creating a sort of double exposure memory. Same places, different faces.

The memory of riding between his father and uncle driving to the rental storage lockers faded into another memory, one more recent and vivid in his mind. In high school. He and his ex, Tina, stealing away behind those same rental storage lockers for some good old, teenage backseat car sex.

Billy now flipping a U-turn at the rural intersection. Not sure why, but deciding to check out their old secret spot. Turning into the entrance, past three rows of metal storage units and slowly following the gravel path around to the backside.

Turning the corner and, like just that, getting a whole new memory for a lifetime—a sheriff squad car parked, engine off. His deputy, Lonnie, snoozing. Stretched out across the front seats, boots crossed and propped on the passenger door.

Lonnie in a deep sleep, not even stirring as Billy rolled up in his SUV. Billy getting out, closing his door quietly. Approaching the driver's side of the squad car. Billy rapping on the glass, Lonnie jumping in the air like an angry rooster.

Lonnie scrambling around to see who it was, what was happening, his hand on his sidearm. Seeing who it was and yelling goddamn it. His voice muffled through the closed car window.

Billy smiling, yelling back. “Having sweet dreams of big ole catfish, Lonnie?”

“Don’t ever do that again,” Lonnie yelled.

Billy laughing now. “So it’s not that I woke you, it’s how I went about it, that’s what you’re upset about? By the way, you can take your hand off your sidearm, deputy.”

Lonnie relaxed his posture, hand moving away from his gun. He sat up. “Scared me half to death, damn it,” Lonnie yelled.

Billy motioning for him to roll down the window. “You seem cranky. Maybe I should let you finish nap time.”

Lonnie stewing quietly. Busted but not giving in, not admitting a thing. Billy sizing up his deputy, trying to figure how to play this one. Big bad boss? Understanding colleague? Extend the professional courtesy of not chewing Lonnie’s ass?

Billy realizing he was less concerned about how he thought he should handle it. Found himself more concerned with how Lonnie would want Billy to handle it.

Billy had no idea about that one. But at that moment, he did have a small revelation about trusting his instincts and this job of his.

"Well, what do we do here, Lon?" Billy said. "Do I play it soft? Or play the hard ass?'

A smirk oozing across Lonnie's face. "Fact that you had to ask me, that says it all."

Billy tamping down that part of himself that wanted to punch his deputy in the mouth.

Instead saying, "I'm serious Lonnie. Because this...this is beneath you. I know how much you care about the job, about law enforcement. But are you so pissed at me for getting elected sheriff that you're willing to let down the job?"

"Just a damn popularity contest, all it is." Lonnie not looking at Billy now, just staring straight ahead.

Billy saying could be but it is what it is. At least until the next election.

"In the meantime," Billy said, "show a little respect for the badge. And while you're at it, show a little respect for yourself."

Lonnie just sitting there glowering. Billy watching him, wondering if any of it was getting through.

Billy thinking: Some people, they won't listen and you

can't tell them.

Lonnie, still not looking at Billy, asking if Billy was going to write him up. Billy hadn't yet decided. Telling Lonnie to head back out on patrol. He'd let him know either way at the station in the morning. Billy stepping back from the squad car, seeing it in his head before Lonnie did it: a fuck-you peel out on the gravel as he took off.

Billy stood there for a minute, listening to the whine of Lonnie's squad car fading down the highway. Billy staring off at the flat farmland that extended out behind the storage lockers. Feeling small in that vast expanse.

A brisk wind blowing across the land. A warm day for early spring, but now the late afternoon bringing a chill. A chill at odds with the fiery sun now setting at the western edge of the world, burning orange and spreading fast toward him.

Billy climbing back into his SUV, bothered anew by the strangeness back at Arlita's. Deciding he'd swing back by. Not sure why. Not sure if he would stop in but not sure what good just driving by would do either.

When he turned onto Arlita's street, Billy slowed his SUV. On the way he'd made up his mind to stop in. Under the pretense of seeing if Arlita had heard from Patty but really just to see if everything was still off-kilter with Arlita.

Then seeing the car out front of her place.

A tricked-out 1974 El Camino, white with blue and gray pin stripes and mag wheels. A big blue Dallas Cowboy star outlined in gray painted on the hood.

Billy at first thinking Arlita maybe had a customer in the shop but didn't recognize the car. But a car like that, he and everybody else in town would remember. Its ancestry of owners too. That car had to belong to someone from somewhere else.

Billy noting the Texas license plate. Despite being alone Billy saying aloud, "Mona, you back in town?"

Billy cruising past, seeing that indeed it was Arlita's black sheep of a daughter. Billy watching the woman stomping up the steps, druggie thin except for her wide ass. Barking over her shoulder at a lanky black guy, making sure he grabbed the damn suitcase from the bed of the El Camino.

Definitely not stopping right now, Billy thought. Best to stay out of the middle of that for now.

Billy taking the next left, deciding to patrol Main a few more times before calling it a day.

Thinking about Patty's wrecked car.

And that reminding him of Paige taking photos. She's grown up cute, funny and smart. Something attractive in the confident way she handled her camera.

Billy forcing himself back to the issue at hand.

Recalling Sheriff Otis Cady's advice that Billy should familiarize himself with the normal rhythms and patterns of his citizens and town. That way, when something out of the ordinary pops up, it stands out like a spotted runt in a litter of pink piglets.

Patty's flipped car. The weirdness in Arlita's shop. Now out of the blue, Mona showing up in a clown car.

Billy wondering what, if any, connection there might be among it all.

Five

"**So guess who** shows up today?"

Sharla asking Chubba, saying it like she's challenging him with a trivia question.

Chubba hunched over a laptop computer at his kitchen island, too absorbed in his online poker game to share Sharla's excitement about her big news.

Sharla certain Horace would be interested, but at the moment he was out back in the barn, feeding his horses.

Sharla pushing for a reaction from Chubba, ready to spell it out if that's what it took. Which, evidently, it did.

"Fucking Mona shows up," she said. "Some black dude with her, too."

Delivering the news about Mona like the big surprise it was, but not getting the reaction she expected. Just a grunt from Chubba.

Sharla had stopped by to give Chubba and Horace an update on the situation inside Arlita's. Arlita canceling all her appointments for the week except for a few of her little old lady regulars. Arlita giving Sharla the rest of the week off. Mona suddenly back in town. And with a black guy.

"Believe that shit? Mona! I mean, if she's asking Mona to come home, you know Arlita's rattled to the tits," Sharla said.

Chubba's attention perking up at the word *tits* but still not sure what Sharla was going on about.

"Yep," he said, just to say something. He raised the pot on in his Texas Hold 'Em game, feeling out a bluff by some dude making ridiculous raises from his computer in South Korea.

Never one to go ignored, Sharla watched Chubba as she considered her next move. Chubba looking soft, losing some definition in his arms, his biceps and triceps hanging flabby from his sleeveless t-shirt.

Sharla thinking his lard ass has probably been parked in front of the computer for days. Swallowing junk food and pop the whole time too. Amazing how quickly his body starts to go spongy if he skips even a few trips to the weight room.

She didn't mind it so much, made him cuddlier. But she knew Chubba well enough to know he didn't like himself that way.

Sharla coming around the island and playfully poking Chubba in his tender ribs. "Hey, fat boy, you hear what I said?"

Chubba clutching at his side, annoyed. Telling her not to do that.

Sharla demanding to know did he know what the hell she was talking about?

"How am I supposed to know what you're going on about if *you* don't even know?" Chubba said.

"Oh, you're a funny fat boy," Sharla said.

"Don't call me that, please."

"Fat boy." Sharla laughing.

Chubba trying to stay mad but starting to chuckle. Chubba standing. Sharla backing away, putting the kitchen island between them.

For the first time since Sharla had walked in, Chubba really saw her. Looking rough, her eyes watery and raw. A little too thin, even for her. Looked like she hadn't slept much.

Still, something about her, even now at less than her best, something about her just seized him inside. He couldn't deny it.

Chubba, laughing now, asking where you going, girl?

Sharla, squealing, saying nowhere. Chubba started after her, chasing Sharla around the island, both of them giggling.

And both out of shape, tiring quickly. Sharla letting him catch her, and Chubba wrapping his arms around her from behind. He kissed her nape. She let him. But as his hand slid to her breasts, Sharla twisting away and turning to face him.

"Your daddy walks in on us, he won't like it none."

"Maybe we better head up to my bedroom then," Chubba said, pulling her close again.

Sharla wanted Chubba heated up but not too hot.

Her plan was to deliver her news, then hit her meth dealer's house to stock up before heading back to KC.

Jutting her chin in the direction of the computer, Sharla changed the subject. "He won't like it, you gambling on the

Internet, neither."

Not gambling, Chubba said, it's a free site. Just honing his game. Sharla saying, whatever, Horace still wouldn't like it.

Sharla knowing Horace had been riding Chubba hard about his gambling as of late. They'd never said it out loud, but Sharla guessed the whole reason they were holding spoiled Patty was to pay down Chubba's gambling debts. And maybe make some profit in the process.

Sharla was certain Chubba had a genuine gambling problem. She just wasn't sure what she could do to help, what with her own expanding cravings to deal with.

Chubba, sensing Sharla on the verge of lecturing him about his gambling, looked away. Chubba not wanting to go there because it wouldn't be long before he came back at her, wondering who the hell was *she* to lecture him on bad habits? Chubba deciding it was better to just avoid it all.

"Tell you what," Chubba said. "Let's go out tonight. Get some dinner, catch a movie or something."

Or something in Chubba's mind being either sex or finding themselves heading over to the casino in Pierette County. Or, perfect world, both.

Sharla thinking about her plans. Asking Chubba if he thought it was a good idea, going out in the middle of everything going on right now.

"Got to keep up appearances," Chubba said, "stick to our usual ways."

Chubba's hands moving down the small of her back, squeezing her boney bottom. "Someone might notice if we start acting different all the sudden. Good times, that's just par for the course for us, right baby?"

Sharla agreeing, absolutely. But asking didn't it make more sense to focus on The Project for the time being?

And now that Arlita had given Sharla the week off, didn't it make sense for her to head back up to KC?

Sharla saying, you know, keep an eye on Pearce and Patty, make sure all goes well up there?

"Smart move is to save the good times for later," Sharla said, "Don't you think, baby?"

She could see disappointment cloud Chubba's eyes, his face hardening.

Sharla sliding her hands down to the crotch of Chubba's sweat pants where she found another part of his body, not at all soft.

Sharla smiling up at Chubba. "Don't have to save all the good times for later though," she said.

Sharla watching as the light came back on in Chubba's eyes.

Clutching him in her hand, leading him down the hall, up the stairs and into his bedroom. Pushing him down on the bed and going to work on him.

Her hands moving with the deftness and precision of a highly-skilled craftsman. Just her hands and, before Chubba knew it, it was all over. This was quite all right with Chubba.

After lying there for a minute, Sharla stepping into the bathroom to wash. Then she and Chubba heading back down to the kitchen, holding hands.

“I guess I better take off,” Sharla said, the timing of it awkward but forcing it anyway. “Get myself up to KC to run things there.”

“Why not wait until the morning,” Chubba said. Chubba thinking it had been a long time since they’d had this kind of fun. An even longer time since it felt like Sharla actually liked him. He’d forgotten how nice it was, having her attention.

Lately, he’d begun to question her motives for being with him. She liked his car. She liked his family’s money. Just didn’t seem to like *him* all that much. And though he tried not to let it, that was affecting the way Chubba viewed himself.

When he found himself liking her, Chubba noticed that

he hated himself for it. And when he found himself not liking her, Chubba felt better about himself. How twisted with that? It was as if their relationship had become an oversized, tangled up knot.

"I thought you said it made sense for me to keep an eye on things up there?" Sharla said.

"Nope, you said that."

Chubba uncomfortable with his girlfriend being alone with Pearce. Suspicious there was more going on up there than meets the eye. Not the first time he'd had his doubts, but this was the first time he didn't deny them. Chubba allowing himself feel the burn of it.

Sharla getting snotty with him now, saying, well you agreed to it.

Chubba just repeating a terse nope.

"Well, you should have," Sharla said, "because it's the right answer."

Over Chubba's shoulder, through the window over the kitchen sink, Sharla saw Horace coming in from the barn. Something in her deciding she wanted to be gone before he made it to the house. Let Chubba tell him the news about Mona showing up.

Sharla turning to Chubba, expecting to find him standing there acting hurt, like he usually was whenever

Sharla did just what she wanted.

Instead, she was surprised to find him checking on his poker game. She hit with the realization tha*t, oh my god, he's putting gambling before me.*

Sharla thinking fuck if he isn't a gambling addict.

The thought reminding Sharla of her own particular hunger.

"Baby, I'll need some cash for while I'm up there," she said. "Couple hundred, if you got it."

Chubba not saying a word, just reaching into the pocket of his sweat pants and giving her all he had. Never taking his eyes off his poker game.

Sharla counting the wad of bills, a little less than a hundred. Better than nothing. Moving up behind Chubba, kissing him on his cheek.

"See you soon baby," Sharla said. "When this is all over, we can go on a vacation somewhere. Just get out of town and have us some fun."

As she said it, Sharla realizing she meant it. Immediately started looking forward to it. Now Sharla a little conflicted about leaving.

Sharla running some quick relationship math in her head, trying to see which had the greater value: Scoring her crystal meth and heading to KC?

Or scoring crystal meth and staying in town with Chubba?

KC promised more brutal fun with Patty. Maybe heat up the quarters before tossing them on Patty's body. Sharla really hating that girl.

Sharla had spent much of her time coming up with more tortures. Minor tortures, all of them involving the slightest of pains: little cuts, tiny burns, petite welts. Hurt after hurt piling on top of one another, putting Patty in agony, pushing her to the brink of mental and emotional breakdown. But just short of actually killing the fatso.

KC promised Pearce. Seeming more and more like total bullshit, that gangsta thing he was trying to pull off with the tats and the metal hanging off his body.

But even knowing it was just a show, Sharla had to admit it turned her on. She'd always been attracted to that roughneck thug look, like in the hip-hop videos. Of course, she knew she could never be with a black guy. That's just not how she was raised. But a white gangsta would do.

Pearce, he wasn't much of a gangsta really. But if she was high enough and squinted at him just right in a fuzzy light, Sharla figuring she could make it work for her.

But then here was Chubba. Now as always, treating her nicer than she deserved. Sharla feeling something almost like loyalty to him.

Sharla's resolve hanging in the balance. Just for a moment. Until she heard Horace clomping up the steps of the deck.

The mere sound of his boots enough to tilt her toward KC. Sharla not in the mood for his ass-holier-than-thou act.

Horace coming into the kitchen through the sliding glass doors, saying howdy to Sharla. Thinking the young woman looks rode hard and put away wet.

Sharla saying hey back at him, then heading out the front door.

From the kitchen, Horace watching her through the big window at the front of his home. Sharla pulling away in Chubba's Mustang.

"Where the hell's she running off to?" Horace said.

"Kansas City."

"What the hell you let her do that for?" Horace said. "Don't she have to work at Arlita's?"

Chubba brought his father up to date on Arlita canceling her work week, Mona showing up with a black dude, all of it.

Horace thinking it over. Things were picking up steam. Maybe it wasn't such a bad idea, letting Sharla go to KC. If something went wrong, it would be easier to pin it on them if Sharla and Pearce were shacked-up together with the hostage.

Of course there really was no doubt in Horace's mind that they'd get away with it; otherwise he'd have never had them snatch Patty in the first place.

But Horace couldn't deny that he was growing more concerned about weak links.

Horace thinking something's going on with that girl. Appeared the drugs were cutting hard into Sharla. Won't be long before she starts getting as sloppy as she looks. That was worrisome to Horace.

Suppose Sharla got popped for drugs? Horace knowing she wouldn't think twice about spilling everything. Do anything to save herself. No doubt about it, Sharla was turning into a serious risk.

Once this deal was over, Horace had no intention of him and his son living the rest of their lives wondering if all this might come back on them somewhere down the line just because Sharla needed to get herself out of a jam.

Horace's best move for his future and that of his son was to minimize all risk. The only question mark on that issue was Chubba himself.

"Son," Horace said, "How much you like that girl, really?"

Six

Arlita arranging the place settings for their late dinner, spacing her everyday China around the oak dining room table. Not expecting any help, so she wasn't overly disappointed when Mona just planted her ass in a chair.

Mona glad to be back in *her* seat. The spot next to what had been her father's seat at the head of the table. Mona sitting and smoking as her mother worked around her. They were alone for the first time since Mona and Gerald had arrived.

With Gerald around, Arlita was only able to give Mona an outline of the situation. She damn sure wasn't giving up any details on how she was handling Patty's kidnapping, not in front of some stranger her daughter had dragged in from God knows where.

Finally Arlita had managed to get rid of Gerald for a while, asking if he minded running out to pick up a bucket of chicken at the KFC. And get a few sides too, mashed potatoes and whatever he wanted. Gave him two twenties to cover it.

Though she was free to speak openly with her daughter now, Arlita hesitated, not certain she even wanted to tell

Mona everything. Arlita loved her daughter but she *knew* her daughter—and with Mona, it was a crapshoot which secrets she would keep.

Arlita circling her dining room table setting out the fine bone china plates, white with blue and gray pin striping. Jesus, Arlita thought, her plates looked like that stupid-ass Dallas Cowboy car-truck of Gerald's.

"Why did you bring him here, anyway?" Arlita said.

Mona blowing out a stream of gray menthol smoke. "You mean why did I bring *him* here? Or why did I bring him *here*?"

Arlita caught her daughter's meaning. "You think I care he's black? Honey, you think that, you don't know me at all."

"Really?" Mona ready to pounce. "So it's just a coincidence then, you sending him out for fried chicken? God, mom, fried chicken? Surprised you didn't ask him to pick up some watermelon then tap dance his way back."

That stopped Arlita in her tracks. "That's ridiculous."

Arlita considered it some more. "I didn't even think of it that way. Think he took it that way?"

Mona just shrugged, letting her suggestion hang in the air like her cigarette smoke. Refusing to let her mother off the hook and enjoying the feeling of winning a round.

Mona couldn't deny she felt electric. Wasn't happy that her daughter had been kidnapped, naturally. But without a doubt it took Mona some effort to hide her excitement at all the drama. Mona thinking life is some weird-ass shit.

Growing up in this place, her life going in the direction it had, so far astray. Now all of a sudden she's back home, sitting next to her father's empty chair. She wondered where her daughter usually sat.

"Which place is Patricia's?" Mona said.

"You're sitting in it," Arlita said.

Recognizing that Mona only used Patty's full name when Mona felt the need to make it clear she was the girl's mother. Mostly when Mona was just trying to say "look at me, I'm a mother." But at that moment Arlita too tired to fight.

Arlita again asking Mona why she brought along Gerald, this being a family crisis?

Mona saying for support. Saying it like it was the most obvious thing in the world.

Arlita finished laying out the plates and silverware. She checked the table one last time. Even before winning the lottery, Arlita had promised herself that in her own home she would eat off good China only, never from plastic and paper plates. Not a problem for her to eat off them at someone else's house or even outside at a picnic. In her own home though, all it did was remind her of her poor childhood.

Arlita sat at the head of the table in her late husband's seat, next to her daughter. She asked Mona where she and Gerald met.

"In rehab."

"Ah, true love," Arlita said.

Mona shooting a sarcastic smile at her mother. "He wasn't in rehab, for your information. He was visiting his sister. Josephine's got a problem with aerosols. She's good people though. Gerald too. He don't drink or do drugs or nothing. Just smokes a little weed is all."

Arlita snorted. "That's all, huh? Well, it's good to know he's well on the way to sainthood."

"I'm serious! G, he's a hard worker. Got a good job out at the aircraft plant. He's current on his child support. He's a good dad to his two kids. Don't ask much other than to be left alone on Sundays to watch his boys."

"Well, it's good that he spends time with his kids."

"The Cowboys," Mona said. "That's what he calls them, his boys. Just leave him be to watch the game. But he does spend time with Emmitt and Deionna. Sometimes they come over, watch the game with him. He and his boys are all into this fantasy football stuff. Telling you, mom, G's a family man."

Arlita just nodded, not sure what to say. Had to admit he sounded better than most of the drugged out losers Mona usually wound up with.

Arlita finally saying, well, long as he treats you right, and Mona saying, oh he does.

Arlita knowing that if she was to have an open conversation with Mona, now was the time. Gerald would be back any moment. Arlita thinking on it, still not sure she wanted to tell Mona everything.

"You on drugs?" Arlita asked.

"Clean as a whistle. Just a little weed."

Arlita rolling her eyes, starting to rise from the table.

"Mom, weed ain't my issue," Mona said. "Booze, meth, those are my demons. I know I shouldn't smoke weed either and I plan to quit it. Cigarettes too. But they help take the edge off."

"You mean they help not deal with things," Arlita said.

Mona not saying anything, just toying with the fork in front of her. "Maybe. But right now, we got some pretty awful things to deal with."

Arlita feeling her anger mounting. Long ago she'd grown tired of her daughter's woe-is-me act. This late in the game it shouldn't have surprised her, Mona being self-absorbed. But it did. Arlita couldn't believe Mona would shrink back into it now when her own daughter was in trouble.

Who was this person? What, Arlita wondered, had she and her husband done wrong in raising this child?

"You're goddamn right things are pretty awful," Arlita said. "Things are in the shit, as you father used to say. But not for you, Mona. For your daughter. For chrissakes, don't you get that?"

Mona's eyes welling up.

Arlita pushing harder. "Your daughter, Lord knows where she is right now. Is she even alive? She needs you to face this mess that's going on. You and me, we're all she's got. Do you get that?"

Mona, head down, nodding that she understood. A tear falling into Mona's lap, and at that same moment a familiar parental desire to take away her child's pain rising up inside Arlita.

Arlita placing a hand on her daughter's arm, telling her everything would be fine.

Mona looking up, taking the napkin her mother offered to dry her eyes. Mona asked what the police were doing to find Patty.

Arlita paused. Mona was Patty's mother. In Arlita's mind, that meant Mona had a right to be let in on the whole picture.

"The authorities haven't exactly been notified," Arlita said.

A look of confusion washed over Mona's face as she stubbed out her cigarette in a bean bag ashtray.

"What do you mean?"

"Well, I didn't actually tell anybody. Them kidnappers said they would hurt Patty if I did."

"Of course they say that!" Mona starting to regain some of her self-righteousness now. "I'm no friend of the cops, but you still bring them in on something like this. Big Jim Olden finds out you didn't call him, you're going to wish the kidnappers had taken you instead."

Arlita caught up Mona on things, namely that Sheriff Big Jim Olden had been dead for more than a year, and Billy Keene was sheriff now.

"Billy Keene?" Mona said. "Little Billy? I thought he was off playing baseball or something?"

Arlita shook her head, said he got hurt. Mona saying she didn't think of Billy as the law enforcement type.

"Nobody does," Arlita said. "Including Billy his own self."

"So what's the plan then, pay them off?" Mona said. "Just let the motherfuckers get away with it?"

Arlita revealed the whole picture to Mona. Telling her about the phone calls, the ransom demand, the instructions for the money drop coming up on Thursday.

Telling Mona about the arrangement with Vic.

At the mention of Vic's name, Mona started laughing. "Oh hell, I feel sorry for those dumb son- a-bitches if Vic catches up to them."

Arlita saying, yeah, that was the idea.

They heard Gerald's El Camino pull up in front of the house. "Don't say nothing to Gerald about all this," Arlita said.

"Why not?"

"He's not family."

"Yes he is!" Mona said. "Put a ring on my finger two weeks ago."

Mona pulling a diamond ring from the front pocket of her jeans, saying surprise! Slipping the ring on the ring finger of her left hand.

Arlita stunned, not sure what to say. Mona, not sure how to read her mother's silence, filled the room with her voice.

"G wanted to get me the wedding band to go with it, but

I was like, hell, just give me the diamond!"

Finally Arlita spoke. "But you didn't say anything to him about this thing with Patty, right? I told you not to. So tell me you didn't."

Mona shaking her head. Arlita demanding to know what Mona did tell him, what reason she gave for coming home?

"Just told him I just need to go home is all."

Arlita not buying it. Figuring that even if Mona hadn't told Gerald the truth about what was going on, she definitely told him something was wrong. No way in hell Mona pass up an opportunity to be dramatic and self-centered.

Mona finally adding, "I told him Patricia was having drug troubles."

Arlita laughing. "Go with what you know, I guess."

"Quit laughing," Mona said. "It tore me up, lying like that. Especially to someone I'm starting a new life with, someone I care about."

Arlita raised her eyebrows in disbelief. "Since when?"

They heard Gerald coming through the front door.

"Anyway, don't say anything about anything to him," Arlita whispered. "All right?

Gerald yelling hello as he made his way through the

house.

"Mona?" Arlita's voice at once pleading and threatening.

Mona, pouting, nodded in agreement.

Gerald finding them in the dining room, saying, there you are. Setting the red-and-white striped bucked of chicken and the plastic sack of sides on the table. His eye catching the flash of the small diamond on Mona's hand.

"I see you told your momma the big surprise," he said. "Baby, I thought we agreed we'd tell her together."

"It just sort of came up," Mona said.

Arlita smiled, a mask to hide behind while her mind raced to catch up.

First thought was why didn't her daughter invite her to the ceremony? She had been there for Mona's first three weddings, why not this one?

Could be because after Mona's last wedding, to that short, bald biker guy, Arlita had let Mona know that the novelty of being the mother of the bride was wearing off. Still, Mona could have at least called to let her know.

Next thought was that this Gerald guy was after money. Which was why Arlita was surprised when Gerald handed back the two twenties Arlita had given him to cover the chicken.

"Dinner's on me," Gerald said.

Arlita laid the twenties on the table and thanked Gerald for treating.

"Sorry you couldn't be at the wedding," Gerald said, as he sat down at the table. "But I'm glad to see you're feeling better. My auntie Loraine, she had the shingles and said it was the most pain she'd had since giving birth."

Arlita's eyes darted in Mona's direction.

Mona with that dumb, whatareyougonnado smile of hers on her face.

"Lucky I'm a quick healer, I guess," Arlita said. "Let's eat."

Arlita passing the bucket of chicken to Gerald. "Mind if I ask you a question, Gerald?"

"Shoot."

"Did I offend you when I asked you, would you mind running out to pick up some fried chicken?"

Gerald looking confused for a moment. Glancing at Mona for some sort of clue as to what was going on. Getting back that same, dumb smile of hers.

"Why would that offend me?" he asked.

"I just, I mean Mona...," Arlita said, not sure how to put it. "Oh, never mind."

Gerald started laughing. "Oh, I get you now. To answer

your question, no, I was not offended at all. I didn't even think about it like that. At least not until you brought it up just now. All I thought was, hell yeah, that sounds good. I could go for some fried chicken."

He took a bite of mashed potatoes he'd mixed with some corn. "I just wouldn't go around thinking every brother you meet likes fried chicken is all."

Mona asked Gerald to pass her a chicken breast.

He pulled one from the bucket and passed it to her, saying, "You should try a thigh. You'll like the dark meat. Got more flavor."

They ate in a brief, awkward silence, everyone trying not to laugh at Gerald's unintended double entendre until, finally, laughter erupted around the table.

"Sorry about that. Wasn't how I meant it," Gerald said, "But since we're being open here on issues of color, Ms. Arlita, do you have any problem with your daughter being married to me?"

Arlita putting down her chicken leg. "To be honest, Gerald, yes I do."

Gerald putting down his fork. Taking a breath. Asking, "Because I'm black?"

Arlita looking at Mona before settling her eyes on Gerald's.

"Because you're a goddamn Cowboys fan."

"Oh, no you didn't," Gerald said, laughing.

Arlita running with it now, saying she had two teams she rooted for: the Kansas City Chiefs and whoever's playing them goddamn Cowboys.

Gerald saying oh hail no, throwing down his napkin and pretending to leave the table.

They ate and talked some football before getting around to the unavoidable subject of the missing Patty.

"So when do I get to meet your daughter?" Gerald said.

Mona moving around mashed potatoes on her plate. Saying Patty was out of town.

"Really? She okay?" Gerald said. Gerald back and forth from Arlita to Mona "I mean, given what all is going on with her."

"She'll be back soon," Arlita said. Using her eyes to order Mona to keep their secret. "Patty took a quick trip up to KC is all. Spur of the moment-like. But she'll be back real soon."

Arlita's words of certainty followed by a long, wordless pause. The only sounds were utensils on china plates and teeth chewing food and throats swallowing.

The awkwardness finally broken by a knock on the door. Not the front door, but the beauty shop door out back.

"Huh, someone thinks I'm working late tonight," Arlita said as she stood up to answer it. But knowing who she would find at the door.

Mona and Gerald sitting in the dining room and eating. Hearing the murmur of Arlita's voice and a man's voice wafting in from the beauty shop. Mona and Gerald catching each other pretending not to eavesdrop and giggling at one another.

When Arlita returned to the dining room, she was followed by a tall man that Gerald thought might be the meanest-looking white man he'd ever laid eyes on.

Arlita introducing Vic to Gerald. Arlita fetching two plates from the China cabinet and fixing them up with chicken and sides before covering them in foil.

The whole time she did this, Vic just standing in the corner of the room, eyes boring into Gerald. At first, Gerald had met the man's gaze, knowing a pissing contest when he was in one. But after awhile, Gerald giving in and focusing on his food.

Arlita went to hand the two plates to Vic. He shook his head, saying that was very nice of her, but he only needed one plate, for his mother. Didn't have much of an appetite himself this evening.

"You just go home and make yourself eat a little something," Arlita said. "Just bring back them plates when you can. Thanks for the update on the thing and let me know what you find out about the other thing. And tell your mother I asked about her."

Vic saying he would do just that and thanking Arlita again for the meals. Exiting the way he came in, through the beauty shop.

After he was gone, Gerald couldn't help himself.

"Ms. Arlita, I know he's a friend of yours and all, and I hope I don't upset you by saying this but—that is one crazy, mean motherfucking white dude. Excuse my French."

Arlita nodding, glad to hear someone impartial agreed with her thinking. "Fucking-A right he is."

Wednesday

One

Pearce standing over Sharla in the darkness of his bedroom.

Up early, heading out the door for work but catching a glimpse of her in the sliver of yellow light spilling in from the living room of his apartment.

Stopping, just looking at her sleeping there. So close he could reach out, touch her if he wanted.

Sharla out, crashing hard. Half naked and twisted up in his sheets. Pearce watching her for a long minute or two.

Then it was five minutes.

Considering it. Not moving toward her but not moving away.

She'd shown up around ten the night before. Driven up from Caulfield, arriving red-eyed and ragged and rambling. Going on about that so-called boy friend of hers. Pearce stretched on the couch trying to hear some show on Animal Planet about spitting vipers.

All the while Sharla's going about how much she loved Chubba. How she always did Chubba wrong. How bad she felt about always doing Chubba so wrong.

Next thing Pearce knew, she had crawled onto his lap and was licking the tattoos on his neck. Leaving wet trails of saliva all over him. Just as suddenly, she'd flopped off of him, started digging in her purse. Snatched up the hard cranberry lemonade she'd walked in with and used it to down four Xanax.

To help her come down, she said. Took Pearce by the hand and lead him into his bedroom.

Stripped off everything but her pink panties. Just spread out on the bed and melted into those cotton sheets. Crashed hard and stayed crashed.

Eventually, Pearce had grown frustrated with trying to revive her and moved back out to the couch. Paying half attention to some show on the History Channel about the shitty daily existence of people during the Dark Ages.

Wondering if all along Sharla's plan had been to tease him? Or had she wanted him to ravage her after she'd passed out? Pearce had fallen asleep before settling on an answer.

And now Pearce just staring at her. At her exposed breasts. The nipples brown and erect in the dim light. The way she was sprawled though, Pearce couldn't really tell if they were rising and falling.

Pearce considering it.

Finally taking a step toward Sharla. She didn't stir. He moved up beside her, touched her shoulder. No movement, but body warmth. Pearce relieved she wasn't dead.

Pearce turned to go, had another thought, and turned back to Sharla. Slowly, he reached down and cupped her left breast. He felt a charge run through him, at the feel of her nipple between his fingers, the firmness of her breast in his palm. She did not move.

Pearce coming alive with the idea that at that moment he could do just about anything he wanted.

And get away with it. That part was key.

It was an intoxicating mix of power and sex, and Pearce's head grew dizziness. Removing his hand from Sharla's body. Taking in a deep breath.

He closed the bedroom door behind him as he left.

Walking through the chilly spring morning, Pearce went around the pool and across the complex to the apartment where they were keeping Patty.

Since late Saturday night, when they'd imprisoned Patty there, he'd been diligent about stopping by to check on her. Make sure she was still secure, still gagged, still breathing.

The basement apartment's small box of a living room exploding with light when Pearce flicked on the overhead fixture. Striding through the sparsely furnished living room, past the two patio chairs and low table he'd dragged in from the pool area.

Pearce snatching up the plastic Bugs Bunny mask off the laminate counter top that marked the start of the apartment's kitchen area.

Slipping the mask over his shaved head and hiding his face, Pearce eased down the dark hallway toward Patty's room. Pausing just inside the bedroom, letting his eyes adjust to the darkness.

Listening to her labored breath forcing its way through her nostrils.

Pearce moving quietly toward her. Having trouble seeing through the eye-slits of the cartoon mask and pushing it up high on his head. Pupils dilating to take in any light. Patty's nearly-naked form spread eagle and tethered to the bed, slowly taking shape in the shadows.

Pearce at the foot of the bed, watching his hostage. No movement other than the regular rise and fall of the torso, the breathing steady and leaden.

Pearce's hand reaching out, fingers lightly playing along the curve of Patty's calf. Her meaty legs unshaved since Saturday and now prickly with stubble. Pearce caressing her calf with his hand, allowing the stubble to scratch his itchy palm.

Suddenly the leg jerking violently away from Pearce's hand. Seized in the ropes binding it to the bed frame. A grunting noise as the entire body twisted and turned, fighting to escape but fleeing only inches away.

Again Pearce feeling a euphoric jarring of his equilibrium.

Savoring the exhilaration and in that moment Pearce coming to believe that all things were possible.

Under properly controlled circumstances, of course.

He grabbed the ankle, pinning it still against the mattress. Holding it there. Observing the other leg flailing helplessly against its truss. Once the thrashing stopped, Pearce knelt down alongside pinned leg.

Opening his mouth, putting his teeth on the ball muscle of the calf. Not biting down hard, just a little. Enough to prove to everyone in the room that he could take whatever he desired.

Except for panting, the body lay still and passive, waiting.

After a moment Pearce rising and leaving for work.

Two

Using the side of his fork, Billy sliced into his over-easy eggs. Watching the yolk seep into its bed of corned beef hash.

Doing his best to ignore the gossip flying back and forth over his breakfast.

"I guaran-damn-tee you she was drunker than snot," the man to Billy's right said. "Or on drugs."

Billy sitting at the long counter in Trace's Place, wedged between two prominent Caulfield citizens.

The man to Billy's left was Kenny Vogel, Caulfield's city manager.

To Billy's right, was a local businessman whom everyone called Dogpatch. Dogpatch ran one of the town's two motor inns, the one sitting atop the hill on the north side of town. But he made his real money as the sole source of janitorial supplies for local businesses.

Every weekday morning, local business leaders and civic types gathered at Trace's Place for coffee to gossip about goings on here and there around town.

On this particular Wednesday morning, everyone in the café was chewing over the possible, if not probable, hows and whys of Patty's car wreck.

And even more tantalizing, her disappearance from Caulfield.

Dogpatch, a passionate conversationalist on even the most mundane of subjects, was particularly keyed up over this succulent piece of gossip. So much so that each time he spoke, he leaned across Billy's corned beef hash to make sure Kenny could hear him clearly over on Billy's far side.

"Know what you ought to do, Sheriff?" Dogpatch said, leaning in.

Billy didn't bother asking what he should do. Knew he was going to find out whether he wanted to or not.

"What you need to do is get one of them hair follicle tests," Dogpatch said, voice urgent, eyes intense. "Them things can tell you what all someone smoked or snorted six months ago. Hell, they can tell you if a person ate a chili dog on the third Tuesday of last October."

Dogpatch said this as if sharing the most important

secret in the world, implying that Billy best heed his words. Billy, uncomfortable, only nodded.

Dogpatch's real name was Dan Lippough. But for the past twenty years everyone in town had called him Dogpatch. He, his sisters and his parents had moved to Caulfield from Arkansas, his nickname springing from the long-dead hillbilly-themed amusement park located in his home state. For his part, Dogpatch wore his nickname as if it were a medal he'd won in a war.

Even now, a full two decades later, some life-long residents of Caulfield still considered Dogpatch an outsider. Despite raising a family and building a successful business there, giving back to Caulfield as much as got from it, there were those lifers who contended an "outsider" like Dogpatch held little claim to, or say in, the direction of their community.

Kenny, the city manager, had resided in Caulfield only a few years. Just barely a step above illegal alien status in some people's eyes.

Sooner or later everybody – especially Dogpatch – always got around to reminding Kenny that he "wasn't from around these parts." Someone was always thoughtful enough to assure him that he didn't understand what the town stood for or "how we do things around here."

As if Kenny was not invested in the community. Never mind uprooting his family from Oklahoma so he could serve as Caulfield's city manager. Never mind his responsibility for the town's day-to-day municipal operations. Doing his best to ensure the sidewalks and roadways and parks and residential waste removal were as reliable as local government could make them in a small town of tax-loathing citizens.

As city manager, Kenny also had an interest in promoting Caulfield as a great place for people to live and businesses to locate. This meant Kenny spent most of his time between bites of raisin bread French toast contradicting or denying the sensational theories Dogpatch kept spewing.

"Now Dogpatch, why do you want to go and say something like that," Kenny said. "You don't know that Patty was on drugs. Don't go slandering the poor girl just because her family's got money."

Dogpatch both insulted and incredulous.

"Did you even hear what I said, Kenny? Don't try to trash my reputation with your inferences. Never said she was on drugs. Was merely recommending to the good Sheriff here that he may want to consider finding out *if* she was on drugs."

Tippy, their waitress, gliding by to check on coffee for all three of them. Tall and broad shouldered, Tippy kept her blonde curls short, making her attractive in a tomboyish way. Like all the servers Trace hired, she was a divorced mother in the late twenties-early thirties neighborhood.

Trace always championing the importance of giving these ladies the opportunity to support themselves and their children. Billy noting that none of them were too hard on the eyes and suspecting there was more to it than Trace's goodwill.

"Oh, you said exactly that," Tippy said. She poured more coffee and also served up a gotcha smirk to Dogpatch. "Believe you went so far as to put your reputation on the line by guaran-damn-teeing she was on drugs."

Shaking his head, Dogpatch denied ever saying such a thing.

Kenny talking over him, corroborating Tippy's version.

Billy, keeping his head down, tucking deeper into his corned beef hash.

Dogpatch thinking it best to change the subject. Running a finger over his scraggly mustache, he shifted back to the mystery of Patty's wreck.

"Most likely she hit a loose cow," he said, "or maybe a deer. Damn deer population's getting out of hand; county game warden needs to up the kill limit."

Tippy pointing out the problem wasn't more deer needing to be shot and gutted. Might be the problem was all the people moving farther out into the country where the deer lived.

"Anyway, you find a deer carcass at the scene, Sheriff?" she said.

Billy shook his head, sipped his coffee.

Trace coming out from the kitchen, making his way along the back of the counter. As he moved behind Tippy, Trace placed a hand on the small of her back, letting her know he was passing.

Billy catching the gesture. Recognizing something overly familiar in Trace's touch. Probably would have dismissed it if he hadn't also caught a flicker in Tippy's green eyes.

Suspicions about the two of them confirmed, Billy took another sip of coffee to hide his smile.

"Know what?" Dogpatch said. "Bet she stumbled onto a back road drug deal and things went bad."

Kenny saying, "Whoa, whoa, I'm getting tired of everyone, the newspaper and whatnot, blowing this drug stuff out of whack. Most people around here aren't into drugs. I'll give you that there's an element that do. But it's a pretty darn small portion of our citizens."

"What would you know about it?" Dogpatch said. "You ain't even from these parts. In the cowboy days, Caulfield was a frontier town, a boomtown. Being outlaws is in our blood. Don't believe me, go to the library and look it up. They got archives on it. I seen them."

"Spend a lot of time at the library, do you Dogpatch?" Tippy said. "That before or after your family unpacked when you moved to town?"

Tippy winking at Billy. It was too easy, sticking it to Dogpatch like that. But Tippy didn't seem to mind because, really, she found it fun to mistreat him.

Dogpatch ignoring her, moving on.

"Could be it was a sex thing gone wrong," Dogpatch said, his voice rising. "Like that choking game all the junior high kids play. But sexual."

From over in one of the booths near the front someone yelling, "Goddamn it Dogpatch I'm trying to eat over here!"

Dogpatch waved an apology. Turning back to his audience at the counter and, voice lower but still loaded with conviction, saying "Sex thing."

Billy heard the bell over the door ring behind him. Turning to see who had come in and wondering just how wrong a breakfast could go.

It was his ex, Tina.

Billy taken aback by how ragged Tina looked. Makeup so heavily layered over puffy cheeks. Eyes tired. Hairstyle constructed around the same part down the middle as when she was in high school, looking dated these days.

He nodded hello to Tina before turning back toward the counter, then feeling her moving behind him. A part of him waiting for a steel blade in his back.

At the same time an image of Paige Figures flashed in his mind. Paige squatting, a craftsman getting down in it, snapping pictures at the scene of Patty's flipped car. It was an image that pleased him, that reaffirmed how glad he was to be free of Tina.

The restaurant went quiet. Everyone familiar with the story of Billy and Tina and watching to see what might happen. Tippy going over to take Tina's order.

Tina taking her time, looking over a menu she'd looked over hundreds of times before. Finally saying, "Know what, Tippy? I ain't hungry after all. Something turned my stomach. I'll just take a cup of coffee, for now."

A few guffaws here and there. Billy let it go. Gradually the noise level rose again in the café.

Helped considerably by Dogpatch, who seemed to be in some gossip brainstorm mode, just blurting out whatever ridiculous idea popped into his head, facts be damned.

"Bet it was a serial killer come along and snatched her up," Dogpatch said. "Cut her up and stuffed her in a suitcase."

Kenny groaning, quick to say there weren't any serial killers in the town, maybe not even in the whole county. Billy didn't think Kenny sound too sure of himself. Definitely not as certain as Dogpatch sounded.

Dogpatch, ignoring Kenny, suggested that if Billy got any reports of suitcases left alongside the road, he best check them out pronto.

Billy nodding in agreement.

Billy about to ask for the check when the bell over the door chimed again. Billy hoping it was the town serial killer coming to stuff him in a Samsonite, anything to get him the hell away from this conversation and all the free advice he was getting.

Turning around to see who it was and finding Dale Longnecker limping into the café. Bluish bruises coloring his cheeks, the blue gradually giving way to the black around his eyes.

Tippy wondering, just loud enough that only their little gossip group could hear, what the hell happened to Dale?

"Looks like he ran straight into a brick wall," she said, "About thirteen times."

Dogpatch keeping his head down. "More like a baseball bat ran into him several times. I'm guessing his wife finally figured out what a great guy he is."

"Maybe she found out about him playing around all over town," Tippy said.

Billy pausing in mid-sip. Remembering all the talk from the other night at The End Zone about Patty and Dale. Maybe Lucinda had found out about it. Any connection between that and Patty's wreck?

Anything was possible, Billy guessed, although he doubted it. Still, he figured it best to chat up Dale.

Excusing himself for a minute, Billy slid off the swivel stool and went over to the two-top in the center of the café where Dale was sitting, scanning the laminated menu.

"Mind if I sit for a second, Dale?"

Dale didn't look up from his menu, just gave a loud

sigh. “Suit yourself, Billy.”

Billy slipping into the empty chair across from Dale, who was hiding his beat up face behind his menu.

Billy started by saying he didn’t mean to pry but how did Dale manage to ding up his face like that?

Dale put down his menu. With a straight, swollen face asking Billy what did he mean?

Billy laughing.

Dale laughed too but it hurt. Dale wondering if Billy had received a call from any witnesses about the ass whipping Vic had given him yesterday morning. Wondering if Billy was trying to trap him. Dale couldn’t figure it one way or the other so he going with his natural instincts and lying.

“Oh hell, my dumb ass went and fell down the stairs,” he said.” Can you believe that?”

Billy chuckling but thinking, no, he couldn’t believe it.

“Lucinda didn’t give you a hand getting down them so quickly, did she?”

Dale didn’t laugh. “My wife knows better than to do something stupid like that.”

“No doubt,” Billy said, but not liking the implied threat of domestic violence he detected in Dale’s words.

"But anybody gets mad enough, maybe they find out something that really sets them off... well, anger can be one hell of a motivator."

Dale putting on his best hard-ass, Clint Eastwood face but wincing at the pain. "You getting at something, Billy?"

"Nope, just chewing the fat," Billy said.

The two men eyeballing one another for a moment before Tippy came over. Flipping the cup right side up and pouring coffee before taking Dale's order. Dale opting for the garlic mashed potato pancakes, scrambled eggs and sausage.

"Links or Patty?" Tippy said.

Dale snapping at Tippy, "What's that?"

Dale misunderstanding Tippy, hearing only the name of the woman he'd been cheating on his wife with.

"I asked: you want link sausage or patties?" Tippy unfazed by his tone.

"Oh, sorry," Dale said, trying to cover. "Links please. And a chocolate milk." Tippy went to place the order.

Billy, sensing a soft spot, leaning in closer to Dale. Dropping his voice.

"Maybe this isn't the place or the time. Maybe you and I should talk somewhere else?

A stupid pride rising up in Dale, his go-to reaction in most uncomfortable situations. Dale looking around the café as if just realizing where he was.

"Hell, everybody in here knows everybody's business anyway," he said, not yelling but not keeping it down either. "Got something to say, say it, Billy."

Billy aware people were listening so he tried to keep it hushed. "I'm saying maybe Lucinda found out about some of your extra-curricular activities."

"My what? Speak up, Billy!"

Billy shaking his head. If that's how the ignorant fool wants to play it, so be it.

"Said maybe your wife found out you were sleeping with Patty Hardy."

Billy not saying it as loud as Dogpatch might have but not whispering it either. Billy going on.

"Maybe Lucinda's upset, drives around until she finds Patty. Starts following her. Chases Patty out to a county road and runs her off the road. Or maybe it was an accident. That kind of stuff happens."

"Do I need a lawyer, Sheriff?" Dale said. "Or my wife?"

"Don't know," Billy shrugged. "Do you?

"My wife don't know nothing about anything," Dale

said. "Be all over my ass if she did. She didn't have anything to do with this." Dale pointing to his damaged face. "Told you, I slipped. Took a ride down the stairs is all."

Billy saw he wasn't getting anywhere and ready to let it go. Feeling someone move up behind him. Looking behind him, finding Tina hovering over his shoulder.

Billy waiting for it, whatever it was going to be. An insult. Maybe spit flying in his direction. A salt shaker against the back of his head. She surprised him by speaking to Dale instead.

"I'm taking off in a sec," Tina said, "but just wanted to say that ain't right, what Vic did. And it wasn't right that no one did anything to stop him neither."

Billy seeing the panic flooding Dale's battered face. Billy turning halfway around to look at Tina, asking her what exactly did Vic do?

Beating up Dale like he did, she said. At the Quik Trip yesterday morning.

Billy raising his eyebrows at Dale, an efficient look asking two questions at once: *This true?* and *Why'd you lie, dumbass?*

Dale still looking for a way to keep the law out of it saying, "Where'd you hear that?"

"Everybody's talking about it," Tina said.

"First I've heard of it," Billy said. "Nobody's talking to me about it."

Billy nodding at Dale. "Not even the horse's mouth here."

"Now that would be some kind of circus show," Tina said. "A horse's mouth talking to a horse's ass. Really be something to see."

Billy thinking, *there it is*. Tina finally getting around to it. Not a bad one either.

Tina excusing herself, saying she was late for work and then the door chiming as she left.

Billy watching through the window as she walked down the sidewalk. Billy wondering if Tina ever made it to work on time at her parent's real estate office.

Billy turning back to Dale and didn't have to say a word.

Dale just starting in on it, beginning with Vic flipping the U-turn and asking him about Patty and the brutal rest of it. Then ending with having to borrow money to pay for the gas.

"I owe Larry Pfeifer seven dollars and fifty-four cents," Dale said. "And I hate that son of a bitch."

"Why didn't you call it in?" Billy said. "People can't

just go around beating up people."

"Can't they? Happens all the time around here. You know that."

"Well, it shouldn't. And I can't help you if you don't tell me," Billy said. "So Vic was asking about Patty, huh? Any idea why?"

Dale shook his head. "Wasn't really in a position to be asking the man any questions."

Again Dale shaking his head, but this time with heaviness to it. Dale going on.

"Thought we was being cool about it, keeping it all on the down low. Thought we were tiptoeing around, but the way everybody knows about it, guess Patty and me were stomping."

Billy saying small towns, and Dale agreeing.

Billy still unsure why Vic had been asking about Patty. Not seeing a connection. Billy guessing he might have to ask the man himself. Not something he was particularly looking forward to but knew it needed to be done.

Dale answering no way when Billy asked if he wanted to press charges against Vic.

At that, Billy figuring it was time to leave Dale alone for a while.

Billy standing, recommending Dale get some ice on his face. Maybe even soak his head in a sink filled with ice water.

"Won't I drown?" Dale said.

"You'll figure it out," Billy said.

Billy returned to his breakfast at the counter. Then realized he wasn't hungry anymore. Paying his bill and fetching his sheriff's Stetson from the coat rack next to the door.

Walking out and hearing Dogpatch, Tippy and Kenny still chewing over Patty's wreck, something about Patty maybe hitting her head and getting amnesia. The door chiming and Billy was gone, leaving the gossip behind in the café.

"Maybe," Dogpatch said, warming up to his latest notion, "just maybe Patty was kidnapped. Maybe somebody's holding her for ransom."

Kenny couldn't take it anymore. "That's plain silly. Dogpatch, this isn't a TV soap opera. This isn't Peyton Place. It's just a nice little town filled with good folks living right."

Dogpatch looking hurt, taking his time to answer.

"Shows what all you know about it, Kenny. You ain't even from around here."

Three

Horace hammering the glass storm door with his knuckles. Stepping back, waiting for Arlita to answer. That morning at breakfast, he'd decided to pay a visit to his old lover. A cruel, vain streak in him wanting to see how Arlita was holding up, all things considered.

He and Arlita had only gotten together a few times one summer, years before. Arlita less plump and Horace with more hair on his head back then. Not much heat between them, just the shared thrill of cheating on their spouses. Nothing more than killing time in a small town.

Still, Horace felt it was enough history to justify swinging by to say hi.

Arlita not answering the doorbell. Horace unsure if that was good or bad. Rapping on the door again, his reflection in the pane warping and bouncing with each knock.

At the sight of Horace standing at the door to her beauty shop, Arlita only managed a surprised, "My word."

"Thought I'd come by for a haircut," Horace said. Taking a half step forward, expecting Arlita to let him pass.

Arlita standing her ground, chuckling.

"All you got is that horseshoe strip around the back of your head," she said, "and it's as short as the bristles on a toothbrush."

"Won't take you long then, will it?" Horace said.

Arlita knowing Horace well enough to recognize that attitude in his voice, a tone telling her he felt entitled to whatever he'd come for. She let him into the beauty shop.

He took a seat in the swivel chair. Watching in the mirror as Arlita draped a black vinyl gown over him, snapping it at the back of his collar.

Near as Horace could tell, she seemed the same, sure and level in her movements. Knowing how tough Arlita was, Horace wasn't sure why he expected her to show the stress of the situation. But he supposed she was churning inside.

"Don't you get your hair cut down at McGee's?" Arlita said. "Them barbershop boys find out you came slinking into a beauty shop, you'll never hear the end of it."

"Variety's the spice of life," Horace said. "Or so they tell me."

"Consider yourself lucky," Arlita said, smiling. "Shop's closed rest of this week."

"Oh, I am a lucky man, yes indeed," Horace said to

her in the mirror. "Hey, I heard Mona's back in town. She around?"

Arlita shook her head, said Mona was out showing off her home town to her new husband.

"You know, all the places that mean something in a girl's life—where she went to grade school and the high school. Where she lost her virginity, where she first smoked pot. Not sure I got the chronological order right but, you know how it is."

"Yeah, I heard she had a fella with her."

"People in this town, I swear," Arlita said. "You mean a black fella, don't you Horace?"

"You know me, Arlita. I don't care one way or the other," Horace said. "It's just the kids I feel sorry for."

Arlita laughing at Horace, not with him. Taking a comb and scissors to the back of his head.

Arlita saying, "If weren't for people like you feeling sorry for the kids, wouldn't be no need to feel sorry for them. Besides, Mona can't have no more kids, thank God. Had her tubes tied when Patty was born. Mona's not much of a forward thinker, but I'll give her credit on that one."

Arlita had brought up Patty, so Horace decided to follow it.

"How is Ms. Patty? I heard about her car. Damn

shame. That was a nice car. She okay? She around?"

Arlita still poker faced, not even a flinch. She stuck to her bluff, saying Patty was staying with friends up in KC.

Horace thinking she's hiding it like a champ. Time to play the card up his sleeve.

"Arlita, I don't mean to offend, but you look a little frazzled," he said. "Everything okay, hon?"

Arlita still not breaking, telling him everything is fine.

"Got to be honest with you," Horace said. "I knew you were closed. Sharla was by the house the other day and mentioned it. She was worried about you. Said you seemed stressed."

The comb slipping from Arlita's fingers, slapping against the tile floor. Arlita bent to pick it up, then moved to the salon counter for a fresh comb.

"Sharla best worry about her own self," Arlita said. "That girl's got her own problems."

All the while Horace watching her in the mirror, noticing the tension creeping around the edges of her face. Horace agreeing with her on Sharla, girl's got issues.

Horace now taking in how heavy Arlita was these days. Remembering her body back then, during their brief time together. Amazed that this big body was the same body from that time in the back seat of his Lincoln in the bowling alley parking lot. Getting old ain't no kind of fun, Horace thought.

"Sure you're okay?" Horace said, surprised at the genuine concern in his voice, almost forgetting he was the cause of it all. "We go back a long way, you and me."

Seeing her remember it.

No way of knowing how much she was regretting it.

Arlita thinking, jackass has to bring that up. Once a pompous ass, always a pompous ass. She was young. She and Pat were having their troubles, like all couples do. It was what it was.

And what it was, was a long time ago. Arlita thinking, let's just leave it back there.

Then it occurred to her that maybe Horace had come by to try to fuck her. For old time's sake or some bullshit like that. Not that she couldn't do for a roll in the sheets.

Not with this one, though. Sometimes you say never again and mean it.

Time for Horace to leave. His haircut was finished because he hadn't needed one in the first place.

Arlita saying all done, unsnapping the gown around Horace's throat. Then telling him to hold on a second while she cleaned him up along the hairline and down the back of his neck.

"Don't mind if I use the electric razor, do you?" she said. "Don't trust myself to bring a straight razor that close to your neck."

Arlita finding herself particularly funny, but Horace had to force a smile.

Giving Horace's neck a cursory pass with the electric razor, then whipping the gown off of him like a matador waving a cape at a murderous bull.

Horace standing, eyes still locked on her face. Looking for a glimpse of pain, a crack in her armor.

Arlita refused the ten dollar bill he offered her, saying it was on the house. Horace about to leave when he figured there was no harm in one last shot at it.

Turning to Arlita, placing a hand on each of her shoulders, softening his eyes. looking deep into hers.

"You let me know if there's anything I can do, you hear?" Horace said. "I mean it. Anything, just say it."

Seeing her eyes melt, just a little.

Before she knew what she was saying Arlita asked Horace if he wanted some coffee. Horace following her into the living room, then waiting as she brought two full cups from the kitchen.

Her fleshy bottom barely hitting the couch cushion before the story came spilling out: Patty, the calls, the demands.

"My God, Horace, what am I going to do? "

Once again it felt good to Arlita, telling it all to someone, a slight weight lifting.

Knowing the relief was temporary, the weight not going away forever, at least not until Patty was back safely. Even then, there would always be a real fear.

It dawning on Arlita that no matter how this turned out, even in the best possible outcome, she and Patty had permanently crossed a line. On the side of the line they'd left, the world was marked Before. Now they found themselves on the side marked After.

Forever and no going back. All they could do was make the best world they could on the After side.

Horace quiet for a long time, contemplating what he'd just heard. And what he hadn't. Asking if Arlita had called the sheriff. Horace growing quiet again when she said no, she had not.

"You going to go through with it then?" he said. "Give them the money?"

Horace almost forgetting that *them* was *him* as he said it.

Arlita set her cup on the coffee table, saying come here. Horace put down his cup, momentarily distracted by a dark stain on her carpet. Looked like coffee or a lot of blood spilled there. But he quickly forgot about the stain as he followed Arlita through her house.

Arlita leading him to what she still thought of as her husband's den. His favorite artwork still hanging on the paneled walls. Directly behind the desk his favorite nature print, a pheasant taking flight in a brown field.

On another wall, a painting in heavy brushstrokes of cowboys and Indians in mid-battle chaos on the plains. Framed family vacation photographs sitting on the desk and a couple on the bookcase shelves.

Of course now the den, like everything else, was all hers.

Following Arlita into the den and immediately Horace's eyes drawn to the money.

His mouth turning dry at the sight of all the neat stacks of bundles of cash atop the oak desk.

"Well, I guess you're going through with it," he said. Horace wishing he could ease himself right down into one of the oxblood leather guest chairs and start counting it.

"Maybe," Arlita said, leaning against the desk. "Maybe not. Depends."

"On what?"

Arlita chewing it over for a minute before deciding to go all in.

Telling Horace the rest of it, about turning Vic loose to play coon dog, sniffing the trail of whoever was behind it. Horace forcing himself to swallow his panic at this news.

Then Horace thinking this might come in handy somewhere down the line. Might be enough just to know it, might be more. If Vic could be used to his advantage, Horace would figure out how later.

Arlita turning to face him and, not sure why other than she needed it, moving in to hug Horace. Arlita taller than Horace, settling for burying her face in his shoulder rather than his chest. The meager tears she would allow herself soaking into his custom-fitted western shirt with faux pearl snaps.

A reflex, Horace hugging back. Holding this woman again after so many years. Her heavy body strange to him now. Almost forgetting he was responsible for her anguish. Almost overlooking his power to stop her pain.

Tracking the rhythms of her soft sobs on his shoulder until his attention was pulled away. Drawn to something on the floor, sitting off to the side of the desk. A black box labeled *Dominez, Cherry 99*. A roll of gray duct tape standing upright like a wheel next to it.

Horace pulling back from Arlita, handing her a clean white handkerchief.

"Arlita, box up that cash as soon as I leave. You hear me?"

Arlita, wiping at her eyes, nodding.

Pulling her back in close, kind of liking the feel of her ample body against his. "Everything's going to be all right. You hear me talking to you, Arlita?"

Rocking her a little as they stood. Catching sight of their reflection in the glass covering a framed drawing that hung on the back wall of the den. A pheasant flapping its wings over a field. Horace had completely forgotten what a hunter Pat had been.

Remembered thinking when he and Arlita were running around behind Pat's back that Pat wouldn't hesitate to use a 12-gauge shotgun if he found out. No worries now though.

Horace holding Arlita and thinking back to the issue at hand—better get Sharla's ass back to Caulfield, right quick.

Time to make some money.

Four

Paige Figures sensing her cell phone vibrating in her purse. Pulling it out, not recognizing the number.

"Mom, how about those sandals down there?" she said pointing down the row of shoes and shoe boxes.

Watching her mother inspect the sandals. It had been a good morning so far. Her mother's mind had been sharp.

Now the voice on the other end of Paige's cell phone brightening her day even more.

"Billy Keene," she said, a lilt in her voice. "How are you doing today?"

Billy on the other end saying,"I'm good!" Billy liking the way she sounded happy to hear from him.

Billy sitting in his department SUV, his sheriff's cowboy hat pushed back on his head. His free hand holding the business card with her cell number that Paige had given him at the scene of Patty's wreck. Billy flipping the card around and around in his thumb and fingers.

Asking Paige if now was a good time and what was she up to?

"Just shopping. Mom and I ran over to the outlets in Pierrette. Looking for some warm weather shoes. What are you up to?"

"Oh, not much," Billy said, playing it casual. "On a stakeout, sorta."

"A sorta stakeout, wow," she said, "then I'm sorta impressed."

Billy laughed, told her she sorta better be. Billy parked in the Dairy Queen parking lot. Up front, near the street, watching traffic run up and down Main as he talked to Paige on his cell.

After leaving Trace's diner that morning, Billy had swung by Vic Shear's house to ask him about beating the tar out of Dale Longnecker. Vic wasn't home, so Billy had walked across the alley to Vic's mother's house to ask her if she knew where her son might be or when he might be home.

The old woman only came back with curt, empty answers, never once looking up at him as she poked around her garden.

After that Billy headed uptown and parked to wait for Vic to drive by. Billy figured that passed for a stakeout.

"Let me guess," Paige said, "you need me to run and pick you up some donuts?"

"No, I'm all set in that department," Billy said, going along with the joke. "Actually, I was calling to ask about the photos you took of Patty's car, out at the scene of the incident. You developed them yet?"

Paige laughed, unsure if he was putting her on. "There's no developing. It's all digital, Billy."

Billy giving off a nervous laugh. Thinking if she likes him, she'll think that was cute. If she don't, she'll think he's just dumb. And there's always a chance for both.

"I guess I need to get out more often," Billy said.

Paige saying it sounds like it. And then a pause.

The pause stretching into awkwardness until, finally, Paige jumped back in.

"I'll have someone from the newspaper send the digital picture files over to your office," Paige said. "Or I could drop them off myself when I'm back in town later."

"No hurry," Billy said, thinking it would be nice to see her. "Just drop them off later, when you can."

"Your deputy give you the casts?"

"What casts? Did Dustin break his arm or something?"

"Of the tire tracks," Paige said. "Both sets."

Paige telling Billy how she'd had Marvin make himself useful by running into town to the hardware store to fetch some plaster. She then had Deputy Dustin make casts of the both sets of tire tracks and all the footprints at the scene, three different sets.

“That’s what they do on the detective shows,” she said. “Could come in handy, never know.”

“No, you never know,” Billy said. Trying not to let his confusion come through the phone. He needed to have a serious talk with Dustin.

“So people just do things for you when you ask them to, huh?” Billy said. “I can’t seem to get anybody to do a damn thing I ask them to. What’s that like, having them jump when you say so? ”

“It’s not bad, I can tell you that. Guess it’s just all in how you ask it.”

Billy saying he bet there’s more to it than that. Then hearing the smile on her face when she said he might be right.

“How about I give it a try?” Billy said. “Three questions.”

“Shoot.”

“All right, here goes. I was hoping you had the pictures in front of you. I can’t remember for sure which side of Patty’s car was bashed in.”

“Driver’s side.”

“You got the pictures right in front of you right now?”

"Nope. But I remember."

Billy said he'd take her word for it, adding quickly, "Still, better drop off those pictures when you can."

Paige saying will do and what's the second question?

"You remember seeing any paint on Patty's car where it was bashed in? A different color, like maybe it came off from another car in a collision?"

"Funny that you ask that," Patty said. "When I was looking at pictures back at the office, I did notice some paint. A reddish color. Darker red. Somehow I missed it at the scene."

"Me too. I missed it too," Billy said, excitement in his voice over this thing they had in common. Probably a little overly excited considering their common ground was missed evidence.

"You're pretty certain of yourself on all this, huh?" Billy said.

"Yep. That's the only way to play it."

"All right then. That brings us to question three."

Billy swallowing. "Would you like to have dinner with me this evening? Or if that don't work, maybe tomorrow evening?"

Another long pause coming back at Billy. Billy thinking maybe she only liked a one-way flow of confidence.

"Yes," Paige said finally. "Tomorrow works."

"You left me hanging there for a bit, huh?"

"Yes," Paige said, that smile coming through again. "Yes, I did."

They made plans for Billy to pick her up around six, take her out for Mexican food.

Both of them saying see you later and Billy canceling the call.

Tickling his lip with a corner of her business card, thinking you got to love a girl who says yes. Little Paige Figures all grown up. Go figure.

Billy removing his hat and setting it upside down on the passenger seat. Sipping coffee from his travel mug. Watching the Main Street traffic flow past his windshield. It was like watching fish in a tank, the same cars you saw a moment ago going thisaway now coming back thataway.

He took deep breaths to help keep his focus. Listening to the police radio, glad to hear the chatter was mostly work related. Turing on the radio, hearing the farm report – the price of wheat, corn, hogs, cattle and whatnot – on the local AM station.

Billy didn't have a stake in agribusiness, but he followed the market for civic reasons. He'd found that the condition of the agriculture market was an excellent barometer of the local mood.

Most farmers and ranchers, living life at the mercy of nature's extremes and the market's whims, tended to be a stoic group. On the outside anyway.

But having grown up in Caulfield, Billy had learned that more often than not there were simmering fears and frustrations underneath those stone faces.

Don't matter who you are, Billy knew, there's only so much a person can take. The farther south the market went, the more sour the local mood turned. Usually resulting in more drinking, more fighting, more domestic abuse.

People feeling trapped by their lives and livelihoods. Turning on one another. Taking it out on the people closest to them. Or taking it out on themselves.

It had been a few years since the last suicide in Caulfield. Neil Postner walked out to his back pasture with his deer rifle. Took off his Tony Lama cowboy boots and white tube socks, stuck the rifle barrel in his mouth. Pulled the trigger with a bare toe.

Everybody knew why Neil killed himself. He was about to lose his farm to a Wichita bank. Their farm had been in the family for five generations so people understood his suicide.

What they couldn't ever understand about his suicide -- and still talk about to this day — was why Neil took off both boots and socks?

He only needed one big toe on one foot for the trigger. Billy thinking maybe at that ultimate moment, a sense of balance was crucial to Neil.

Billy shaking off the thought of Neil Postner just in time to spot Vic Shear's red truck passing in front of his windshield. Vic's truck skidding to an abrupt halt, tires squealing on the asphalt.

Billy looking at Vic look at him. Watching Vic jam his truck into reverse and backing up in his lane.

Vic hanging a quick, rubber-burning left turn into the Dairy Queen parking lot. Billy thinking, *evidently Vic's looking for me too.*

Billy calmly stepped out of his SUV. Vic's truck sliding to a stop at a right angle to Billy's vehicle, throwing gravel and dust everywhere.

Vic jumped out, leaving the door open and the truck running. Vic making a hard line for Billy.

"Hi Vic," Billy said, all friendly despite the adrenaline he felt pumping through his body. "Glad I ran into you."

Billy thinking Vic was looking pale, thin and weaker than usual.

Or maybe not *that* weak. Instinct telling Billy the punch was coming before he actually saw it.

A haymaker right. All in all a surprisingly wild and useless punch from a guy with as much experience in bar fights as Vic.

Billy quickly connecting the dots. If Vic was so keyed up that he forgot how to throw a decent punch, this must be personal.

Billy easily slipping the wild right. Then, using Vic's own momentum, Billy forced Vic face down on the hood of the sheriff's SUV. Pinning him there, Billy's elbow digging in between Vic's shoulder blades and twisting Vic's left arm up along his spine.

Amazing what a man can pick up in a week-long course from the training unit of the Kansas Bureau of Investigation, Billy thought.

A few people inside the Dairy Queen watching through the windows. People driving by on Main slowing as they passed, craning their necks to see the excitement. Billy feeling every muscle in Vic's wiry body struggling to break free.

"Lost your religion for a second there, Vic."

"You ever harass my mom again, I'll kick your ass!" Vic said.

"You're doing a fine job of it right now," Billy said, pushing Vic's arm higher up his back. The pain of it causing Vic to submit a little.

"Now, if you calm down we can talk," Billy said. "Otherwise, we'll just take a ride to my office so we can talk there."

Billy keeping the pressure applied even after he felt Vic relax. Not going to be suckered by a false surrender. Protocol demanded Billy cuff Vic, if only for the sake of controlling the situation.

Billy decided against it, figuring Vic would be even less reasonable wearing bracelets. In the past and on more than one occasion, Vic had shown himself to be one of those guys who, when cuffed in the back of a squad car, thinks it helps the situation if he bangs his forehead against the window.

Billy only hearing the stories from years before. Didn't mean Vic wouldn't do it now though.

"What's this I hear about you knocking around Dale Longnecker?" Billy said, leaning in, voice composed and affable. "He bother your mom or something?"

Vic saying he didn't know what the hell Billy was

talking about. The rope-like muscles in Vic's body going taut with anger again.

So Billy pushed the forearm up Vic's spine again until he relaxed a bit.

"Here's your lesson for today," Billy said. "This arm of yours is kind of like a lever. Your anger goes up, so does your arm. That there's called a direct relationship. Bonus lesson for you: don't lie to the law. It always comes back on you. Understand?"

Vic ignoring the question with fuck you silence.

Billy pushing up the arm a little farther.

"Ow, goddamn it," Vic said. "I didn't do nothing!"

"That's right, you didn't. You didn't answer me. The less you work with me here, the more your arm goes up. That there's called an indirect relationship. Ain't learning fun? Now, what's this all about with Dale?"

Again Vic claiming he had no idea what Billy was going on about.

Again Billy cranked up the arm. "Works like a bullshit meter too, doesn't it?" Billy said. "Tell me, would that be a direct relationship or indirect?"

"Why the hell you keep going on about direct this and indirect that?" Vic said, trying to look back over his shoulder at Billy.

"I don't know," Billy said. "Guess I want to show you how smart I am. On account of you keep treating me like I'm dumb as a box of rocks. You really think I'm going to ask you a question that I don't know at least part of the answer?"

"Dale say something to you?"

Billy knowing where this was going. "Whether he did or he didn't, nothing better happen to him."

Billy pushing hard on the arm. Vic stifling a yelp.

"Now you pissed me off, Vic. You put me in a situation where I got to stand up for a jerk like Dale."

"Guess it ain't easy protecting and serving the public when the public's full of assholes," Vic said. Grimacing in serious pain but not fighting back nearly as forcefully as Billy expected.

Billy easing up on the arm a little, taking Vic's humor as a small white flag.

Their mutual dislike for Dale proving to be the common ground on which to negotiate, if not a lasting peace, then at least a temporary truce.

"Vic, I'm going to let up on you. But I swear, you try anything, I will not hesitate to shoot you in the face. Understand?"

Vic nodded.

Slowly Billy eased up completely on Vic's arm and backed away. Putting a good amount of space between them. Telling Vic to stand up, turn around, but keep his hands in plain view.

Vic's truck still idling. Every now and then a car or truck rolling by along Main. Vic working the pain out of the arm Billy had been using against him.

"I'm not even going to ask you if you did that number on Dale's face," Billy said. "I know you did it. What I want to know is why you did it?"

"Just never liked the guy, that's all," Vic said.

"Is that right?" Billy said. Wondering what it would take to get people in this town to quit yanking his chain. "So then you *weren't* asking him about Patty Hardy the whole time you were wailing on him?"

Billy watching Vic's face go slack, mouth open. But the man's eyes lighting up like a caught animal searching for a way out.

Billy saying, "Told you I ain't asking something unless I got a good idea of the answer. So what's up with the Patty thing?"

"Just thought he might know something about Patty, given everything between them," Vic said. "You know about them two, right?"

"Hell, who doesn't?"

Billy thinking it over before saying, "Asking Dale about what specifically?"

"Pardon?"

"I mean, you're cleaning his clock, shouting questions at him. My guess, you weren't asking him general knowledge questions—Patty's favorite color, her favorite TV show, favorite song, whatnot. Am I right?"

Vic folding his arms across his chest. Looking down at his the gravel dust covering his boots. "Hell, I thought he might know something about her wreck is all."

Billy smiling and breathing through it to hide his suddenly racing heart. Four count breathing in, a four count hold, four count breathing out. Repeat.

Billy doing the math in his head

"You were asking Dale about Patty's wreck?" Billy said. Making sure he heard right, circling back to get Vic to confirm it.

Vic nodding, saying yep.

Billy deciding to move on before Vic figured out he'd just stepped in a hole. "All right, well, do us both a favor. Stop assaulting people."

"Anything you say, Billy," Vic said, relaxing a little now. He'd spent enough time in front of the law to sense when he was getting run in and when he was getting off.

Billy telling Vic to go on, get out of here. Not sure what, but Billy sensing something different about Vic. Something weaker.

Vic saying thanks, heading for his truck. Just as Vic reached his driver's side door, still hanging open, Billy called after him.

"Hey Vic! Why you?"

Vic stopping, his guard coming back up. "Why me what?"

"Why did you feel the need to ask about Patty in the first place? No offense, but what business is it of yours?"

Vic shrugging. "Friend of the family is all. Arlita's been cutting my hair all my life. Always good to mom. I've known Patty since the day she was born. They're good people."

"So Arlita, she didn't ask you to go ask Dale?"

"Nope."

"You just did it all on your own, out of personal concern?"

"I guess you could put it like that."

"I think I just did, Vic."

The two men facing each other, not so much a macho staring contest as two bona fide predators sizing up each other. Finally Billy's face breaking into a grin, saying "Go on, git."

Vic smiling, climbing into his purring truck. Closing his door before shaking the forearm that Billy had worked over.

Saying with a smile through his open passenger window, "Growing up, huh, Billy Keene?"

"They tell me it's about time," Billy said.

Vic laughing pulling slowly out of the gravel lot. Reaching the asphalt and gunning his truck too fast down Main.

Billy shaking his head at Vic's taunting. Watching that lifelong criminal race down the street.

Billy wondering just how in the hell Vic was kicking Dale's ass and asking him questions on Monday about a wreck that hadn't even been reported until Tuesday?

Five

Mona reclining on one of the padded reclining seats in her mother's home theater. Sock feet up on the extended footrest. Ample bottom stuffed into black stretch pants and, on top, wearing a pink T-shirt embroidered with silver rhinestones spelling out PORN STAR.

Smoking a menthol and watching QVC in HD on her mother's huge-ass flat-screen.

The home theater was a post-lottery-win addition on the back of Arlita's house. Mona thinking that giant TV's got one goddamn clear picture. The giant woman with the orange tan on TV making her sales pitch for those cute hand-painted glass dolphin figurines, but Mona unable to concentrate. Goddamn Gerald kept yelling questions at her from somewhere else in the house.

"Want it in the bedroom?"

Silence.

"Or want it in the hallway?"

The two of them alone in the house for the moment.

Ten minutes earlier the phone rang and Mona answered it. Vic on the phone for Arlita, excited.

It was a quick call. Arlita's said *Hello. Say again? Damn it. Be there in five. Bye.*

Then Arlita hung up, headed right out the door.

Now Gerald, bored, finding a way to fill the time. Yelling again from another room. "Tell me, where you want it, girl?"

"In your ass!" Mona yelling as she flicked ashes into her Diet Dr. Pepper can from breakfast. The can now sitting in the theater chair's cup holder. Mona thinking maybe that came out harsher than she meant. "Sorry, babe, just...will you please shut it."

Gerald coming into the home theater, wearing jeans and a Tony Romo jersey with a white long-sleeved T-shirt underneath. Gerald holding up a smoke detector for her to see. Big grin on his face.

"Baby, I don't think this is gonna fit in my ass."

Mona not looking away from the big TV, saying, never know 'til you try.

"You leave it up to me," Gerald said, "I be putting one in the bedroom, one in the hallway, one in the den... one in every motherfucking room in this house. But that's just me. Really, if you only got the one, I say put it a central location, like a hallway."

Mona finally taking her eyes off the TV. Considering Gerald, then blowing a stream of cigarette smoke at the detector in his hand. Mona waiting for the alarm to go off.

"Thing don't seem to work," Mona said.

Gerald shaking his head, unsure if Mona was serious or messing with him. "Haven't put the battery in it yet."

Mona dropping her cigarette into the mouth of the can, making a *duh* face at him. "No shit, Sherlock. I was joking."

Lifting her bare foot off the recliner's footrest. Pointing her toe and aiming to run it seductively up Gerald's leg. "Don't need no alarm, G. I detect a fire right here."

But Mona misjudging the distance between them. At the last second her body doing a clumsy flop-lunge trying to get close enough to graze Gerald's kneecap.

Gerald looking at her there, comically stretched out in the theater chair with the hem of her PORN STAR shirt hiked up, exposing an apron of pale belly flab.

Gerald saying that's sure a tempting invitation and all but let's get the alarm up first.

Mona saying fine, but hurry it up goddamn it. The idea of doing it in her mom's home theater without her mom knowing now making her super horny.

Guess that's a good thing," Gerald said, "because if us going at it in here *with* her knowing turned you on, that would be some weird shit."

Mona laughing and trying another lunge at him, this time to kick him in the balls, and missing.

"Way short," Gerald said.

"You got that right," Mona said.

Gerald catching her meaning and telling Mona she *knew* that wasn't true.

Laughing and telling her she was a cold, cold swamp witch. Both of them laughing now and sharing, for a moment, that free and easy feeling that often comes over a couple on vacation. Except they weren't in Caulfield for a vacation.

The sound of the doorbell putting their affectionate moment on pause. They were in Caulfield for a kidnapping, even if only one of them knew it.

"Who's that?" Mona said.

"Fuck do I know?" Gerald said.

"Go check."

"You go check," Gerald said, pointing at her with the alarm. "Like I'm going to recognize who it is. I don't know nobody in this backwards-ass town."

Mona nodding, point made. The doorbell rang again as Mona made her way to the front door.

Through the pizza slice glass panes in the door, Mona thought she saw Billy Keene wearing a gray cowboy hat. Didn't think anything of it until she opened the door, saw it was Billy Keene. And he was wearing goddamn cop clothes.

"Well, Billy Keene," Mona said, still trying to reconcile her memory of the jock kid she'd known all her life with the uniform he was wearing now. The uniform instinctively putting Mona on edge.

"Hey Mona," Billy said. "Heard you were in town. How you been?"

"Getting by." Mona pointed to the badge on his chest. "I see you're up to no good."

Billy smiling, said he guessed that was one way of looking at it. Asking Mona if her mother was home?

"No, she's gone out to the store." Mona comfortable in her own skin now, lying to an officer of the law.

"Mind if I come in," Billy said.

For a moment Mona forgetting about the whole kidnapping secret. Reflex taking over, Mona doing a quick mental check of just how many felonies she might have in her possession at that moment. Some weed in Gerald's bag. They were married now; they couldn't force her to testify against him.

With her acquired, practical knowledge of probable cause and search and seizure laws, Mona also understood that allowing Billy to enter was all he really needed to go poking around.

"Sure, come on in," Mona said, holding open the screen door with one hand and inviting Billy across the threshold. She couldn't get past the idea that this was Billy Keene. What the hell kind of harm could he do?

“Look at you, Sheriff,” Mona said as they stood in Arlita’s living room “You wear that uniform about as well as anybody can. Nice hat.”

Billy feeling himself blush, almost removing his hat, but deciding to keep it on for effect.

“Thanks. Looking good yourself.”

Billy noting Mona’s t-shirt, thinking Mona’s still working hard at being Mona. Even if it’s not working out so well for her.

“Ain’t you sweet? I’ll take it where I can get it,” Mona said, flirting. “Even from a cop.”

Billy smiling politely. Asking what Mona was up to these days? Where was she living now?

“Well, I was in a facility for a while, dealing with some personal issues,” Mona said, trying to make rehab sound glamorous. “Nice place. Excellent staff. Living down in Dallas now. Everything’s going great. I’ve turned a corner, I really have.”

Billy saying that was great to hear. Mona saying it looks like they had both grown up, and the way she said it, soap opera-thick with innuendo, almost causing Billy to laugh at her rather than with her.

Billy about to ask if Mona knew when Arlita might be back when he was interrupted by a booming voice coming from the next room.

"Mona, your momma got a drill?"

Mona rolling her eyes at Billy before she yelled, "Probably, yeah. She's got everything else."

"Any idea where I might find it?"

The voice with an edge to it. The man with the voice stepping into Arlita's living room. Billy not hearing any footsteps, only the voice and then suddenly there's the man. Billy figuring the guy had been eavesdropping from the adjacent room.

Mona moving toward the man and introducing him to Billy as her brand new husband.

Gerald shooting a look toward Mona that said, yeah, I heard how you left me out of the latest chapters in the Mona Saga you were telling this man. Then an easy smile as he crossed the carpet to shake Billy's hand.

"Do I know you from somewhere?" Gerald said. "Seems like I've seen you before."

Mona jumping in, "Billy here used to be a big baseball star."

Gerald's eyes lighting up. "That's right. Couple years back with the Yankees. Had a ridiculous rookie season."

Billy shifting into his usual patter. This was a conversation he'd had many times before. A conversation that, mercifully, was coming up less and less often.

"I did all right," Billy said "A little luck and a lot of great players behind me."

"Yeah, that was something else, man. Really tore it up there for a while."

Billy smiling, waiting for it.

"So, uh, you don't mind me asking, what happened?"

"Shredded rotator cuff," Billy said, pointing to his right shoulder.

"Damn shame."

"It is what it is," Billy said.

Mona stepping between them, saying you boys going to talk baseball all day long or what?

"Gerald here's decided my mom needs more smoke alarms."

"More?" Gerald said. "She don't have but the one in the kitchen and that thing's damn near old as you."

"Very funny," Mona said. "What you need a drill for? Can't you just glue it up there or something?

Gerald shaking his head, saying if he was going to do it, he was doing it right.

"All of Daddy's tools are probably still in the garage," Mona said. "Mom doesn't change much of his stuff around.

Check in that big red tool chest on wheels out there."

Gerald saying he'll go do that. Telling Billy nice to meet him, shooting another look at Mona before walking back through the house toward the garage.

Mona saying, "G's got a thing about fire. Got an alarm in every room of his house. Carbon monoxide detectors all over the place, too."

"Sounds to me like he's got a thing about dying in his sleep," Billy said.

"Yeah, well then he better treat me right. Otherwise, it's a frying pan upside his head one night while he's off in beddy-bye-land."

Mona catching herself.

"I'm just joking, you know that right? I mean, if really I was going to do it, I wouldn't tell a cop – no offense – how I would kill my husband. I'd just do it. But, again, I'm not."

"You sure?"

"God no," Mona said. "I mean yes. Yes, I'm sure I'm not going to kill him."

The uniform making Mona nervous. Couldn't Billy at least take off that goddamn cowboy hat?

Billy telling her he was just teasing. Asking if Mona had any idea when her mom might be back?

The whole kidnapping secret coming back to Mona now. Thinking she'd fucked up many times—but she knew where the line was with Arlita. It was right here. Let this slip out and her mother would cut her off.

"Really don't know," Mona said. "Momma didn't say if it was a big shop or not." Mona breathing easier now that she was back to deceiving a cop. Felt natural.

"Is there anything I can do for you?" Mona flirting the only way she knew how, too obviously.

Billy shaking his head, saying no problem, he'd catch up with Arlita later.

"You in town long?" Billy said.

"Few days."

"So you expect Patty back from KC soon, I guess?"

Billy seeing Mona's eye flit from side to side before settling back on him.

"Yeah, I guess," Mona said.

"I mean, I just figured she'll want to visit with her mother."

"You would think," Mona said. "Then again, it's no secret we're not close as a mother wants to be with her daughter. Partly my fault, I realize that. But Patty, she's never been easy. Wasn't an easy delivery, not an easy child and definitely not an easy young woman. Like I said, it's mostly my fault. That's what they tell me, anyway."

"Mona, your momma got any batteries?" Gerald's voice coming from somewhere in the house. "The transistor kind with the connectors on the top?"

Mona not taking her hard eyes off Billy as she yelled back to Gerald wherever he was. "How the hell should I know?"

"Used to live here, right?" Gerald yelled. "Well, where did your momma keep the batteries? Before she kicked you out?"

"She didn't kick me out!"

Gerald not even bothering to answer Mona's last comment. Instead yelling back that wherever it was she used to keep batteries, Arlita probably still keeps them in the same place because people don't change much.

"Well, I'll leave you two to it," Billy said, putting his hand on the storm door latch.

Then stopping, turning back to Mona. "Hey, I was wondering? Vic Shears been around?"

"Huh?" Mona said. "Vic Shears?" Mona playing dumb. Saved by Gerald walking into the room again.

"Sheriff, do you know who in town does good radon remediation work?" Gerald said. "Someone certified? Going to put a couple test kits in the basement. If they come up high, it would be good to know who could handle the job."

Billy giving Mona a smile. "Radon won't kill you in your sleep, will it?"

"No, but it will kill you," Gerald said. "Dead is dead, am I right?"

Billy agreeing and suggesting Keith Velnor for the remediation work. But sensing more going on here at the moment. Billy going on.

"So anyway, Mona, about Vic. He dropped by since you been in town?"

"You mean that tall, skinny dude?" Gerald said. "Crazy, scary looking guy?

Billy saying that's the one.

Mona jumping in, only one way to play it now. "Yeah, he dropped by the other night."

Billy clarifying that by "the other night" Mona meant last night. Mona confirming it. Billy asking what Vic wanted.

"Just saying hi," Mona said.

"What you all talk about?"

Mona's eyes flitting again. "Nothing, just catching up."

Bells going off in Billy's head, sensing something's

not right. “He and Arlita talk about Patty at all?”

Mona shaking her head. “Not that I remember. Again we was just catching up is all.”

Billy pausing. Realizing he was the reason behind all the tension in the room. Surprised at how much he enjoyed dictating it. Giving credit to Mona for treating him like a real sheriff, if only by lying to him.

“Well, let Arlita know I stopped by,” Billy said.

Closing the door behind him as he stepped out onto Arlita’s port. Knowing the tension inside hadn’t left with him. Knowing it was still back inside Arlita’s house like an invisible, odorless gas eating away at these people who were so blatantly hiding something from him.

Back inside the house Gerald silent, giving Mona a level, heavy-lidded glare.

“What?” Mona said. “You going to hit me?”

“I ever put my hands on you before?” Gerald’s voice as level as his gaze, both of them grave. Mona just standing there.

“I asked you, have I ever put my hands on you?

Mona shaking her head.

“Ain’t going to neither,” Gerald said. “But you ever pull that shit again, lying to the police, I’ll dump your ass. That bullshit, I do not need.”

Gerald went back to installing the smoke alarm, leaving Mona in her mother's living room. Mona standing there all alone, struggling to identify what she was feeling right at that moment.

Mona unsure if it was what Gerald said or how he said it. But something in what her husband said causing Mona to understand something about herself: She didn't want to fuck up and chase away yet another person.

This person. This man. Her husband.

"Well, I'll be goddamned," Mona said.

Six

Inside the sheriff's station house, everyone keeping busy at not doing much.

Dustin cleaning his service revolver, gun parts spread out over newspaper atop his desk. Nodding and saying, yeah, uh-huh, at Lonnie, who was kicked back in his chair, feet up on his desk, spinning a golf story.

Cookie at her desk dividing her attention between Lon's story and her computer solitaire game.

Zane, the only one doing actual work, filling out activity reports covering his shift.

Billy coming through the doorway, seeing them all there in the shared office space they called The Corral. Billy thinking damned if it's not standing room only. Thinking it but saying nothing. Billy moving into his office partitioned by half-walls and glass. Leaving the door open so he could hear them.

Grabbing a legal pad and a cheap pen, then Billy hunching over his desk. Jotting down names, days and approximate times. Going over it again and again, each time adding an item or two to it.

Outside his office, Lon dragging out his story while Dustin and Cookie followed along. Zane finishing up his reports, double checking them to make sure they were correct.

After a while, Billy set aside his legal pad, got up from his desk and stepped outside his office. Lon not skipping a beat as he went on with his story.

"I'm in the rough, right? Tall, hairy, ugly rough. Like your mother's diddly-do."

Dustin laughing, working a long, oily brush in and out of the cylinder holes. Holding it up and saying, me and *your* mom.

Cookie scolding them both with a you-boys-cut-that-out. Lon ignoring it, going on with his story.

"So I'm about a hunnert and fifty yards out from the pin—."

"—Dustin," Billy said, "I don't think you're supposed to be cleaning your gun at your desk."

"It's all right." Dustin not looking up. "Almost done."

Billy standing there a little burned, but not sure if he should push it.

After a moment, turning to go back into his office. Hearing the pointed tone in Lon's voice as he says, "So anywhooo... I'm about a hunnert and fifty yards out."

Back at his desk. Leaning back in his chair now, legal pad in his lap, cheap pen ready. Billy moving from what he knew to what he thought.

Staring at the ceiling for a few moments before writing on the pad. Once or twice mumbling just to hear his thoughts out of his head and in the air of the real world.

Some of it made sense. Some of it might make sense. Much of it was nonsense.

Billy unconcerned with how wild or silly it sounded. Think it, write it down. Judge it later. A few words to capture it, a spare phrase to remind him of the entire idea.

About twenty minutes of this before the chatter and the laughter in The Corral pulled him out of his deep thoughts. Billy again stepping out of his office.

"About finished there, Dustin?" Billy said, again interrupting Lon, whose story had finally made it onto the green. "Supposed to be out on patrol right now, aren't you?"

"I will in a sec," Dustin said. At least glancing up at Billy this time as he spoke. "'Bout done here."

Billy eyeballing Lon now and not even having to say it.

Lon grinning at him, saying, "I was just about to head back out."

Lon still sitting where he was when Billy walked in earlier and making no move now.

Someone coming through the front door, and Billy suddenly feeling a positive charge run through him as Paige Figures entered The Corral.

Paige looking around at the entire law enforcement team gathered in one spot.

"The gang's all here," Paige said. She turned, pretending to leave. "Excuse me while I go rob the bank."

Everyone laughing. Billy impressed by the way she takes over a room. Billy led Paige into his office.

"How did your shopping trip turn out?" Billy said.

"It was a good day." Paige smiling at his interest. Unconcerned whether it was genuine or not. Just liked that he was making the effort.

Paige showing off the black slip-on flats she bought, describing the sandals, blouses, skirts and jeans she and her mother bought.

Billy nodding, not so interested in the words coming out of her mouth but enjoying that she was saying them to him. Enjoying the sound of her voice. The shape of her mouth itself. Enjoying having a good reason to not take his eyes off of her.

All sounds like a good deal, Billy said.

Paige handing him a disc with the high-resolution pictures of the scene of Patty's incident.

"Noticed it wasn't much of a story in the paper," Billy said. "Just a small bit in the police notes."

"What makes you say that?" Paige said. "Should it be something else?"

Billy smiling, trying to play it off. "You a reporter now?"

"Never know," Paige said. "I keep my ears and eyes open."

Billy wanting to compliment her on her brown eyes. Knowing this was neither the time nor the place.

"I just figured that, given whose vehicle it was, it might get made into something bigger."

Paige laughing. "You think I work for a small-town tabloid?"

"Well, the other day you did run that juicy story about infighting among the county commissioners," Billy said. "Blew it all way out of proportion."

"Just selling the sizzle." Both of them laughing now.

"So tomorrow night," Billy said, "still good for you?"

"Looking forward to it. I've been craving tamales ever since you suggested Mexican food."

Billy saying all right then, he'd pick her up around six. Then an awkward moment, Paige standing to go, Billy standing to walk her out. A hug didn't seem right. Neither did shaking on it. Certainly not a kiss. Paige finally tunneling a way out for them both.

"So see you around six then." Paige turning and walking out.

Billy watching her walk away until she was gone. Everyone else in the room not saying a word, just trading glances that said it all.

After a few more minutes in his office, Billy came out and walked over to Cookie's desk. Cookie not looking up from her card game but asking, "What can I do for you, Sheriff?"

Billy asking if she could log on to the FBI's National

Crime Information Center database, run a couple of searches. The database was another handy law enforcement tool he'd picked up during his two-week training session with the Kansas Bureau of Investigation.

In Caulfield they didn't have much call to use it. Everyone was pretty much familiar with everyone else's rap sheet. Billy asked Cookie to run a search on one Gerald Wright. Lives in Dallas. Run one for Mona Wright too.

"Mona who?" Cookie finally tearing herself away from her computer solitaire game.

Billy clarifying that he was looking for a sheet on Arlita's daughter.

"Oh, I'm sure she's got all sorts of things on her sheet," Cookie said. "Under more than a few different last names too, as many times as that girl's been married."

"No doubt," Billy said. "Maybe only look for anything recent. Within the last year or so. Under whatever married last names you can find for her."

"Thing is," Cookie said, "I'm not so great with that system. Only been on the NCIC once or twice. Honestly, Sheriff, it's a wonder I learned to do all our computer stuff. Me and computers don't really mix."

Billy glancing at the solitaire game on her screen. Smiling at Cookie, this lifelong friend of his mother's.

Cookie, who had worked at the station house as long as he could remember. Deserving respect. But also owing respect to the job.

Billy saying, “Black four on red five there.” Gently making his point.

Lon still kicked back in his chair, hollering across the room, “What's up? Got a lead on a hot case?”

Billy ignoring the sarcasm. “Don’t know yet. Just looking right now.”

Lon sitting up, putting his boots on the floor. Something in Billy’s voice that caused him to set aside his bullshit for a second. “Seriously what’s up?”

Dustin and Zane looking up at him. Lon and Cookie still looking at him. Everyone looking at Billy.

In his life, Billy had stood on the mound in packed major league stadiums with everybody looking at him, most of them screaming at him. Yet he had never been as nervous as right now in the station house, about to pitch a case theory to his team.

“Something’s going on,” Billy said. “What exactly, I don’t know. But something’s just not right.”

He laid it out for them, starting with Patty’s wreck. Patty leaving town. Vic knocking around Dale, asking him about Patty a day before her car wreck was even reported.

Mona just showing up out of nowhere. And with a new husband.

"Okay, that last part about Mona with a new husband isn't so out of character, I'll give you that," Billy said. "But put in the context of the other stuff, it could be something."

"So what do you think's going on?" Lon said. "Patty ducking the accident? Maybe she was drunk, ran off the road."

"Possible," Billy said. "But why's she still not around? She's sober by now."

"Maybe she's on drugs," Cookie said. "Like her mother. Maybe Arlita sent her off to rehab but don't want anyone to know about it. They need to look into getting themselves a family pass to rehab."

"Okay, but if that's the case," Billy said, "then why is Vic giving Dale a beating, asking what he knows about it all?"

Lon coming over, saying, "So what do you think is going on?"

Billy taking a breath, collecting his thoughts.

"I'm not sure really. Somehow Arlita found out about the wreck before everybody else, but I don't think she really knows where Patty is. If Patty's in KC, then what is it exactly that Arlita's got Vic running around trying to find out for her?"

"Hell, why Vic Shears?" Dustin said. "That thug sure ain't a people person."

Billy hadn't even felt Dustin move up beside him. Nor Zane, who'd moved over from his desk. Zane picking up the conversation.

"Because it's not delicate work she's asking him to do. Maybe she's looking to find out in a hurry. Maybe someone knows something and maybe she wants to scare it out of them."

Billy saying exactly. Noticing that no one was laughing. All of them gathered around Cookie's desk, kicking the tires on Billy's idea.

"Think Dale's got anything to do with Patty being gone?" Dustin said. "Given everything with those two?"

"Could be," Billy said. "But if Dale had anything to do with anything, my guess is he'd have crapped his pants and told Vic straight up."

"So what about Mona," Cookie said. "How's she figure into it?"

Billy shaking his head, saying no idea yet or if she figured in at all. But maybe her new husband was a piece of it too, maybe not.

"Hence the NCIC search," Billy said.

"Sounds like Patty's just run off," Lon said. "Spoiled little brat."

Billy ignoring that last part.

"Could be as simple as that. But I can't shake the feeling there's more to it? Why's Arlita keeping it so quiet? Why didn't she call us?"

"To save face," Cookie said. "Doesn't want everyone in her business."

"Good luck with that in this town," Dustin said.

"No," Billy said, "there's got to be more to it than that. Something we're missing. I bet you though: We find out how Arlita found out about Patty's wreck before anyone else – and why she didn't call us – we find out what's really going on"

"What's really going on?" Lon with a funny look on his face, like a child just told him there's a monster in the closet. "Like what?"

Billy shrugging his shoulders. "Maybe Patty took off on her own. Maybe not."

Lon saying you mean maybe she'd didn't leave town. Billy saying maybe. Or maybe she left but not of her own will.

"How you mean?" Lon said, talking slowly. "Like she

was kidnapped? You're serious?"

Everyone watching him. Billy feeling his confidence slipping away, scrambling to cling to it.

"Sounds kind of silly, when you say it out loud like that, I guess," Billy said. "But I don't think we can rule out anything at this point."

Lon laughing now. "Oh, I think we can rule out that we're not living in some Mexican soap opera. Aye Dios mio!"

Everyone laughing now. Billy plastering a good-natured smile on his face. Burning inside. Hide it. Hide the burn. Or maybe just hide.

"You're right, we must consider all options," Lon said. "Have you considered the vampire option? Maybe they took her. Or the Hare Krishnas?"

"Hell, you're starting to sound like old Dogpatch over at the café," Dustin said, laughing.

Billy ready to wrap this up. "All right, all right. Let's get back to work. Zane, your shift is over so have a good evening."

Billy turning to Dustin but Dustin speaking before being spoken to. "I'm about done with cleaning my gun. Just be a sec."

Billy saying hurry it up and don't let him catch

Dustin cleaning his gun in The Corral again.

Then Billy and Lon locking eyes. Lon turning slowly saying, “I’m going, I’m going.”

Lon picking up his deputy sheriff’s cowboy hat off his desk, placing it lightly on his head. “Better swing by the grocery and get myself a garlic necklace. Can’t be too careful out there.”

Billy ready to run up behind Lon, put a foot up his ass sideways. Instead Billy turning toward Cookie still seated in front of her computer.

Telling her to close out of her card game and he’ll show her how to use the NCIC.

Seven

Horace rounding the corner of the supermarket aisle and surprised to find Vic Shears standing in the frozen food section staring at the diet meals.

It wasn’t finding Vic in the grocery store that surprised him. Horace had followed him there. It was the diet meals that threw him. What was a gaunt, hollowed-out son-of-a-bitch like Vic mulling over diet meals for?

Horace had been tailing Vic for most of the latter

half of the afternoon. He'd started out watching Arlita's house. Horace following her as she left in a hurry. Turned out she was headed for a quick meet with Vic in the parking lot of the Baptist church.

Horace had parked about a block away, watching their cars pulled up alongside one another, nose to tail. Both of them agitated about something. Horace figuring it had something to do with their "private investigation" into Patty's kidnapping. From there, Horace had picked up Vic's trail.

After leaving the Baptist church, Horace had followed Vic to the pool hall. Horace considered approaching him over a game of straight pool but decided against it. Too many big ears in there.

So Horace had waited down the street in his Cadillac until it was getting on to suppertime. Finally Vic emerged, took a lubricated stroll to his pickup. From the pool hall, Horace followed Vic to the grocery store.

Horace figuring the grocery store was as inconspicuous of a place as any to approach the man about something like this.

"Hey there, Vic," Horace said. Sidling up next to him. But not too close.

Vic saying hey back. A quiet moment while both of

them eyeballed the frozen dinners.

Vic wondering why the hell Horace Fucking Self, The Fourth was speaking to him? Both men knew of each other but they hardly ran in the same circles. Horace, a pillar of the community, one of those assholes in town who thinks they're better than everybody else.

"Know which of these diet meals are any good?" Horace said. "Need to pick up a few for the wife."

"They're all pretty much the same, I guess," Vic said. "Which ones does she normally like?"

Horace shaking his head. Saying hell if he knew.

"She don't even realize she needs to go on a diet. But indeed she does. Thought I'd pick some up for her. What good's a husband if he won't drop a hint? Am I right?"

"I'm sure she'll appreciate the gesture," Vic said.

"I'm a thoughtful guy," Horace said. "Don't look like you need to shed any weight though, Vic."

Vic saying, yeah, well, doctor said to try to eat better. The part about the doctor slipping out, but Vic talking past it like it was nothing. Saying normally he'd be over there picking up a Hungry Man or two, but figured these diet meals got to be better for you, even if they aren't as good as home cooking.

Horace agreeing, attempting to build as much

common ground between them as possible until he was comfortable enough to get to it.

"Nothing's as good as home cooking, of course," Horace said, shaking his head. "You have to wonder about all this crap, though. Even these frozen diet dinners. Sure they're convenient. But good for you? I'm doubtful."

Vic chuckling, saying they'd find out eventually. Vic still feeling warm from the beers at the pool hall. Pleased to finally have a bit of an appetite for the first time in days. Vic never one for small talk but enjoying this friendly conversation with Horace, of all people.

Horace stepping closer to the glass door of the frozen food freezer and at the same time edging in closer to Vic too.

Horace dropping his voice a little, saying "Talked with Arlita, earlier today."

Glancing over at Vic to see if anything registered on his face. Nothing, just raw and blank.

"About the thing," Horace said. "The way you're helping her out."

Still nothing from Vic.

Horace clarifying that he *appreciated* what Vic was doing for Arlita. Goddamned horrible situation it was. Good that Arlita had people she could lean on. Someone she could confide in, like Horace. And someone she could depend on, like Vic.

"I guess," Vic said, his tone as frosty as the freezer in front of them. Vic checking this way and that, making sure no one was close by.

"When was this?" Vic said, looking at Horace for the first time. "I just talked with her an hour or so ago. She didn't say nothing about filling you in on it."

Horace explaining they had spoken earlier that morning. Arlita sort of broke down about it all.

Vic turning to Horace at that, not saying a word. But the look on his face asking if Horace was bullshitting him because breaking down, that didn't sound much like Arlita.

"I know," Horace said. "I never seen her like that. Don't think she was planning to tell me. Just having coffee. But something like this, I mean the weight of it has to just get to a person. Even someone as strong as Arlita."

"I guess," Vic said again. Thinking he needed to have a talk with Arlita to see who else was in on it. Too many people and she could count him out.

At least he understood now why Horace was chatting him up. Still uncertain where their conversation was going, though. Maybe Horace, like most people in Caulfield, enjoyed being in the know. And what good was being in the know unless people knew you were in the know.

"I hate to even bring this up," Horace said. "But the thing is, since Arlita told me, I been thinking about it nonstop. Who could it be and all that."

Horace pausing, like the next thing to come out of his mouth would take everything he had just to get it out.

Finally Horace saying, "Man, I hate to even say this but...as it relates to this whole...predicament...have you taken a look at Sharla?"

Vic frowning, pretending to look over the frozen dinners. "She's your boy's girl, right?"

Horace saying yeah, that's why it kills him to even bring it up. "I mean, we like her and all, but she's a strange girl sometimes. Very strange. More so lately."

Vic looking at Horace to catch his meaning.

Horace whispering, "Drugs."

Vic went back to contemplating the frozen dinners.

"Sharla, huh?" Vic said. "Why you think she's got anything to do with it?

"Oh, I'm not saying she does," Horace said. "Not saying that at all. Just saying maybe she's worth a look. I mean, lot of times these things turn out to be somebody close, somebody the person knows, wouldn't suspect. And, you know, she works at the shop and all. And like I said, she's been a little off lately, even for Sharla."

"Off?" Vic said. "How so?"

The two men facing each other now, keeping their voices down. People passing by with shopping carts but nobody disturbing them.

Horace saying he thinks maybe Sharla's got some guy she's been seeing up in KC. Been running up there all the time, back and forth.

Horace mentioning KC tripped a trigger in Vic, but Vic made sure not to react one way or the other. Vic remembering what Arlita had shared with him, about Patty saying her favorite restaurant was Stroud's, a chicken place in Kansas City, rather than the seafood place she really liked. Arlita taking that as her granddaughter tipping her location.

"Why you telling me?" Vic said.

"Because of what you're doing for Arlita," Horace said. "Looking into it for her."

"No, I mean *why* are you telling me? Just because she might be screwing around on your son?"

Horace clarifying, he didn't know if she was cheating on Chubba. But it wouldn't surprise him. And no, he wouldn't be happy about it. Wouldn't want to see his boy hurt.

"Like I said, I'm not saying she's got anything to do with what's going on with Arlita and Patty," Horace said. "I'm just saying maybe she deserves a look, is all. Something is just not right about that girl."

A pause as Horace made sure the coast was clear before going on.

"And if it turns out there is something there, well, if she's doing something stupid, even more stupid than her normal bullshit, then I don't want it getting on my son."

"You mean the Self family name," Vic said.

Fucking guy thinks he's better than everybody else and wants to make sure he can continue thinking that way.

Horace having to stop himself from telling this white trash piece of shit to watch his mouth. Clarifying to Vic that it was more than that. Much more. Reiterating that Sharla might be worth a look, that's all Horace was saying.

"And, God forbid, it does turn out there something to it, Sharla and this guy up in KC," Horace said, opening the freezer door and pulling down a couple of three-cheese ziti meals off the shelf, "well, then you got to do what you got to do to take care of it. I recognize that."

Horace looking at the shiny pictures of the pasta and stringy cheese and red sauce on the packaging. Thinking the picture on the box didn't look half bad. But willing to bet that the food inside would taste like horseshit. What the fuck did he care? Wasn't like he was going to eat them.

Horace looking up at Vic, square in the eyes. "Just so you know, if that turns out to be the case, I won't have a problem with the outcome. Whatever it may be."

Horace eyeballing Vic. A slight nod before turning and walking off with the diet frozen dinners for his wife.

Leaving Vic there in the aisle wondering if he'd really heard what he had just heard from the mouth of Horace Fucking Self, The Fourth.

Eight

"**Sharla, that's brutally** fucked up," Pearce said. "I mean, that's just not right."

Pearce sitting on his ratty couch, looking up at Sharla standing over him. Pearce wearing only black shorts because Sharla had ordered him to take off his shirt.

Said she liked the look of his tats and piercings, the definition of his muscles. Hear that from Sharla and who wouldn't strip?

Not staring at her tits as usual, Pearce now checking

out her eyes. Trying to see if she was serious about this plan of hers, making home videos of torturing Patty.

Hoping like hell it was the meth talking, not her. Did he even know her well enough to tell the difference?

"You are such a pussy, I swear," Sharla said. That meth cackle escaping her mouth again.

Pearce thinking maybe they both needed some fresh air.

It had been like this all evening, the two of them in Pearce's cramped apartment. Sharla buzzing around the room in a v-neck t-shirt and Daisy Dukes, smoking meth, yammering. Changing crazy topics as fast and often as she flipped music channels on the television. Talking all kinds of shit.

Like early on, she'd given her glass pipe a name, dubbed it Mr. Puff. Found that hysterical. At some point during their small party, her pipe got a medical degree and became known as Dr. Puff. Sending Sharla speeding off on another laughing jag.

Now she was giggling and calling for Prince Puff.

The whole time Pearce's eyes seldom left Sharla's tits and ass as she bounced off the walls. Not bothering to keep up with her thoughts, catching maybe half of whatever she was rambling on about.

But that last bit about torturing Patty coming in loud and clear.

Pearce figuring Sharla's savage brainstorm has passed. Giggling now, calling for Prince Puff.

Pearce thinking her pipe may be royalty but Sharla is royally crazy.

And Pearce hoping her lunacy didn't royally fuck them both with The Project.

No sooner did he have that last thought, than Sharla went abruptly still. Her face nearly sober except for those untamed green eyes. Christ, even her cleavage seemed to harden.

Her sudden seriousness putting Pearce on edge, freaking him out. Pearce held still, wary of spooking her. As if a mountain lion had wandered into his apartment. Pearce sensing this could go south quick, turn ugly in one fluttering heartbeat.

Sharla bending forward, down toward Pearce, who was looking up at her. Her pupils were saucers. Pearce feeling his chest pounding like it was trying to escape.

Her hand reaching out. Flicking the loopy hole in his left earlobe with her middle finger.

Then turning on a dime, giggling her way back over to the kitchen bar where she'd left her pipe, her lighter and her precious dope.

"Here's my baby," Sharla said. "Prince Puff don't ever leave me again. You know I will always find you."

From the couch, Pearce watched Sharla, thinking this bitch is crazy, no doubt.

Sharla with her back to him, leaning her elbows on the bar. Igniting the butane torch lighter, the lighter making a whoosh sound. Ass cheeks hanging out from her cut-offs.

Pearce couldn't help thinking, *crazy...but fucking hot.*

Out of nowhere Sharla saying "I'm serious!"

Taking a deep pull on glass pipe, rolling the bowl over the flame so not to burn the liquefying crystal.

Sharla sucking on her dope. Pearce wondered aloud what she was serious about?

Sharla holding the smoke in her lungs as she croaked, "The home videos."

Sharla eyes closing tightly now, feeling it. Oh fuck yeah.

Pearce thinking oh shit, she's back on that again.

"I don't doubt you're serious," he said, "and that makes it worse." Laughing uncomfortably, trying to sell it as a joke.

Sharla turning around, eyes open and watery. Venting a stream of smoke from the corner of her mouth.

"Fucking laughing at me?" she said.

Pearce watching to see if he'd played it wrong.

"You *know* there's people who'd get off on it."

Sharla getting into it. Liking her idea. Falling in love with her idea. Her idea making her happy now. That and the meth.

"Hell, could probably charge a shitload for it," she said. "Some sick fucks out there, you know?"

"I know there's one sick fuck in here," Pearce said. Both of them laughing at that, back to being good friends now. But Sharla not letting it go.

"I'm not saying anything big, like they do to them fucking Taliban motherfuckers," Sharla said. Moving over to the remote, changing to a channel that played hits from the 1970s. Lee Michaels wailing and wondering Do You Know What I Mean? Sharla going on.

"Not saying we hook her up to a car battery or nothing. Just make her suffer a little. Like tossing quarters at her. Or paper cuts. Slowly break her down. Use my phone to video it. Give it that raw feel."

Pearce saying okay, fine, say they go ahead and do all that. What sense does it make putting it on the Internet for other people to see?

"See, that there's the insane part, far as I'm concerned, Pearce said. Realizing how insane *that* statement was even as he was said it.

Sharla coming back at him, adamant.

"We *have* to put it online. That's the whole goddamn point! Not just videos though. We blog about it. Tweet it and shit. Talk about what it feels like to be in control. Follow her breaking down. See, it's kind of a reality show on the web. We could be, like, YouTube stars."

Pearce shaking his head. "You mean we could be, like, on our way to jail."

"Uh, hello, we could go to jail as it is," Sharla said. Pointing to the floor. "See that big red X?"

Pearce looking at his worn carpet as if actually expecting to find an X like on a treasure map. Thinking maybe she's hallucinating now.

"That big red X says, 'You are here, ya kidnapping motherfucker,'" Sharla said. Now pointing to the front door. "And that way the hell back there, that's the line you done crossed a long fucking time ago."

Pearce thinking this is true. And had to admit that, inside, he hadn't thrown out Patty's idea altogether. Remembering how he'd been turned on by having complete control over Patty. Drunk on the idea that he could do anything he wanted.

But that was mostly fantasy. Doing it? That was something else. Pearce wondering how a person even gets to that level of crazy.

Pearce dead set against videoing, no question. Saying to Sharla, recording it? Creating evidence? Putting it on the Internet? That's just plain stupid.

"Sweetie, you need to loosen up," Sharla said, heading back to the bar.

Pearce assuming she was going to hit the pipe again.

Instead she scooped up all her gear, carried it over and laid it out on the cluttered coffee table. Looking at her pipe and baggie of meth and lighter next to some tattoo magazines, her personal cell phone and her Project cell phone, a wireless game controller, a pair of toenail clippers. Sharla just standing over the mess, smiling down at Pearce.

Pearce knowing where she was going with this. Looking up at her, saying, "Told you, I don't do that shit."

"I know, you told me, Mr. Straight Edge." Sharla holding up her glass pipe. "But our new Senior Vice President of Loosening Up has an idea."

"I ain't smoking meth."

"He knows you're not," Sharla said, setting pipe back

down on the coffee table. "You haven't earned the right to put your lips on him. But...."

Sharla picking up her plastic bag full of chunks of crystal meth. Unbuttoning her cutoffs, letting them fall down around her ankles. Stepping out of them as she eased herself down on the couch.

The whole time Pearce stunned and staring. All that thinking about it and wondering if it would happen between them. And now, just like that.

Sharla leaning back against the arm of the couch, legs apart. Showing herself to Pearce. Then, careful not to let any meth crystals fall out of the bag, she tapped a little powder out of the bag. A tiny, wicked pile just below her belly button.

"But," Sharla said, "If you put your nose on this, then you earn the right to put your lips...." That meth cackle jumping out of her mouth again.

Pearce unsure if this was a joke, a dream or a nightmare. Looking to Sharla for a clue, but only getting back her saucer eyes and insane laugh.

"Why's it so important to you that I do this?" Pearce said.

Sharla not even sure herself why. Could probably figure it out if she thought long and hard about it. But why think about it? It just is.

Sharla smiling and saying, “You want to talk? Or you want to do this?”

Sharla’s hand reaching out, taking him by a loop in his earlobe and pulling him into her. She held his buzzed head, pushing her stomach into his face.

Pearce inhaling, snorting. Eyes watering. Sinuses scorched like he’d just sucked in fiberglass. The harsh burn soon giving way to a numbness that spread across his face. A rush of euphoric energy flooding his body.

Sharla’s stomach undulating as she laughed at the feel of him feeling it all.

Pearce responding to her hand pushing on the back of his head, directing him. Letting her lead him down.

Sharla reclining, enjoying the ride. Making out shapes in the rough texture of the cheap popcorn ceiling. A fat man’s face. A snail. A tyrannosaurus rex. Like that. Marvin Gaye’s funked up falsetto on “Got to Give It Up, Part 1” coming from the music channel. Had heard that song before but Sharla thinking now it might be her favoritest song ever.

Thinking, oh fuck yeah, it’s a party now. Could use another hit though on...on...the Sultan of Smoke!

A loud ringing, her project cell phone going off. Had

to be Chubba. Sharla noticing Pearce had stopped.

"You keep on," she said, reaching over to the coffee table for the phone. She hit the button. "Hi baby, what's up?"

"Not much," Chubba said. "What's up there?"

"Oh, nothing," she said, peering down at the top of Pearce's head. "Just watching some TV."

Chubba asking what the hell she was watching that played disco. Sharla saying she didn't know.

Chubba suspicious, saying you're watching TV but you don't know what you're watching?

"Just flipping channels," Sharla said. "Some stupid movie, how the fuck do I know the name. You call just to pick a fight? Or do you actually need something?"

"Daddy says you need to come home," Chubba said. "The drop is on. So you need to do your thing tomorrow."

Sharla with her eyes closed, feeling so good, mind drifting a bit. Hearing herself humming lightly, which she did when things were taking off for her.

"Are you humming?" Chubba said.

Eyes popping open, Sharla telling herself to focus. "The drop still set for before lunch, like we planned?"

"Yeah, 11 or so. But you need to be— "

"—I know where I need to be and when I need to be

there," Sharla said.

She looked down at Pearce looking up at her. A playful smile that said to him "What are you looking at?" Jutting her chin at him, get back to work.

Then into the phone: "Be back soon as I can. Just want to make sure things are set here before I leave."

Chubba asking if there was a problem on her end, anything he and his daddy should know about. Sharla saying no, just making sure.

Chubba asking sure of what? Sharla saying just sure is all. Telling him she'd see him soon enough and hanging up before Chubba could spit *I love you* at her through the phone.

She put the phone next to her on the couch, then reached for her pipe and lighter. Pearce about to pull back until she made sure he understood he was to keep at it while she lit up.

She lit up. A delicious concoction of physical and chemical pleasures jolting her body rigid.

Thinking she was glad she'd held out this long with Pearce. Made it better for both of them. Holding out, holding back, made it easier to get what she wanted. Want something from someone? Just hold back something they want from you. Don't give until you get. The way the world worked, as far as Sharla could tell.

Her mind flying on waves of thought now. Realizing she was still clutching her lighter and...and... Baron Von Burnit!

Laughing at that as she put them down on the coffee table. Picking up her personal cell phone, switching the camera to video mode. A soft beep as she started recording, capturing Pearce's head down there on the job. Getting a different kind of thrill from watching him on the little camera screen.

Sharla thinking that's what it's all about. Different thrill. More thrill. Any kind of thrill.

"We're definitely partying now," she said. Glancing at her pipe. Another hit? See just how high she can get? But something else catching her eye. Something shiny on the coffee table.

Trying to keep Pearce' bobbing head in the video frame as she switched the cell phone to her other hand. Leaning over to grab the toenail clippers.

Lying back, Pearce still in the frame of the camera phone in her left hand. But Sharla's examining the sharp teeth of the toenail clippers in her right.

Thinking *a different kind of thrill.*

Nine

Patty suffering, really needing to pee. Then hearing when someone coming through the front door of her apartment-prison.

The thought *thank God* flashing through her mind. Then Patty thinking, that right there, being happy to hear her captors coming, that was definitive proof of how badly she needed to go to the damned bathroom.

Could simply let it go, of course. But then she'd have to lay there in it. Patty maintaining, so far, her sanity and strength by controlling what she could. Just trying to find a way to live with what was happening to her.

Her bladder she could control. Letting it fly now was like admitting they'd beaten her, Bugs and Daffy. Fuck them. Maybe wet those two characters down the next time they paid her a visit.

It had been several hours, Patty guessed, since her captors last checked on her. Fed her a cheeseburger, fries and a large pop. Untied her so she could sit up, blindfold in place, eating and slurping a Diet Coke. That big-ass soda tormenting her bladder now.

Someone coming through the door to her room now. Him? Her? Both? Whoever it was keeping quiet, keeping Patty uncertain.

Patty realizing it was Both when she sensed movement on either side, circling her.

Patty had managed to work her blindfold slightly askew on her head again. She could see that whoever it was had left off the overhead light. Normally when they paid a visit, the room light turning on was the first thing to happen.

Patty unsure what to make of that.

Hearing the flick of a lighter. Not a regular cigarette lighter but one of those drug lighters, making that whooshing sound. It went on and off several times.

A cloying, waxy aroma tickling Patty's nostrils above her duct tape gag. Through her sliver of vision beneath her blindfold, Patty catching a glimpse of warm, yellow light dancing on the wall. Candle light. Patty thought she heard a soft beep, like from some kind of electronic gadget.

Patty flinching as a razor sharp fingernail grazed a line across the small of her back, tracing the top of her thong underwear. Scaring her. Patty almost letting go of her bladder.

Next a large hand, His hand, roughly working its

fingers into her hair. Patty distracted by the hand in her unkempt hair but certain she'd heard that beep again from somewhere in the room. Then a finger snapping. Then Both suddenly leaving the room.

Patty thinking, damn it, they took off before giving her a bathroom break. Realizing she was hoping her kidnappers would return. Mad at herself for that.

Arguing with herself to just let her bladder go, then she wouldn't need them. But countering herself, had absolutely no desire to lie there in her own filth, degraded.

Patty so tired of living in her mind. Her emotions raw. Hating all of this and just wanting it to be over. And all the while having to urinate so badly.

He or She or Both returned. The drug lighter firing several more times. Patty thinking it could be more candles but her nose unable to tell because the air was already thick with scented wax.

Patty turning her head this way and that. Catching a glimpse of Bugs. Patty hearing that electronic beep again.

A firm hand grabbing Patty's left ankle. Him. Lifting Patty's leg behind her. Pressing it against his naked chest. He was body hairless, skin moist with sweat. Holding her foot out straight.

Now fingers. Hers. Pinching Patty's big toe. Patty

confused now. A light clip. They were trimming her nails? Patty thinking this is one hell of a time for a pedicure.

Patty struggling, grunting. Trying to say *bathroom* through her gag. Both laughing at her. Then a stinging sensation shooting through Patty's toe and up her leg. The clippers chewing the nail agonizingly low. Then gnawing it even lower.

Tears filling Patty's eyes as she wet herself. As they tortured her toes. Patty understanding she had no way of knowing how horrible the night would get.

Thursday

One

Billy coming through the front door of his parent's house expecting to smell bacon and eggs cooking. Counting on his mom to fix him breakfast. Greeted instead by his mother heading out the door.

Sara Jane wearing a light blue fleece pullover and matching hat, saying she was meeting some of the girls. Since winter broke, they'd been walking down at the high school track every weekday morning. Telling Billy to feel free to fix himself something to eat.

Calling him by her pet name for him, Chipmunk. Telling Chipmunk she'd be back in an hour or so.

Billy found his dad at the kitchen table, reading that morning paper.

"Believe this?" his dad said, as if Billy had been reading along with him.

Billy figuring his dad was doing some last minute research for his golf radio show later that day.

"Nope," Billy said. "Don't even know what *this* is. Just I know I don't believe it."

"Smart man," Bill Sr. said, not looking up from his newspaper. "Eat breakfast yet?"

Billy saying he had not. Grinning, saying that was his whole reason for stopping by.

"Figures," Bill Sr. said. "Guess you'll have to grab something at the café."

"Nah," Billy said. "Too many ears down there. Too much helpful advice."

Bill Sr. finally looking up from his paper. "Well, heaven forbid you fix your own breakfast, boy," his dad said, rising. "Sit down. Eggs and bacon all right?"

Billy took a seat at the table, the two of them talking while his dad fried the bacon and three over-easy eggs in the same pan.

"Now what's got you so worked up?" Bill Sr. said.

"Ah, it's nothing"

"It's something," Bill Sr. said. He dropped two slices of sourdough into the toaster. "I can tell."

Billy not even sure how to say it. Getting up to pour himself a cup of coffee, telling his dad he couldn't get into specifics of who and what but there is this one situation.

"Something's up," Billy said, "but I'm not sure yet what it is. Thing is, I'm looking into it but people didn't take me seriously. Or worse, they flat out lie to my face."

Billy adding that, generally, he found most people refused to take him seriously. Saying he guessed it bothered him the way people viewed him.

Bill Sr. setting the plate of eggs and bacon and toast in front of his son. "Sounds like you're waiting around for permission to do your job."

Billy keeping his mouth closed other than to eat his breakfast, listening.

"By and large, your mother and I raised you not to care too much what other people think," Bill Sr. said, "long as they know they can trust your integrity. But the rest of it? Hell, son, it's your job. You've been elected to do the job. No need to wait around for permission you already have."

Billy sipped his coffee. Shook his head.

"What?"

"Nothing," Billy said. "Just thought it was funny is all. Sitting here, me needing to hear you give me permission not to ask permission."

"It is what it is, I guess," Bill Sr. said. Neither of them spoke for a bit.

Finally Billy saying, “Hey, mind if I borrow your truck this morning?” Explaining that he needed to do a thing and it would be easier to pull this thing off if he wasn’t driving a vehicle that screamed Sheriff down the side.

Bill Sr. saying no problem, as long as the county was prepared to pay to fix any damages.

He wasn’t joking about that, Billy could tell.

“How are the eggs?” Bill Sr. said.

“Runny.”

“Well, next time feel free to fix your own damn breakfast.”

“Didn’t let me finish,” Billy said. “I like them runny.”

Bill Sr. went back to his newspaper. “All right then, there you go.”

Two

Mona sipping her Diet Dr. Pepper, wondering what bug crawled up everybody’s ass. Her momma and Gerald being everybody.

Sitting at the kitchen table, hands busy folding, unfolding then refolding a dish towel. Gerald outside, up a ladder cleaning the gutters. His stubborn ass still mad at her for lying to Billy Keene, of all things.

Mr. Make Himself Useful finding any chore he could to keep himself out of the same room with his new wife. Mona figuring the honeymoon was over.

Arlita with no problem being in the same room as Mona, but refusing to sit down. Arlita in constant motion around her kitchen. Loading the dishwasher with dishes from breakfast. Wiping down the counter. Sweeping the floor. Mopping the floor. Straightening her spice cabinet.

Mona seeing that and thinking *fucking spice cabinet? Seriously?* Wondering what she'd done to make everybody do anything just to avoid her.

Eventually, it dawned on Mona that maybe the tension in the house had nothing to do with her. Might be all the stress built up from waiting around all morning for the kidnappers to call, give them the go for the money drop.

Mona taking another sip of her soda. Yeah, probably that. Nothing to do with her.

Mona craving a cigarette, but not bad enough yet to get up and go all the way outside like Arlita insisted. That's something, huh? Won't even let her own daughter smoke in her childhood home. Love you too, momma.

Another thought occurring to Mona: Bet her momma wouldn't pay all that money for *her*.

Mona picturing in her mind all that money in the hair color box in her daddy's den. If Arlita wouldn't let her daughter smoke in the house, no way would she hand over millions of dollars for Mona's freedom.

Oh, she knew Arlita would pay a ransom for her. But Mona suspected there was a limit. But what was the number, the street value of her freedom?

That number suddenly very important to Mona. If her life was ever on the auction block, Mona wanted to know at what point her momma would invoke final offer, not a penny more and be fully prepared to walk away from the deal?

Whatever that number was, she was damn sure it was well below the price her mother was willing to pay for Patty's freedom. Mona suspecting there was no price in dollars, sweat, tears or even blood that Arlita wouldn't pay for Patty's freedom.

"Momma, can I see the money again?" Mona said.

This morning Arlita had twice refused Mona's requests to sneak a peek at the ransom dollars. But Mona sensed her momma might be wearing down on the issue.

"For heaven's sake, no," Arlita said. "I told you, the

box is all taped up, ready to go. Don't ask me again, Mona Louise."

Getting the middle name. Mona knowing the issue was completely off the table now. Maybe. Might circle back to it later. Mona saying fine, whatever.

Silence between them. So quiet that, there in the kitchen, they could hear Gerald outside exchanging hellos with someone. A moment later the sound of that someone entering through the front door.

Then Sharla standing there in the kitchen with them.

Mona taking one glance at the girl and recognizing it. The bloodshot eyes. Face twitching now and again and a slight tremble in her hands even when resting at her sides. That raspy warble to her voice as she barked a too-enthusiastic hello.

Mona thinking that bitch is tweaking like a motherfucker.

Arlita recognizing it too. Seen it a hundred times before in her own jacked up daughter. But ignoring it now. Arlita telling herself she was too wrapped up in her own shit to walk over and step in someone else's fresh pile.

Instead Arlita asking, What are you doing there today. Shop's still closed until I decide to open back up."

"Looking for a barrette of mine," Sharla said. "Can't find it anywhere. Thought I'd check over here. Might have left it in the bathroom. Mind if I check?"

Mona thinking Sharla needed more than a barrette with that mess of hair. Even a hat wouldn't be enough. Need one of them rubber Halloween masks that goes completely over the head, Mona thought. Just cover it all up.

Arlita telling Sharla go ahead. The tone of her words also letting Sharla know to hurry it up.

And with that, Sharla cutting across the clean kitchen floor toward the guest bathroom, heading deeper into Arlita's home.

Mona and Arlita exchanging glances. *See what I saw and can you believe it?*

Mona about to remark on Sharla's sorry condition when the ring of the telephone exploded in the kitchen. The ringer on its loudest setting so Arlita couldn't miss it.

Arlita's big body across the across the kitchen in a heartbeat, pouncing on the phone on the counter. But not answering it right away.

All morning long she'd been ignoring familiar numbers, knowing most of them were little old ladies looking to pass the time with conversation, gossip. She checked the caller I.D. *Unknown.*

A part of Arlita wondering if that was really true. Was whoever behind this nightmare unknown to her? Finally Arlita picking up the phone.

Mona watching her mother, looking for a sign that this was The Call. Something in her momma's voice, her eyes. Interestingly, the sign revealed itself in Arlita's shoulders, they way they relaxed when she recognized the caller.

Mona realizing all the waiting around drove her momma nuts. Arlita finally able to relax, now that she had something to do.

Mona listening to her mother's side of the conversation. At first a little surprised by her momma sassing the kidnapper. But when she thought about it, not really all the surprising. Arlita gave everybody lip. That was just her way. Why should this jackass be any different?

As she listened, Mona noticing Sharla in the living room, searching in between the couch cushions. Taking her time with it, like she was maybe trying to eavesdrop.

Mona stood, heading in to help Sharla look. But mostly to distract her.

"No luck, huh?" Mona said. Disappointed she didn't surprise Sharla like she expected. Must have heard her coming.

"Hell no," Sharla said, flipping up a cushion. "Probably gone forever. But it's my favorite one."

Mona asking Sharla what the barrette looked like and when was the last time she had it and so on. Mona not really giving a rat's ass, just keeping Sharla from listening in on Arlita's call.

The whole time Mona watching Sharla. Seeing the girl was tweaking hard. Mona figured Sharla must have been hitting it for some time now, maybe days. Knowing Sharla would need to smoke up again, keep the crash away as long as possible. Mona knew.

Mona had a feeling Sharla's surprise visit was about more than some bullshit barrette. More like pop over to steal some cash or maybe something to sell for cash so she could buy more crystal. Mona knew that's what she would have done back when she was using.

"Sharla, you okay?"

"What?" Sharla said, thrown by the question. "Yeah, fine."

"I ask because you don't seem fine is all," Mona said. "Seems like maybe you could use a friend. Someone who's been there."

"Been where?" Sharla on point, paranoid from the

meth.

"Where you are right now. That dark place," Mona said.

Slipping into that blunt been-there-done-that-but-there's-a-better-way patter that was familiar to her from her twelve step meetings. Liking the way it made her feel, reaching out to someone.

Mona sliding into self-righteousness, really bringing it now. "Oh, I know how it is. You look around, don't see a door. Well, I'm here to tell you the reason you can't find no door is there ain't no door."

Sharla continuing to look around the living room, lifting magazines, looking under chairs and tables. Mona following her around, talking at her.

"And the reason there ain't no door is because you're not in a room. Girl, you're at the bottom of a deep, dark hole. And it's hell. I know, I been there. But look at me now...."

Mona pausing there, all dramatic. Hands open, palms up, a visual aide re-enforcing her command to Sharla to look at her before she continued. Sharla didn't look at Mona like she was supposed to.

Mona went on anyway.

"I'm here. And because I'm here, that tells you

what?"

Mona not waiting for an answer.

"Tells you there must be a way out of that hole. I'm proof of it. And if there's a way out for me, then there must be a way out for you. You hear what I'm saying, Sharla?"

Sharla finally stopping her search, turning to face her would-be sponsor.

"Mona, I hear what you're saying," Sharla said. "I just got no idea what the fuck you're talking about. I'm going to check the dining room."

Sharla left Mona burning in the living room, both of them thinking *stupid bitch.*

Mona not sure what to do with herself now. Maybe go outside, yell at Gerald up on the ladder.

About to go do just that, then hearing her momma still on the telephone jawing with the kidnapper. Asking for clarification on things, then what does she do, then what happens and can she talk to her granddaughter?

Mona moving into the kitchen, hoping she might get to talk with her daughter.

Arlita shaking her head.

Mona recognizing that look on her mother's face, half scared and fully pissed off. Mona having seen it hundreds of times growing up whenever things were out of her momma's reach. It meant they weren't going to put Patty on the line.

Arlita advising the caller that soon after she coughed up the money, her granddaughter's ass better be back home in good shape.

"Otherwise you can count on your world turning into a shitstorm for the foreseeable future," Arlita said, then killed the call. Turning to Mona. "Why wouldn't they let me talk with her?"

"Think something's wrong?" Mona said. "I mean this whole thing is wrong. But think something is wrong-wrong?"

Arlita shrugged. "Just have to find out the hard way, I guess. Do me a favor, go fetch the box from the den. I need to call Vic, give him time to get in place."

"So when he sees them pick up the money, he ain't going to beat the shit of them then and there, right? He's just going to follow them, see where they go?"

Arlita shrugging again. "That's the plan."

No need to say the rest of it out loud. Both of them knowing there was no telling just what that feral son of a bitch might do.

On her way to the den for the box with the ransom money, Mona caught Sharla coming out of the bathroom again. Mona's nose suddenly on the alert for the burning cat piss stink of meth smoke. Not detecting any odor and Mona couldn't help her heart racing at that.

Lack of an odor meant that if Sharla was smoking, she had some really good shit. Mona hearing her group counselor's bird voice singing once an addict, always an addict.

"Any luck in there?" Mona said. "I mean, finding that barrette?"

"No, and it's driving me nuts," Sharla said, a little too loud. "Hopefully it'll turn up. But I should get gone. You and Arlita got things you want to get done today probably."

Mona thinking, yeah, they had some things to get done all right.

Sharla heading for the front door. Mona listening to make certain Sharla had left the house before getting the box from the den.

The box sealed up just as the kidnapper had instructed. Gray duct tape along every edge, top and bottom, with one strip across the middle of the top. The box heavy with cash. Mona struggling with it as she brought it back to her mother in the kitchen. Plopping it down hard on the kitchen table.

"Goddamn, momma, you paying in quarters?"

"What can I say, honey?" Arlita said. "A lot of money's got a lot of weight to it." Arlita, strong, picking up the box like it was empty and walking out the door with it.

Mona standing in the suddenly quiet kitchen and not liking it. Not liking the taste in her dry mouth. Not liking the way her stomach felt empty, not so much hungry as vacant. She decided she would go yell at Gerald, see if that made her feel any better.

Found him at the top of a ladder on the west side of the house. Yelling up to him to be careful, don't fall off. But sounding more like scolding than concern for his safety.

"Good idea, will give that a try," Gerald said. "Saw your mother leaving. Had the box with her. I take it everything is happening?"

Mona looking up at her husband, her heart not in yelling at him anymore. Wanting him to come down right then and hold her.

"G, come down off that ladder for a moment, okay?"

Gerald not catching the desperation in her voice. Saying just let him finish this gutter, then he'd be right down. Damn gutter covers were a bitch to get off and put back on.

Mona about to whine, stomp her feet, throw a hissy

fit. Had always worked for her in the past. Well, maybe not worked for her, but at least had gotten people's attention. But her heart just not in it.

Suddenly felt tired and depressed from all the excitement of the day. Ignoring the signs of her vast mood swings.

Wandering back into the house and through the rooms. Unsure what to do with herself in that big old goddamn house. Goddamn quiet, empty house.

Then the house not so quiet, a noise coming from the shop. Something knocked over. Mona checking in the shop and surprised to find Sharla there.

Had let herself in the shop, her keys still dangling in the doorknob. Sharla holding up a shiny piece of black plastic.

"Remembered where I left it," Sharla said, pointing. "Set it on that shelf under the counter over there the other day."

Mona eyeballing the girl, seeing that make Sharla uncomfortable. "So about our conversation earlier.

"Yeah?" Sharla thinking here we go again with the Just Say No bullshit.

"You're obviously drugging and all that" The words out of Mona's parched mouth almost before she realized what she was saying. "Wouldn't happen to have any on you, would you?"

Three

Billy parked his dad's silver pick up just down the street from Arlita's house. Waiting for Vic to show up. Waiting for Arlita to leave.

Waiting for something, hoping he'd recognize it when he saw it.

For a while watching Mona's new husband, that Gerald guy, clean out the front gutters. Then killing time by messing with the menu on the GPS in the dash of his dad's vehicle.

Laughing at his old man: Lived in this small town most of his life, so now where could he need to go that he would need directions? Bill Sr. could find his way to any part of Caulfield with his eyes closed, simply intuit his way there. Billy shaking his head at the the riddle his father sometimes was.

Pushing the on-screen buttons on the GPS, trying out alternate voices, hoping to find one sounding like Kacey

Musgraves.

Out of the corner of his eye, catching sight of Sharla pulling up in front of Arlita's. Seeing her, realizing lately he hadn't seen Sharla around much.

When she stepped out of Chubba's Mustang, Billy wondered if *she'd* seen herself lately. She looked haggard, hair all a mess. Tramping on unsound legs up the walkway to Arlita's house, giving a big hello on the fly to Gerald as she passed below him. Sharla walking straight up to and through the front door.

Billy not thinking anything of it, Sharla showing up. After all, she worked there. But something about her entering through the front rather than around the side to the beauty shop struck him as odd. Wasn't sure why, just did.

Billy growing bored with waiting. He was parked on a hill and from his vantage he was able to take in the clusters of budding trees and the roofs of the houses in Arlita's neighborhood.

As if for the first time, he saw how slanted and steeped the roofs were. Nothing level, nothing sure. Yet almost touching. It looked like some giant Rube Goldberg contraption. Like a person could drop a marble on the tallest roof and the marble would roll from one roof to the next, no idea of its next move or ultimate destination, just blindly descending as fast as nature's laws would allow.

Billy went back to playing with the GPS. Remembering that when Bill Sr. bought the truck, he'd joked that it came with a special setting so the thing would bitch about his driving whenever Sara Jane wasn't along for the ride. Order him to slow down, speed up, change lanes, hang a right or a left just as he passed the turn he needed.

Sara Jane's backseat driving was a long-running joke in their family and, like all jokes with legs, there was some truth to it. Sara Jane never backed down though, defending herself by saying she wasn't bitching, she was mentoring.

Billy's attention pulled back to the job by Sharla coming back out the front door, waving goodbye up to Gerald, hurrying to her car.

Billy watching as she drove away, turning right and out of sight at the end of the block. Considering following her but deciding to wait it out, see if Vic shows up or Arlita takes off somewhere.

He didn't have to wait long.

Next one out the front door was Arlita, carrying a large box. Billy couldn't make out the picture and writing on the box, but he saw it was sealed with gray duct tape. Arlita stowed the box in the backseat of her Mercedes S-class sedan before heading off down the street.

Billy started up his dad's truck and put it in gear. Pulling away from the curb and the digital voice on the GPS said cooing at him in Japanese. Billy reminding himself that he better reset that later.

Starting out after Arlita, following from a two-block distance.

Moving through the intersection just past Arlita's house, Billy checked traffic to his right. Surprised to see Sharla in Chubba's Mustang down the block, heading back toward him. Figuring she must have flipped a U-turn. Again struck by a vague, anxious feeling about her.

Billy wondering where they were both going, Arlita and Sharla. He wasn't sure which one to follow but instinct told him to stay on Arlita's trail. Wishing the GPS could tell him where both Arlita and Sharla were headed.

Billy laughing to himself, letting that silly wish go. Realizing that even if the GPS could tell him where they were going, it would say it in Japanese.

Four

Vic squirming in his truck, trying to discern if his bladder was fooling him again. Rolling down his window, hoping the fresh air might help.

Parked in the used car lot adjacent to the DQ at the end of town, where Arlita said she had been told by the kidnapper to drop the money. Vic had slipped into a spot at the back of the car lot, one that offered an advantageous view of the dumpster out back of the DQ. Other than a lack of giant numbers pasted to his windshield, his raggedy truck blended in nicely among the rows of beaters.

Both the DQ and the used car lot backed up to a small copse of trees, a network of farm pastures stretching out beyond them. A creek cut through the small woods, alive from all the recent rain—cold, blackish water trickling and gurgling along.

These sounds were not soothing to Vic, fidgeting in his truck and trying to out-guess his bladder.

After hanging up Arlita's call, he'd bolted from his house, not stopping for a try at the toilet. Thanks to the cancer, a trip to the bathroom before leaving any place was part of his routine, a precaution. As if chewing away at his prostate weren't enough, his cancer had a vile sense of humor, pestering him with random, insistent urges to take a piss.

Sometimes Vic really did have to go; other times it was a phantom urge. Valid or bogus, the urges always felt real. But Vic had been in a hurry to set up on the DQ before anyone else showed up. But now wishing he'd stopped to hit the head first.

Vic shifting his feet along his truck's floor boards. Still unclear if this was a real alarm or just the cancer tricking him. Vic thinking it's pretty damn pathetic when a man can't trust his own bladder.

Considering sneaking back into the trees. Call his bladder's bluff, see if it was playing straight with him.

But Arlita would be showing up any minute, maybe the kidnappers too, picking up the money. Vic fought the pressure to take a leak.

When she called, Arlita had said the ransom caller told her to drive behind the DQ and drop the duct-taped box with the money into the dumpster. After dropping the money, she said, the caller's exact instructions were to "drive the fuck off, do not look in the fucking mirror and do not fucking come back if you ever want to see your granddaughter again, alive or dead."

Vic figuring that meant the kidnappers would be nearby, ready to move in quickly to snatch up the ransom money before getting gone.

Trying to take his mind off his untrustworthy bladder. Eyes relentlessly scanning the area, on the look out for...well, anybody. Not like they'd have on black hats or name badges. Could be anybody.

A question occurring to Vic: Had Arlita called the fast food joint by its initials because that's what everyone in town called the Dairy Queen? Or had the kidnapper called it DQ too?

And if the kidnapper had used the initials, did that mean anything, like maybe it was someone in town?

Vic unsure how widespread that was, calling it the DQ. Just a Caulfield thing? Or did everybody in every hayseed town that had a Dairy Queen refer to it as the DQ? He didn't know and he went a little dizzy comprehending how little he had traveled in his life.

Out of nowhere the weight of all that he had not seen of this world — hell, this county even — closing in on him at once.

Vic shaking his head, pinched hard on his penis. Partly to clear away his grave realization, partly to keep from pissing his pants. His bladder was being straight with him.

"Fuck it," he said, climbing out of his truck.

Rushing into the cover of the woods. Positioning himself behind an oak tree so that he had coverage but maintained clear sight of the dumpster. Unzipping and enlivened by the tickle of fresh air.

Vic breathing deep, trying to relax. Nothing. Nothing flowing other than the burbling creek behind him. Closing his eyes, trying to submit to its peaceful song.

And then it came, slowly at first but gaining power. The sensation of relief was like a promise kept. Felt so good Vic smiled. Then his smile fading, mumbling a curse as Arlita's Mercedes pulled into the DQ lot.

Vic pushing internally, trying to empty his bladder as the Mercedes prowled around back toward the dumpster. Vic unable to stop the stream, didn't want to. Figuring get it all out then get on with it, he thought.

Another vehicle, a silver pickup, pulling into the DQ.

Somewhere in the back of his mind Vic knew the truck but not thinking much about it. Had a lot going on at the moment.

Vic watching, still going, as Arlita pulled alongside the dumpster.

Sitting in her car, taking a moment. Surveying her surroundings. Arlita spotting Vic's empty truck, empty. Looking around for Vic but not finding him.

Arlita climbing out of her idling car. Pulling the duct-taped box from her backseat.

Vic hurrying to evacuate the last of his bladder. Anxious to get in position to pounce on whatever sorry motherfucker showed up to fish that box out of the dumpster.

Reminding himself that the smart move was to play it cool, follow the dumpster diver back to whatever rock he lived under.

But not completely ruling out attacking the son of a bitch as soon as he pulls the box from the dumpster. Beat the Who, Where and Why out of his sorry ass. More than one way to skin a cat, his mother always said.

Vic almost finished answering nature's call when his whole body locked up on him. Seizing up at the sight of the silver pickup pulling up behind Arlita's Mercedes.

Arlita consumed with her task, not even noticing the truck.

Just like that, it hit Vic whose truck it was. Thinking *you sneaky little prick.*

Billy Keene stepping out of his dad's truck.

Five

"What's in your box, Arlita?"

Billy sliding out of his dad's truck and easing his sheriff's Stetson onto his head with that fluid, all-in-one motion of his. Big *caught ya* smile plastered over his face.

Walking toward Arlita, who was holding the duct-taped box over the mouth of the dumpster like a sacrificial virgin over a volcano.

Arlita surprised by the voice, turning her head, seeing Billy. Regaining her composure quickly. Meeting Billy's grin with a big *fuck ya* smile of her own.

Arlita trying to hide her unease, saying, "Your come-on could use some work, don't you think?" Arlita said.

At that, she let go of the box, pretended not to hear it bang and echo inside the empty dumpster.

"Not very subtle," she said.

"Depends on the woman."

Billy sensing that behind her smile Arlita was worried. Something in the way she kept glancing around, distracted. "So what's going on?"

"Running errands and whatnot." Arlita said.

Arlita casually throwing a glance one way, then the other. Still not finding Vic. Afraid the kidnappers might be watching now, maybe thinking she'd defied them, called the law.

Pushing panic as far back in her mind as she could, Arlita decided it was best to end this little get-together. Or at least move it elsewhere. Arlita moving to get back into her car, wishing Billy a good one.

"Hold up, Arlita," Billy said. "Need you to haul that box out of the dumpster."

"What box?"

Billy smiling, unbothered by her contempt. He'd come to expect it. Knowing it wouldn't change until he changed it. Knowing it might never change.

"Box I saw you drop in the dumpster. That's how it's going to read in the report when I write you up for illegal dumping."

"Illegal dumping? Tossing something in a dumpster's littering? Not that I'm doing that. Just how many years does illegal dumping get you in the state pen, anyway?"

Billy keeping up his smile. Clarifying her offense as a misdemeanor, a hundred-dollar fine on the first offense.

Arlita saying hold on she'd take care of it right now, had some spare change somewhere in here. Then making a show of leaning through the open window of her Mercedes to search her interior.

"Arlita, I'm going to need you to shut off your car, step away from it."

The sudden edge in Billy's tone catching Arlita off guard. Allowing her no time to consider not obeying him. Immediately killing the engine before pulling herself out of her car window. Arlita turning to face Billy.

"No need to be a crab about it, Billy," Arlita said. "Get crabby when I'm hungry too. Tell you what: let's head down to Trace's, grab some lunch? I'm buying."

"Thank you much, but I had a big breakfast this morning. Not hungry," Billy said. "Tell you what I will let you do for me though—pull that box out of the dumpster, please."

"I truly do not know what box you're talking about, Billy?"

Billy still holding his smile, nothing getting to him. But taking a moment to slow things down.

Reminding himself not to confuse controlling Arlita with controlling the situation. His eyes making a quick pass of the area before dropping his head, looking at his boots. Laughing to himself.

Arlita asking what's so funny?

"Just people," Billy said. "Like you claiming to know

nothing about that box I just saw you drop in the dumpster. Or Vic Shears over there with his dick in his hand."

Billy jutting his chin in the direction of the woods behind the DQ and used car lot.

Arlita turning, finally seeing Vic half-hidden behind a tree. Wondering how she'd missed him and, yeah, why's he holding his penis?

Vic, realizing he'd been spotted, jumped fully behind the tree. A reflex. As if that might undo being discovered.

Billy shaking his head at Vic's lame attempt to hide, saying, "See, told you: People are funny."

"That move right there, that was pretty goddamn weak," Arlita said.

Billy whistling at Vic, waving him over.

Vic stuffing himself back into his pants as he joined Billy and Arlita at the dumpster.

"Probably won't do much good to ask *again,*" Billy said. "Up to this point both of you done nothing but lie to me. But, hell, it's worth a shot. Either of you care to catch me up on what's going on here?"

Arlita shrugged. "Nothing to catch you up on, Billy."

"Had to take a piss is all," Vic said.

"Pretty much what I figured," Billy said.

Billy instructing Arlita to go stand next to the hood of her car. Ordering Vic over to the far side of the dumpster, away from Arlita. Then Billy leaning in and hauled up the box from the mildewed dumpster.

The box surprisingly heavy, landing with a thud on the ground at Arlita's sneakers. Billy pulling out his pocket knife, opening the blade.

"Last chance," he said to Arlita.

Arlita grim now, giving him an icy glare. She obviously wasn't talking.

Squatting, Billy gently sliced the top seam of duct tape on the box. Flipping open the top flap. Billy frowning at the contents of the box.

"Got something against the environment?" Billy said, looking up at Arlita. "You're supposed to recycle newspapers, not throw them away."

Billy reading the horror and confusion on Arlita's face when she saw the old newspapers inside the box.

The confused look on her face betraying to Billy that her situation, whatever it was, had just gotten more jacked up than even she expected.

Six

Now Arlita and Vic leaning against her Mercedes, talking it over.

Billy had finally gone on his way after a lot of questions but no answers from either of them. But both Arlita and Vic knowing Billy was on to them, wouldn't be leaving them alone anytime soon.

Vic kicking the duct-taped box of old newspapers with the toe of his cowboy boot.

"So what's the idea here? You playing a game? Don't cross me, Arlita."

"No game, that's not me," Arlita said, pointing furiously at the box. Layers of dread and anger and confusion all blending in her voice. Letting Vic know that accusing her wasn't the best approach to take with her right now.

"You didn't do this?" Vic said. "So where the fuck's the money?"

"That there's the three million dollar question, ain't it?"

Arlita walked Vic back through her steps up to that point: sealing up the box with duct tape the night before, taking the call this morning, Mona fetching the box....

Vic shaking his head, saying no way would Mona

steal the money meant to save her daughter's life. Would she?

"I can't see even Mona doing something so low down as that. Not even at her drugged up worst." Arlita said. "Least I don't think so. I guaran-damn-tee you I'm going to find out."

Vic could see that Arlita was wound up, itching to leave. When he insisted they go over it again, she pushed back, saying she needed to get going.

"I got kidnappers expecting a box of money," Arlita said. "And not a whiff of an idea where my money might be."

"I hear you, Arlita. Things are uglier than an old cowtown whore right now. And that's exactly why we ought to slow down, figure all the angles before we make our next move on this."

Arlita nodding her head, taking a deep breath.

Vic asking her about Mona's new husband, Gerald.

"Now I ain't bringing him up just because he's black," Vic said. "All I'm saying is we don't know him. Only color that matters in this here deal is green."

Arlita saying she didn't see it, he didn't seem the type. But agreeing that they didn't know him. Suggesting maybe Vic chat him up while she had a talk with Mona.

Split up the two of them, see if their stories fit back together.

"So we got Mona and Gerald," Vic said. "Anybody else at the house, last night or this morning?"

"Sharla dropped by this morning."

Vic's eyebrows arching at Sharla's name. Recalling his conversation about her with Horace Self in the frozen food aisle.

"Sharla huh? What'd she need?"

"Just looking for something, headband or scrunchie or some shit like that," Arlita said. "Wasn't there long. Looked like warmed-over death though. That girl better bring it down soon, else she's heading for a crash."

Vic saying he'd heard as much from Horace. Filling in Arlita on his conversation with Horace.

"Why are you just telling me this now?" Arlita said. "You never said you talked to Horace."

"I could say the same damn thing to you," Vic said. "The wheels are starting to come off. You need to decide right now, you going to be straight with me? I feel for you. For Patty. But play me any way other than straight, I'm out."

A long silence between them. The sound of cars, the early lunch crowd pulling in and out of the gravel lot, the traffic trolling along Main.

Finally Vic proposing their next steps: Arlita would go home and hope the kidnappers called soon. Try to get them to wait while she pulled together another three million. That was the priority.

Meanwhile, Vic would try to find Sharla and have a talk with her. He thought they could put off talking with Mona and Gerald until later.

"Thing is," Vic said, "You go home and she and her husband are still there, you pretty much know they didn't do it. Pull something shitty as that, they'd be looking to get gone right quick."

Arlita about to agree with Vic on that when she saw him wince. "Something wrong?"

"Urine trouble," Vic said.

"I'm in trouble?" Arlita said, "Hell, we're all in trouble."

"No, no," Vic said. "Urine trouble. Gotta piss."

"Again?"

Vic wincing again, rolling his eyes, saying, "Your guess is as good as mine."

Seven

Chubba saying, "Ever seen so much money all in one place?"

He and Sharla standing in the barn out back of Horace's farm house. Facing each other, a duct-taped box on the dusty concrete floor between them. Flaps open, contents exposed.

Chubba unable to take his eyes off the money.

Sharla's eyes too staying locked on the fat stacks of cash. "Yeah. I have."

"The hell you have."

Both of them overhearing snippets of Horace's half of the cell phone conversation he'd taken outside. Sounded like he might be talking with Arlita.

"Fine, don't believe me," Sharla said. She was rocking back and forth on her feet, unable to still herself.

Her restlessness annoying Chubba to no end.

"Christ, even a simple conversation with you has to be a goddamn hassle?" Chubba said. "I just meant, that there's a lot of money."

Tom, the fat gray cat, was curled up yet balancing on a rafter above. Half-dozing, unconcerned with Lola, the black Labrador, and J.J. the terrier mix. Both dogs running around excitedly, wet nose to the ground, taking in an all-you-can-smell buffet of barn aromas.

"Okay, maybe I ain't seen this much," Sharla said. "That *is* a shitload of money."

A second passing before it occurred to Chubba to ask the question. "Where else you seen a big box of cash?"

"At Cole Peter's", Sharla said.

Chubba saying you mean your drug dealer.

Sharla saying whatever.

Sharla going on, telling Chubba how this one time she dropped by Cole's and he told her he'd come into a bunch of money. Didn't specify how he had come into it. Asked if she wanted to see it.

"So he showed it to me, a big ole pile," Sharla said.

"Tough to compare a pile to this nice, neat stack."

Sharla agreeing Chubba might be right about that. "Know the real difference though?" she said.

Chubba shook his head.

"Never seen this much money that belonged to me!" Sharla let out an obnoxious rasp of a laugh. "Well, part of it belongs to me anyway."

In their individual stalls, the two horses picking up on the weird energy of the humans around them. Delilah, the chestnut quarter horse, agitated. Head poking out of her stall, bobbing violently. Throwing whinnying calls to Chief, the Appaloosa in the stall on the far side of the barn. He had retreated to a far corner of his space, turned away and giving everyone his pale hindquarters, as if trying to ignore this whole sorry state of affairs.

Everyone, people and animals, hearing Horace coming back into the barn. Wrapping up his call, telling whoever it was on the other end that he'd take care of it. Then killing his call, joining them at the box of money.

The three of them gathered around it as if warming themselves by the heat it gave off.

"We got a problem," Horace said. "Arlita knows she dumped a dummy box."

"How the hell she know that?" Sharla scratching nervously at her cheekbone.

Horace giving her the once-over before launching into Arlita's version of events at the DQ.

"So it would seem our dutiful Sheriff has gone and stepped in it," he said. "I better get over to see him, set him straight."

"Did Arlita, did she say anything...." Sharla's stopped, her voice wavering. She cleared her throat and started again. "Arlita mention me at all?"

"Yeah, your name come up," Horace said. "Said you

stopped by this morning, then next thing her money's gone. She thought that was kinda funny. Not ha-ha funny, of course."

"Told you that was a bad idea," Sharla said.

She began pacing around the barn like one of the cooped up animals and rambling.

"Didn't I? Didn't I say that? We should have just let Arlita drop off the money, then pick it up."

Horace shaking his head. "They were watching, like I said they would be. They'd have spotted us when we picked it up. Made more sense to make the switch before."

Sharla moving around the barn like a boxer trying to hide in a ring, saying, "Not sure it made sense for everybody."

"For chrissakes Sharla, will you hold still a second!" Chubba said.

Sharla stopping in one place.

Chubba turning to Horace. "Daddy, you said *they*. Who's they? Billy?"

Horace didn't say anything, letting them wait before finally telling them about Vic helping out Arlita.

"Oh man, I am sooo fucked," Sharla said, starting up her hopping again. "Hell with it, I'm taking my share and going."

Sharla making a move toward the money. Chubba stepping in to cut her off with a calm hand on her shoulder.

"Hold up. Going where?"

Sharla thinking it over.

"Hell, I don't know, Kansas City, anywhere," she said. "Just away from here for a while."

"You run, it's going to look bad," Chubba said, a whine in his voice. "Right Daddy?"

Chubba trying to play it that way, like it was about the situation. Hoping his worries about Sharla and Pearce weren't too evident in his voice.

"Everybody keep your britches on," Horace said. "We're all fine. Arlita's confiding in me. She'll listen to me."

Horace walking over and pulling down a calf rope from its hook on the barn wall. Standing, thinking a good long moment. Holding the rope in one hand while paying out the lasso in his other, the loop growing.

"Now at some point, Sharla," Horace said finally, "you *are* going to have to face her. Just stick to your story, you'll be fine. But it might make sense for that conversation to take place after Arlita's had a chance to cool down. After her granddaughter's back home safe and sound."

"But as far as she's concerned," Chubba said, "she think's the kidnappers don't have the money. So why would they let her go?"

"Good point," Horace said. Pausing again to think.

Trying to figure how to turn these unexpected developments into something that works for him. All the while working the rope in his hands. He'd long considered this ability to turn things his way to be the essential benefit of the pioneer spirit that ran through his bloodline.

Once the lasso was big enough Horace began to twirl it above his head in a tight, deliberate circle. His wrist and elbow gyrating in a counter-sync rotation.

With a practiced, striking motion, Horace cast the lasso toward a dark corner of the barn. The lasso ensnaring a pair of steer horns nailed to a sawhorse. Horace yanking the rope taut around the horns with a downward, sideways jerk at his hip.

"Here's what you do," he said to Sharla. "Head back on up to KC—"

"—Now you're fucking talking," Sharla said.

"Hold on," Chubba said.

"Both of you shut the hell up," Horace said.

Dropping the rope, walking over to the box of money before going on.

"Do this right and we'll come out of this scot-free and richer for it. So pay some goddamn attention to what

I'm about to say, both of you."

Horace instructing Sharla to call Pearce, have him call Arlita. Have him start out all pissed off at her about the cops being there, like he was watching all along. Ask if she was dicking him around, did she think this was a joke, must not love her granddaughter, that sort of thing. Really rattle her.

"But I want Pearce to eventually give her more time to get the money," Horace said. "Tell her same place out back of the DQ. Same time, but on Saturday."

"Same box and duct tape situation?" Sharla said.

Horace shook his head.

"Naw, this time just a duffle bag or whatever will hold that much cash. I want her to be able to check to make sure it's got money in it, so she'll feel comfortable dropping it off."

"We're going to double down on Arlita?" Chubba said.

"No, no," Horace said. "No, this goes like it should, all this will be over with long before then, and Arlita will never have to deliver it."

Horace turning to Sharla, ordering her to get her ass up to KC.

Chubba interrupting to protest but Horace cutting

him off with a look.

Horace saying tomorrow night, Friday, Sharla and Pearce need to find a quiet, residential side street. Dump Patty there.

"Dump her body?" Sharla said.

"No goddamn it!" Horace said. "Make her feel like she escaped if you can. But just let her out and drive off if you have to."

"We can do that," Sharla said.

In her mind, Sharla already plotting out her trip up to KC. Swing by her dealer before heading out of town.

Sharla starting again toward the box of money, saying, "I'll just grab my share. Take Pearce his share too."

Again Chubba cutting her off, this time grabbing her by her stick-thin forearm, a twig in his vise grip.

"Hold up a sec," Chubba said. "Honestly, I ain't so crazy about how bad you seem to *want* to go."

"Don't be dumb," Sharla said. Laughing, trying to make him feel silly. "You heard your daddy."

A long moment of Chubba going under, feeling submerged and powerless against the combined undertow of his girlfriend and his father. Letting go of Sharla's arm.

She patted his belly, saying "We gotta play this out."

"Smart girl," Horace said. "But nobody gets their

money until the job is done, and this ain't over just yet. Not until Patty's home safe and sound."

"I call bullshit on that," Sharla said. "You got your money. Hell, you got *all* the money! Fuck if I'm leaving here, goddamn it."

Horace listening. Like he expected the torrent of drugged-up white trash crazy-ass bullshit spilling out of her mouth. Letting her go on a bit before finally conceding she had a point.

Horace telling her okay, take a couple hundred thousand.

"Consider it a good-faith gesture to you," Horace said. "And Pearce."

Sharla scooping up as many bundles as she could fit into her purse. Horace fetching a plastic grocery bag so she could carry more out to Chubba's Mustang.

Sharla with a quick goodbye to Chubba but not even a peck on the cheek. Then the sound of his Mustang firing up and prowling down the long driveway.

"I don't get it, Daddy," Chubba said. He knelt down, folding the flaps, boxing up the rest of the money, going on about it.

"I mean, no need to send her up there. That freakshow can handle letting Patty escape. Shit, I'm surprised she hasn't gotten loose already."

Horace striding over to retrieve his calf rope from the dummy horns.

"Just trust me. It's better this way."

"Tell you something else," Chubba said, getting to his feet. "Arlita still don't have a good answer for where her money went. She's going to want to know who left her holding a box of old newspapers. How do we explain that away?"

"Not our place to explain anything away," Horace said, replacing the calf rope on its hook.

"I don't know," Chubba said, looking at his daddy walking toward him. "I don't understand it all."

"What you don't understand could fill a set of cyclopedias, boy."

Horace refusing to look his son in the eye as he passed him. Chubba turning to watch his father walking away.

"You mean encyclopedias, right?" Chubba said.

"I don't know," Horace said over his shoulder, leaving the barn, "Do I?"

Eight

Back at the sheriff's office, Billy sitting at an open desk in the bullpen. Struggling to concentrate on a report from the Kansas Bureau of Investigations. For once his staff wasn't the distraction.

Lon quiet at the moment, an unnatural state for him. Kicked back at his desk, replacing the six D-cell batteries in his black flashlight. Rather than carrying a lighter flashlight, Lon opted for the long, heavy Maglite that doubles as an unsettling nightstick.

Cookie over at her neat desk keeping to herself, going toe-to-toe with her computer solitaire. Deputies Dustin and Zane out on patrol.

Instead, it was the mild anxiety in his stomach distracting Billy. Nervousness before a date.

Billy' eyes repeatedly clocking the couple of hours until he would pick up Paige. Chiding himself for being all worked up like some teenage kid.

It's what he'd always felt like before taking the mound in a game. Remembering a minor league pitching coach laughing, telling Billy: "If you're not nervous, then you're not paying attention."

Billy receiving this advice while bent over a locker

room toilet, puking up every last bit of his nervousness before a game.

Anticipation for his evening with Paige interfering with his ability to fully absorb the print-out of the KBI report. It wasn't even overly long even, just a two-page brief on the pictures of the evidence found around the scene of Patty's vehicle that Cookie had sent up to Topeka.

The tread pattern on the pictures and plaster casts indicated the tracks were made by sixteen-inch Michelins. The kind most often used as original equipment and most often by foreign car makers. That meant there was a good chance the car had rolled off the lot on those tires.

If that was the case, then given the wear on the treads, the car was likely somewhere between two and five years old. That particular tire was most found often on wagons, coupes and mid-sized sedans. Given the spread between the left and right tracks, it looked to be a sedan.

A side note in the report complimenting the excellence of the photos taken at the scene. Billy smiling at this, stomach fluttering, thinking again of seeing Paige in a few hours.

Billy considering the contents of the report again, making sure he hadn't missed a detail. Really nothing in it pointing in any particular direction. But if something developed in the case, then he might be able to match tracks to tires, tires to car and then maybe tie that car to someone at the scene.

And after that odd business at the dumpster out back of the DQ, Billy was convinced there was more to Patty's upturned car than just an accident.

Billy glancing up at the clock again, just a minute and a half since the last time. Then catching sight of Horace Self entering the sheriff's office like he owned it.

Billy lowering his eyes back to the KBI report even though he was finished with it. Sensing Horace making a beeline for him anyway.

"Hey there, Mr. Self," Lon said, rising from his desk to shake Horace's hand. Lon setting his long flashlight on the empty desk.

Finally Billy looking up to Horace, also rising to shake the man's hand. The two men exchanging pleasantries as Lon hovered nearby. Horace starting with small talk, asking how's business.

"Sorry, Mr. Self," Billy said, "but I have a few things I need to finish before an appointment later. Busy man such as yourself, sure you understand."

Horace nodding, saying certainly understands. Then easing himself down into an office chair. Making himself comfortable, sitting to chat for a spell.

"Thing is, I got a call from Arlita," Horace said. Picking up Lon's flashlight from the desk, looking it over. Clicking it on, shining it across the room. "I tell you, whatever you did, you got her panties all twisted."

Horace tossing a sugary cherry of a laugh on top of his words. Lon laughing along too enthusiastically.

Billy giving an effortless smile to these two. Just guys, all of them shooting the shit about how silly women can be, right?

But Billy noticing how all the sudden it was about what *he* did, not what Arlita was up to. Not going to follow Horace down that way. And Billy wondering what the hell Horace has to do with anything anyway?

"She's upset all right," Billy said. "Get the feeling though she's got more eating at her than me doing the job that people elected me to do."

Horace clicking off the flashlight. Horace willing to overlook the tone Billy was using with him. For now.

Instead, Horace giving Billy a wise, patronizing smile, as if about to reveal to a child how a magic trick works.

Horace saying, "Know what made your predecessor so good at this job?"

Click, flashlight back on.

"His ability to walk in heels?" Lon said, working hard to score cheap points with Horace.

An annoyed glance, Horace deducting points for interrupting him.

Click, flashlight off.

"No, not Bob Gaffney. That skirt-wearing degenerate was an aberration in more ways than one. I'm talking about Big Jim. That man, he had a talent for fitting himself to people, to situations."

Lon jumping in, seconding Horace's point. Horace ignoring the uncalled-for backup, continuing on with his explanation.

"Let's say Big Jim was in the face of some drug pusher down at the trailer park. In that case he was The Sheriff. Capital T, capital S."

"That's so true," Lon said. "I seen it many times. One time Big Jim and I—"

"—But now if he was chatting up one of Caulfield's prominent citizens on the tee box at 17...," Horace said.

Click, flashlight on.

"...or better yet," Horace went on, "pulling over that same prominent citizen as he weaved home from the country club, well then Big Jim knew how to be the sheriff."

"Little t, little s, right?" Billy said.

Horace holding that father-knows-best smile while allowing his wisdom the quiet time to sink in.

Click, light off.

"See," Horace said, "it was that talent for fitting himself to the context of a situation, recognizing who he was dealing with—that's what earned Big Jim the respect and loyalty of our prominent citizens."

Click, light on.

"You are exactly right about that," Lon said. "You paying attention to all this, Billy?"

Billy giving Lon a curious smile, plain but chocked full of questions. A smile asking:

Did you really just say that?

You really just call me by my name?

You really just try to dry-fuck me in front of a civilian?

Billy letting it go for the time being. Getting back to Horace and the point he was trying to drive like a nail into Billy's head. More interested in how odd it was that Horace came all the way down to the sheriff's office just to make his point.

"Oh, I hear you. Arlita's a prominent citizen," Billy said, straight-faced. Watching to see if a self-centered jackass like Horace would be able to let that slide.

The smile evaporating from Horace's face. Heating in a slow burn now.

Click, off.

"Yeah, well, don't forget that some citizens are more prominent than others."

"No doubt," Billy said, really needling Horace's ego now. "Given all her money, she's probably sitting on top of the pile. Of prominent citizens, that is."

Horace putting the flashlight back down on the desk where he'd found it.

"There's more to it than money," Horace said.

"Is that right?" Billy said.

Watching Horace's eyes blinking rapidly atop his flush cheeks, truly rattled. Billy thinking he never realized Horace was so thin skinned.

For his part, Horace wondering just where the hell this conversation was heading? This smart-ass kid think he knows something? Horace hesitating, and for once glad to hear ass-kissing Lon's foghorn of a voice.

"Billy, I think you might want to apologize to Mr. Self," Lon said.

The room suddenly quiet, nothing but the faint whir of computer fans.

While the three men had been talking, Deputies Dustin and Zane had returned to the office. Both now crowding around Cookie's desk. The three of them trying not to get caught eavesdropping. Billy knowing they were watching him.

"Lon, I'm going to need you to wait in my office for me," Billy said. "I'll be with you as soon as Mr. Self and I are finished here."

Everybody watching Lon now. Lon hesitating before finally skulking into Billy's office, sent out of the room so the adults could talk.

"I appreciate you stopping by, Horace," Billy said. "That's good advice. I'll swing by Arlita's soon, smooth things over. Make sure there's no hard feelings."

"Actually I was suggesting you leave her be," Horace said.

"Horace, just why in the hell are you here?" Billy said.

"Think I just told you, kid," Horace said, getting up from his chair. Leaving it at that, heading out the door.

After Horace had gone, Billy joined Lon his office. Shutting the door behind him. Lowering the blinds on the windows.

On the outside, Cookie, Dustin and Zane unable to

see anything, only hearing Lon's raised voice. Billy's voice muffled but calm. But no way to make out exactly what was being said.

Then the office door banging open and Lon scowling as he stormed out.

Glaring at everybody as he stomped wordlessly across the floor. Anyone looking bound to notice the empty holster on his right hip, the bare spot on the left breast of his tan uniform.

Lon turning to face the room, barking, "Fuck. All. Y'all!"

Then he was gone.

Billy unruffled, coming out of his office. Picking up the KBI report from the desk in the bullpen. Feeling all eyes upon him.

Cookie having the nerve and the seniority to speak up. "What was that all about?"

"I just fired Lon," Billy said, his eyes lingering on the report before looking up at his staff. "Don't think he liked it very much."

Nine

An oversized six-by-three-foot mirror rested on the painted hardwood floor. The mirror framed in mahogany and leaning against the wall of what in the 1920s was the bedroom of the middle daughter of the wealthiest farmer in Wheaton County.

Billy thinking that only goes to show you how much things can change Billy trying to steal a tactful glimpse of himself in the mirror.

Checking that his hair wasn't sticking up all funny as he sat in that one-time bedroom but at a dinner table, intimate, draped with a white tablecloth.

The magnificent Victorian farmhouse now converted into a restaurant. Billy seated across from Paige on the upstairs floor of The Oasis.

Finally catching a sly glimpse of himself and struck with a vain relief. Damn, he actually looked pretty good.

Didn't need a magic mirror to tell him how good Paige looked tonight.

Billy still having a hard time wrapping his head around little Paige Figures all grown up. Thinking right here, across the table, sipping a glass of white wine, sits living proof of our ever-changing world.

"Kinda neat how they turned this big old house into

a restaurant," Billy said, matching her with a pull from his green bottle of beer.

Kinda neat? Billy embarrassed by his lame conversation. Thankful Paige was polite enough to cover for him, agreeing enthusiastically, yes, it was very neat.

Billy wondering how much time she'd give him to either make a good impression or eliminate himself altogether. Maybe his time was already up.

Maybe she was just sticking around for the free meal and because he had driven and because she was a polite person.

Earlier, when Billy picked her up, she'd greeted him at the door with a smile. One word popping into his head at the sight of her: *Delicious*.

Dark curls down on her shoulders, carrying herself well in her black sweater and jeans, hitting a perfect note of casual but nicely put together.

Billy, in his jeans and sport coat and white dress shirt, feeling a little overdressed but glad of it. Better than being under-dressed, giving Paige the impression he was taking her for granted.

Before they left, he'd gone in to say hello to Paige's mother. Surprised at Julie looking better than expected, though he wasn't sure exactly what he expected.

Vicky was there too, a friend of Paige's mother. She and Julie about to sit down at the kitchen table for an evening of cutthroat dominoes. An unspoken understanding in the room that Vicky was there to watch Julie while Paige was out for the evening. Maybe not necessary at this point, but it would allow Paige to truly step out in both body and mind for an evening.

On the drive over to Eden from Caulfield, their conversation had kicked off swiftly. Only a few awkward pauses during the twenty minutes riding high in his sheriff's Escalade.

Billy driving and listening to her voice. Glancing back and forth between the two-lane black top and her warm brown eyes. Thinking how nice it was seeing her as she was now, not a little kid anymore.

It was a bonus that they didn't have to start from scratch, Billy decided. The two of them sharing a slim history, acquaintances since the days when the few years difference between them might as well have been a lifetime.

Then both had gotten out of town for a while. They had followed dissimilar paths away from Caulfield so now they both had something fresh to talk about.

And, of course, their separate paths had led them

both back to town. And together.

"Hope you didn't mind the drive over," Billy said, fiddling with his silverware on the table, giving give his hands something to do. No matter where he put them – folded on the table, in his lap, at his side – his hands felt meaty and out of place. "Thought it might be nice to get out of Caulfield for while."

"You're embarrassed to be seen with me in public, aren't you?" Paige said.

"What? No!" Billy putting up his hands and even that feeling odd. Resting them back on the white table cloth. "I just thought—"

"—Relax, I'm kidding," Paige said. "You're too easy, Billy Keene."

"You might be right about that," Billy said.

"Seriously, thanks for bringing me here," Paige said. "Everyone's always saying how great this place is. I've been meaning to get over, try it out."

"Well, I hope you like it," Billy said. "Good food, quiet place. We might actually get to have a conversation. Back in Caulfield, I doubt we'd go more than a minute or two without an interruption."

Paige with a quizzical look on her face, unclear on what he meant.

Billy saying, you know, people stopping by the table to say hello, asking how he was doing, how the job was going?

"Interesting," Paige said. "A big baseball star such as yourself, I assumed you would be used to the limelight. Sign a lot of autographs?"

"Not many," Billy said, checking to make sure she was only teasing. "No harm in being neighborly. I mean, I do work for them. But eventually they always get around to asking if I could look into something for them. Noisy neighbor. An unkempt yard. A funky smell coming from next door."

"Heavy hangs the head," Paige said.

Billy nodding, not sure what she meant but playing like he did. Rescued by their server stopping by to take their order; mushroom risotto for Paige, filet mignon and smashed Yukon Gold potatoes for Billy.

After the server left, Paige saying, "So rough day?"

"I guess. Odd, anyway. A little bit of crazy here and there. Plus I had to let Lon go."

"You did?"

Billy nodding. "He's been over the line for some time now. Least as far as I'm concerned. I'm sure he'll take it to the county commission, see if they feel the same about it.

That's his right."

"That must have been hard, firing him."

"Don't want to give you the wrong idea, it was ultimately harder on him than me. Didn't think it would be all that hard. But it really was. Even though, I'm serious, he's been nothing but a dick to me since I took over."

Billy catching Paige's blurred reflection in his knife as he buttered the bread their server had left.

"But yeah," Billy went on, "it was hard. Taking away a person's livelihood. He's a little obnoxious, sure. But you get right down to it Lon's not a bad guy. Really does enjoy the job, even if he doesn't always go about it the right way. But some things...I don't know, you just can't let them slide. Someone once told me never to pass up a legitimate reason to fire someone. Because it will always come back to bite you in the ass."

"Sagacious advice," Paige said.

"We'll see," Billy said. Then briefly lost in thought, a quick rewind of the whole strange day playing in his mind.

Paige noticing him gone off for a moment, saying. "You okay?"

Billy nodding, ready to change the subject. "Oh, meant to tell you, you have fans up in Topeka?"

Billy relaying the KBI's compliment on her pictures

of the scene at Patty's car.

Paige playing it humble, like *oh. those old things?*

"Still, I'll take a compliment wherever I can get it," she said. "Especially if it will get me out of a speeding ticket the next time the highway patrol pulls me over. Recognize me, officer? It's me, the Diane Arbus of crime scene photography."

Before he could stop himself and fake it, Billy asking who?

Paige, laughing, saying yeah that's probably the same reaction she'd get from a highway patrolman.

"So what's up with Patty and all that?" Paige said. "She turn up yet? That is, if you can talk about it. Not sure why but something just felt, I don't know, not right about things out there."

"Good instincts," Billy said. "Officially I can't talk about it. But between you and me, I can't talk about it because, honestly, I still have no idea what's going on."

"Yet," Paige said, smiling.

Billy liking how she stated it like a fact rather than a question. Billy telling Paige he's glad she has confidence in him and his department.

Paige saying what other choice did she and the tax-paying residents of Caste County have?

Making a joke, but the truth in it burrowing into Billy. Again Billy changing the subject. Telling Paige that her mom seemed in good spirits.

"Good days," Paige said. "Others less so. Doctors say it's still early. Takes time to heal."

"It was pretty bad, huh?" Billy said.

Paige nodding, looking down.

"It's better now though," Billy said. "She's on the mend. She's got you looking after her."

Billy pausing before the next part, making sure it was the right time.

"And it's good to see you."

Paige blushing. A sip of wine for something to do. Then that smile again.

"Good to see you too, Billy."

Everything much looser from that point on. Conversation less self-conscious, coming easier.

Sharing an artichoke fritter appetizer, the golden puffs crispy and savory. Their main courses layered with flavor. Their eyes flashing with interest, lips wet with wine.

Both Billy and Paige leaving behind their day and escaping to an uncharted borderland where their worlds intersected.

Making it all the way to coffee and a shared slice of

key lime pie for dessert before finally being interrupted.

A couple coming up the stairs from the first floor, a lean, rugged-faced man and his striking wife. The two of them comfortably middle-aged in a way that made people who witnessed them, if not look forward to that time of life, at least feel less afraid of its inevitability.

"See you decided to come over for a real steak," the man said, stopping with a hand on the banister of the stairs as he spotted Billy.

"Otis, be nice," the woman with the man said. Smiling brightly, gently touching her husband on the arm.

"Just stating a fact," the man said, as the couple made their way toward Billy and Paige to say hello.

Billy grinning, then standing as he introduced Paige to Otis Cady, sheriff of Eden County, and his wife, Elaine. Otis telling Billy to sit and Billy doing so.

The four of them chatting for a moment about the food and the restaurant before the Cadys proceeded to their table in a back bedroom. Before he left, Otis Cady suggesting he and Billy have coffee the following week.

Then offering a teasing bit of advice for Paige, make sure Billy picks up the check.

"He's been known to forget his wallet," Otis said.

"Otis, for heaven's sake, let them alone," Elaine said

from the hall, where she was waving at her husband to come on. "Our table's ready."

Billy and Paige hearing him say, "Where the hell are we sitting, in the bathroom?" as he followed her down the hardwoods of the hallway to their table.

"He's a character," Paige said. "Is he who I think he is? The deal with woman everybody thought was already dead? A few years ago?"

"That's the one," Billy said.

Paige remarking that Billy and Sheriff Otis Cady seemed to get along well. Billy agreeing, mentioning that they had coffee from time to time.

"Sort of a mentoring-type situation, I guess you could say," Billy said. "He's seen a lot, been around awhile. Told me he started as sheriff here when he was about the same age as me."

"That was smart of you, hooking up with him," Paige said. "I'm guessing maybe you like the job more than you let on?"

"No need to read into it," Billy said, shaking his head. "He reached out to me. Having been in my shoes, he said it would be helpful for me to have someone to talk it out with. Said it like that. Not a question and do I agree but just the truth, plain and simple, no argument. Said to consider it his payback to Big Jim for the listening and all his advice over the years."

"How's that working out for you?" Paige said.

"Well, it was him that told me never to pass up a chance to fire someone who's asking for it," Billy said. "So we'll see."

Ten

"**Where the hell** you been?"

Pearce hopping up off the couch to meet Sharla coming through the door. Not even a knock, just hip checking it open like she lived there. Seven hours since he'd heard from her.

She'd called to tell him they had the money but he needs to call Arlita and act like they didn't. Sharla promising to explain everything when she got there.

Now finally showing up, looking like shit and lugging four purses and two overnight bags in his apartment.

Pearce closed the door behind her. "What's with all the gear?"

Sharla ignoring him, putting the purses and bags on the bar in his kitchen. Instead, asking him if he'd called Arlita like he'd been told.

"Done. Went fine. I started off all pissed like you said. By the end I thought she might actually thank me for giving her more time. So she knows about switching the money?"

"Yeah, but Horace says not to worry. He'll handle it."

"How?"

"Fuck do I know how? That's the old buzzard's problem," Sharla said. "Look here."

Sharla fanning her hand across the purses and bags displayed on the bar, a game show hostess presenting a contestant with what he might win, if he's lucky.

Pearce saying great, very nice. But so what?

Sharla waving him closer to have a look inside.

Pearce not playing along. "Just tell me what's with all the bags?"

"Get your ass over here," Sharla said, pulling him by the hand.

Opening one of the purses for him, a black leather one outlined with heavy white stitching. At first Pearce's face wrinkled in confusion.

Sharla flicking him on the dangling loop in his

earlobe.

"It's the money, dumbass. Our money"

Now Pearce's face growing eager as he unzipped and pulled open another purse, then one of the overnight bags, the one with the garish, flowery design in pink and green.

"This all f it?" Pearce said. "Seems way short?"

"No, just some of it," Sharla said. "Horace let me take it. Show us we could trust him for the rest of it."

"But there's money in all these bags, right?"

Sharla giggling now that he was finally as excited as she was.

"Yeah, except the one with the gold studs on it. Fake gold, though. I asked the salesgirl if they had any with real gold but they didn't. She called it faux gold but I call it fake."

Pearce confused now. Asking Sharla where she got them.

"At the outlet malls," Sharla said.

Pearce thinking this over. Asking Sharla *when* she got them.

"On the way up to see you, baby."

Sharla rummaging around in the large black purse with the fake gold studs.

Pearce thinking, must be her new everyday purse.

Or maybe just her This Day purse.

"So in the middle of a kidnapping, one that's not going exactly to plan," Pearce said, "you decide it makes sense to go on a little shopping spree?"

"Not like I can't afford it."

"I don't know what's worse," Pearce said, shaking his head. "You stopping to shop, or that you went to an outlet mall and bought cheap. Ever hear of Nordstrom's?"

"Yeah, I heard of it," Sharla said, a defensive edge in her voice. "I can buy that whole hoity-toity shitbox now if I want."

Pearce giving her a sure thing, you bet smile even though she never looked up from her purse.

Considering how messed up Sharla looked, her herky-jerky movements, Pearce figured it was probably a good thing she hadn't gone upscale. A gaunt, jittery bitch of a drug addict flashing cash might stick out.

Unless of course she was gaunt from Pilates and diet and the drug was Klonopin backed by a legit prescription. Then it was, "Would you like to sign up for our customer loyalty program?"

A good time to change the subject, so Pearce asking what comes next?

"We party!" Sharla said.

Sharla pulling a freezer bag of blush chunks from another purse, this one brown leather. Her mood brightening now just as quickly as it had darkened before.

Jumping up and moving in close to Pearce. Holding up the baggie for his viewing pleasure.

"No, I mean with her." Pearce nodding in the direction of the apartment across the complex where Patty was stashed. "What's the plan?"

"Oh, she's invited to the party," Sharla said. "Trust me."

Pearce a little turned off by the funk coming from Sharla. "You probably want to shower, huh?"

Sharla giggling, giving him a mischievous look.

"What? Don't care for my natural aromas?"

Sharla rubbing up against him like a stray cat.

"I think you just marked me with your musk," Pearce said.

His eyes landing on the baggie she now held against her shoulder like a newborn. He'd managed to come down from their last party while Sharla was gone. Got some sleep, cleaned up. Got right. But he couldn't deny that his mouth was watery with excitement.

Pearce taking the bag from Sharla and tossing it on the counter. Pushing her into the bathroom. Watching her strip while he ran the shower for her. Her collar bones jutting out beneath her skin. Starting to lose some heft in her boobs. Skin taut over her knobby knees.

Pearce thinking she's still attractive but, she keeps this up, not for much longer. Did she even realize that, one way or another, this would all end soon?

"So really," Pearce said, speaking to Sharla's naked form, obscured and distorted by the shower door's frosted plexiglass, "what about the package across the way?"

"Horace says let her go," Sharla said over the running water. "Make it like she escaped on her own."

"When, before or after we collect the second ransom?"

Sharla rinsing her hair under the shower head, suddenly freezing in place. Then cursing.

"I didn't even think of that! You know, I bet that son of a bitch is going to double-dip Arlita, cut me out of it."

"You?"

"You know what I mean," Sharla said. "Us, baby."

"Really think that's what he's up to?"

Sharla turning off the water, opening the door and signaling for a towel. Saying she wouldn't put anything past Horace.

"No idea what that short fucker's planning to pull

out of his ass," she said, wrapping the towel around her, "but I'll find out."

"So when do we let her go?" Pearce said.

"Horace told us to let her go." Sharla signaling to Pearce for another towel to wrap her hair. "But he didn't' say when we had to let her go. I say it's fucking gravy time."

"Gravy time?"

"Look it, we got some money. We got our full shares on the way. Maybe even more than that if that old man's really going to hit up Arlita a second time."

Sharla with her damp hair up in a towel turban now, water drops on her shoulders, slinking up to Pearce.

"And we got our squeak toy all tied up and ready to be played with. In my book, that's gravy."

Sharla planting a deep, hungry kiss on Pearce. Her tongue excavating the back of his mouth.

Then Sharla pulling away, telling Pearce to go fetch her new purse.

"Which one?"

"The black with the faux gold. Faux sure," she said. "And grab that bag of Go Fast too."

Pearce doing as he was told, almost dropping the large purse when he pulled it from the counter. Asking her what was in it that was so heavy. Handing her the purse.

Sharla set it on the back of the toilet. Reaching in, pulling out a curling iron and a clothes iron. Holding them up for Pearce to see alongside the bag of blue meth in her other hand.

Pearce's wide eyes bouncing between dope and the irons held up by their cords like rats by the tail.

Sharla making a show of inspecting them both. Coughing out her raspy laugh before saying, "This party's about to heat the fuck up, baby."

Eleven

Billy licking his lips, the traces of scotch there woody, biting. Drinking it neat, taking another sip.

Alone and leaning forward on the edge of his couch. His house sat just outside of town and was still, both inside and out, with a quiet that can only be found in the country.

Replaying his evening in his head. He and Paige having so much fun doing just routine things like eating, driving and talking. Always talking. Conversation seemed to come easy for them. Not much else to do in a small town but get to know one another.

Less than half an hour before, he'd dropped her off at home.

Now Billy found himself resisting the urge to call her. Wanting to hear that voice of hers again. Long time since he'd felt anything so strong as this.

Another sip from the rocks glass of 15-year-old single malt. A Christmas gift for Billy every year since turning twenty-one. A man's gift, giving or getting.

This made Billy laugh because he knew it was his mother who actually bought it, wrapped it and put his father's name on it.

Billy thinking back to the quick, good night kiss with Paige. It was nice, no doubt. But it was the embrace that got him. Being so close to her, the scent of her hair, the reality of her body against his.

Billy had been around enough to know that just because it felt like the real thing in the beginning didn't necessarily mean it would turn out to be that in the end.

Certainly didn't mean it didn't feel nice when it was happening though. And definitely didn't necessarily mean it *wouldn't* turn out to be the real thing either.

Only one way to find out.

Billy glancing at the cordless telephone on his coffee table, wondering if it was too late to call. Instead opting to send another swallow of scotch burning down his throat and into his chest. Feeling that comforting warmth trickle somewhere inside him near his heart.

Thinking what an interesting day all the way around. This job of his starting to feel like it *was* his. Like he was a new goddamn man.

Tomorrow he would pay another visit to Arlita. Beyond figuring out what was going on with Patty, he'd also poke around and try to find out just why Horace was in the middle of things all of a sudden.

Poke gently though. Billy knowing there was more than a little truth to Horace's advice.

But that was tomorrow. There were still a couple of hours left in today, and Billy couldn't tear his thoughts away from Paige. Didn't want to.

"Hell with it," Billy said. He leaned forward, picking up the phone.

But before he could dial the number of the young woman he was pretty sure he was in love with, he was distracted by the sound of a car turning off the road and into his drive.

Billy getting up to look out the window. A pair of headlights creeping down his drive toward his house. For a moment tempted to believe that it might be Paige.

Flipping on his porch light for his visitor. Recognizing the car, and Billy's heart sinking more than a little.

Billy thinking what the hell does she want?

Opening his front door as his ex-girlfriend climbed the three steps up to his wooden porch. The two of them talking through the storm door screen.

"Hi, Billy," Tina said.

Billy knowing her so well that he could tell by the way she said his name, the way she sidled onto his porch, the firmness in her jaw, that she'd been drinking. Still, Billy asking her so it would be out in the open.

"Yep, been drinking. Ain't drunk though," Tina said. "Not that drunk anyway. Going to invite me in?"

"I don't know, Tina," Billy said, trying to soften his next words with a smile. "Seems like every time we bump into one another, all you want to do is insult me. Unless you're drunk—then you just want to knock me upside my head."

"Like I said, I'm not drunk, I'm not sober. So let me in," Tina said. "Let's find out what I do to you when I'm in between."

Billy standing there considering it.

Taking longer than Tina liked so she opened the

storm door herself.

Billy stepping back to let her in.

"Where's Cody?" Billy said. "You know, your boyfriend."

"Out. Boy's night," Tina said. Giving Billy's living room the once over. "They all probably went over to the casino."

Tina, still wearing her suede jacket. Noticing the glass of scotch on the coffee table. Picking it up and taking a sip. Shivering as it went down.

"Mmm, damn that's good. Drinking from the top shelf, tonight huh?"

"That's what it's for, I guess."

Tina giving him a heavy-lidded stare. "Think you're hot shit, don't you Billy?"

"Okay, time for you to go," Billy said.

Starting for the door but careful not to touch her. "Not sure you should drive, though. I'll give you a ride home."

"I'm not going anywhere with you," Tina said. "Drove myself here and when I go I'll drive away myself."

"What do you want, Tina?" Billy said. "It's getting late, and I got a busy day tomorrow."

"I want to know why you dumped me, goddamn it."

Billy sighing, looking around. Telling her they'd been over all that and she knew it. It was something he had to do. At the time, where he was in life. He'd needed to focus all his energy on baseball. It took all he had to compete at that level.

Billy saying it was a terrible thing, breaking up with her like that. But it was done. And again and forever, he was sorry.

"But you're back," Tina said. "So what's your excuse now?"

"I don't know," Billy said. "Things change, I guess. People change."

"Not around here they don't," Tina said. "Folks won't let you."

"So don't let them not let you," Billy said.

Tina smirked at Billy. Shaking her head before taking another sip of his scotch. Telling him, you'll see.

Tina setting the glass on the table and peeling off her jacket. Bending over the coffee table to fill the glass halfway with the amber liquid.

Bringing the glass to Billy, who was still waiting by the door to escort her out. Handing him the glass.

"Don't tell me you don't miss it," she said.

"Miss what?" Billy taking the glass.

"Us." Tina looking up at him with drunk, coaxing eyes. "How we used to be."

Billy saying sometimes, sure. Finally taking another sip. "But that was then."

Tina agreeing, nodding. Yep, it sure was. Then reaching out her hand, running a finger over the top of his jeans.

"And this is now. Right. Fucking. Now."

Almost every voice in Billy's head telling him to back away. Almost.

One voice full of a bravado that covered up a fear of looking weak.

Another voice compliant, reminding him of his obligation to play the roles expected of him.

Yet another voice nothing more than a lustful animalistic growl echoing from the base of his brain.

All these voices conspiring to keep him in place.

It was only later, lying naked in bed and watching Tina dress to leave, that Billy would have to admit it was his choice to let the voices trap him.

Feeling like his old self again.

Letting things happen to him. Not liking it one bit.

"I don't regret this, Billy. Don't you either." Tina said, hooking up her bra behind her back. Knowing him well enough, able to read everything by the look on his face. "Don't mean we got to tell Cody though."

"You okay to drive?" Billy said.

"I'm good. Told you I'd drive myself when I left." Tina always so determined like that.

Billy walked her into the living room, a blanket wrapped around him. Wondering what this meant to her. What it meant to him. Again, Tina reading the look on his face.

"See you around," Tina said. "Not like this though. One-time deal here. Ever happens again, it's because we're together."

"And Cody?"

"He's got his good points. Things are smooth with us. We get along. But who knows where it'll go? Only one way to find out, right?"

Billy nodded, smiling at a private thought. "Yeah, I was just thinking that."

"Won't lie to you, I'd like us being together again," Tina said. "If things worked out a certain way. But only if you did too. That's how it works, ain't it?"

"That's what they tell me," Billy said.

Just then the telephone ringing. Billy and Tina both turning to look at the phone on the coffee table. Another ring.

Billy walking over, picking it up. Checking the number, recognizing Paige's cell number.

His heart jumping at first, then sinking as he came back to where he was, who he was with and what had just happened.

"Calling after midnight, it must be awful important," Tina said.

Billy setting the phone back on the coffee table, and walking Tina all the way to the door. "I'll talk to them tomorrow."

Tina turning, checking the clock on his wall. Using that smoky voice, saying, "Billy, it is tomorrow."

Friday

One

A buzzing sound going off somewhere near Patty's ear, close enough to scare her awake. Eyelash crusted shut with dried tears, straining behind her blindfold before finally forcing themselves open.

It had been a long night.

Only darkness behind her blindfold, but Patty thought it might be morning. Hoping it was. For once, she did not try to move her blindfold to see. After three short bursts, the buzzing near her ear stopped.

Patty lying there, tied to her prison of a bed, thankful to finally be left alone. Patty on a sliding scale of wants and needs now. To be left alone, that's all she wanted. Go home, yes. To live, yes. But just to be left alone, that was enough for the moment.

No pressing urge to use the bathroom. But knowing

that when the need arose she would not hesitate to go right there on her mattress, on herself.

It had been a crushing night.

It had started with music. Some hard-beat, death growl metal noise. Coming through the tinny speakers of a cheap sound system.

Both of Them were there, Him and Her. For the first time Patty had heard Her speak.

Patty not recognizing the woman's voice. Could tell the woman was young though and there was something about her disguise of a stage whisper seeming familiar to Patty.

Then Patty had felt Them around her and heard the usual electronic beep, like something being put on record. Patty thinking a video camera, maybe.

Then Him and Her randomly touching Patty, gentle at first, but soon turning into pinches here and there. Then slaps. And sick and sickening laughter. Another beep, the recording stopped.

More movement before Patty was left alone. Over the death metal, Patty had been able to make out an argument between Him and Her in another room. Something about extension cords. Why didn't He have any? Which of Them would go buy some?

A door closing as one of them left, the other staying behind.

Her.

Patty recognizing Her by the nails as they dug into Patty's flesh. Hers were longer than His.

Now three more short buzzes exploding in the early morning, and Patty jerking her head as far away as her bindings would allow. The hum coming from below the bed, on the floor. Again the buzzing stopped after three beats.

Patty lay still in fearful contemplation. Was it an electric razor? An electric carving knife? She'd learned to fear anything electric now. Didn't matter what device it might be and its intended use—she knew now that if it could be plugged in, it could cause pain.

Last night, after He returned with the cords, was when it had really turned ugly. Patty had heard the electronic beep again. The death metal music had grown louder.

Then the whoosh of a lighter, the bitter smell of smoke filling the room. Someone blowing in her face, and Patty choking on second-hand smoke.

Then came The Heat.

To Patty it was just that, The Heat. Random and

remorseless.

They'd made small burns on her body in places outside and in. Patty had choked on the odor of her own singed body hair and blistering skin. Her screams muffled by her gag, drowned out by hammering beats and awful growling anti-melodies.

Then the worst of it, Him and Her climbing atop Patty. The two of them moaning with pleasure while Patty groaned in pain. Their writing bodies tormenting the seared patches of her flesh. Tears flooding Patty's eyes.

Eventually, He and She had left Patty alone, and the tears had dried. But only after a long night.

The three buzzes again near Patty's ear, sending her heart racing with fear. The buzzing stopped. Patty holding still, terrified.

It would go on like this for most of the morning, Sharla's cell phone – the one she was using for the job and that had accidentally fallen to the floor near Patty's bed – exploding with three buzzing bursts, signaling yet another urgent text message from Chubba.

And each time the noise jump starting Patty's heart with panic.

Two

Billy sitting at the counter at Trace's Place, wondering how long it takes to cook up some French toast?

Fingers looped around the handle of a white cup, sipping his coffee. Reading over yesterday afternoon's *Caulfield Pioneer*. Checking his phone again on the off chance he'd received a text message or email since checking it a few minutes before.

Just something to do. Anything to keep him from listening to the chatter going back and forth at a high volume around him. Nothing blocking it out, though.

The regulars packed the café this morning. Among the ones Billy was trying to ignore were Gil the tow truck driver, Kenny the city manager, Anthony and Marvin in matching blue uniforms and, of course, Dogpatch.

It was as if someone had called a town hall meeting for the expressed purpose of scattering rumors like fertilizer.

At the moment they were debating Gil's hypothesis that Patty had been run off the road and snatched up by federal agents in a silent, black helicopter. Not just stealth but *completely* silent.

Gil had been very adamant about this part of his story. *"Think the Feds don't have 'em? Get your head out of your hiney!"*

All this was done, Gil said, in retaliation for her grandmother's refusal to pay taxes on her lottery winnings. Billy having to stop himself from pointing out those taxes were deducted long before Arlita ever received a dime.

Not wanting to get in the middle of it. Besides, why let the truth get in the way of a juicy rumor?

"That just might be the most asinine thing I ever heard."

Billy, no need to look up to see who was talking, recognizing it was Anthony.

"Well now, there's no call to get all foul-mouthed about it." Gil said, his bald head growing redder the more people discounted his idea.

Not only was he annoyed that his idea wasn't accepted at face value but he was offended by what he assumed was profanity. Gil never cursed. What's more, he was intolerant of other people's vulgarity. That did not motivate people to clean up their mouths around him. Made it worse, in fact.

"You know asinine ain't a cuss word, right?" Marvin said. Standing up for his business partner, Anthony.

"Course I do," Gil said.

The cafe instantly quiet, everyone waiting for it.

"Okay, not really."

At that, the café exploding with laughter.

"I promise you, Gil, it's just a regular old word-word," Marvin said. "Means dumb as shit."

Laughter roaring even louder.

All this noise around Billy taking his mind off the previous evening. At least, until it didn't.

Every time he blocked out their rumor mongering, started floating atop pleasant thoughts about his date with Paige, his conscience would sweep him under with a reminder about his late-night hook up with Tina.

Billy scolding himself. *Really fucked yourself into a corner this time, bozo.*

Then to get his mind off how stupid he felt, Billy would grab on to a jagged branch of the idiot conversation around him. That made him feel a little better. Until it didn't.

Eventually the talk would get to be too much for him and it was back to thoughts of Paige.

The past fifteen minutes spent going back and forth like this up in his head.

Someone tossed out the idea that maybe Patty was

taken as payback for Mona's drug debts.

Dogpatch picking up this thread of kidnapping, but weaving it into a story that involved casino debts and the Indian Mafia.

Everyone conveniently overlooking the fact that Arlita, being the wealthiest person in the county — maybe the entire state — could easily pay off any gambling debts.

Kenny, the city manager, wondering aloud why they would be called a mafia? Because they run casinos? As Indians or Native Americans or what have you, shouldn't they be just like braves or warriors or something?

Billy thinking, so that's where the Indian Mafia theory falls apart for you? What name they go by? Looking around, again wondering just how goddamn long it takes to make French toast?

Seeing Trace standing at the far end of the counter rather than where he should be, back in the kitchen cooking. Standing up close to Tippy, the waitress. The both of them carrying on a side conversation with a customer, John Hawkins, one of Caulfield's three chiropractors.

Billy catching Tippy saying something about "maybe they should bring in a psychic."

Billy dismayed, shaking his head. Wanting to get up, walk around the counter and put a size-twelve cowboy boot sideways up Trace's ass for being out front gossiping rather than back in the kitchen fixing his French Toast. And for nodding in agreement with Tippy just because he was sleeping with her.

Trace knowing just as well as Billy who Tippy meant when she said "they." The authorities. The law. Him.

Billy thinking here it comes. Telling him how to do his job.

Suggestions on what he should have done.

Recommendations on what he should do.

Soon, all around him there would be talk of sniffer dogs and CSI, like on those TV shows. Putting together a search party.

Or maybe a posse. That would fit right in with the town's vestiges from its frontier days and Old West ways. But rather than a posse on horseback, now running amok on all-terrain vehicles.

Billy thinking it was time to leave. Looking to see if the coast was clear for him to slip out the front door.

Too late. Seeing a dark blue, duel-axel truck whip into in an empty spot in front of the café. Billy recognizing it as Cody's vehicle.

Cody stumbling into the café. Billy not sure if Cody was drunk or tired or both, but definitely looking rode hard and put away wet.

Billy turning back around to the counter, not wanting to let his eyes linger on Cody. Afraid to give away anything about last night with a look.

Another sip of coffee and not needing to look to know that Cody was now standing behind him. No one else seeming to notice as they carried on conversations around him.

"Ats it. Iss time. Less go."

Billy knowing he was the person Cody was talking to and even able to understand what Cody was saying through his thick slur.

Billy turning on his stool to face Cody. Wonder just what, if anything, Cody knew about last night.

"Long night, Cody?"

"Went to the casinos. But it ain't over. C'mon, I'mma kick your ass."

"Right here? Right now?" Billy said.

The place quiet now. Everyone watching.

"Thing is, I'm waiting on some French toast." Billy pausing to look over at Trace. "Been waiting awhile, in fact"

"Be tough to chew with no teef," Cody said.

"Guess I better eat before you knock them out then,

don't you think?"

Cody a little confused, trying to follow Billy's logic. Losing some of the wind in his sails.

Billy taking the break in the confrontation to suggest some coffee, maybe something to eat. Picking up a menu off the counter and handing it to Cody.

"Eggs are good as always."

Cody's face turning pale at the mention of eggs. Crashing hard now. Standing there wavering like the ground under him was moving.

"Shoub sit dowmb." Cody reaching out a hand, falling forward toward Billy.

Billy standing, catching Cody before he went all the way down.

"Okay, time to go home," Billy said. He propped up Cody with an arm around his shoulder as if they were buddies. "I was just leaving anyway."

"You going to let him drive, Billy?" Kenny said. "He's in no shape."

"No, Kenny, you're right about that. Definitely in no shape to drive."

Billy remembering Cody parking in front of the café. Not sure if anyone else saw him pull up behind the wheel. Billy going on, loud enough so everyone could hear.

"You know, it was good of your friends to drive you home this morning."

Cody looking up at him, even more confused.

"I mean, if you had driven," Billy said. "I'd have had to arrest you, driving under the influence and all. But your friends did you right, dropping you off back at your truck out front there."

Cody still not understanding what exactly was going on, and Billy knowing there was more going on than Cody needed to know.

Billy figuring it was the least he could do for the guy, considering. Not really sure if he was doing it for Cody or his own guilt.

"Come on, I'll drive you," Billy said, dragging Cody toward the door. "Was just fixing to leave anyway. Can't wait around all morning for French Toast that's never coming."

Three

Chubba driving like a madman up the interstate toward Kansas City.

Dressed comfortably for his road trip, jeans and a black t-shirt with the sleeves cut off. Wearing his one-of-a-kind running shoes that he'd custom designed on a web site. Red, gold and white with black accents. Chief's colors but could have been McDonald's.

One chunky hand on the wheel, sausage fingers of the other checking his cell phone for a text back from Sharla. Must have sent twenty messages to her personal cell this morning and not a word back from her.

Chubba thinking something's not right up in KC. On the road about half an hour now since deciding to find out just what the hell was going on up there.

Driving his daddy's Cadillac because Sharla had taken Chubba's Mustang, left him with her Pontiac. Chubba doubtful that heap of bolts on bald tires would survive the trip.

Horace wasn't around when Chubba went to ask his permission to take the Caddy. Tammy saying Horace was on his morning walk with the dogs. Surveying the land, he called it.

With his mind all made up, Chubba didn't feel like waiting around. His daddy might be gone "surveying" for an hour or more.

And Chubba damn sure not about to ask *her*

permission to take *his* daddy's car. Not bothering to tell Tammy where he was going either. She didn't know anything about anything, but even if she did, as far as Chubba was concerned, it was none of that bitch's business.

So he'd taken the Caddy. Hadn't asked, just took it.

Driving and listening to sports talk radio out of Kansas City. Getting the occasional direction command from the lady's voice on the GPS. Chubba forgot to grab his own music before he left, in a hurry once he decided to leave.

Now only half-paying attention to a sports radio host in love with the sound of his own voice. The endlessly coming up with topics, slanting them one way to give everyone something to argue about. The callers calling up to point out the obvious.

Tooling along the interstate estimating how mad his daddy might get. But knowing that Horace would get over it. His daddy always getting over anything Chubba did.

Better remember to clean out the fast-food breakfast wrappers and the paper sack rolling around the passenger floorboard though. Otherwise Horace would be pissed about that too, the mess and the lingering smell of grease. But Chubba not worrying too much about that either at the moment.

More concerned about what he would find when he reached Kansas City.

First thought was that she was cheating on him. That had been nagging at him for some time now. Even in a sober state, Sharla wasn't the most faithful of girlfriends.

Chubba not sure why he put up with it. She just had him in a way. When she paid attention to him, she made it seem like he was the only person in the world. It felt great and he felt great.

She had him in a way he couldn't shake free of. At least he hadn't been able to yet.

But this, if she *was* cheating with this Pearce freakshow, this might push Chubba over the edge.

Chubba wondering aloud just who does this Pearce fucker think he is anyway? All the tats and holes in the guy's skin? What kind of person does that to himself? Either sad or twisted or a funky cocktail of both.

If Pearce was half the twisted-fuck-badass-criminal he claimed to be, then maybe Sharla was in trouble.

Chubba feeling guilty now for suspecting maybe she was cheating. Thinking that if Pearce had hurt her, Chubba was going to jack him up even worse than if they were just messing around behind his back.

Chubba staying in the left lane, reminding himself to

bring it down around the speed limit. Getting pulled over was that last thing he needed right now.

There was no question Sharla was in trouble. Whatever he might find in KC – them cheating or Pearce out of line or everything fine – there were still the drugs.

Chubba noticing how the drugs had gotten hold of her lately. Not pretty. Chubba promising himself that when this was all over, he'd get Sharla some help.

Chubba passing a sign indicating the next exit had a rest stop with gas and food. Despite having eaten two breakfast sandwiches as he pulled out of Caulfield less than an hour before, Chubba felt an emptiness in his stomach. His mouth began to water.

Chubba easing the Caddy over into the right lane, breaking and then guiding the vehicle along the curve of the exit ramp.

There was no restaurant, only a grubby little gas station not doing much business other than an old farmer pumping gas into his pickup truck. Chubba, okay on gas, parked and went inside the gas station.

Coming through the door, announced by the ding of an electronic bell. The heavy-set girl behind the register not saying a word.

She was around Chubba's age. Didn't even look up

from the cell phone in her hand. Just kept on tapping at her phone with fat fingers as Chubba made his way down an aisle of salty snacks.

Chubba scanning the shelves. Stopping to check his phone again, hoping for a message from Sharla. Nothing.

Chubba laid out two bags of BBQ corn nuts, a giant soda and three different candy bars on the counter. Finally, the girl putting aside her cell phone and stepping up to the register.

Chubba getting a little embarrassed now at buying all this junk food. Caught himself eating a lot like he used to lately. All that crap he ate back before he got a handle on it. Aware that stress was causing him to reach for empty calories, saturated fats and sugars. Promising himself he'd get back on track once everything was back to normal.

"Breakfast of champions," Chubba said to the girl, trying to make a joke of his purchases.

The girl not looking at him, just giving off a courtesy smirk and a grunting murmur as she scanned his items and rang up the total.

Chubba running his card through the reader and surprised at just how pissed off he was that this girl wouldn't look at him. Like she was something special. Like he wasn't.

The girl dropping his junk food in a plastic bag. Not handing it to him, leaving it on the counter for him to pick up. Already back at her cell phone.

Chubba standing there, slurping his soda, watching her work her phone. Eventually the girl feeling his eyes on her, finally looking up at him.

"Need something else?" She said. Not helpful, but like a smart-ass.

The door dinging behind Chubba as the farmer came in to pay for his gas.

"Well, thank you too," Chubba said to the girl. "And fuck you very much."

With that Chubba turning to make a grand exit but bumping into the farmer. Chubba shoving the old man. Telling him to get the hell out of his way.

Chubba pissed as hell and gunning the Caddy. Getting back on the interstate, speeding toward Kansas City. Going to find out just what the fuck was going on up there.

Four

Arlita finding it difficult to swallow even a tiny bit of bagel, swallowing hard to force the dry crumbs down her throat.

Not hungry and couldn't remember the last time she had been. This whole ordeal finally starting to wear on her.

So tired of everyone looking to her for what they should do next. Tired of running this sorry show. But Arlita knowing she'd never agree with anyone else's choices unless they matched her own.

First round of ransom money vanished. Still unsure what had gone wrong there, but Arlita had an idea. Goddamn if Sharla didn't have something to do with it.

The kidnapper or kidnappers had given Arlita more time to get more money. Getting it together wasn't a problem. But Arlita knowing the delay couldn't be good for her granddaughter.

Afraid to let herself wonder if Patty was still alive.

Taking a sip of coffee to wet her mouth. Arlita thinking maybe it was time to go to the law, let Billy and the KBI handle it. For the moment keeping her own counsel. Not sharing these thoughts with all the people gathered around the small table in her kitchen.

Vic standing by the kitchen door like a sergeant-at-arms. That is, when he wasn't running to the bathroom every five minutes. Looking frail, Arlita thought, but still mean as hell. Muscles and veins in his neck and jaw tightening every few seconds as he checked out the window for whatever might be out there in the clear morning.

Horace sitting to her right, talking in reasonable tones. Arlita surprised by Horace, the way he'd stepped up in a time of need. Volunteering to deliver the second round of ransom money, make sure it made its way to the kidnappers.

At first Arlita was unsure, said the kidnappers might not like it. Horace pointing out they wouldn't give a shit who dropped the money so long as they got their money. Arlita seeing he was right.

Also believing he was right about not watching the second drop. Arlita convinced now that had something to with jinxing it, having Vic stake it out. Horace a smart man, turning out to be a better person than she ever thought he was.

Still a cocky little son of a bitch, and Arlita still not convinced he wasn't trying to get in her pants. But Arlita thinking people can surprise you. Never know what's inside them, what they're capable of.

Mona fidgeting across from her. When she wasn't

outside smoking. Arlita watching her daughter seem to get it now, that this thing was real, not some show for her to act in. Noticing how her daughter constantly looked to Gerald, making sure he was still there. Like she was desperate for her husband's approval.

Gerald hovering in the background, not saying much, recognizing small things that needed to be done, like taking out trash or washing dishes. Doing it all without being asked.

Arlita sitting there wishing her husband wasn't dead, if only so he could tell her what he thought. Didn't mean she'd do what he said; she seldom had. But damn if it wouldn't be nice just to talk with him.

Allowing herself for a moment to indulge in something other than this tragedy. A memory of a vacation they took to the Gulf of Mexico, just the two of them. Tequila, beaches and blue water, jokes about the drinking water and their ample pink bellies.

Arlita jarred back to reality by a knock at the front door. Ashamed for letting her mind wander from the awful present. Like doing so was a betrayal of her grandchild.

Five

Billy coming through the front door and following Vic through the house to the kitchen. Finding everyone gathered around Arlita at the small table in her breakfast nook.

"See you all brought food, "Billy said, "and dour faces. It's like a funeral in here."

"That's not funny," Vic said.

Billy shooting a look at Vic. "Why, did somebody die that I don't know about? If only I had known..."

Vic coiling. "I ought to take you outside."

"Go on out. I'll be out in a second."

Billy noticing how pale Vic looked but not bringing it up. The man was about to pounce on Billy but cut off by Horace.

"See our little conversation yesterday failed to take."

"Hey there, Horace," Billy said. "Running into you two days in a row. Imagine that. Saw your wife's Yukon out there. Tammy here too?"

Horace said no, he was driving it. Leaving it at that, no need to share how he returned from his morning survey of his land to find his son had taken his Cadillac. No idea where, either.

When Billy asked if something was wrong with the Caddy, Horace ignored the question. Instead, Horace pressing Billy on just what they could do for him.

Billy, still hungry from lack of breakfast and eyeing the food on the table, said he wouldn't say no to a bagel. Onion, if they had it, or an everything

Mona pulling an onion bagel from the box on the table, asking Billy if he wanted cream cheese? He did, and she fixed it up with a layer before turning around in her chair to hand it along with a napkin to him.

While Mona was doing all this, Billy telling Arlita he'd come to apologize about yesterday at the DQ. Sorry if he'd been a little too forceful.

"It was just kind of a funny circumstance, is all," Billy said. "Like this too, everyone over here. But I guess it's just me, thinking something's going on when it isn't. My mistake."

Arlita saying it was not a problem and not to worry about it. The woman distracted, missing or ignoring the hint of sarcasm coming from Billy.

"Not to change the subject," Billy said, "but how is Patty, anyway? Heard from her? Really need to get this business with her car straightened out."

Arlita's face flooding with color. "Yeah, the other day

she called."

"Other day?" Billy said.

"Yesterday." Arlita taking a drink of her coffee. "Was yesterday."

"Say when she'd be back in town?"

"Honestly," Arlita said, "I expected her back home by now."

Billy sensing something more in what Arlita said. Not sure what though. It was like her words had clotted the air in the room. Billy took a bite of his bagel. It was disappointing.

Billy saying how in New York, they got the best bagels. Something to do with the water up there. Makes the dough firmer.

"It's like the bagel bites back," Billy said. "Bagels here in the Midwest, all airy and bready."

"So what?" Vic said. "You ate a bagel in New York so you think you're better or something?"

"No, Vic, I don't think I'm better," Billy said, "Just shooting the shit about bagels."

Mona piping up, saying "I got no idea why the hell we're talking about bagels. Billy..." Pausing to glance at her mother.

Billy standing behind Mona, looking at the back of

her head. Unable to see her face but reading her mother's face, a look saying *don't you dare.*

"Billy, why don't you have a seat?" Mona hopping up, offering her chair. "I been sitting all morning."

Billy thanking Mona, taking her seat directly across the table from Arlita. Settling in, laying the remaining half of his bagel atop his napkin on the table. Billy noticing Gerald leaving the room without saying a word.

Mona noticing it too. Saying she needed a cigarette but following Gerald out to Arlita's beauty shop rather than outside to smoke.

The kitchen uncomfortably silent now. Billy hoping the sound of his chewing was only loud in his head.

"So what do you think, Arlita?" Billy said between bites. "Got something to tell me?"

"Nothing to tell," Horace said, voice rising. "Nothing to say."

"You don't speak for her!" Vic jumping in.

"Quiet, both of you," Arlita said.

Billy locking eyes on her like it was just the two of them alone in the room.

Billy saying, "Arlita, I'm going to tell you what I told Horace yesterday: People around here elected me to do a job. I am going to do that job."

Arlita looking up and around the room. At Vic and Horace. Down into her lap. Anywhere but at Billy.

"You don't need to look at me," Billy said, leaning in toward Arlita, "but you do need to hear me. Thing is, I find out something's going on...and you didn't work with me on it...Arlita, I've known you a long time, but I can't look away from that."

Billy feeling like she was about to break. Telling himself to push the damn button on her.

"Last chance, Arlita. Now is something going on with Patty?"

Seeing Arlita's shoulders soften. Her jowls tremble.

"Time for you to go," Vic said. Billy feeling the man move up behind him.

"Vic, you don't speak for her either," Billy said, not turning around. "I'll leave when Arlita asks me to."

All eyes on her now, waiting. The woman fighting back tears. Stuffing down her emotions as difficult as swallowing a dry hunk of bagel.

"You should probably go," Arlita said. "Got things I need to do today."

Six

Mona walking into the beauty shop to discover Gerald crouching underneath one of the sinks. Busy loosening a goose neck trap with a pair of channel lock pliers.

Mona plopping down in the adjacent barber's chair, started slowly spinning in circles, one way then the other. Neither of them speaking.

Gerald giving her the silent treatment, obviously upset with her.

Mona waiting to see how to play it. Deciding to pretend he wasn't shutting her out or maybe she just didn't notice.

"When I was a kid," Mona said, "my ass got yelled at all the time for spinning in these chairs."

Gerald, too pissed off to keep up the silent bit, saying, "Then your ass probably shouldn't be spinning in them now."

Mona hiding her delight in getting him to crack so easily.

"Yeah, well now my ass is too full grown to be told what to do."

"Then your full-growed ass shouldn't act like it

needs to be told."

Mona coming at Gerald with her voice, but keeping it low so the people back in the kitchen could hear her. Asking what did he want her to do? Tell Billy what's going on?

"With momma sitting right there shooting daggers at me? Family is family."

"Sure it is," Gerald said, "Spin in the chair, fuck you mama. Take drugs, fuck you mama. Marry a black man, fuck you mama."

"That's not how it is, G."

"So you say. Go against that woman in every way you can. Except when it matters. Tell me, am I the only one in this house thinking of your daughter?"

"That's not fair."

"What is?" Gerald said. "Ain't never met the girl but here I am, the only one thinks it might be in her best interests to, I don't know, maybe go to the damn police? Let them do what they're supposed to know how to do."

"It's not easy like that," Mona said. "What do you want me to do?"

"You're bullshit, you know that? Got enough bullshit people in my life. No need to add one more."

Gerald getting up from the half-finished plumbing

job and leaving the room. Leaving Mona alone, spinning in the chair.

Seven

Billy sitting at the butcher block island in Paige's kitchen, still not sure if this was the right thing to do.

Paige across the island from him, trying to get the cover off the back of the TV remote.

Paige's mother off in the family room, watching that afternoon's *Jeopardy*. Every now and then calling out an answer at the screen. *Who is Rosie Ruiz? Who is Titanic Thompson?*

Billy wishing he had some kind of an answer. Category: Big Dumbasses. *Who is Billy Keene?*

Billy thinking if a guy's able to get himself in a jam, he ought to be able to get himself out. That had been the idea when he texted Paige right after leaving Arlita's earlier in the day. Asking to see if they could get together.

But not adding: So they could talk.

A phrase like that left hanging might ruin your

whole day. No sense ruining Paige's day *before* they talked.

Now it was not quite like he'd planned it. Him coming over to her house, that was Paige's idea. Inviting him for supper. Paige about to fix everyone a plate of chicken and cilantro rice just as soon as *Jeopardy* was over and she finished replacing the dead batteries in the remote.

Billy wondering when is a good time to tell her he cheated on her after only one date? Before they ate or after?

Watching Paige fiddling with the remote, unable to budge the release tab of the battery cover with her fingernail.

Hell, did he even need to tell her?

Been going back and forth on that one all day. Just the one date; wasn't like they were exclusive yet. There it was again, the "yet" part.

Every time Billy thought about her, that word kept working its way into the conversation in his head. Like he expected more to come for them as a couple.

Still, it seemed like a dick move, telling her something like this over her dinner table. Maybe even a bigger dick move than sleeping with an old girlfriend. Maybe.

Billy not even sure he would tell her—right up until

the moment he started to tell her.

"Paige, before we eat, there's something we need to talk about."

Something serious and pained in the sound of his voice causing Paige to glance up from the remote. Asking him what's on his mind?

A deep breath before laying it out for her. But keeping it brief, no need to go into details. Just the facts, saying more than once how much he regretted it and apologizing.

Then Billy catching himself over explaining, starting to run on at the mouth. Wrapping it up quickly.

"So anyway, I want you to know I am so sorry."

Paige had kept at the battery cover on the remote as she listened to what Billy had to say. Now there was a silence between them. Broken once by Paige's mother yelling *who is Barry Minkow?*

Billy with no idea who that was.

Wishing he could find words to fix things. Watching Paige struggle with that damn remote. Maybe her obsession with the stubborn battery cover was the only thing keeping her from looking up long enough to throw him out.

"Mind if I try?" Billy said, reaching for the remote.

Paige ignoring his offer. “Why did you tell me this?”

“Well, it’s a small town. Things get around. Usually a distorted version of what actually happened.”

“No, I mean what made you think you had to tell me something like this? It’s not like we’re a together or anything.”

Billy thinking about that for a moment.

“No, we’re not,” Billy said. “I guess I have the feeling there might be something. Between us. It’s too early to be talking like that, I know. But I feel some things, good things. And I think you do too. I hope you do anyway. I mean, who knows if it will turn out to be anything more—”

“—You do realize,” Paige said, now trying to pry open the battery cover with a flathead screwdriver she’d pulled from a junk drawer under the island, “telling me something like this very well could lead to there not being anything more, right?”

“Trust me, I know the smart play is to just keep quiet,” Billy said. “But the thing is, if it does turn out there’s really something here... I figure it’s better if everything’s built on solid ground. Seriously, can I give it a try? Before you stab yourself with that screwdriver.”

Paige glaring at him.

“Only one around here needs to worry about getting

stabbed is you."

But she passed them over, the remote and the screwdriver.

Billy wedging the screwdriver in between the cover release tab and the back of the remote. The hard plastic tab resisting. Billy not wanting to break it. A few tries before finally prying the cover open, popping it off.

Paige passing him two fresh AA batteries. Billy making sure to install them correctly before replacing the cover. Saying he'd take the old ones because they have battery recycling at the station house. Passing the remote back to Paige.

"You fixed it," Paige said.

"Wasn't broken," Billy said. "Just made it work again."

"We'll see."

"We still talking about the remote?" Billy said. "Or we talking about something else now?"

"Yes." That flat look on Paige's face eventually giving way to a slight smile. "Hungry for some supper?"

Eight

What she would do is, she would try to trick him.

Horace knowing this about Tammy. Ways she would try to fool him into eating healthy. Like with the turkey burger on the dinner plate she'd placed in front of him.

Horace didn't like being tricked. But who the hell does?

The two of them sitting down to supper. From his chair at the head of the dining room table, Horace able to see his barn, his land extending out beyond. In his mind picturing the hole he'd dug in his ground that morning on his surveying walk.

Far back near the southwest corner. An open-mouthed hole in the ground awaiting the possibility of a second helping of Arlita's ransom money.

Horace tasting the first bite of his turkey burger, thinking something's different. Tastes like a trick.

"What's going on here with the fake burgers?" Horace said as he chewed.

"New recipe," Tammy said. "Like it?"

"No," Horace said. "Didn't care for the last one neither. Bad enough you got me eating ground up tom turkey instead of real hamburger."

Tammy sighing, saying now Horace you know you need to eat better, what with your cholesterol and all. Stressing how this new recipe is healthier than the other. Like that made everything all right.

Horace about to reply that at least the old recipe had some kind of flavor to it, but instead letting it go. Arguing about turkey burger recipes seeming as pointless to Horace as just about anything he could think of.

What did he care? Horace already having made up his mind to head out later, sneak a real burger from a fast food joint.

Horace picking at his microwaved sweet potato, thinking he'd grab some fries too.

All in all Horace feeling pretty good about things. This whole deal about over and cleanly so.

Sharla and Pearce do their job right, Patty will turn up later tonight, no problem.

If they don't – and honestly Horace was counting on Sharla screwing up, not releasing Patty exactly as planned because, well, that drugged-up little bitch never did what she was told – then Horace would double dip Arlita.

Should Sharla and Pearce find out, they wouldn't like it too much being cut out of a second helping.

Then again, if all went right those two might be in

jail. Or dead.

Horace taking another bite of his turkey burger, not liking it any more than the last. Wondering where in the hell his kid was with his Caddy?

For a while there, he'd been concerned he might have to sell off his Caddy and a whole lot of other things to help cover Chubba's debts over at the casino. Not now. Now everything was wrapping up as nicely as a present under a Christmas tree.

Horace looking up from the plate he was picking at, thinking he heard tires on the highway. Just an old truck grinding by.

Horace deciding he'd had enough of poultry's poor impersonation of beef. Getting up from his seat. Taking his plate.

"Where you going with that plate?" Tammy said.

Horace not answering her as he slid open the glass door, went outside. Leaning over the deck railing, scraping the food off his plate into the yard.

Tammy calling out to him, "Shouldn't feed scraps to those dogs."

"Why not?" Horace said. Grinning as he came back to the table. "It's healthy, ain't it?"

Laying a hand gently on the nape of Tammy's neck.

Like that made everything all right.

Nine

From the spot in the apartment complex parking lot, Chubba could see the outer door to Pearce's building.

Good view of the unused pool, the stacked patio furniture, other doors leading into other buildings. In his rearview mirror he could see the ass end of his Mustang, where Sharla had parked it.

But Chubba keeping his eye on the outer door to Pearce's building, watching.

Somewhere behind that door lay the door to freakshow's apartment. Behind that apartment door, freakshow and Sharla were having incredible wall-to-wall ape sex.

At least in Chubba's mind they were.

The reality of it was Chubba still with no idea what the hell was going on up here. Obviously wasn't in too big of a hurry to find out either. Been parked there for some time. Had freakshow's apartment number.

Just hadn't made his move yet.

Earlier, when he first pulled into Overland Park, it hadn't taken him long to find Pearce's complex thanks to the GPS. Once he found it, he'd had to wander the sprawling complex for some time before locating Pearce's exact building. Easing the Caddy through the maze of cul de sacs, Chubba was pleased to find the place more than a little shabby.

Getting dark now. Chubba had been watching the outer door for hours, not once seeing Sharla or Pearce.

Chubba was starving. His gas station snacks finished off long ago back on the interstate. Putting off a quick run for something to eat for fear of missing one of them coming or going.

Chubba not sure what he was waiting for, why he didn't just barge in.

His stomach growling, urging him to check the snack bags for any remnants. Chubba caught in a shame spiral now. Ready for all this to be over so he could leave behind the stress, start eating better again, get himself right. Help Sharla get right again.

Telling himself there's always the possibility the two of them weren't up to anything.

Or worse, maybe he'd been wrong all along and

freakshow did have a little badass in him. Was he up there mistreating Sharla right now? Oh, she'd be pissed if she found out Chubba had been there and waited it out. That idea seemed almost like a wish to Chubba. Better she's a victim than a cheater.

But knowing Sharla's ways, that wasn't likely.

Besides, he'd had to beg her to return to Caulfield. She couldn't wait to get back up here. All that pretty much sank his Sharla-as-victim theory.

Left with two options now—either she's fucking him or she's not. Chubba knowing there's only way to find out and it ain't by asking.

So just storm in then, damn it. Chubba pumping himself up. Get in, beat the living hell out of freakshow and move on. Catch her red-handed at something she ought not to be doing.

If nothing else use that as leverage to get her to clean up, get right. Rub her nose in it for her own good.

Stomach turning hollow with adrenaline, not hungry now. Chubba climbing out of his daddy's Caddy. Lumbering through the complex toward Pearce's building.

Chubba suddenly halting his march, looking around. Wondering which building Patty was hidden in.

Thinking of Patty for the first time since he'd

arrived. Chubba knowing she was somewhere in the complex but no idea exactly where they had her stashed.

Wondering how she was holding up, the poor girl. Stuck up as hell, but Chubba feeling bad for her anyway. She'd be free soon enough though. Sharla and Pearce supposed to let her escape later tonight.

Patty should be okay, long as freakshow had fed her, taken care of her like was supposed to happen?

Chubba deciding he'd better check on Patty while he was in town. First things first though.

Quietly through the outer door he'd stared at all afternoon and evening. Then up one flight of stairs until he found Pearce's door.

Pausing. A deep breath.

Kick it open? Really surprise them?

Might not give with one kick though.

Grabbing the knob, turning it slowly but not opening the door. A slight push, checking if the dead bolt was set. The door gave, unlocked.

With one foot, Chubba kicking the door as he let go of the knob. A loud thump and the door swinging open.

Chubba thinking now that's motherfucking barging in!

Scanning the apartment as he moved inside, closing

the door behind him. The place a mess, clothes and trash everywhere.

On the coffee table, neat stacks of money, Chubba assuming that was the money his daddy had let Sharla take.

Next to the money, a nest of electrical cords and small appliances—a clothes iron, maybe a curling iron. Chubba's eyes not lingering long enough to untangle and identify each item.

Catching sight of Sharla and Pearce looking up at him.

Both of them in front of a laptop computer set up on a small bar off the kitchen. Pearce shirtless, his chest all ink and metal studs.

Sharla barefoot in hip-hugging sweatpants and a short T showing her belly. Slutting it up a bit but Chubba always liked that about her. Girl could turn a white wedding dress into whore-wear. But otherwise, both of them fully clothed.

"What the fuck?" Sharla coming at Chubba. "The fuck you doing here?"

Chubba feeling stupid now, not catching them up to anything. Noticing more wires on the bar. A video camera next to the laptop. Cables running from the video camera to the computer.

Pearce lowering the lid on the computer.

Chubba's eyes landing on the meth pipe next to the video camera.

"I knew it," Chubba said. "Up here smoking the old peace pipe. Sharla, damn it, you got to stop all this."

"That why you come up here?" Sharla said, eyes open with contempt and drugs. "To Dr. Phil me?"

"Am I wrong about it?" Chubba said.

"Bullshit," Sharla said. "That ain't why you came up here."

"I come up to make sure you all unload Patty tonight. And I see it's a good thing I did, too."

"It's early," Pearce said. "Waiting until midnight or so to cut the strings on her."

"Shut the fuck up, freakshow," Chubba said. "Wasn't talking to you."

Pearce rising from his barstool. Asking who was Chubba telling to shut the fuck up? His place so how about Chubba shut the fuck up?

Chubba stepping toward Pearce, telling Pearce that he was going to have to make it happen.

"Both you lames shut the fuck up," Sharla said, keeping herself between them.

A brief, tense standoff until Sharla ordered them both to sit down. Pearce moving toward the couch; Chubba choosing to remain standing. Both young men eye-fucking each other as Pearce moved past.

"Let me guess," Sharla said to Chubba.

Chubba's eyes still locked on Pearce sitting on the couch.

"Hey, over here," Sharla said, snapping her fingers. "Look at me when I'm talking to you."

Chubba finally looking away now that he had permission and wouldn't look like a pussy. Turning toward Sharla, who started in again.

"Bet I know why you showed up out of the blue. Your jealous mind has you all convinced something nasty's going on up here, right? Two of us up here getting to know one another?"

The way Sharla was saying it, like a question but really making statements, tripping the breaker on Chubba's anger, cutting the power to his rage. Chubba quiet, eyes toward the floor. Feeling silly now for even thinking it.

Sharla moving in close to him, telling him it was okay.

"You're just over-protective, is all. Kinda sweet. At least, when it ain't so fucking frightening. Scared me, coming through the door like that. Like John Cena or some shit."

Mentioning Chubba's favorite professional wrestler, the image making him smile.

"John Cena, huh?" Chubba said.

Chubba moving up to Sharla standing by the bar, his body language asking for a hug.

"Just like him," Sharla said. Hesitating before accepting that an embrace was required to sell it.

Hugging Chubba but throwing a fleeting look at Pearce.

Pearce stewing on the couch, one leg up on the chaotic mess covering his coffee table. The blue-green coiled snake tattoo on his lower leg, her favorite, peaking out the bottom of his pant leg.

Sharla relaxing, letting Chubba know their cuddle was over. Moving away from Chubba, leaving him standing beside the bar. Sliding onto a barstool but keeping herself between him and Pearce.

"So how come you never texted me back?" Chubba said.

Sharla saying with a shrug she never got any texts. Chubba adamant that he'd sent, like, a hundred messages earlier.

Sharla snatching her project phone off the bar, checking it for messages from Chubba. Showing it Chubba, saying see? Nothing.

"No, the other one," Chubba said. "Your personal cell."

Sharla looking around for her other phone. Checking down to the bottom of her purse. Getting up to check on the coffee table, under the couch, between the cushions.

Not finding it and exchanging another look with Pearce, a nervous one this time.

"Shit," Sharla said, "hope I didn't leave it in Patty's room."

"How is Patty?" Chubba said, turning to Pearce. "Better have been taking care of her like you're supposed to."

"Wouldn't hurt that cow to miss a meal," Sharla said, chuckling.

The only one in the room laughing at her joke. That had been happening a lot, she'd noticed.

"Anyway, yeah," she said, "Patty's fine."

"Didn't know you cared so much," Pearce said to Chubba. "Like her so much, maybe you shouldn't have kidnapped her."

"Think I'll have a look at her," Chubba said. "Make sure she's okay."

Sharla and Pearce speaking at the same time.

"How come?"

"Why's that?"

Chubba sensing a fresh current of tension in the room. Different from the previous but Chubba not quite sure how.

"Daddy told me to," Chubba said, pulling rank of sorts. "Said make sure she's all right."

Aware now of the glances bouncing back and forth between freakshow and Sharla.

"A week into this thing," Pearce said, "and *now* your Daddy's all concerned? He's that concerned, maybe he should come up and see for himself."

"Daddy's a busy man," Chubba said. "So where is she?"

"You and I step outside, it's only for me to kick your ass," Pearce said, still sitting back on the couch but ready to hop.

Chubba giving a laugh, in his head thinking *John-Cena-John-Cena-John-Cena.* "Let's go, freakshow."

"For god sakes, will you two just shut it," Sharla said.

Reaching for her meth pipe on the bar. Needing a hit right now. Never smoked meth in front of Chubba before but thinking, hey, got to stretch your boundaries, right?

"Now you're going to make me watch you kill yourself?" Chubba said.

"Nobody's making you look," Sharla said, pulling a sapphire-colored hunk of meth from a baggie on the counter. "And I don't need no lecture right now."

Sharla turning on her bar stool to Pearce.

"How about you? Want a hit?"

Pearce smiling, waving her over. Happy to be in the drug club with Sharla, no Chubba allowed. Sharla stepping through the clutter layering the carpet.

Chubba watching in disgust. The two of them with their backs to him, shutting him out of their party.

Focused on the ritual and the paraphernalia. Their hungry brains firing signals of sweet, brief relief in sight. Chubba recognizing it, felt the same way whenever he heard someone open a bag of chips. So ready for all this to be over.

With Sharla and Pearce occupied with their dope, it was as if Chubba had left the room. They didn't notice when he cleared his throat.

Paid no attention when he went to the sink for a

glass of water.

Didn't see him lift the lid on the laptop.

At first Chubba was unsure what he was looking at on the screen. Couple of different boxes with images in them. Not images, but videos. Lots of skin. Porn maybe?

Using the touch pad on the laptop, rolling the cursor over the Play button of one of the videos. Hitting it.

Chubba still unclear on what he was seeing but definitely not happy that his girlfriend and freakshow had been checking out porn together.

Looked like a three-way. Low-quality amateur stuff but a warped scene.

Two girls, fat one lying face down on a mattress with a skinny girl lying on her back to back. The cherry on top of them both was a lean guy with tattoos.

He was humping away at the skinny girl in the sandwich, her legs spread wide, mouth almost as wide, yelling something. The sound down on the laptop.

All at once everything coming into focus for Chubba.

Recognizing who it was. What was going on. A flood of adrenaline so brutal his stomach went queasy. Head spinning. Gasping for breath, mouth dry.

Unmuting the sound on the computer.

Sharla's voice coming loud and tinny through the

machine's built-in speakers. Swearing, barking out perverted threats and commands over the sound of Patty crying in pain. Pearce grunting and thrusting to the hammering beat of some kind of death metal blaring in the background.

Sharla's live voice now coming loud from across the apartment.

"Chubba get away from that computer!"

Sharla and Pearce both struck by the wounded fury in Chubba's dampening eyes.

Chubba thinking it's one thing to think you're being cheated on and it's another thing to know it.

But some other kind of twisted thing to see it being done.

Pearce didn't know a wide body could move so quickly. But Sharla did.

Sharla ready for it, almost able to slip Chubba's grip when he came at her. Almost.

One thick hand clamping tight on her bony wrist, yanking her back toward him.

Sharla pulled in close now, and Chubba clutching her throat in one hand. The skin of her neck bulging up in between his knuckles like it was bubbling. Chubba's other hand pinning Sharla's arm at her side.

Sharla's clawing at Chubba's neck and face with her free hand, fake nails flying off this way and that. Chubba drowning in rage, not feeling a thing.

Pearce jumping up, cussing, trying to pry Chubba off Sharla.

With Sharla's throat firmly in his right hand, Chubba let go of her wrist. Swinging his left hand, popping Pearce in the throat.

Pearce shrieking, falling to the floor. Trying but unable to wail in pain.

Chubba, wanting to do that for a while now, wishing he was able to enjoy the moment more. Looking deep into Sharla's desperate eyes, letting her know he was going to take her all the way there.

Chubba thinking it might be the only way to help her. Just put her down like a broken dog that can't be fixed.

Pearce writhing near Chubba's feet, hands at his throat as he tried to take in air. Chubba with enough hatred left over to give Pearce a hard kick in the ribs.

Pearce letting out a howl, rolling away.

Sharla's face purple now, eyes starting to roll back. No longer scratching at Chubba, the fight leaving her.

Chubba thinking do it or don't but now's the time to decide. Easing his grip on her throat but keeping his hand there. Her eyes coming back down, leveling on him. Gulping for air, trying to say something.

Chubba not ready to release her yet, hand firmly on her throat. Chubba asking, “What did you say?”

Sharla shaking her head weakly.

Chubba confused by the sight of her eyes growing wide again. Confused by the sudden sharp pain around his throat. Surprised by his inability to take in air. Letting go of Sharla, tearing at whatever was around his neck.

Feeling a body behind him. Had to be freakshow.

Chubba feeling himself pulled close to Pearce by whatever he’d wrapped around Chubba’s neck. His mind flashing to the extension cords he’d seen on the coffee table.

Chubba trying to shake the taller body off him. Frantically ramming backward into walls. Throwing his head back into the face behind him. A nauseating meeting of skull and bone as Pearce’s nose explodes in crimson. Chubba feeling the warm, stickiness of blood matting his cropped hair.

But Pearce hanging on tight, powered by drug-strength. Leaning back, almost lifting Chubba’s one-of-a-kind sneakers off the floor.

Last thing Chubba saw was Sharla looking at him.

Unable to tell if she wore excitement or shock on her face.

Realizing he always knew, in his heart, that the two were pretty much the same thing to her.

Chubba's final thought was a hopeful one. Hoping Daddy wouldn't be too mad about the car.

Saturday

One

Patty abruptly wide awake.

Heart jumping at the muffled sound of someone entering the apartment. About to cry, not wanting to suffer through another night (was it night?) like last night.

She'd been left alone for hours, no food, no drink, but happy just to be left alone. A long time since she'd last heard the buzzing. Now many heavy steps, grunts, a racket coming down the short hallway toward her.

Patty lying still, pretending. Asleep. Unconscious. Not there.

They were in the room with her now. Straining and breathing hard but no talking. A meaty thud. Dead weight dumped on the floor.

Then one of them, Him or Her, moving around the room. Moving closer to her.

Patty waiting for a touch somewhere on her body to tell her who it was. Feeling and hearing hot breath on the back of her neck. Him or Her kneeling down by the mattress.

"Found it," He said to Her.

His voice sounding different. Stuffed up, pained. Like He was having difficulty breathing and speaking at the same time. Patty expecting His touch, but it never came.

Instead, He moved away. Then wordless movement out of her room, down the hall and out of the apartment.

Patty listening intently for them to return. The room around her quiet for a moment.

Then a soft, guttural sound, like someone choking. The suddenness of it startling her. She'd heard a sound like that before. Coming out of a hog, dead but before it was butchered. A death rattle.

Patty afraid but sensing no movement. Turning her head, scraping her face against the mattress. Edging up her blindfold just enough to see.

In the darkness making out a pair of legs splayed awkwardly on the carpet. On the feet, a pair of red and gold running shoes.

Looking familiar, but Patty not quite able to place them.

Two

Pearce inspecting himself in his bathroom mirror. Unsure which hurt more—his torn up face? Or looking at his torn up face?

Pearce feeling all kinds of sick now. Coming down off several days of meth. Killing a man. Dumping the body in the same room where he'd helped torture a woman that he'd kidnapped for ransom.

Thinking it had been an out-of-the-ordinary week, definitely.

Catching sight of Sharla in the mirror, barefoot and perched on the edge of the tub. Twitchy hands loading up her pipe. No sign of quit or coming down in her.

"So what now?" Pearce said.

"Get high," Sharla said, putting the pipe to her dry lips and the fire to the pipe.

Pearce not answering but thinking no thanks. Crashing hard. Needing sleep. An ache in his stomach like being stabbed with a dull knife over and over.

His body crying out for something healthy. Orange

juice maybe. Trying to remember if there was any in the fridge. Might need to run to the store real quick.

The store. Pearce missing quite a bit of work this week. Wondering if he even still had a job. Part of him wishing he could get the week back. Rewind to standing behind the deli counter and getting treated like crap by his bitch of a boss, Dana. Start from there and do it over differently.

Never make that ransom call.

Never kidnap that rich fat girl.

Never try to pretend with Sharla that he was a stone-cold criminal. Look where posing had gotten him.

"Real deal, now," Pearce said to the reflection of his battered face.

Sharla, eyes clenched and choking back smoke, asking with a squeak what did he just say?

"Nothing," Pearce said. "I think I need some OJ, something with vitamins."

Sharla finally spewing out a stream of meth smoke. "Got all the vitamins I need right here."

"You might want to give that a rest," Pearce said to her in the mirror.

"Don't talk to me about my drugging. You saw what happened to the last guy who did."

Sharla laughing at her own joke.

Pearce not laughing, amazed and appalled she found any of it funny.

"You do realize I just killed a man," Pearce said. "Oh, and that man just happens to be your boyfriend."

Sharla's laughter petering out. "Yeah, that wasn't so funny, I guess."

"We are both, you and me, we are both in this." Pearce turning to face her. "You get that, right?"

Sharla not caring for Pearce harshing her buzz.

"What bug crawled up your ass?" Sharla said.

"Whatever," Pearce said. Shaking his head. Turning back to the mirror and his fucked up face again.

"Think I need to go to the ER?" Pearce said. "I think I need to go to the ER. Don't get this taken care of, could be some nasty scars."

Sharla laughing at that.

"So, you'll put holes in your earlobes and everywhere else," she said, "But you're afraid you might have some scarring ?"

Pearce not liking being laughed at but letting it go. Watching Sharla already loading up another bowl.

"Seriously, you need to take a break from that shit. We better come up with a plan," Pearce said. "We need to clear our heads."

"Do my best thinking on it," Sharla said, caught in a manic rush now. "It's high octane for the brain! Firing on all motherfucking cylinders now, whooo!"

"Okay Einstein," Pearce said. "Then what about Horace? We can forget about getting the money he owes us."

"Relax," Sharla said. "He's in this thing, much as any of us. He ain't going to like what happened. But maybe he don't have to know who did it. I ain't figured that out quite yet. But fuck him. He's paying, trust me on that."

Pearce thinking that over, trying to play the scenario out in his mind. Not knowing Horace well enough to know if Sharla knew what she was talking about.

Pearce confused by it all, a little nauseous. Needing to lie down. Moving past Sharla as he climbed into the empty bathtub.

Stretching out, closing his eyes, feeling ill all over his body.

"Daylight now," he said. "Guess we'll have to wait until tonight to let Patty go."

"Oh, that ain't happening," Sharla said.

Pearce keeping his eyes closed. "Well, what then?"

Sharla saying, "Patty, she just goes away."

Pearce opening his eyes slowly. Looking up at her, asking what do you mean Patty just goes away?

Sharla shrugging.

"She just...goes away." Sharla doing a bird flutter thing with her hand that had the lighter in it.

"You mean kill her?" Pearce said.

"Ain't buying her a fucking ticket to Disney World. Makes you feel better, I'll do it. Here, take this."

Sharla handing the loaded meth pipe to Pearce.

"Doctor Sharla's orders," she said.

Pearce pausing with the pipe in hand. Letting it all sink in.

Wondering if the drugs were what made Sharla so ruthless or if that was just who she was. Wondering where it ended with her. Then a horrible thought occurring to Pearce.

"Don't tell me you want to film it?" Pearce said.

Sharla scrunching up her face at Pearce.

"That's fucking sick. Should be ashamed of yourself."

Sharla tossing the lighter at him in disgust, hitting him in the chest.

"Even I ain't that twisted."

Pearce thinking uh-huh, that's where the line is and

I crossed it. Right., sure. Pearce hitting the pipe but keeping an eye on Sharla.

Afraid to take his eyes off of her.

Three

The telephone ringing and ringing.

Arlita listening to the phony digital purr in her ear. What the hell's taking Vic so long to answer?

Hanging up when the line finally kicked over to his voice mail. Not leaving a message, preferring to talk to him on this.

Still sitting at her dead husband's desk where Horace had left her. Stumpy little bastard showing himself out with her money. Arlita looking at the address written on a scrap of paper he'd given her.

Thinking that Horace might have the nicest handwriting she'd ever seen on a man. Strong lines, airy loops giving it a nice size. An almost too perfect slant to his lines.

At first, thinking how fortunate it was that Horace had found the address and passed it along.

Horace saying he'd found it after Sharla had left his

place. Must have fallen out of her purse. Said he thought it could be where they're keeping Patty.

Hell of a lucky break, he'd said.

Something in Arlita coming all the way around from *wasn't it fortunate* to *wasn't it interesting?* Not sure why, simply instinct talking inside her.

Listening to her instincts and absentmindedly checking the drawers on the desk. The knob on the top left drawer was loose. Arlita thinking she'd ask Gerald to fix it. Not that she couldn't do it herself, but the man seemed to like to help out by fixing things.

All the sudden she had a lot of people around her anxious to help out.

Horace offering to drop off the money, make sure it got delivered. Before he left, having Arlita check it one more time to make sure there was money inside the large duffle bag.

And Horace awful enthusiastic that something bad should happen to Sharla. Not that Sharla hadn't earned it by just being Sharla. Arlita damn sure wouldn't want her son dating her. But Horace adamant that Sharla was involved and made a convincing case for it to Arlita.

"How else is she going to know what box to use to swap the newspapers for the money?" Horace had said.

Arlita had to admit it was a good question.

If Sharla was involved in all this in some way...well, Arlita just couldn't see that. She couldn't understand how someone could do something like this, even a mean little bitch like Sharla.

But if it turned out Sharla is in it, Arlita swearing to herself that she'll be more than happy to kill the girl with her own hands.

Arlita realizing this wasn't an idle threat. Over something like this? No doubt in her mind, she would do it.

Arlita dialing Vic again. This time Vic answering on the first ring.

"What the hell took you so long?" Arlita said.

"Goddamn, Arlita, I answered before it even finished ringing."

"I mean before. I just called and you didn't answer."

Arlita fiddling with the loose drawer knob as she talked.

"I just come back from my mom's," Vic said. "Was getting her some breakfast."

His voice sounding kind of puny to Arlita. And there was some kind of echo on his end.

"You on the toilet?" Arlita said. "Sounds like you're in a bathroom. Please don't tell me you're taking a dump while you're talking to me on the phone. I do not need that picture in my head all day."

Technically speaking, no Vic was not on the toilet. He was on the bathroom floor.

Spending most of the night after getting tired of running in there every time he felt he needed to take a leak. More false alarms than anything.

Vic lying to Arlita about being over at his mom's place because it was just easier that way. His bones ached, and the first time she called he hadn't been able to move quickly enough to the phone. Bringing the phone back to the bathroom with him, so he could answer it the next time it rang.

"Well, you sound like shit," Arlita said.

"Love you too," Vic said. "Now, what the fuck you need?"

Arlita telling him about Horace giving him the address and saying Sharla might be there. So might Patty. Asking if he had a pen to write it down.

Vic looking around as if there might actually be pen and paper somewhere on his bathroom floor. Nagged again by the urge to urinate. Needing to sit still for a bit to calm the dull throbbing in his bones.

Telling Arlita to text him the address. He'd get on

the road shortly.

"You got a GPS?" Arlita said.

"Nope and don't need one," Vic said. "Get to leaning on those things, next thing you know you need a GPS just to find your own asshole."

Vic listening to Arlita on the other end of the phone telling him she knew she didn't have to remind him but she would anyway—he gets up to KC and finds something wrong, really wrong, then he knows what to do.

Vic half-listening, distracted. Noticing cracked tiles in his bathroom floor. The filth collected in the grout between tiles. The rust around the edges of the fixtures.

The whole goddamned room rotting away. Vic thinking it might be time to renovate his bathroom, but then laughing at himself.

Like he had that kind of time left.

Four

Arlita hanging up the phone after talking with Vic. Looking up to find Mona had come into the den during the conversation.

Handing the scrap of paper Horace had given her to

Mona, telling her daughter to make herself useful.

"Fetch my cell phone out of my purse," Arlita said. "Purse is on the kitchen counter. My fingers are too fat for texting on them itty-bitty things. Text that address to Vic. His number's already in there."

Mona looking at the address on the scrap of paper.

"So you think Patty's here?"

"We'll see," Arlita said.

"And Sharla's got something to do with all this, more than just swiping money?"

Arlita reprimanding her daughter with a look.

"Mona, I don't know a damn thing. But I'm planning on finding out. Now just go do what I ask, please."

Mona rolling her eyes at her mother, turning for the door. This grown woman acting like a teenager who's been told there is no way she's going out wearing *those* shorts.

Before Mona was through the doorway, Arlita remembering the loose knob on the desk drawer. Arlita calling after her daughter.

"Where's Gerald?"

"Upstairs," Mona said, in the doorway, turning back to face her mother. "Packing."

Arlita confused and angry, giving her daughter a hard look.

“Not even going to stick around, say hi to your daughter when she comes home from being kidnapped? Should be a big moment for you, being the mother and all. Seems like your kind of thing.”

Arlita sarcastic as all hell.

Mona unsure if she was more pissed off at her mother for her accusation or for being sarcastic as all hell. But keeping it hidden, stepping back into the den, knowing she was up on her mother now.

“No. I’m staying,” Mona said. “G’s heading back to Dallas.”

“What did you do?”

“Goddamn it momma, why’s it got to be something I did, something I didn’t do? Can’t it just be all this? It’s like ‘Hi, welcome to the family, you got here just in time for the kidnapping.’ I mean really, momma.”

Both quiet now, letting all that sink in. Exchanging a long look before, finally, Arlita nodded. Neither of them saying anything.

Arlita fiddling again with the loose knob on the drawer. Mona picked up a framed picture from one of their family vacations.

Looking at it for a long moment. Mona around eleven at the time. It was a sepia tintype of their family dressed in Old West garb. Her daddy a gunslinger, Mona and her mother both saloon girls.

"'Member this?" Mona said, holding up the tintype for her mother to see.

"Sure I do. That was Branson," Arlita said, smiling. "Silver Dollar City. I remember you threw a fit because you wanted to be a saloon girl."

"Well, you wanted me in some kind of *Little House on the Prairie* get up. What fun is that? You just wanted to be the saloon girl, nobody else. I know you."

"Oh, that's not true," Arlita said, laughing. "You were too damn young to be dressed up like a floozy. But your daddy, he said let you have your fun. Got your way as usual."

Both of them smiling now, missing the man.

Arlita saying about Gerald, "He's just heading back home, right? What I mean is, you two—"

"I don't know, momma," Mona said.

Mona not wanting to tell Arlita that it was more than just the kidnapping. It *was* something she did, going along with her mother's plan. It *was* something she didn't do, not spilling everything to Billy.

"It don't look good though."

"That's too bad," Arlita said. "Seems like a decent

guy. I think your daddy would have liked him."

Arlita considering it, then laughing.

"Damn sure better than all them others. You've found yourself some real dandies along the way."

Mother and daughter some how able to laugh now at all the drug dealers, thieves, white supremacists and bikers (sometimes all rolled into one scary motherfucker) that made up the contestants in Mona's own personal dating game.

"Don't know what to tell you, girl," Arlita said, "other than to do whatever it takes not to let the good ones squirm away."

Mona nodding and thinking about that advice as she headed to the kitchen for her mother's cell phone. Holding in her hand the scrap of paper with the address she would text to Vic, just like her momma asked.

Trying to figure what it might take to get her man upstairs to unpack his suitcase.

Five

Mona strolling into the Sheriff's office, right up

to Billy as he ate his breakfast at his desk.

Saying she wanted to talk.

Billy so shocked he almost dropped his homemade breakfast burrito on the newspaper he was reading. He'd picked up the burrito on his way into work from a sharp-tongued Mexican lady named Flo who sold them out of her house. Billy glad he didn't let the burrito slip through his fingers.

"Mean you're not coming to turn yourself in?"

"I'm serious," Mona said.

"Since when's that count for anything? Like I've been playing around all along."

Mona standing there looking sad and sloppy in her baggy gray sweat pants, hoodie and flip flops. Hair up in a ponytail to hide some of the crazy.

Billy motioned for her to sit.

Mona sitting and starting in on it. Coming clean on as much as she knew. Her daughter not coming home, then Arlita getting calls from a dumbass saying he had Patty and wanting money.

Billy listening to Mona, not asking questions yet. Letting her tell it her way. Seeing she's enjoying herself. Showtime.

Mona putting her spin on things where she saw fit.

Like how Arlita always gave the caller a rough time. That couldn't be too helpful to the situation, could it?

Telling about Vic being in the middle of things. Mona spicing it up, saying how everyone knows he done killed people before and that's why her momma was working with him. Telling it all like gossip happening to somebody else.

"At your momma's yesterday," Billy said, "Vic didn't look like he could do much damage to anybody. Looking thin, even thinner than usual. Pale."

"Momma says he's got cancer pretty bad."

"No," Billy said, genuinely shocked by the news. "She say what kind?"

"Prostrate."

"You mean prostate?"

Mona saying whatever, Vic gives her the creeps.

Mona going on, saying at this very moment Vic's probably on his way up to KC. Pulling out the scrap of paper with the address where Vic was headed.

Billy taking it. "What's Vic expecting to find at this address? Patty?"

"Oh, I hope so," Mona said, dramatic as she could. A pause before going on.

"Or, you know, could turn out it's just Sharla doing

drugs and fucking some guy, excuse my French."

"Sharla Ricketts?" Billy said. "What's she got to do with anything?"

Mona rolling her eyes.

"Duh, I'm pretty sure that's what Vic went to find out. Look, are you going to do something about all this? My child's in danger."

Billy wanting to smack her for that one. For the tone and the attitude and because she wouldn't talk before but now that she's decided to run her mouth she suddenly feels entitled to a taxpayer's right to demand action.

But Billy waiting out his anger. Thinking of what Sheriff Cady told him—the job is about people, but it's not personal.

"So when did Vic leave for this address?"

Mona shrugging. "Maybe an hour ago?"

Billy thinking, damn, don't hurry in or nothing, Mona. But again keeping quiet. Instead asking how she knows it was an hour ago?

"Couldn't be much longer than that," Mona said. "That's when I texted it to him, after Momma called him. Was right after Mr. Self left."

"Yeah, I noticed Horace and Arlita been close recently. What's that all about?"

"Just being neighborly, I guess," Mona said. "Momma says he's been a big help to her through all this. Like today, he's dropping off round two of the money."

"What money?"

"Oh yeah, I forgot that part," Mona said.

Explaining how the box filled with old newspapers that Billy had caught Arlita tossing into the dumpster behind the DQ was supposed to be full of money. Arlita pretty damn sure it was Sharla who took the money. And how Horace volunteered to deliver the second round of cash this morning.

Billy didn't say anything for a long time, processing it all. He and Mona the only ones in the sheriff's office.

Billy always enjoying Saturdays because no one else was around. On weekends Cookie usually only checked in for a few minutes in the afternoon. Zane was off until the afternoon when he would come in to relieve Dustin. Now that Lon was out and they were a man down, everybody would be working overtime until they found a replacement.

Including Billy, whose mind was working overtime at the moment.

Mona unable to tolerate the silence any longer.

"Momma don't know I come up here. She finds out, she'll skin me. But G, he says it's the right thing to do."

"He does, does he?" Billy said. "Sounds like a smart man."

"You're not going to arrest momma, are you?"

"Not right this second," Billy said. "But I'm not making any promises long term. We'll see how it shakes out. Seems like first things first, ought to put the brakes on Vic."

Mona asking if Billy was going to call the police up in KC, and Billy saying tell them what? Might could be a guy looking to hurt someone who might could have kidnapped someone?

"Lot of might be's and could have's in that story," he said. "A bit flimsy."

Billy not telling Mona that he wasn't in a hurry to involve another law enforcement agency, only to have all this turn out to be less than she said or, worse, something she just made up in her head. Billy with no desire to come off looking like a small-town, hick sheriff who didn't know his ass from apple butter.

"Story? Wait one goddamn second," Mona said. "You saying you don't believe me? I come in here – me, of all people – to talk to you, and you think I'm lying?"

"Simmer down," Billy said. "There's what I believe and what I can prove. Two entirely different things."

His words smoothing out Mona's hackles. Telling her to go on home.

"But aren't you going to do anything?" Mona said.

"Yes. I am," Billy said, having already made up his mind to head up to KC, check out the address she'd given him. Maybe bump into Vic and Sharla. "But honestly I see no upside in telling you what I plan to do."

"You don't trust me," Mona said, not offended but smiling, almost flirting.

"Imagine that," Billy said.

Billy telling her one more thing: don't leave town. At least not until all this is sorted out.

Mona thinking that over, seeing an angle.

"You know my husband, Gerald? He's waiting out in the car. G can back up everything I told you. Probably he shouldn't leave town either, right?"

Billy saying sure, have him stick around too.

Mona smiling at that.

"Mind if I bring him in here?" Mona said. "So he can hear it from you?

On his way out of town Billy stopping by the DQ

but not finding any money in the dumpster out back. Pulling back onto Main Street and pointing his sheriff's SUV toward KC.

Wondering if somebody picked up the money already, or if Mona's story was just trash too.

Six

Somewhere between Caulfield and Kansas City, another urgent need to piss hitting Vic, this time it set him off on a laughing jag.

Vic wondering is this really who I am now?

Before leaving on this road trip, Vic had little doubt that real and false urges would plague him along the way. But he was in a hurry. Had no desire to pull over every five minutes. So once he'd cleared Caulfield, Vic stopped at the first convenience store he found and picked himself up a box of adult diapers.

Pulled around back of the store and diapered himself in the cab of his truck, jeans down around his cowboy boots, head on a swivel checking no one was watching. Quickly taping the sides before trying to pull up his pants. His dingy underwear wouldn't fit over the diaper so he'd ripped them off and tossed them back into the bed of his truck.

Then stuck the .38 Smith & Wesson revolver he'd brought along for the trip down deep in the diaper box.

Following the interstate and fighting the urgency stirring inside him. Vic sensing this one was the real deal but Vic not wanting to let it go. Finding it harder to piss himself than he thought it would be.

Looking himself in the eye in the review mirror. Gaunt face staring back at him. Again, thinking is this really who I am now?

Taking a deep breath, trying to relax. Giving in and letting it fly.

A warm feeling spreading over his midsection before disappearing, absorbed into the lining of the diaper. His diaper. Leaving Vic feeling dry and not half bad down there.

But in his head, Vic fuming about the sorry state of things for Arlita and Patty. And for himself. Growing angrier as he drove.

Thinking some motherfucker's gonna pay. Boot heavy on the accelerator.

Seven

"You know me," Sharla said, sitting glassy-eyed on Pearce's couch.

Bare legs up and apart on his coffee table, intentionally giving him a peep up her shorts. Rambling on.

"I do it, I'm taking my own sweet time with it."

Pearce at the bar loading up the pipe again, thinking, yeah, definitely getting to know you. Not liking you much either.

Then Pearce turning on the barstool and— hello! Catching the show she was putting on for him.

All morning long and now into lunch time, the two of them smoking meth and arguing about killing Patty.

Not should they kill her—that wasn't even on the table.

Question was, what's the best way?

Sharla insisting they have some fun before putting Patty out of her misery. Pearce arguing they should do it quick, as painless as possible for everybody involved.

Pearce adamant that Sharla should be the one to do it. Bring balance to their relationship, given that he'd done Chubba, even if it was self-defense. Sort of.

Sharla coming back at him, that's why *he* should kill

Patty. He was experienced.

"It's something you're good at," she said. "Might be you found your true calling."

Sharla too high to feel bad about her dead boyfriend. Or feel much of anything.

Pearce thinking it didn't feel that way to him. He knew he was feeling terrible somewhere under all the dope. Kept hearing the same thought in his head over and over: This is not me.

Not sure who he was trying to convince, though. Peace hitting the pipe again because why the hell not?

Getting a little rush but not like before. Figuring he was so damn high there might not be any such thing as higher. Nowhere to go but down.

"Okay, fine," Pearce said. Deciding he'd do Patty, if only to make sure it went fast and easy for the poor girl. Thinking he might have to do Sharla too, just to get clear of this mess. Not definite yet, but not against the idea.

Pearce getting up and taking another hit off the pipe as he crossed the apartment to Sharla. Bending down to kiss her, grabbing the back of her chaotic hair and forcing smoke down her throat.

Sharla taking it all in. Then Pearce coming up for air.

"Let's do this."

Sharla blowing out the smoke.

"That's my baby!"

Sharla knowing why he was giving in without him having to say it. Sharla thinking this one's a punk, just like all of them turn out to be.

Trying to decide if she should let Pearce do Patty before she killed him. Or kill him while making Patty watch. Picturing his big kitchen knife, the one she's slipped into her purse the last time he'd gone to the bathroom.

Sharla hopping up off the couch, began scooping up the curling iron, extension cords and handfuls of the ransom money. Stuffing it all in a plastic shopping bag.

"What you needed all that for?" Pearce said.

"Something fun. Want to show the money to Patty before we killed her. I mean, least we can do is let her go out knowing her grandmother loved her enough to come through for her even though, you know, sorry, it just didn't work out."

Pearce shaking his head.

"Don't need any of that stuff," Pearce said. "Just leave it all. I'm the one doing her and I plan to end her quick."

"Fine with me," Sharla said, swinging her purse and

the shopping bag in one hand as she made for the door. "But you're talking about the end. Don't mean I can't have some fun with her before we get to the end."

Eight

Vic eyeing the building, double checking the text from Arlita. Wanting to be certain before he made his entrance.

Didn't doubt he had the right place. Had parked his truck parked alongside Horace's Cadillac. Chubba's Mustang visible in his rearview mirror.

Vic just taking his time, making sure everything was right.

Watching the apartment complex. The pool empty for the winter, lounge chairs stacked around it. Springtime creeping up on them, and soon they'd fill the pool back up again.

Vic wondering if he'd even see the summer.

A short silly regret passing through him at never having a pool of his own in his backyard. In-ground, anyway. Vic thinking that a thing like that tells the world you made it. Vic guessed he'd never made it.

Of course, he once heard the only thing better than having a pool, was having a neighbor with a pool. Then that way that poor bastard's got to take care of it instead of doing it yourself. Wouldn't have done Vic much good though. Never was much for neighborly chit-chat.

"Bet I could fill that sumbitchin' empty pool from my bladder though," Vic said aloud.

Vic wanting to be ready for whatever happened next, so deciding it was best to change his diaper now.

Peeling down his jeans, thinking can you fucking believe this?

His mood growing nastier as he undid the taped ends and stripped off the urine-logged diaper. Chucking it out the window of his truck onto the asphalt parking lot. Doing his best to ignore the pain hammering his bones from the inside out at every movement.

Fetching a fresh diaper from the box and sliding it under his bare ass. Affixing the tape, doing a better job of it this time.

Vic with the passing thought: what they ought to do, instead of this sissy white tape, should use duct tape on the diapers. Man it up a bit.

Vic laughing but not feeling any better about it.

Buckling his belt and feeling like, okay, now he really needs to kick the living hell out of someone.

Might make him feel better. Might not. Good thing was, instead of some random jack off at a bar mouthing off over a pool table, he actually had some folks that deserved an ass-kicking to one degree or another.

Vic reaching into the box of diapers and pulling out the J-frame .38.

About to step out of his truck, go find out what there was to find out. Just then the door of the building opened.

Sharla and some guy he'd never seen before coming out.

Sharla with her mouth running, but Vic unable to make out what she was barking at the guy. Swinging her purse and a plastic shopping bag.

Vic thinking that idiot girl's looking feral. Hair's a mess. Wearing shorts and a tight t-shirt—under-dressed as usual. Vic thinking, nice day and all, but nowhere near warm enough for showing off your titties like that.

Then checking out the guy with her. Dude wearing some kind of fruity rock-star get up, black jeans, black long-sleeve shirt and black boots. The sun glinting now and again off the various pieces of metal in his face. The two of them moving in herky-jerky steps across the complex.

Vic tracking the two of them with his eyes. Where's Chubba? Maybe they're on their way to see him. Sharla and the rock star heading toward an apartment building across the way.

Vic stepping out of his truck, slipping the .38 into the front of his jeans and following them.

Nine

Patty hearing the front door to the apartment open then close. A sense of relief washing over her. She'd been waiting for Them.

Enough was fucking enough. The past few hours spent running through a checklist of weapons at her disposal.

Fists.

Teeth.

Legs and feet.

Spit.

Puke

Head.

Anything and everything.

Patty's mind made up, getting free today one way or

another. All in.

Hearing those sick bastards coming down the hall. Usually, they came quietly but not this time. The woman jabbering a mile a minute. The voice sounding kind of familiar, but Patty not concentrating on it too long.

The sound of footsteps on carpet getting closer, and Patty readying herself.

Eyes tight behind her blindfold. Big breath through her nose. Her gagged mouth on fire. Hearing movement outside the door to her room. Then an explosion.

Like someone kicking in a door.

Ten

Pearce and Sharla's panicked eyes locking for a split second.

Then both of them rushing back down the short hallway to see about the noise at the door. Pearce pulling up short near where the hallway opened up into the front room.

A gaunt, mean-looking guy with a craggy face standing by the door that he must have just kicked in.

Pearce noticing the guy's jeans fit him funny around the waist, puffy.

Pearce scared stiff and silent.

Afraid of the guy; no idea who he was but could tell the man wasn't somebody Pearce wanted to mess with.

And Pearce afraid that someone outside their little circle of kidnappers had just kicked his way inside. Everything ripping apart now. Pearce with a free-falling sensation even as he was frozen in place alongside Sharla.

Noticing Sharla seemed fine though. Almost like this guy had an invitation to their party. Maybe because, evidently, Sharla knew him.

"Vic!"

Sharla sounding surprised to see him, then catching herself and making it conversational.

"What the fuck you doing here?" she said, smile. Putting it back on the guy like that, trying to control the situation.

Pearce thinking it just might work until he spotted the gun.

The guy, Vic, holding it at his side, pointing it down.

"Could ask you the same thing, Sharla," Vic said.

"Just partying is all," Sharla said. "Me and Pearce here."

Sharla giving Pearce a glance. Pearce seeing her recognize the fear running through him. A look of disgust flashing across her face.

At the moment Pearce not all that concerned with Sharla's opinion of him. More concerned with what comes next.

This guy Vic scanning the bare room. Place looking unlived in. Two high-backed wooden bar stools at the bar separating the living room from the kitchen. Not much else other than a few rolls of gray duct tape and a couple of cheap, plastic cartoon masks on the counter, Bugs Bunny and Daffy Duck.

"Going trick or treating?" Vic said.

Sharla not getting it at first, then following his eyes to the masks.

"That's funny, Vic. No, that was just...."

"Just what?"

"Just playing around," Sharla said. "Me and him."

Pearce catching the way Sharla sounded embarrassed to say she'd been with him.

"I'll bet," Vic said. Noticing her holding her purse and the plastic bag. "Whatcha got there?"

Sharla saying nothing then asking Vic if he wanted to sit down, have a beer

"The beer's back at Pearce's apartment," Sharla said. "Let's all head over that way."

"Yeah," Pearce said, finally getting his bearings. "Vic, right? I got a twelve pack in the fridge. We can all go over. Or I can go grab them for us. Won't take but a minute."

"Oh, we could all go," Sharla said. "Got a little crystal left too. You party, right Vic?"

Vic raising his .38, pointing it at Sharla.

"Toss the goddamn plastic bag on the floor."

Sharla saying all right, fine, no need to be an asshole about it and tossing it on the carpet halfway between them.

With his cowboy boot, Vic nudging the bag open, seeing the extension cords and curling iron.

"Was going to fix my hair," Sharla said. "You can see it's in need of a little attention."

"Now that's the first true thing out of your mouth since I got here," Vic said. Then something catching his eye.

Keeping the gun on Sharla and Pearce as he knelt down. Pulling the curling iron from the bag, examining it. Something all over it, white and papery thin. Reminding Vic of snake skin.

Vic realizing it *was* skin.

"What the fu—"

Sharla springing on Vic before he could finish his sentence.

Pearce not sure where the knife came from, out of her purse maybe. Later he would wonder why she had a knife on her in the first place.

Pearce, his fear still holding him in place, watched Sharla slash a deep gash in Vic's shoulder. Guessing she'd been going for his neck, the artery, and missing.

Vic reacting, exploding from his crouch. Throwing Sharla off of him, knocking her to the floor.

Pearce just standing there watching as Vic went over to Sharla scrambling on all fours to get away.

Vic cornering her, then bringing the gun down hard on the side of her head. Her body going still like somebody unplugged her.

"Holy shit, did you kill her?" Pearce said.

Vic turning around like he forgot Pearce was there.

"Don't think so. Not yet, anyway."

Vic inspecting the slice in his shoulder. Long but not too deep. Vic thinking it wouldn't kill him and laughing at that. Turning around and kicking Sharla's defenseless body in her ribs.

"Look, I don't know you," Pearce said, words

pouring from his mouth. “This whole thing was her idea—”

“—Shut it,” Vic said. “Put her on one of those barstools. Tape her up good. Otherwise, I’ll knock you out and tape you both up myself.”

Sharla’s meth-diet frame gave Pearce no trouble as he lifted her and set her like a rag doll on the barstool. Placing her arms at her side before wrapping duct tape around her several times so her limbs were pinned against her. She sat affixed to the chair, head drooping, mouth half open.

“All done,” he said, like he was proud of his handiwork.

“Remind me to give you your duct tape badge,” Vic said. “Now get on the fucking barstool, Webelo.”

After he had finished taping up Pearce, including his mouth, Vic ripped off a few strips of tape and used them to bind the cut on his shoulder.

Then leaning in close to Pearce, eyeball to eyeball.

“Now that I know you two lovebirds ain’t going nowhere, think I’ll have a look around,” Vic said. Reaching up and flicking the big hole in Pearce’s earlobe. “That okay with you, rock star?”

Pearce’s sobs muffled by the duct tape.

Vic stepping back, surprised and a little

disappointed this kid broke down so soon, not that it mattered. Noticing the wet spot on the kid's jeans, a blacker spot in the crotch of his black jeans.

"You pissed yourself," Vic said. "I got something can help with that."

Vic laughing to himself, then having a look around.

Eleven

All the noises in the other room. Patty alert to it all.

That door crashing in, then hearing Her call out "Vic!"

And Vic (she'd recognize Vic Shear's gravelly voice anywhere!) at one point saying the name Sharla.

At that Patty thinking, so that's who She is, *goddamn Sharla Ricketts.*

Patty mad as hell. Then came the disbelief. How someone could cause all this pain to another human being was bad enough. But to someone familiar, someone you've known most of your life....

Patty unable to wrap her head around that. It kicked

her in the chest like heartbreak.

Then hearing some sort of scuffle out there. Then nothing but the screech of duct tape being ripped off the spool, again and again.

And Patty wondering what the hell is taking so long.

Heavy steps coming down the hallway. Someone entering the room, and Patty sensing it was someone other than her usual visitors.

"Jesus Christ."

Again recognizing Vic's voice. Her heart racing, ready to finally be free of all this. Light at the end of the dark tunnel behind her blindfold.

Vic bending down to her ear.

"My god, Patty, you okay?"

His voice soft like it sometimes was when he was talking to his momma.

Patty nodding vigorously. Crying. Thinking why in the hell don't you take off this blindfold, pull away my gag, let me loose?

"It's okay now," Vic said. "Everything's going to be all right." Pausing. "Are you in pain?"

Patty shaking her head, pleading into her gag to be set free.

Vic saying I know, I know. But she would have to

wait just a little bit longer.

"Can't let you loose just yet, honey. Sorry, but it's for your own good. What's about to happen, I don't want it coming back on you. The cops saying you should have stopped me, if it gets to that. Cops can be all fucked up sometimes."

Patty struggling, yelling into her gag.

"You have to trust me," Vic said. "You're safe. Just got to do something I promised your grandmother. She's been worried sick."

Patty thinking this was the most she'd ever heard Vic talk at one time.

A stroke on her hair and Patty flinching, a reflex. And then Vic was gone, closing the door behind him.

Twelve

A shock of cold and wet hitting Sharla's face. Yanking her from her dreamy darkness.

Suddenly aware that she was coughing up some of the water that had landed in her throat. Then realizing she couldn't move.

Trapped by the duct tape wound tight around her torso. Each of her bare, skeletal legs taped to a leg of the barstool. Where she was and what was going on, all of it coming back to her, feeling like falling off out of a tree.

Eyes making out two fuzzy Vics, both waving money in her face. Her head woozy. Blinking, her head clearing a bit.

Vic saying, “Sloppy, very sloppy.”

Sharla able to focus on just the one Vic now, sharper but still waving the bills in her face.

“Win the lottery, Sharla?” Vic said. “I guess in a way, you did. I mean, someone else wins the lottery and then you rip her off, that’s as good as winning the lottery yourself, ain’t it?”

Sharla fully back in her head now. Seeing Pearce taped to the barstool beside her. Noting the duct tape over his mouth and thinking that works.

“This was all him,” Sharla said, tossing her head in Pearce’s direction. “Grabbing up Patty. What he did to her in there. All of it.”

Pearce offended, irate. But his defense stifled by the duct tape over his mouth.

Vic not really listening but not saying anything either.

Sharla talking fast to fill the silence.

"Thank God you showed up when you did," Sharla said. "Said he was going to kill Patty. I think he was fixing to kill me right after."

"He kill Chubba too?"

"He did!" Sharla said. "I tell you, Pearce here's a grade-A fucking lunatic."

Vic shaking his head, laughing. "You forget about trying to gut me like a hog just now?"

"Vic, you gotta listen to me—"

"—Shut it," Vic said.

Leaping on her to stretch duct tape over her mouth before she could get out another word. Then stepping back, amused as both of them struggled.

"No sense in all that," Vic said. "See, right now it don't matter what you say. Tell me the truth, tell me a lie. Won't matter."

Vic suddenly stopping, his face screwed up in pain.

Pearce way too busy crying to notice but Sharla seeing it. Vic suddenly seeming weak to her. Wishing her mouth wasn't taped shut so she could ask him what's the matter.

After a moment Vic letting out a breath.

"Anyway, we'll get to all that near the end, all the He

Said, She Said," he said. "First, though, we have a little fun."

Sharla's eyes following Vic as he moved to the far side of the living room. Vic picking up the curling iron. She hadn't noticed it had been heating up.

Vic Walking back toward them with the hot curling iron.

"This first part, it's just for Arlita," Vic said.

Then stopping and wanting Sharla to know just how despised she was. Looking her in the eye.

Vic saying, "Pretty sure Horace won't mind, neither."

Thirteen

"**This must be** the place."

Billy parking his sheriff's Escalade in the apartment complex parking lot so that it penned in Vic's truck and Chubba's Mustang. They'd have to ram him to get away.

Figuring Sharla drove the Mustang, so she must be around here some place. To his left, Horace's Cadillac where Chubba parked it. Gang's all here.

Billy looking around, wondering if Patty was here too. And if so, in what condition?

He'd made good time from Caulfield to KC, cutting the trip from a law abiding ninety minutes to a siren-and-cherry-aided hour or so. Plenty of windshield time for thinking.

Seemed unlikely to him that someone would kidnap Patty. That sort of thing happened, sure. But it happened to other people in other places.

Billy guessing that's probably what the people it happened to always thought too.

Then there was the Arlita issue. Why hadn't she told him? Could be she figured it was nothing more than Patty being difficult or breaking the law and Arlita maybe not wanting to involve him.

Still, Billy's mind kept going back to the scene where they'd found Patty's car. Something about all that just not adding up.

During his driving and thinking, Billy also hadn't discounted the notion that maybe Patty had just run off, that all this was a production of Mona's soap opera mind.

Or say it really was a kidnapping and Arlita chose not to come to him because she didn't trust him to get the job done? Billy not feeling good about himself at that.

Didn't make it untrue though. If it really was a kidnapping situation, it might make some sense for Vic popping up everywhere. His family and Arlita's had always been close.

And Billy still had no idea how Horace fit in.

Walking now across the complex to the building that housed the apartment number. Billy double-checking the piece of paper Mona had given him. Unable to ignore the butterflies in his stomach.

Considering if he should call in the local authorities, but deciding against it. Billy refusing to give up on what he felt was the most plausible explanation—that all this would turn out to be very stupid but, probably, not very criminal.

Only one way to find out.

Standing in front of the apartment door number that matched the number on Mona's paper. Trying to control his breath like he was on the mound in the last inning of a game.

Listening first, hearing nothing coming from inside the apartment. Knocking but not identifying himself.

Billy with no jurisdiction here, so deciding he had none of a lawman's obligations either. A gray area, maybe, but more and more it seeming to Billy that life was full of them.

Knocking again but still nothing coming from inside. Surprised at how glad he was of that. Checking Mona's note again. Now what?

Maybe they were all out, tooling around in someone else's car. Billy hadn't thought of that, of how many other people might be involved in addition to the people he knew.

Billy heading back downstairs to wait for them in the lot. Whenever they showed back up, he'd watch and get a better sense of what he was up against.

Fourteen

Arlita fiddling around out in her beauty shop, keeping busy to keep away her anxiousness. Windexing the mirrors when her cell phone rang.

Vic's name popping up on the screen, and Arlita almost dropping the damn phone when she tried to touch the answer button with her fat thumb.

"You find her?" Arlita said. "She okay?"

Arlita able to breathe again when Vic said he'd found her.

But something odd in his voice. Like he was in pain. Maybe the cancer getting to him. Or sick at what he found?

"She's alive? Goddamn it, Vic, you tell me she's alive."

"She is. She's been through hell though." Vic figuring it best to keep it vague for now. "She needs a doctor."

"Can you get her home? I mean, if you have to take her to a hospital up there, then do it. We'll worry about the rest of it later. But can you get her home? Or should I come up there?"

Vic saying he thought Patty would make it home. Then telling Arlita "You'll never guess who and what I'm looking at right now?"

"Not in the mood for games, Vic."

"Sharla. And a small pile of your money."

"Is that right?" Arlita growing calmer now as her questions were answered.

"So, we've been having a little chat. A hot time you could say," Vic said. "Oh, and Chubba Self's up here too, in the other room. But he's dead."

"Dead?" Arlita said. "Vic, what the hell's going on up there?"

"Probably best to avoid the details for now," Vic

said. "But there's no doubt Sharla's in on it."

"She tell you that?" Arlita said, about to give Sharla some credit for at least admitting her sins. A good idea before her next stop.

"Hell no," Vic said. "Her rock star boy friend did. This voice sound familiar?"

Arlita hearing some kind of thump and then a voice crying out. Then Vic back on the line.

"I guess you'll have to excuse him. He's not himself at the moment, so you might not recognize him. But he claims he's the one called you. Says his name is Matt but Sharla keeps calling him Pearce. Never guess what else he told me."

Arlita about to ask what when Mona and Gerald walked into the beauty shop. The two of them looking for her, see if she'd heard anything yet.

Mona seeing Arlita on the phone, knowing the look on her mother's face meant something was happening.

Mona asking who is it, is Patty okay, is that Vic, is her baby okay?

Arlita shushing Mona, telling Vic to go on.

Vic telling Arlita about Horace being behind the whole thing. A long shocked silence as Arlita let that sink in. Complete disbelief.

"They telling the truth?" Arlita said.

"Trust me, they're telling the truth," Vic said. "If Sharla had said it first, I wouldn't buy it. Nothing but horseshit coming out of that girl's mouth. But the rock star said it. He's too goddamn piss-pants scared to lie."

Another pause, and then Arlita telling Vic to put Sharla on the line. Vic saying okay, he'd put the cell phone on speaker. Arlita hearing what sounded like tape being ripped from skin, then hearing Sharla swearing.

"Sharla?" Arlita said.

"Arlita, goddamn it this was all Horace's idea," Sharla said.

Arlita thinking she'd never heard Sharla sound so desperate.

"It was, huh?" Arlita said. Going on, talking louder, they way people do when they're on speaker.

"Maybe, Sharla. But that don't mean you had to go work it for him, now did it? You done what you done because you wanted to. Just like always, all your sad little life. What a sorry waste."

"Arlita, please..."

"Vic, shut her up."

A thud and a yelp coming back over the line to Arlita. So loud Mona and Gerald heard it too.

Arlita covering the phone and telling Mona and Gerald that Patty was okay. Now leave her alone, she'll come in to tell them everything in a minute.

After Mona and Gerald left, Arlita waiting another few seconds to make sure they weren't listening outside the door to the shop.

"You there, Vic?"

"What you want me to do now?" Vic said.

Both of them knowing he was giving Arlita her final out before they crossed a line none of them could uncross.

Arlita could tell she was still on speaker, glad everyone there could hear her. No hesitation on her part.

"Handle it."

"Consider it done," Vic said. "Then I'll head back home with Patty, handle things there."

"Just get your ass home safe with my grandbaby," Arlita said.

The sounds of cussing and pleading coming through the line. Arlita talking louder so that Vic could hear her over all the racket on his end.

"I'll handle things on this end," Arlita said.

Fifteen

Vic hit the end call button on his cell phone before dropping it to the floor. Pulling the .38 from the front of his pants, where he'd tucked it down into his heavy diaper.

Watching Sharla struggling against the duct tape, Pearce crying, begging. Both of them making a hell of a lot of noise.

"Quiet!" Vic said.

Both of them quiet, though Pearce was unable to stop gasping for breath.

"Now this has all been real fun," Vic said. "And you, rock star, I do appreciate you filling me in on the details of everything. Because if I'd had to depend on Sharla here for the straight story, we'd be dancing around forever. But as it is, party's over."

Raising his .38 and, just like that, Vic shooting Pearce in the forehead.

Pearce's body slumping, twitching as his organs raced to catch up with his dead brains, now splattered on the kitchen wall.

"Damn, that was loud."

Vic stepping closer to inspect the damage, talking to

Sharla.

"Tore a good chunk out the back, but that's a neat little hole in the front there. Got holes everywhere else; bet he'd like having a hole right dead center of his forehead."

Vic turning to Sharla. "If he weren't dead anyway."

"Vic, please, I will do anything—"

"No doubt about that," Vic said. "We've established you're capable of anything." Then Vic stopped, bent over, grimacing.

"What the hell's wrong with you?" Sharla said.

Vic willing away the pain.

"What's wrong is I'm dying," Vic said.

"Sorry to hear that," Sharla said. "Any chance you're going to drop dead right this second?"

"No chance, don't worry," Vic said. "By the way, you're not going as quickly as rock star here either. It's going to be a long slow ride for both of us."

Vic proceeding to tell Sharla how it was going to go:

Five shots in his .38, one of them already spent out the back of rock star's skull.

That left two bullets for a painful gunshot in each of her knees.

Then two more for an agonizing shot in each elbow.

"Now here's the tough part," Vic said. "You'll have to

wait — in excruciating pain, I might add — while I reload. Empty the cylinder, reload the cylinder. Be surprised how long it can take. I just hope I don't get all nervous and drop the bullets when I'm reloading. Would hate for it to drag on, cause you to suffer."

Vic pausing, pleased that Sharla was able to feel fear, feel anything.

"But I promise," Vic said, "right after that, I'll shoot you in the face a time or two. Put you out of your misery."

Sixteen

Billy walking back across the apartment complex to his SUV when he heard the gunshot.

Ducking behind a stack of lounge chairs by the pool. Peeking up, surveying the area. Pretty sure the shot had come from the apartment building directly across the way.

Hitting 911 on his cell, unsure if the local police used the same radio codes as his department so telling them shots fired, shots fired.

Reading off the location from the note Mona had given him.

Telling the 911 dispatcher, more than once, his name and that he was the sheriff of Caste County.

The dispatcher saying units were on their way and trying to keep him on the line. Asking Billy, what was he doing right at the moment? Was he in a safe place?

Another gunshot, definitely from the building right in front of him. Time to move.

"I been in safer places," Billy said into his phone, then killing the call.

Pulling his Kimber Custom II .45 and running in a crouch up to the side of the door leading into the building where the shots had come from.

Still no sirens in the air. Billy telling himself to breathe. Four count in, four count hold, four count out. Pushing open the heavy door, slowing moving inside the three-story building.

Billy snapping toward a sound coming from his left, gun up. Scaring a small, bent old woman even more than she already was. Lowering his gun, pointing out his badge.

The woman still scared, just not of him now. Wordlessly pointing to the stairs that led to the basement apartments.

Billy nodding, whispering for her to get back inside her apartment and stay away from her door. Assuring her the police are on their way.

Both Billy and the old woman ducking at another ear-splitting gunshot. Hearing the wail of someone in agony. The old woman scurrying back into her apartment, slamming the door behind her.

Billy creeping down to the bottom of the stairs. At the bottom, two apartments. Seeing where the framing around one of the doors was splintered as if it had been kicked in and slightly ajar.

Billy guessing the prize was behind that door. Having this confirmed with another loud gunshot and more shrieking.

A giant breath before kicking open the door. Coming in fast, gun up, yelling.

"Freeze! Sheriff!"

Billy coming face to face with Vic. Telling Vic to drop the gun he was pointing at a woman taped to a chair.

Taking a split-second for Billy to register that it was Sharla in the chair. In tears, covered in blood. Both knees blooms of muscle and bone and blood. One of her elbows in shreds too.

"Wow," Vic said. "Have to say you were the last motherfucker I expected to see coming through that door."

"Drop the gun, Vic," Billy said. "Now."

"Billy, he's crazy," Sharla screamed. "He's torturing us, me and Patty. She's in the back. Killed Chubba. Killed Pearce. He's...."

Sharla running out of steam, out of life.

"Mean Matt, don't you?" Vic said, grinning. "I tell you Sharla, I am impressed. Three bullets in you and your mind is still working like a rat on a wheel. Instinct is strong in you."

"What say we talk it out," Billy said. "First though, I need you to put the gun down."

Vic laughing, then gritting his teeth as if something was chewing at him from the inside.

Then Vic saying to Billy wait until you hear this shit. Telling Billy what rock star had told him about the whole situation, who was involved.

"You believe that, Billy?" Vic said. "I mean I am a nasty, cold-ass son-of-a-bitch. But something like all this? Horace-goddamn-Self? Bastard played us all. I just don't understand rich people sometimes."

"No telling about people," Billy said. "Now put the gun down."

Billy and Vic locking eyes for a moment as they both heard the approaching sirens outside. Vic smiling.

"Yeah it was true," Vic said. "I killed rock star. But

Chubba, he was dead when I found him."

Billy seeing the smile fall from Vic's face.

"Patty's back there," Vic said. Cocking the .38, still leveled at Sharla. "They did some awful things to her. It ain't right. Make sure Patty gets home, all right?"

"Put the gun down, Vic, please," Billy said. The "please" just coming out, and Billy wishing it hadn't. Billy knowing a man like Vic only took the word as a sign of weakness.

"Sorry it had to be you," Vic said to Billy.

"Why, think I don't have it in me?" Billy said.

"Hell, we all got it in us," Vic said. "Just a shame to have to bring it out in some people is all. Tell mom not to forget to feed Fred."

Billy looking confused. "Who the fuck is Fred?"

"My cat," Vi said, the lines in his sinewy arm pulling taut as his finger tightened on the trigger.

Billy thinking *damn it* and shooting Vic in the chest, knocking him to the floor.

Billy found Patty tied to the bed in the next room. Immediately calling out her name, lifting her blindfold.

Patty squinting even in the dim light.

Billy trying to shield her from Chubba's corpse rotting on the floor. Gently as he could, removing the tape from her mouth.

"Billy, are you real?" she said.

Billy saying nothing. Wondering how to answer a question like that.

Seventeen

The paramedics taking Patty off in an ambulance, Sharla in another and Vic in yet a third.

Billy standing in the apartment, talking with one of the detectives from the Overland Park PD when word came in that Vic died en route to the hospital.

The detective watching Billy's reaction, deciding his grief at the news was fitting.

"It happens," the detective said.

Billy nodding, saying nothing. Fighting to hide a case of random, post-adrenaline hiccups. Watching the forensic photographer snapping photos of the body they'd IDed through the building manager as Matt Hart.

Another photographer in the back bed room taking pictures of Chubba's body and the hostage scene.

"Seventeen years on the job," the detective said, "I never shot anybody."

Just then one of the forensics techs, a woman in a white lab coat and rubber gloves, picking up a cell phone near where Vic had been standing when Billy shot him.

Billy with another hiccup, this one jarring loose a thought in Billy's head.

"Excuse me," Billy said to her, then checking with the detective to make sure it was okay he talked to her. The detective nodded.

"Can you tell me the last number he called?" Billy said.

The woman working the buttons on the phone.

"It's one in his address book," the woman said. "Comes up as Arlita."

"What time did he make the call?"

"Says here, 1:54 p.m."

Billy looking at the detective look at him. Billy asking him if he wouldn't happen to know what time Billy had called 911?

The detective checking his notes.

"Looks like your call came in at 1:59 pm."

Billy saying oh hell and rubbing his eyes.

Eighteen

"**Pick up the** damn phone."

Billy racing down the highway, lights flashing and sirens howling. Heading southwest across the rolling plains, back to Caulfield as fast as possible.

The afternoon sun hanging low in the sky, staring him in the eyes. Out of radio range so trying the station house on his cell again. Again, no answer.

Didn't make sense. Right about now everyone should be there for shift change, even Cookie. Billy deciding to call someone else, test that his phone worked while it was roaming out on the prairie.

Paige answering her cell phone on the second ring with a neutral hello. At the moment, Billy not caught up in whether she sounded happy to hear from him.

Instead, asking her if she could do him a favor, go over to the station house, see if anyone was there.

"I guess, sure," Paige said. "Why?"

"No one's picking up there. And, damn it, there's

supposed to be someone there right now."

"Billy, what's wrong?"

"Nothing and everything," Billy said, realizing he sounded frantic. Which he was, but no need to wear it like a loud western shirt with fake pearl snaps. Resetting himself.

"Dunno, yet," he said. "That's why I'm trying to get hold of whoever is supposed to be there right now."

"Well mom and I are heading to the grocery store right now," Paige said. "We can swing by on our way."

"Yell at whoever's there to answer the phone," Billy said. "Better yet, have them call me, and I'll yell at them."

He and Paige saying goodbye, then Billy immediately trying the station house again. Still no answer.

Taking a chance, dialing Arlita's beauty shop. Calling the landline number in his cell phone address book that he used when he needed to make an appointment for a haircut. Ringing several times before being picked up with a "hello" rather than the usual "Arlita's."

"Who's this?" Billy said

"You called here," Mona said, "who the fuck is this?"

"Mona, goddamn it, this is Billy."

Mona not bothering to apologize, of course. Instead launching right into a string of desperate questions.

What did he find in KC?

Who was there?

Was her daughter really okay, like Arlita said?

Mona not pausing long enough between questions for Billy to answer. Not even a breath, just running on to the next thought that popped into her head, until finally Billy said for her to quiet down a second so he could tell her what he knew.

"Patty's okay," Billy said. "It was pretty rough for her but she's in the hospital now. She'll be fine."

"Hospital?" Mona said. "Momma said she was coming back with Vic?"

"When was that, Mona?"

"Right after she spoke with Vic. That's all she said though. Wouldn't stop and tell me nothing about nothing, just ran out of the shop."

Billy asking how long ago was that and where did Arlita go?

Instead of answering, Mona smart-assing him, saying now look who's asking the next question before the last one's answered.

"Mona, I'm trying to help your mother," Billy said. "She may be about to mess up. Something she'll regret. Now you said she left soon after she talked to Vic. That was around two this afternoon, right?"

"Right, how did you know?" Mona said. "Damn cops, always jacking with you, asking questions they already know the answer to."

"Well, I don't know the answer to this one," Billy lied. "You have any idea where Arlita was headed?"

"No idea," Mona said. "Like I said, she wouldn't stop long enough to tell me jackshit. Just grabbed one of Daddy's shotguns and took off like a bat out of hell."

Billy wishing he could reach through the line and throttle Mona right then.

"Did you say shotgun?"

"Yep. And a box of shells." Mona leaving it at that.

Billy getting Arlita's cell number from Mona, then telling Mona to stay put before hanging up.

One eye on the road as Billy punched in Arlita's cell number. No answer, straight to voice mail. Billy leaving a message, asking Arlita to call him as soon as she got the message.

Again Billy trying the station house as his vehicle sped along toward Caulfield.

Still no answer.

Nineteen

The phone at the station house ringing and ringing.

"Now just who could that be?" Lon said, sarcastic as hell.

No one making a move to answer it. Not with Lon waving his .357 around every time he opened his mouth.

Dustin and Zane both handcuffed to their desks. Lon with their side arms tucked in his pants.

Cookie trying not to appear afraid. Lon waggling his gun in her direction now and again as a clear reminder of who was in charge.

The phone halting it's ringing for the time being.

"Bet our noble sheriff's panties are all in a bunch, no one picking up," Lon said.

"You should be ashamed of yourself, Lon Harmon" Cookie said, sitting up straight in a chair next to Dustin and Zane. All of them lined up so Lon could keep an eye on them. "Lord knows what your mother would think if she were alive."

Lon flashing a grin at Cookie. "Maybe you can ask the Lord and my mom real soon."

The phone started up ringing again.

"A tenacious little prick," Lon said, "I'll give him that."

"Want me to answer it?" Cookie said.

"Want me to put an extra hole in that plump rump you're always shaking all over the place?" Lon said. "You know, you act like you're the damn boss around here. Like your shit don't stink and this place runs on your farts. Hell, you ain't nothing but a glorified secretary, you know that? Now if what was supposed to happen had happened – namely, I being sheriff – first order of business would have been you landing on your fat ass out on the bricks."

The phone stopped ringing.

"Lon, you don't want to do this," Dustin said.

Dustin trying to use whatever friendship he and Lon had left to take the heat off Cookie. Maybe talk some sense into Lon. Telling him he needs to think for a minute now.

"How the heck would you know what I want or don't want to do?" Lon said. "We get along and all, Dustin, but that don't make you any brighter than you are."

Lon pausing, using his sleeve to wipe the seat from his forehead. Going on, tone nicer now.

"But don't be hard on yourself. Not like it's reasonable to expect you to know," Lon tapping the barrel of the black .375 against his temple, "what goes on up in old Lon's head."

Lon noticed Zane looking away.

"How about you, boy?" Lon said. "You're supposed to be so smart. Any idea what I'm planning here?"

"No idea," Zane said.

Talking quietly, not look directly at Lon. Zane wanting to make himself as near to invisible as humanly possible. Watching and waiting for a moment, for a mistake, that he could use to change the situation.

"Figures," Lon said. "So smart you can't even string two sentences together."

The phone ringing again.

"Now I like all y'all well enough," Lon said. "But if our punk sheriff – hitting the redial there over and over – thinks he can fire me and *not* have anything come back on him for it...."

Water coming to Lon's eyes as his voice cracked. After a moment that grin returning to his face.

"Heck, then he's even dumber than everyone thinks," Lon said, forcing a laugh.

Lon so caught up in his jumble of emotions, and everyone else caught up in where Lon's gun was pointing at any given moment, that no one saw Paige and her mother walk in through the glass front doors.

"Need a warrant to answer a phone around here?" Paige called out.

Then grabbing her mother by the elbow, pulling them both up short. Paige first seeing the fraught looks on everyone's faces, then the big gun in Lon's hand.

"What a nice surprise," Lon said, waving them over with the gun. "Come on in, have a seat."

Twenty

Arlita watching Horace's place. From the front seat of her Mercedes, she had a good view of his house and his land behind it.

She'd parked down the country road a ways, pulled off on to the shoulder. Waiting for Tammy to leave so Arlita could confront Horace, just the two of them. Arlita waiting a couple of hours now.

She was in no hurry. Waiting on Tammy to leave gave Arlita time to get her head around it all. She still wasn't quite there.

None of it seemed certain to her. Maybe because she hadn't seen any of it, she thought. Seeing is believing.

Except when your eyes trick you, of course. So then nothing is certain.

Down a rabbit hole of thought now. Deciding she believed it all because it's what Vic had told her. That was that. But knowing she needed something tangible to make it real to her.

Looking at the clock on the dash and thinking Vic should be pulling into town with Patty any moment now. Bringing her grandbaby home where she belonged. Arlita considering a quick call to Vic, check where they were.

Then deciding against it. Enough to deal with right here right now.

She'd turned off her cell phone earlier. Mona kept calling. And some other number that seemed familiar to Arlita but that she couldn't quite place. Mona and that other number calling over and over.

Arlita not answering either number. Her ringtone, Alabama's "Mountain Music" playing over and over until finally Arlita had had enough.

Keeping her eye on Horace's house. His two dogs, the fat lab and the little terrier mutt, lounging about the front yard. Arlita reaching over, touching the cool gunmetal of the shotgun lying across the passenger seat. Her dead husband's pump action Mossberg twelve gauge.

She'd fed three shotgun shells into its underbelly right after parking her car. Figuring two should be plenty but one more just to be safe.

For the about the billionth time since Pat had passed, Arlita wished her husband was there with her. Good times, bad times, didn't matter. She wanted him right there beside her.

Resigning herself to the idea that his gun on the seat next to her was as close as she was going to get to him. For the time being, anyway.

All of the sudden the dogs stirring, up and barking. Arlita watching Tammy exit the house, shooing away the dogs before they could jump up and get their dirty paws on her jeans. Tammy climbing into her white Yukon and rolling down the long driveway.

Arlita had driven past Horace's place before turning around to park, figuring when Tammy left she would head into town, the direction opposite of Arlita.

Tammy did just that.

Arlita waiting for the Yukon's taillights to disappear down the hill before firing up her Mercedes, easing it closer to Horace's place. Rather than pull up the drive and set the dogs to barking, Arlita parking on the road and walking up, shotgun pointing to the ground.

The dogs running out to greet her, tails wagging. Following her as she made her way up the drive.

Neither dog barked until she got close to the house. Then the black lab let out a deep, friendly bark. The other little yippy one joining in.

Arlita hearing Horace out back of the house, shouting for the dogs to shut up. Arlita going through the unlocked front door.

Making her way through Horace's house toward the deck. Spotting Horace through the sliding glass doors. Sitting in a chair, his back to her.

If she were certain of it all, she could shoot him now, be done with it. If she were certain, no problem at all with shooting him in the back.

Arlita walking slowly with her husband's shotgun in front of her. Still not certain enough for her to put the butt of the gun against her shoulder.

Sliding open the door and causing Horace to jump. Probably expecting Tammy but shocked to find Arlita with a shotgun.

Arlita seeing the duffle bag of her money at his feet. Raising the Mossberg, tucking it tight against her shoulder.

Everything at that moment becoming certain for Arlita.

Twenty-one

Now, this didn't make any sense. Billy pulling into his reserved space out front of the station house.

Two Crown Vic squad cars. Cookie's Buick. Paige's mother's Ford. All lined up in the diagonal parking spaces out front of the station house.

Billy thinking surely somebody in there had a free hand to pick up a telephone. Redialing the station house on his cell phone as he walked up the steps to the front doors.

Wanting to make his point, walk in as the phone's ringing and catch them all sitting around on their asses.

Hearing the landline ringing as he came through the glass doors. Seeing Lon holding everyone at gun point.

Lon, head turned away, laughing at the ringing phone and not noticing Billy come in.

Billy pulling his Kimber before Lon finally caught sight of him.

Rather than turn on a reflex and put his gun on Billy, Lon kept his gun on his hostages. Figuring there was more leverage in it this way.

"Hey, lookie who's here," Lon said.

"Everyone okay?" Billy said.

Noticing Paige's mother looking pale. "Miss Julie, you all right?"

"They're all fine," Lon said. "It's you I came to see. So Sheriff – and I use the word as loosely as the elastic on a fat man's underwear – you might want to drop that gun before someone other than you gets hurt."

"Don't think I'll do that, Lon," Billy said. "But you might want to put your gun on me instead of them. From this angle I got a good view of your finger. Telling you, I see you even think about squeezing the trigger, you're getting two in your chest, one in your head before you hit the ground."

The threat throwing Lon off a bit. Not fear, but surprise. Expecting Billy to drop his gun, maybe even fill his pants.

"You sure that's how you want to go about it?" Lon said. "Not exactly what the playbook calls for in this situation."

"Seems the book's out the window today," Billy said. "And honestly, I was done taking suggestions from you the moment I gave you your walking papers."

Lon's face showing confusion now. Like he was the

one who was trapped rather than everybody else like he'd planned. Looking at his former co-workers and Paige and her mother looking weak.

None of them looking as scared as Lon suddenly felt.

"That's what I want to know," Lon said, "who the hell are *you* to fire *me*?"

"Sheriff, duly elected by the people of Caste County," Billy said. "And if anything, right now I'd say you're proving the collective wisdom of the people."

"Kiss my ass," Lon said.

"If that's what it takes," Billy said. "I'm all about serving my constituents. They are customers after all. Customer service is key, am I right? Then again, I already shot one of the customers today. What's one more?"

"I don't know what you're talking about, and frankly don't care," Lon said. "I just—"

"—Just what?" Billy said. "What did you think was going to happen, coming in here like this? You going to shoot everybody? You got more people than bullets. So what then? Shoot just me?"

Billy watching the wheels turn in Lon's head.

"I'm pretty sure you'll have to point your gun at me before you can shoot me," Billy said. "But you're the expert."

A long, tense moment of Lon running his options through his head.

Billy deciding now was the time to give him a way out. Billy saying of course Lon could always lower his gun and they could talk.

"That's the great thing about talking," Billy said, "it applies to anything. Hell, sometimes it even helps."

Lon sweating heavily now, confused, not sure where all this was heading. Billy ready to close this deal, one way or another.

"Thing is, Lon, we kind of got a situation we need to deal with immediately. Now I know how you feel about the job, so I know, personal issues aside, you wouldn't ever want to get in the way the job. But I have to tell you, right now, there's some place else we really need to be."

"You tell me what's going on," Lon said.

"Tell you what," Billy said, "drop your gun and after I cuff you, you can listen while I fill in everyone else."

Lon thinking it over. "So I'm guessing there's probably no way I can get my job back? Right?"

Billy puzzled that could even come up at this juncture but hiding his disbelief.

"It's doubtful," Billy said. "But you can always run against me in the general election, come fall. I'm guessing all this doesn't help your chances, but who knows? Anything's possible when you leave it up to the people."

Lon brightening at that. "You think?"

"All I know is, if this situation here or the other situation you're keeping me from goes south, then there's nothing I or anyone else can do for you."

Lon nodding, seeing the sense in it. A long moment before finally laying his .357 on his old desk.

Billy ordering Lon to his knees, hands on his head. Billy grabbing his deputies' service weapons from Lon's waist before cuffing Lon while Cookie freed Dustin and Zane.

Billy hugging Paige, asking if she was okay.

"I think so," Paige said, pulling back. "Mom, are you okay?"

Her mother nodding she was okay, but Billy not so sure.

"Better get her over to the hospital," Billy said. "We have to hurry. I'll call you soon as I can."

Another quick hug between them before Billy let go of her.

Billy turning to his deputies, telling them they all needed hustle over to Horace's Self's right now. Explaining the situation he expected to find there, telling them he'd fill them in on the rest when there was time.

Lon sitting in an office chair, wearing cuffs. Looking up at everyone and taking in every word like a kid listening to his favorite bedtime story.

Twenty-two

"**Well, here they** come," Arlita said.

Turning her head to watch out the picture window in Horace's living room. The sheriff's SUV and two squad cars flying up the long driveway, all sirens and flashing lights.

Horace sitting in his leather recliner, just a slight nod of his head. About all he cared to move with the barrel of Arlita's Mossberg stuck in his mouth.

"I suspect they'll want to talk about all this," Arlita said.

With a free hand, Arlita turning on her phone. Putting it on the coffee table before giving her full attention back to Horace.

Watching the pain in his eyes. Knowing she'd cut him good when she told him Chubba was dead, who did it. Horace trapped somewhere between disbelief and grief.

Arlita taking no joy in that. Earlier, waiting in her car down the road, she'd wondered if maybe his pain over losing his son would be enough for her.

Now that she'd told him, saw it ripping into his soul, she realized it wasn't enough for her. Nothing more than pain he brought on himself and his family.

At the moment, Arlita more concerned with her pain and what had been done to her family.

"Ask you one more time," she said. "And it'd be nice if you gave me a real answer this time."

Arlita extracting the shotgun from Horace's mouth before asking, "Why?"

"I don't...," Horace stopping and then starting again, "What the hell's it matter? My boy's dead."

"Matters to me!" Arlita said.

Pressing the shotgun against Horace's forehead. Dying to pull the trigger but somehow holding herself back.

"Look it was stupid, all right?" Horace said. "We shouldn't have ever—"

"—That's not an answer," Arlita said, pressing the shotgun hard against Horace's damp forehead. "I want to know why."

"Is there even a reason I could give you?" Horace said. "What do you want me to say?"

"Just tell me why, like I asked."

Arlita waiting but Horace refusing to give her the satisfaction. Evidently prepared to die thinking he was her better.

"Wasn't just the money, was it?" Arlita said.

"There are debts," Horace said.

Arlita backing the shotgun off his skull. Thinking maybe they were getting somewhere now.

"Hell, you could have asked me for the money. Everybody else does. Got more than I know what to do with as it is. I'd have given it to you. Or loaned it, if that's what your pride needed to call it."

Arlita paused, watching Horace's face. Eyeballing her, defiant even now.

Arlita saying again, "Wasn't just the money, was it?

Horace not saying a word, knowing the truth would not set him free. But Arlita not needing to hear it. Been living it her whole small town life.

"Couldn't just climb down off your high horse to ask someone like me for help," she said.

Arlita laughing at the stubbornness of some people. Laughing at herself and the thing inside her that always made her want to prove to stubborn people that they had nothing on her.

"Ask me for the money," she said.

Horace kept his mouth shut.

Arlita pressing the barrel against his lips.

"I said ask me for the damn money."

Pulling back so Horace could speak.

"Can I have the money," he said.

"Say please."

"Please, can I have the money!"

Arlita pressing the shotgun against his lips until Horace opened his mouth. The taste of the gunmetal sending a zing through the fillings in his teeth.

"Now ask me for your life, you miserable son of a bitch."

Arlita's cell phone began ringing on the coffee table.

She didn't look at her phone, just kept her eyes on Horace. That scared, pleading look on his face that still somehow came off as arrogant.

"Think I should answer that?" she said.

Billy surprised Arlita answered her cell phone. "What's going on in there, Arlita? Everything okay?"

Billy nodding to Dustin and Zane. Standing by his

vehicle trying to see into Horace's house.

Thought he made out the shapes of Arlita and Horace through the picture window. Hard to see for sure though, the room growing darker every second as dusk crept over them.

"We're fine," Arlita said over the phone. "Horace and I, we're just chit-chatting. He's hitting me up for a loan."

"Going to give it to him?" Billy said.

"I might," Arlita said.

"Let's keep it friendly in there, okay?" Billy said. "I mean, Patty, she'll be home soon enough, a day or so. Want to make sure everything stays friendly, right?"

Billy pausing, waiting for something back from her.

"Am I right or am I right, Arlita?"

"Good talking with you, Billy," Arlita said. "But I got to go."

"Arlita!"

Billy realizing she was gone. Hitting redial as he told Dustin to circle around the left of the house, Zane to flank the right.

Neither of them taking more than two steps when they all froze. A single shotgun blast coming from inside the house.

“Damn it, Arlita,” Billy said.

The three of them meeting Arlita coming out the front door.

She’d thrown the Mossberg into the yard and now stood on the porch, her hands in the air. Blood spattered over her clothes, her face, in her hair.

Face to face with Billy.

“Wasn’t nothing you could’ve done, anyways,” Arlita said.

Billy wincing at that. Reaching for his handcuffs.

“Sure wish you’d have let me try.”

Epilogue

"**More** coffee?"

Five months later on a sweltering August morning and Billy beating the heat in an air conditioned booth at Trace's Place. Sheriff Otis Cady sitting across the table.

The two of them having one of their regular pupil-mentor breakfasts.

Billy and Sheriff Cady both nodding to more coffee, saying please to the waitress. Carmen, a new hire, started about a week before. She'd been a few years behind Billy and Trace in high school.

Now her baby daddy's run off to who knows where. Carmen finding herself to be the latest member of Trace's Home for Single Mothers.

Billy slyly glancing around the café, looking for the other waitress, Tippy.

Finding her wiping down a spot at the counter. Billy

figuring that grim look on Tippy's face most likely had something to do with Carmen. Billy catching sight of Trace working quickly back in the kitchen.

Billy finally pulled away from his thoughts by Sheriff Cady, asking if there was any news on Arlita's up-coming murder trial.

"Lots of talk," Billy said, his head gesturing toward the usual gossipy crowd at the café counter. "But nothing to put stock in. She's hired some big shot lawyer out of Kansas City. She'll be fine."

"Money does buy you things, I guess," Sheriff Cady said. "What about the granddaughter?"

"Patty's doing okay," Billy said. "Talk about buying things—she's driving around in a new Audi. That don't solve things, but it don't hurt neither. She seems okay, all things considered. She's like her grandmother, strong as a bull. Heard she and her mother are a little closer now. So maybe there's something good come out of it."

Sheriff Cady thinking that over. Saying he wasn't sure if that was enough to justify it all but you take what you can get.

"What about that other guy," Sheriff Cady said, "What's his face?"

Billy grinning, knowing he meant Lon. Billy saying

evidently Lon's doing fine, getting the help he needs at the state mental health hospital over in Osawatomie.

"Taking time and doing time at the same time, you might say," Billy said.

"What about you? Still seeing that pretty little thing I saw you dining with over at The Oasis? What's her name again?"

"Paige," Billy said, shaking his head. "No, she's back living in Boston now that her mother's pretty much recovered from her heart attack. We talk on the phone now and again. Text and email and whatnot. Probably see her if she ever visits. Hard not to in a small town."

"Indeed it is," Sheriff Cady said. A sip of coffee before changing the subject, "So you're running for the position proper. Should make for an interesting fall."

"What else you going to do?" Billy said.

Sheriff Cady not buying it, knowing there was more to it than that.

"It's a good gig," Sheriff Cady said. "Like I told you, once you get elected, it's hard to get unelected. Really got to mess it up."

"Thought I managed to do that last spring."

"You have days like that," Sheriff Cady said. "Can't let it eat at you. I mean, it will. Probably always. But you got to try not to let it."

Billy taking a sip of coffee.

"Yeah, I guess. People are gonna do what they're gonna do."

"And when they do, all you can do is try to keep everyone around them safe," Sheriff Cady said. "Nobody bats a thousand, though."

"As an ex-pitcher, I have to say I damn sure hope not."

Both men laughing at that before Carmen came over with their check. Billy grabbing it before Sheriff Cady could reach it.

"I got this one," Billy said.

"You sure?"

"My county, my check," Billy said, smiling like he does.

ENJOY THIS EXCERPT FROM *BROKEN HEARTLAND*

(THE 2ND BILLY KEENE BOOK)

One

Two something in the morning.

Half a moon hanging in the sky, surrounded by stars. Enough light to see but not be seen.

Rubber-gloved hands unfolding homemade stencils so large they need to be laid out on the grass like a dead body.

The stencil's menacing message opened to full size.

A coyote howling in the distance. The violent rip of masking tape. The gloved hands affixing the stencils to the side of a bright white house.

Tink-tink of a metal pellet rattling around inside a spray paint can that's ready to burst.

Hissing as the built-up pressure releases a blood-red spray over the stencils and onto the house.

Two

Sheriff Billy Keene behind his desk at the sheriff's department.

Cell phone to his ear, listening to the woman who held his heart *not* answering her cell phone.

Paige back in Boston for well over a year now. Been back home a few times, and he'd gone to visit once. Had a nice dinner at an Italian fish place in the North End, *The Daily Catch*. Saw the sights, Fenway, Old North Church and such. A nice stroll through The Public Garden.

But over the months they'd gradually talked less and less. Each understood the other was busy—Paige working as a photographer's assistant and trying to build her own photography career; Billy with sheriffing back in Caulfield.

Lately, Paige not returning some of his calls. Answering fewer of them, too.

Her phone still ringing, and Billy thinking *halfway across the country yet still close enough to break my heart.*

Then telling himself at least that was some version of close. Would have to do for now.

Billy killing his call before again having to listen to her recorded voice tell him to leave a message. A feeling in his chest like a rusty blade sawing up through him.

Taking a sip of his morning coffee, trying wash that sawing feeling back down. Jumping a little as he spilled a few hot drops on his light brown uniform pants. Billy dabbing at the stain with a paper towel before finally giving up.

Thinking Tuesdays are getting to be about as bad as Mondays.

Paige not texting, that was becoming a regular thing too. And Billy knowing that when a person of a certain age - hers, his - won't text you back, something's got to be wrong.

Billy leaning back in his leather office chair, considering the cell phone in his hand. As if it might have an answer for him. Dandling it like it was a Magic 8 Ball.

Try again later.

Or now.

Billy fighting the urge to hit redial. Thankfully saved by Cookie Reins, the office admin, walking past the glass walls of his office with a folder clutched to her bosom.

Reversing on her heel, popping into his doorway. Cookie's lips pursed with a mixture of pity and disgust.

"Put down that damn phone."

Billy with a *what, me?* look before laying his cell on his desk.

Every inch of Billy's six-foot-three frame leaning way, way back in his chair as Cookie moved into his office. All thick thighs and tight skirt, as usual.

Just Cookie dressing like she does. Closer to retirement age than she was to Billy's age, but dressing like she was younger than him even though Billy was still a few years shy of thirty.

To her credit, Cookie still kind of pulling it off in the right light.

Billy listening to Cookie going on at him.

"You're doing nothing but driving that girl nuts, everyone around you too. And allowing yourself to be treated this way, that ain't making you feel any better, is it?

"No ma'am."

"Then, all due respect, boss? Cut the shit."

"Feel better?"Billy said.

"Some. Depends on if you do like I say or not," Cookie said, smiling, flirty but not meaning anything by it.

Billy pretty sure that was the only way she knew how to smile. Asking Cookie if she invaded his office just to lecture him or was there anything else? As always, there was something else.

“Want me to run down all this for you?”

Cookie meaning the thick folder she was now holding out to Billy.

Billy shaking his head.

“Will it keep?”

“It’ll keep,” Cookie said, frowning, “for a bit.”

Billy eyeing the folder.

“Budget stuff for next fiscal year?”

Cookie nodding, turning so everyone else in the office could hear her.

“But hell, nobody here needs to get paid anyway," she said. "We’re all in it for the fun of it.”

Cookie turning back to Billy. Setting the folder on the far edge of his desk next to his baseball cap. A fitted cap, dark brown with a flat bill. The front emblazoned with "Caste County Sheriff" around an embroidered sheriff's badge.

Cookie keeping on him.

“Better get your head in the game, right now. Hear me?”

Billy nodding, saying nothing.

Still unsure he and the job were meant for each other. Same as when the local power brokers had convinced him it was a good idea to leverage his celebrity as a local sports hero in a run for sheriff.

In the short year and a half he'd held the office — first as interim sheriff in an emergency election, then elected sheriff proper in a general election — he'd seen and learned some things about the people he thought he knew.

And done some things that change a person forever.

Lately, Billy coming to realize fully that the job of saving people from themselves, it almost never stops.

A sudden small flash. Billy's cell lighting up, vibrating atop his desk.

Both he and Cookie seeing it was Sara Jane calling.

Billy unable to hide his disappointment that it wasn't Paige reaching out. Still, doing a fair job of hiding his self-loathing from Cookie.

For her part, Cookie unable to hide her glee that it was Billy's mother calling.

"Better take that one," Cookie said. "Do you good to give a little of your time and attention to a woman who actually gives a damn about you."

"Find one, let me know," Billy said. "Because I'm sure this one wants something from me like all the rest of you do."

Shooing Cookie out of his office with a look. Picking up the call.

"Morning, Mom. How're you today?"

"I'm good, chipmunk."

Calling him by his nickname. His mother and his two older sisters the only ones who still called him that.

"How are you?" she said. "You busy?"

Billy thinking there it is, working up to what she's calling about.

"I'm good, Mom, I'm good."

Eyeing the folder of budget paperwork Cookie had left on his desk.

"About to get busy, though," he said, despite having little intention of getting to it right away. "Stuff's piling up around here."

Sara Jane saying that's good to hear.

Billy wondering if she was even listening to what he said. Then his mother getting right to it.

"I'm down here at the track at the high school with the girls. You know how we get together, walk two, three times a week?"

"Yeah."

"Well, Dixie hasn't shown up yet. "

Billy knowing his mother was talking about her friend, Dixie Hamm.

A big-boned and big-hearted woman. Quite possibly the kindest person Billy had ever met. Hell of a baker and hell of a talker. When his mother and Dixie were in the same room, Billy was amazed they could find enough space for both of them to talk. Probably why they walked and talked outside.

“Hasn’t called or texted to say she didn't plan on showing,” his mother went on. “And you know Dixie. That’s not like her.”

“Maybe she got caught up with something in the kitchen, lost track of time. You try calling her?”

“I did. She didn’t pick up."

Billy thinking there's a lot of that going around. Then hearing the lilt in his mother's voice, wary of it.

"Chipmunk, would you have time this morning to run by her place, check on her?”

“Mom, I’m sure Dixie’s fine. Maybe she’s busy. Or her phone died.”

“I thought of that.”

An edge creeping into his mom’s voice, feeling like her only son was condescending to her.

“So, I tried her home phone too,” she said. “Home phone’s don’t die, you know.”

Billy wondering to himself who still has a landline? Letting it go.

“Mom, you really got no reason to worry.”

"You won't do it for your mother?"

"Mom, I'm an employee of the county, paid by taxpayers to enforce the law, not run errands for my mother because she's got an unreasonable notion in her head."

His mother saying nothing.

Billy hearing her breathing heavy. Figuring his mother must be on the move while talking to him in the morning heat. All the girls at the track worried about Dixie. Starting without her, though.

Finally, his mother saying, "Am I not a tax payer?"

Billy conceding she was right on that point. Knowing where this was heading.

"So, you work for me. Do I have that correct, Sheriff Keene?"

Billy conceding it all to himself. Admitting now what he knew all along--he would give in.

Still, no reason to let his mother know that right away. As if she didn't already.

"Fine, fine, I'll run out there, Mom."

"Now?"

"Yes, Mom, now." Billy catching himself sounding like he was twelve, feeling foolish. "But I'll have to get off the phone with you first, won't I?"

“Not really, it’s a cell phone. Goes where you go. That’s the beauty of it.”

Billy sighing. His mother using his own words against him.

That’s what he’d once told his mother a few years back, when she'd gotten her first cell phone. For some reason, she'd been under the impression that cell phones only worked when she was in the car, like a car phone in the movies and television.

"Anything else I can do for you?” he said.

His mother pausing again. Her voice going soft, aware that she was about to touch on a sore subject.

“Heard from Paige?”

Billy saying nope. Keeping it short. Not wanting to get into it.

“Well, honey, I’m sure she’s busy," Sara Jane said. "Boston’s a busy place. Only don’t you be calling and texting her all the time.”

“I’m not, Mom.”

That twelve-year-old's voice again. Billy finding no end to the ways to be disgusted with himself today.

“Ok, I’ll let you go, chipmunk. I know you’re busy.”

“Have a nice walk.”

His mother saying you too before getting off the line.

Again Billy wondering if his mother ever truly heard the words coming out of his mouth.

Laying his cell phone on his desk next to the folders of budget paperwork. Reclining in his office chair. Trying to work up the energy to move.

Do the paperwork?

Go check on Dixie like he promised his mother?

Find other busy work to pass the time?

Eyes falling on his cell lying there quietly atop his desk. Billy fighting the urge to speed dial Paige's number real quick.

Or maybe a short, light text asking how she was doing today.

Snatching up the phone. Looking at it in his hand.

Then slipping it into the front pocket of his stained uniform pants as he stood up from his desk.

Grabbing his sheriff's baseball cap. He'd stopped wearing the Stetson cowboy hat soon after the Arlita Hardy case. As much as the people around the county seemed to respond to the power of the cowboy hat and what it represented, Billy knew it wasn't him.

Trading the cowboy hat for the flat-brimmed baseball cap was one way he'd tried to come to terms with the job. Besides, he also had a gun on his hip that people now knew he wasn't afraid to use. Billy hoping that was enough and he'd never have to use it again.

Billy placing the cap on his head, heading out to check on his mother's friend.

Visit www.mrchadsanborn.com today to find out where you can get Broken Heartland *and take the next suspenseful ride in this thrilling crime fiction series!*

Can I Ask A Favor?

Now that you've reached the end of the story, I hope you'll leave a review wherever you acquired this book. Good, bad, indifferent, just say what you feel.

Readers say other readers' reviews are the most important factor when deciding to try a new author. So I'd really, really appreciate it if you'd be so cool as to post a review of the book on its page with you favorite online bookseller. Thanks and hope all is well in your world.

And if you would like to connect, please get in touch with me at www.mrchadsanborn.com.

Chad

Want to Know When The Next Billy Keene Book's Out?

Visit www.mrchadsanborn.com and join my email list to be notified you about a new release in *The Billy Keene Stories.*

To sweeten the deal, when you sign up I'll give you an exclusive, free ebook copy of *Getaway*, a crime novella prequel to *The Billy Keene Stories.*

So that's your exclusive, free crime novella ebook AND you'll be among the first to know when the next Billy Keene book is out.

Sound good? If so, sign up today at www.mrchadsanborn.com. Thanks!

Chad

(*Please note that while the print version of* Getaway *is available online for a cost, the ebook version is free and available only to subscribers to my mailing list.)*

Made in United States
North Haven, CT
27 July 2023

39595921R00339